SHE'LL LEARN

SYBIL BARKLEY-STAPLES

Janet,
Thank you so much for your support and it was great seeing you.

Peace,

Sybil Barkley-Staples
sb_staples@yahoo.com

SHE'LL LEARN

SYBIL BARKLEY-STAPLES

Writersandpoets.com, LLC

Published by Writers and Poets.com, LLC
Cover design by Marion Designs
Printed in the United States of America

Publisher's Note:

This is a work of fiction. Names, characters, places, and incidents either are the product of the author's imagination or are used fictitiously, and any resemblance to actual persons, living or dead, events, or locales is entirely coincidental.

Library of Congress Catalog Card No. 2004114075

ISBN Number 0-9703803-8-0

Writers and Poets.com
P.O. Box 1307
Mountainside, NJ 07092
http://www.writersandpoets.com

First Printing

Acknowledgments

I give thanks to God first and foremost. He has filled my life with so many blessings letting me know that all things are possible through him.

Special thanks to: My mother Lena Barkley, who has been more than a mother but a friend at times when I needed one the most. Thanks for everything. My husband Paris, I love you and I am thankful everyday for the blessing of having you in my life. To our daughters Peri and Sanai, you are my motivation and my hope for the future. To my grandparents, Harry and Mable, for loving me unconditionally and for always being a source of strength to myself and to our entire family. Lovell and LueNell, for all of your love and support. LaQuita, thanks for always laughing with me and for working so hard to help my books be a success.

Thanks to my loving family in Detroit: Martha, Betty, Brenda, Michelle, Shirley, Great Aunt Betsy, David, Dennis, Eric, Harry, Ray and Great Uncle James. Hope, Shaun, Karen, Gary, Eugene, David Jr., Darius, Ray Jr., Tyler and Eric Jr., Dedrick, Jasmine and the Barkley family. Mark Young and family thanks for your support. Detroit's finest DPD, Robert, Andre', all of Dexter, Katrina, Ayanna Kilpatrick, Diehl Boy's & Girl's Club, Paul Barton, Cass Technical H.S. Alumni (89') and faculty, Dina Harrell, The Truth Bookstore, Bob Kerse, Birmingham Border's Bookstore, WCCCD, Fanchon Stinger and bookclub, Charles Pugh and FOXTV2 News.

Thanks to my family in Atlanta and Alabama: Ms. Annette, Erica (Dee Dee), Valeria, Kevin, Carol, Dondee, Eddie, Jermaine, Ben, The Staples, James, Wares, Smiths, and Daniels families, Frank Seals, Bishop Jean Davis, Mary, Cynthia, Shannon, Cassandra and Hair Masters Salon and Barbershop, Monique Johnson my friend until the end, to The Weather Channel and weather.com for your ongoing support and friendships. Alabama State and Clark Atlanta (94') Universities Alumni and staff.

Thanks to the many bookclubs for having me, Rashan Ali and HOT107.9, Laura at Waldenbooks, Debbie at Hidden Talents, Nia at Medu Books, Tia Jakes, Booksamillion staff, Glen Fisher, Monique at flavahreviewers.com, Tee C. and RAWSISTAZ, APOOO.org, Angie and ReadInColor, LaShaunda Hoffman at Shades of Romance, Wayne Jordan at Romance in Color, Janet Johnson, Emma Rogers at Black Images, Sisterfriends, Gevell and RealSistaWriters, Shunda Leigh and Booking Matters Magazine, Paul Buckner, Cheryl at Avid-readers.com, Brenda Thomas and many thanks to a host of authors, book clubs, reviewers and readers that I have met along the way.

Thanks to Keith Saunders for the beautiful cover, my editor Audra Barrett Shivers and Earl Cox for all of your support and dedication to the book industry. If I have forgotten anyone, please forgive me!

She'll Learn

CHAPTER ONE

Early November in Detroit, the city is blanketed in snow as Maxine impatiently awaits the arrival of her two best friends, Indira and Sydney. Maxine takes on the task of picking up a little around the house before they get there. She has been looking forward to this night all week. Thursdays belong to Maxine, Sydney, and Indira. It is the one night they have to get away from everything and everybody. Maxine has been down and out because all she's done is work, work, work, and no play. Sometimes the big old house her grandmother had left her could get real lonely, and having company always did her good. Maxine ran her fingers through her short hair then gave the place the once over.

"Looks good to me," she said to herself. She began looking at her watch just as she heard the doorbell. She knew it had to be Sydney since she was never late.

"Right on time as usual, Sydney," Maxine said.

Sydney stepped through the doorway with a tightly wrapped bundle in her arms.
"I came right over after I got Jasmine from Mrs. Lee's."

Maxine closed the door behind her.

"Girl, it is cold as I don't know what out there," Sydney said as she laid her daughter on the couch and began taking off her three layers of clothing. Maxine watched her friend from the foyer. It was so funny to see little Sydney with a baby, considering she was twenty-two and still a baby herself.

"Has Indira called?" Sydney began taking off her own coat.

"No, but she said she'd be here. Girl, show me some love," Maxine walked over to Sydney with outstretched arms.

"Uh, oh, what's wrong now?" Sydney knew what the problem was beforehand, but she knew Maxine needed to tell her anyway.

Maxine looked up at Sydney. "Don't act stupid, you know what's wrong with me. I need a man."

Sydney shook her head because neither of them had such a prize, but Maxine's need was much greater.

"Maxine, you ain't telling me nothing different from my own problems. You seem to forget that I don't have a man either," Sydney sat down on the couch next to Jasmine, who was still asleep. “Oh, but you are thirty, so time is running out,” Sydney knew that would get her.

"What you talking about? I’ve got plenty of time. And, I’m twenty-nine, thank you,” Maxine mumbled.

"I heard that, but anyway this is the same thing you get all depressed about every week," Sydney straightened Jasmine’s sweater, causing her to squirm.

"When my status changes I won't have nothing to be depressed about," Maxine began to laugh at herself.

"Don’t be so sure about that girl. Oh, did you get the invitation to the art gallery from Indira?" Sydney sounded so excited.

"Yeah I got it, but I don't think I'm gonna go," Maxine looked down at the carpet and picked up a candy wrapper from the floor. Sydney had dropped it out of her coat pocket only moments before. Maxine liked for her house to be clean at all times. She was born and raised in the house bequeathed to her by her grandmother. After her passing a year ago, Maxine, Indira, and Sydney continued to support each other in their web of relationships.

“Why not? We haven't been anywhere nice like that in a long time.” Sydney sounded as if they were an old couple as she looked at Maxine oddly.

"I just don't feel like getting all sharp and shit for some man to make me feel like nothing," Maxine was really down tonight.

"I thought you wanted one so bad, and who says you have to go with a man anyway? You can go with me; you know I ain't got no date," Sydney thought she had a good idea, but Maxine still wasn't down.

"Uh, yes you do,” Maxine tried to look innocent. “I took the liberty of getting you a date." Maxine had been constantly trying to get Sydney on a date ever since Anthony flew the coop two years ago. Maxine sometimes felt guilty about not being there for Sydney when she needed her most. She had been busy with the salon and had left Sydney on her own. The neighborhood had turned to something fierce as drugs took it by the collars. With a half-witted mother and dope-head brother, it had almost been too much for Sydney.

She'll Learn

"A date? With who?" Sydney couldn't believe what she was hearing. She took Jasmine upstairs to Maxine's bedroom. Maxine got up to look out the window for Indira.

"Don't worry, I'll tell you about him later."

Sydney continued up the stairs. A faint drizzle of snow began to fall from the night sky and the street was soon covered.

Where in the hell is Indira? Maxine thought to herself.

*****

Indira sat at her desk and looked out the glass doors of the gallery, watching as cars hurriedly dashed down the slushy street. There was a bitter November wind blowing the people who walked up Jefferson Avenue. The wet drizzle that continuously fell turned the white snow to a gray mush along the sides of the street. Omari walked out of his office and came toward Indira as he slung his scarf around his neck.

"Good night, Indira, I'm on my way home," Omari smiled and pulled his hat farther down on his head. Indira smiled back awkwardly at her boss. "Good night, darling," Omari gestured again as he switched and swayed his way down the stairs. "And please don't stay in here too late. I'm pretty sure that handsome husband of yours is waiting for you."

Indira looked over the balcony and saw Omari blowing a kiss up to her.

"You think?" she sarcastically mumbled. Indira waved goodbye. Omari stepped out the front door to join the ranks of pedestrians combating the wind. Indira could only pray that her husband would be at home waiting for her. She knew that would take a lot of prayer. Robert was probably at his hangout, the Dexter Bar, or just at home drunk.

"Stop it, Indira," she said aloud. She didn't feel like getting herself down, so she turned her focus back to her notes for Saturday's showing.

"Eldridge Moss, you are on the way up," she proclaimed. Last year she had traveled to Atlanta for an art festival with some college friends, and came across some wonderful oil paintings. The artist wasn't anywhere to be found. Indira returned to Detroit in dismay and wondered about the artist of those paintings. After some detective work, she tracked him down.

"Eldridge Moss. What a talented man," Indira had never met Eldridge, but had spoken to him on the phone.

“You are going to be a hit this weekend,” Indira was glad to have found him, and after some extended phone calls, she finally convinced him to show his art at the gallery. He was what she needed. Indira couldn't wait to see the man behind such passionate works of art. She was so impressed with his paintings, especially the paintings he’d chosen as gifts for her office. The painting that lay against her desk was her favorite. It reminded her of Maxine, Sydney, and herself when they were little girls. When she looked over at it on the floor, she sort of got lost in it and began to think about how much fun they used to have together at Ms. Mable's house.

From as far back as Indira could remember, her mother would leave her and her baby sister at Maxine’s grandmother’s house. No matter how tired and worn she was, her mother went to work. Ms. Mable kept most of the children in the neighborhood, and also served as the neighborhood hairdresser. She gave them her love and taught her girls, as she called them, all she had in her heart. Indira knew that Ms. Mable was trying to fill the void of each of their mentally distant mothers. Indira’s mother had problems of her own, Indira's father. She didn’t have time to see about Clarissa and Indira. The girls grew up together, and vowed to stay together.

Indira leaned back in her chair and noticed the time on the clock. She nearly fell out of the chair.

"Boy, I can hear Max's mouth already," Indira locked up the gallery and headed for the parking lot. She hoped it was too cold for somebody to be out robbing people, but she watched her back anyway.

The busy sounds of the city filled Indira's head as she opened the door of her Mercedes-Benz 230 and got in. She tossed her purse and briefcase on the passenger seat and turned the ignition. Indira flipped through the radio stations as the car warmed up. Warming up a car was a must if one expected it to make it through a Motown winter. Indira stopped when she heard the voice of Barbara Jones, Detroit's hottest talk-radio hostess. Indira didn't care much for the show, but she managed to find her way to it damn near every night.

"Hello, caller, you’re on the air," Barbara’s soothing voice coerced the silent caller.

"...Hello, Dr. Jones," the woman sounded frightened.

She'll Learn

"Don't be afraid, honey, I only want to help you," Doctor Jones was lying through her teeth. She thrived on cutting up her callers, especially women.

"My husband and I are starting to have a lot of problems." The caller sounded like she had been crying.

"What kind of problems are you having?" Dr. Jones wasn't holding back.

".... My husband has started beating me whenever he gets angry."

"Yes, you do have a problem. But listen. The solution is easy," Dr. Jones sounded confident, as if the solution to all problems could be easy.

"What should I do Dr. Jones?"

It was only the first week of November and Christmas was already being pushed on the city. Indira rode down the lit-up streets lined with glowing trees decorated with holiday lights until she reached the interstate.

"The only answer for you is to leave him. He'll never stop abusing you if you continue to give him the opportunity."

Indira knew how hard it would be for her to leave Robert, and knew the doctor didn't know what she was talking about.

"Oh no, I couldn't leave him. We have two small children. Plus he'd go nuts," the caller wasn't buying the solution the doctor had given her.

"No one deserves to be beaten like an animal. And do you want your children to see this happening to you?" Dr. Jones made her point-of-view clear and the woman fell silent.

"I...I know you're right. But I just can't do that." CLICK!

The woman caller was gone.

"Listen ladies, you have to think about yourselves sometimes or there won't be any you left to think about. We'll be right back."

A commercial for some movie began right on cue. Indira pushed in her Jill Scott CD and began to think about what the doctor had said. Robert had changed so much over the years. One thing was for sure, he wasn't the same man she had married. She was living with a total stranger. She couldn't believe she was letting it happen. As a child, she watched her father paint her mother's face black-and-blue until the day he died. If she didn't learn anything from that front-row lesson, what would it take?

Indira drove through the slick, salted streets of her old neighborhood. There weren't many stores left on Dexter Avenue, unless you counted the liquor stores, which were on every corner. Once known for the shops and boutiques that lined the street, it was now only known for the crime, burned-out buildings, and abandoned houses. Most of Indira's memories were bad, but she kept a place in her heart for Ms. Mable's house on the corner of Burlingame.

When Ms. Mable died two years ago of breast cancer, Maxine used the money she'd left her, and opened their dream shop. Fashion Hair stood out a step above all the other salons and it never lacked for clientele. The house was one final gift to all of them.

What would you think of me today, Ms. Mable? Indira wondered. She knew that she would love her no matter what, unlike her own mother Arnelle. Indira loved her mother, but her mother never had much time for her children. Arnelle's life was plagued with pain and abuse.

Floyd was a horrible, mean-spirited man who didn't know how to love anybody, not even himself. Arnelle only had time for the man in her life, and he used up all the love she had. Indira and her baby sister watched the drama unfold daily like an onstage play. Indira loved her mother, but hated the woman she had become; the woman her father had reduced her to. Ms. Mable was the mother that Maxine, Sydney, and Indira needed.

Indira slowed her Mercedes sedan and turned onto her old street. She pulled in front of the house she grew up in with her father, mother, and sister. Indira had found her way out when she got accepted to Spelman College in Atlanta. She left the daily dose of her father beating her mother and watching his drunken taunts toward her baby sister. Clarissa was left alone to outrun her father.

Indira's stomach began to turn the longer she stared at the rundown house. Her mother had suffered a heart attack in her sleep and died after many years of being beaten down by a life of drudgery and abuse. Indira felt a sense of relief for her mother. She took her eyes off the house and got back on the street to drive another block to Maxine's.

Indira eased out of the car and carefully stepped across the snow. After all these years, Mrs. Jones still sat in her bay window watching the world go by her house. The recluse waved the minute she caught eye contact. Indira smiled and waved back. She went up the steps of the porch. The crunching under her feet was a sign that Mr. Brown from across the street had salted the steps. Though Mr. Brown was old and tired himself, he continued to keep things for Maxine as he had done for her grandmother.

Maxine saw Indira through the window and hurriedly opened the door. Indira's light-skinned face was nearly blue from the cold. Maxine hugged her before she could get in the door good. Indira was overwhelmed by Maxine's actions. Though like sisters, they were always off and on with each other. Indira was assuming they were on today—true sisters.

"It's about time you got here, girl. We were starting to think you wasn't gonna come," Maxine stated. She took Indira's coat to the closet. She looked the fur-lined leather coat up and down and saw that it was new. Well, at least, it smelled new. "Must be nice," she mumbled.

After hanging the coat, Maxine strolled back into the living room. Sydney was bringing Jasmine back downstairs when Indira dropped on the couch.

"Hey, Indi, I'm glad you finally got here," Sydney said. She leaned over and kissed her cheek.

"Oh, let me hold this big girl," Indira said.

Jasmine yawned then looked at Indira and smiled.

"Say, hey, Aunt Indira," Sydney spoke in her baby voice. Maxine walked in with a tray of flutes filled with white wine.

"Will you please stop talking like that!" Maxine put the tray on the table and slid into the recliner.

"She's a baby, Maxine, how else am I supposed to talk?" Sydney picked up her glass and sat next to Indira on the couch.

"Lord, help this girl please, if she ever has any kids," Indira said jokingly.

Sydney laughed with Indira.

"Where's the hot wings?" Sydney asked as she stopped laughing and got up.

"I forgot to bring them out of the kitchen," Maxine watched as Sydney rushed out of the room.

"And she don't need to eat not a one of them," Maxine whispered to Indira and laughed. Indira ran her fingers through Jasmine's thick, black, curly hair, and thought about how much she wanted a family. She knew that could never be with Robert, not only was he a stone drunk, but he had a vasectomy six years before she met him. She began to feel like her life was going nowhere.

Maxine and Sydney ate chicken wings and watched Indira hold the baby and daydream. The two looked at each other. Indira could never hide anything from them. Jasmine was fast asleep on Indira's chest.

"Why don't you take the baby upstairs and lay her on my bed?" Maxine knew something was wrong and she had a good idea of what it was. Indira walked up the stairs with the baby.

"I think something is definitely wrong with Indira," Sydney gave her opinion in between downing hot wings.

"I can see that, Sydney," Maxine licked her fingers and got up from her chair.

"Do you think it has something to do with Robert?" Sydney didn't care for Indira's husband very much.

“She does have a new coat,” Maxine said sarcastically under her breath.

“Shut up, Max,” Sydney snickered.

"What else could it be, but him?" Maxine asked. She didn't like him from the day she met him. "For one thing he’s old as dirt. He treats her like shit and then buys her shit to make up for it," Maxine got quiet when she noticed Indira coming back down the stairs.

"You must have been talking about me, because you both sitting here looking all crazy," Indira sat down on the couch.

"We're just worried about you, that's all," Sydney confessed. She looked at Maxine and then picked up her glass again. Indira looked at Maxine queerly.

"Come on, Indira. Drink up and relax," Maxine gestured for Indira to pick up her wine glass.

Indira reached for her glass, "I am relaxed and nothing is wrong with me, thank you."

The room fell quiet for a few moments.

She'll Learn

"I can't sit here all quiet and shit," Maxine got up and went over to the stereo.

"Let's see what we got here," Maxine looked to the girls for suggestions.

"I don't know. Just as long as it's not Luther," Indira shrugged her shoulders.

Maxine looked through her collection of CDs and then picked one. "Luther is always good," Maxine put in one of her favorites.

"Is this old Luther or new Luther?" Sydney asked. She didn't care too much for his stuff since he lost weight.

"Old, and don't be talking about my man." Maxine sang with Luther while Sydney and Indira watched.

Sydney turned to Indira, "I got the invitation to the gallery."

"Good. Are you going to come is the question," Indira smiled at Sydney.

"I promise I will be there, but I need a date."

Maxine stopped singing when she overheard Sydney. "Don't forget I already got somebody lined up for you," Maxine never stopped dancing.

"Oh, yeah," Sydney sat up quickly.

"I am kind of tired of you dating me, call her sometime," Maxine said as she pointed to Indira.

"Well, who is he?" Sydney was getting excited.

"Don't worry, he's a friend of Derrick's," Maxine stopped dancing and sat back down.

"Derrick is the married guy, right?" Indira stepped in. She didn't approve of any of Maxine's many acquaintances.

"Yeah, so what! Sydney ain't had a date in damn near a year, so it shouldn't matter much," Maxine threw up her hands.

"Well this man ain't married is he?" Sydney asked.

"No, he's not married. You just need to get some," Maxine laughed then drank her wine.

"What?" Indira looked at Maxine.

"Maybe I don't want none." Sydney and Indira began to laugh and touched hands.

"Well I don't know about you two, but I am in dire need of some," Maxine jumped in on Luther's singing.

Indira sat back and thought about the last time she and Robert made love. She could barely remember that far back. It wasn't worth the time; he drank so much his equipment barely worked.

Sydney sipped on her wine and thought about the way she and Anthony used to make love. She missed him more and more each day.

Maxine needed to be with somebody tonight, but which man could she call? All her men were not really worth the call.

"This is a damn shame." Reality began to set in on Maxine again. "I am alone again for the holidays. Thanksgiving is in three weeks."

Sydney and Indira looked at each other.

"Aw hell, here she goes again," Sydney said as she sat back and got ready for the show.

Maxine turned her glass up to her lips for a final gulp, and then slammed down it down.

Indira threw up her hands in disgust. "Maxine, we sit here and listen to this same speech every week, don't we Sydney?" Indira looked to Sydney for help.

"Maxine, I'm alone too," Sydney tried to make Maxine feel better.

"Yeah, but you got Jasmine, and Papa Joe. I don't have nobody," Maxine got quiet and sat back down.

"Well, if it'll make you feel better, you got me and Sydney," Indira looked at Maxine and smirked, "and Jasmine, too."

Maxine looked at Indira awkwardly. "I know that, but I need a man's love. I need to feel loved and wanted by a man," Maxine picked up her empty glass. "Anybody need a refill besides me?" Maxine picked up the tray and got Sydney's empty glass. "You want a refill Indi?" Maxine looked impatient.

"No, I better not. I need to be sober when I get home," Indira didn't want to drink too much because she already knew what kind of mood Robert would be in.

Maxine headed toward the kitchen. Sydney broke the silence that rested between her and Indira.

"Jasmine will be two years old next Sunday. Can you believe that?" Sydney opened her eyes wide with excitement.

Maxine walked back into the room with the glasses.

She'll Learn

"I want to have a little party for her, but I don't want to have it in my apartment," Sydney turned to Maxine.

"Oh, so you wanna have it here?" Maxine began to frown.

"Please, girl. It'll only be for a couple of hours." Sydney looked like a pleading puppy.

Maxine watched Sydney plead and beg the same way she did as a child to get her way with her grandmother. It was working.

"Okay, but both of you have to do all the work."

Indira looked at Sydney.

"I'm going to need you here to help too, Indira," Sydney didn't have to beg.

"I'll be here," Indira touched Sydney's hand.

Maxine put on some more music, but faster this time. "Come on now. I know you can dance," Maxine was a regular at the clubs, so she could do enough to get by.

"I never could dance all that great no way," Indira said as she tried to duplicate Maxine's moves.

"This is about all I can do, and I learned it from Jazzy," Sydney clapped her hands and moved from side to side.

"Girl, you doing much better than me," Indira admitted as she started to relax and enjoy her time with her friends. That's what their night was for—to be at peace if just for a few short hours.

"Indira, married life done faded you out," Maxine got in front of her and showed off her dancing skills.

"I'm not faded, whatever that means," Indira began to try a little harder.

"Uh oh, get it Indi," Sydney said as she and Maxine started doing the bump.

Maxine stopped dancing, folded her arms and stared at Sydney and Indira who were still dancing.

"Don't tell me you two don't hear that baby crying upstairs?" Maxine fanned her face and sat down. Indira did the same. Sydney ran up the stairs to get her daughter. Maxine watched as Indira patted her face dry with a napkin.

"So what's been up with you, Indi? I haven't heard from you in a while." Maxine continued to fan her face.

"Nothing much, except working day and night to get this showing together for Saturday."

"Oh yeah, I got your invitation. I don't think I'm gonna make it though," Maxine prepared for Indira's response.

"Well, I know you're busy," Indira tried to sound understanding.

"I still might come if I'm not dead tired. The shop is a madhouse on Saturdays," Maxine kicked her shoes off under the coffee table.

"Come on, Max, doing hair can't make you that tired."

Maxine shook her head from side to side in disbelief. Indira had spoken without thinking again, and realized it too late.

"Why shouldn't I be tired, Indira?" Maxine was becoming upset.

"I mean, you've been doing hair almost all your life," Indira realized that was a stupid thing to say, too.

"You trippin' and I ain't in the mood for your shit," Maxine put up a hand for Indira to stop talking to her.

Indira knew she had offended Maxine by downing her profession. Whenever she got nervous her words made no sense.

"Girl, I'm sorry I am trippin' tonight. I don't know what I'm about to go home to, and I am not prepared for whatever it is," Indira took a much needed sip of Sydney's wine. Sydney came back down the stairs with Jasmine sitting up wide awake in her arms.

Jasmine waved her hand sleepily and said hi. Her words were becoming clearer every day.

"Bring her over here to me," Maxine reached for the baby. "Hey, Pudgy, did you sleep good?" Maxine played with Jasmine.

After another hour of talking and laughing, it was time for Indira and Sydney to get home.

CHAPTER TWO

Robert sat drinking bourbon as the television watched him. He couldn't stop thinking about his wife. Robert had convinced himself that Indira was cheating on him.

"Where is that bitch?" Robert took another gulp from his glass and staggered up the stairs to the master bedroom they shared. He gazed around the room looking through his wife's things. He'd convinced himself that his young wife was out somewhere having an affair.

His internal hatred for Indira had surpassed his high blood pressure. Robert went over to Indira's closet and ran his hands roughly over her clothes in disgust. She'd been spending his money on Donna Karan, Calvin Klein, and Versace suits. Indira dressed with style.

After five years of marriage, Robert had begun to despise his wife and her beauty. It was the very thing that led him to her that spring day in Atlanta. The entire time Robert was delivering his speech on financial security, he couldn't take his eyes off the beautiful young woman in the audience. Indira hung onto Robert's every word, as did the all-female audience he was addressing. She would welcome the chance to meet him, she thought. The crowd applauded as Robert stepped off the stage in the center of Spelman's campus. He was shaking hands and signing his book when he noticed the woman from the audience walking away.

He thanked his well wishers and made his way over to her. "Miss. Excuse me," Robert had called out to Indira as she walked off the curb. She turned around to see Robert Carr coming toward her. He was handsome, educated, and well built.

"Hi," Robert stopped in front of Indira and gasped for breath. "You were walking so fast, I had to run to catch you," Robert gazed into Indira's heavenly brown eyes.

"And why were you running after me?" Indira folded her arms across her notebook. Robert laughed. Indira prepared her ears for some lame response. All she seemed to get from the guys around there was stupid jokes and childish games. She was beyond that and those guys.

"I noticed you during my speech, and to tell you the truth, I couldn't take my eyes off of you." Robert looked down at Indira as she looked up into his eyes. Their difference in height was like their difference in age.

"I…I don't know what to say," Indira was so ready for the same routine she was rendered speechless by his approach.

"Just say you'll have dinner with me tonight," Robert noticed the streets filling up with students who eyed the two as they passed. He realized that he was lusting after more than just a beautiful woman. Her eyes said that she was maybe twenty-three years old, he guessed.

"Yes, I would like that." Indira kept her cool. Robert Carr was interested in her. It didn't matter that he was old enough to be her father.

"Good. I'm glad I chased you down after all."

Indira smiled as she gave Robert her phone number and address.

"Then I'll see you tonight," Robert watched Indira walk away. His eyes followed the sway of her hips until she was too far out of his sight.

"What the hell am I doing?" Robert asked himself as he opened the door of his Jaguar and got in. "Finding the new Mrs. Robert Carr," he surmised.

Robert stopped reminiscing and picked up a bottle of perfume that he had bought for Indira last Christmas. It was nearly full.

"She don't even wear this shit no more," he said angrily as he threw the perfume bottle against the wall, smashing it to pieces. The room awakened with the smell of wild flowers. Robert caught a glimpse of himself in the vanity mirror as he passed it. He was getting older and sicker, while Indira was growing more beautiful with each passing day. He ran his fingers through his thinning salt and pepper hair.

As a young man, he had had a head full of black curls and soft skin. Now his face hadn't been shaved in nearly two days. He cringed at the sight of himself in the mirror. He was an old man and he couldn't take it. Robert spotted a stream of sweat running down his face, and realized how bad he looked. He was killing himself, or was she killing him? He gazed into the mirror.

"What does she want with an old man like me?" Robert swallowed the last of his drink. "Damn this house is hot." Robert went into the hallway to check the thermostat. Indira liked the house to be warm because her petite frame was always cold.

She'll Learn

"Seventy-eighty degrees? This bitch is trying to fry me." Robert turned the heat down to seventy and went back down the stairs. He looked at his watch.

"I swear I'll kill that bitch if she's with another man." He didn't want her anymore, but he didn't want anyone else to, either. He filled his glass with bourbon and sat down in front of the TV. He would greet his young wife at the door.

*****

Indira sat staring at the empty glasses on the table. She couldn't help but think about her husband. She knew he was at home right now drinking himself to death. Her marriage was crashing and burning, but she wondered if it was worth saving. She looked up at the clock on the wall, which read nine forty-eight. She jumped up quickly.

"Oh, I didn't realize it was so late." Indira hugged both Sydney and Maxine. The two watched her in amazement.

"Is everything okay, Indira?" Sydney asked as she rushed around the room.

"Yes, I'm fine I just need to get home." Indira got her coat from the closet.

"What a minute, girl. Let me at least walk you to the door." Maxine rushed over to her friend and opened the door.

"You know I've got a long drive," Indira tried to make up an excuse. She began to walk out the front door as Maxine touched her shoulder.

"Hey, if you need to talk to somebody tonight, I'll be up." Maxine and Indira stood looking at each other.

"Thanks. I'll remember that."

Maxine closed the door behind Indira and went back to the living room. "Dang, did she run out of here or what?" Maxine couldn't believe how quickly Indira had left.

"She sure did. I hope Robert ain't drunk when she gets home," Sydney held Jasmine and shook her head.

"Grandma used to tell me that my daddy used to beat my mama, and he damn-near killed her once." Maxine's grandma told her a lot of things. "I also remember her saying that they only do it if you let them," Maxine now worried about her friend.

"Why don't she leave him?" Sydney stated and began to wonder.

"She probably can't leave him. She's been with that man for five years, plus she's in love, remember?" Maxine spoke with much sarcasm.

"Anthony used to get real mad sometimes, but he would never hit me." Sydney was thinking about Anthony again.

"Oh no, I don't wanna hear you talk about Anthony, the runaway, tonight." Maxine got up and took the glasses into the kitchen. Sydney got angry.

"Well what makes you think I always want to hear about your sad-ass life?" Sydney rolled her eyes at Maxine.

*****

Indira cruised through the neighborhood that Robert chose for them to live in. He said that he had made it and he deserved to live in Bloomfield Hills, where the rich white folks lived. They were the third black couple living in their subdivision, along with a couple of the Detroit Piston's players. Robert and Indira were also in the odd category because of their twenty-three year age difference. No one really cared. Everyone out there kept to themselves. One could only guess at what went on behind the doors of the other homes. Indira took a deep breath as she pulled into the driveway and cut off the ignition.

There was only one light on in the house and it was in their bedroom. Indira knew exactly what Robert was doing in their bedroom. Whenever she left Robert at home, he'd get drunk and go through her things. Indira got out of the car and walked up the carefully shoveled walkway. She would have to remember to give some money to Russell, the kid next door, for shoveling their sidewalks, too. Robert sat slumped over at the bottom of the staircase waiting for his wife to come through the door. He didn't know what he was going to do when he saw her. He was harboring so much anger he was unpredictable, even to himself.

Indira opened the door with her key. The house was dark and smelled of strong liquor. After closing the door, she switched on the Tiffany lamp in the hallway. She jumped when she saw Robert sitting on the stairs. Just looking at him answered her question of whether he was drunk or not. He was holding a half-full bottle of bourbon in his hand to back it up.

She'll Learn

"I didn't expect you to be waiting for me." Indira took off the new coat that Robert had given her after their last fight. She hung it on the brass coat rack behind the door, and then hesitantly turned to face her husband.

"Where have you been all night, Indira?" Robert remained calm and turned the bottle up to his mouth.

Indira could feel that trouble was ahead and she didn't want any part of it.

"You always forget that on Thursdays I go over to Maxine's house to spend some time with my friends." Indira had no reason to lie to Robert, although she wondered sometimes why she still loved him. No one could understand her reasons.

"Stop lying to me and admit that you were out fucking around," Robert truly believed that. He was becoming enraged and could feel himself losing control. He didn't want to hurt her, but sometimes the thought of her being with another man ate him up inside.

"No, Robert, I wasn't out with another man. I love you, I don't need anyone else," Indira saw her words take effect on him.

Robert thought about the time when Indira did love him. What he wouldn't give to go back to those days with her, but he knew it was too late for that. She had her friends, the gallery, and another man. He rushed over to Indira and grabbed her by her arm tightly.

"What do you want with an old drunk like me?" Robert pulled Indira over to the mirror in the hallway. "Look at me!"

Indira held her face down as the burning tears covered it.

"Look at me, Indira!"

Indira looked in her husband's fiery-red eyes. He was frightening her. She slowly looked up at him in the mirror.

"You can't love a man like me, Indira." Robert took another look at himself and let go of his wife's arm. Indira said nothing, she only massaged her arm. Robert leaned on the banister with his face cupped in his hand. Indira felt so sorry for Robert and wanted to help him. She wanted to work their problems out, but he had to let her help him.

"Robert, please don't push me away. I want to help you," Indira stood on the bottom stair rubbing her fingers lightly over his graying mane, the way he used to love for her to do. Robert knew his wife was lying to him and wasn't going to let her make a fool of him.

Vera was right, he thought, she only wanted me for my money and status. She doesn't love me.

"Let go of me, Indira." Robert stood up, forcing Indira's hand to fall from his head. "I don't need your fucking help or your love." He stumbled as he got his coat and opened the door. "Don't bother to wait up for me." The door slammed hard behind him.

Indira stood shaking, staring at the door. She went into the kitchen and ran cold water over her face to calm down. After grabbing a paper towel, she leaned over the sink.

Why does he hate me so much? she wondered.

It seemed like only yesterday when he loved her, and then things suddenly changed. Indira locked the front door and headed upstairs to take a hot bath. It was only a matter of time now. Who would be the first to leave?

*****

Jasmine lay fast asleep in Maxine's arms while Sydney danced and lip-synched to *Angel* with Anita Baker. Maxine kissed Jasmine's forehead as she slept. She was the spitting image of Sydney. They both had thick black hair, bushy eyebrows, and a chubby face. Sydney flopped down on the couch the minute Anita's concert was over. She loved Anita and did a fairly decent job of portraying her.

"I had fun tonight with you tricks," Sydney said as she lay slouched on the couch.

"I hope Indira's okay at home with that retarded husband of hers." Maxine shook her head at the thought of him. "Boy, if he ever laid his hands on me, I would kick his balls inside out," Maxine had her fists clenched tightly.

"I don't see why women put up with that shit," Maxine went on and on. She would never let a man do that to her, she thought.

"I think I'll give her a call when I get to the apartment," Sydney said.

Maxine sat up with the baby. "Girl, are you out of your mind? Robert might be drunk as hell and actin' crazy," Maxine checked Jasmine to make sure she was still asleep.

"He used to be so nice to her," Sydney stared at the glasses on the coffee table. "I remember that time he took us all to that movie opening and we met uh, uh…. what's his name?" Sydney tried to remember.

"Lou Rawls," Maxine had heard this story a million times.

"How in the world could I forget his name? My mother played the mess out of his songs when I was a kid," Sydney got quiet when she realized she was talking about her mother.

Maxine watched as Sydney's happy attitude quickly turned to sadness when she spoke about Virginia. Maxine realized that they all had problems in some way or another, and depended on each other to help them get through it.

"Well, me and Jazzy better get out of here before I fall asleep myself. Oh, I have to get something out to wear to work. What, I don't know." Sydney had already gotten Jasmine from Maxine and dressed her before Maxine could say anything.

"Now you trippin' on me, too. First it was Indira!" Maxine stood up to face Sydney.

"Girl, things will work out for all of us, one day."

Maxine helped Sydney put her coat on. "I pray every night for that to happen real soon."

Sydney smiled at Maxine then hugged her. She lifted Jasmine onto her hip and walked toward the door with Maxine following.

"Will you please come over Saturday and help me get ready for my blind date?" Sydney tried to laugh.

"It'll count on how many heads I have to do. You know the shop will be on jam Saturday, but I'll try my best to help you out girl," Maxine gave Jasmine a quick kiss goodbye.

"Well try and make it because I'll be a total wreck without you," Sydney covered Jasmine's face and walked out the door.

Maxine stood in the window and watched Sydney as she got into her car that they called Little Red. It was Sydney's brother's car before he died, and then Papa Joe fixed it up for her to get around in.

Sydney was out of Maxine's sight before Maxine had realized she was gone. Maxine let the curtain drop and cleared the glasses from the table. It was getting late, but she wasn't the least bit tired. She locked the doors and headed up to her room to snuggle up to a book.

I'd rather be snuggled up with a big black man, she thought.

Maxine stomped up the stairs and changed into her nightgown. She fingered the tabs of each book she had, and finally stopped on *Sparkle*. She'd been waiting for some time to read it. She propped her pillows up on the bed and concentrated on her reading, hoping to block out the realities of her loneliness.

*****

Robert had been driving for nearly a half an hour when he finally reached his destination. He'd driven around the neighborhood in circles before he found himself pulling up to the Dexter Bar, his faithful hangout. He was so drunk he couldn't remember actually driving to the bar. Just as he was opening his car door, he saw a policeman at the stop sign across the street. He closed the door and pretended to be buttoning his coat, the police car pulled beside him, and then continued on. All he needed right now was to get another D.U.I. charge. He got out of his Jaguar, barely closing the door behind himself.

The cold wind that cut into his face helped in his venture to straighten up. He rushed into the door of the bar. The place was a dump as usual and the same crowd for the last fifteen or twenty years still went there. Robert fit right in. There had been many changes in his life, but this was the one thing that would never change. Vera was another. She would love him no matter what. Robert heard the words in his head as he searched the room for her. He found the middle-aged woman sitting in the corner of the bar with two other people. He couldn't focus his eyes enough to see the group from where he was standing.

"Bobby, what's going on, my man?" Genie, the bartender and Robert's friend of more than twenty-five years, extended his hand out to him. Robert hesitantly obliged him.

"Nothing much, Genie," Robert continued to look toward Vera as Genie talked to him.

"Bourbon?" Genie knew exactly what he was having.

"Yeah, man, I sure could use it." Robert turned up the glass before Genie could get out another word. Before starting up again, Genie filled Robert's glass. He always knew when something was troubling Bobby, but Bobby was a mean son-of-a-bitch so he didn't ask.

She'll Learn

"What you been into tonight, Bobby? That pretty little wife of yours?" Genie laughed aloud, showing the gold on his front tooth. Robert didn't laugh. He only swallowed his drink and slammed his glass on the bar. Genie turned up his mouth and went back to drying the glasses at the other end of the bar.

Robert found his way over to Vera. She knew he would be there sooner or later, whenever that little girl of his turned him away. Vera flashed a wide smile when she saw Robert standing before her.

"Hello, handsome. I was hoping you'd be coming to see me tonight," Vera motioned for Robert to kiss her. He only eyed the man that was sitting at the table with Vera along with some woman. Vera could see that Robert was already drunk, and it was up to her to keep him from taking his anger out on everybody.

"Oh, Robert baby, this is Sweets, a friend of Ida's, and you know Ida." Vera held onto Robert's hand to calm him. He was giving in.

"Well slide over everybody, so my man can sit down," Vera waved her hands to her party. She took her time sliding over because her dress was fitting so tight on her hips that the slightest move would be the end of it.

Robert sat next to Vera and waved for Ming to bring him another drink from the bar. Ming wasn't very young anymore herself, but she looked better than everybody in there did. The group of acquaintances all looked tired and rundown, unlike Ming. Genie had married her in Vietnam and had brought her back home with him. Her life had been dedicated to that place as much as his had.

"Bring one for the table, Ming." Robert loved to flash whenever he came to the old hood. He was a big time speaker and writer, but his flow wasn't like it used to be. He had his young wife to thank for that. He couldn't blame Vera. He rarely helped her out. She was struggling to make ends meet. Even still, Vera snuggled up against Robert's arm.

He didn't come to the bar to impress anyone. He came for Vera. He had messed up so many things in his life. His first wife Bridget left him after he lost all of his money gambling and drinking. After a brief marriage with his second wife, he wrote three best sellers and got his life back on track. Ten years later, he was on that road again with Indira.

Vera turned to talk to Ida when Rosary blew in on the arm of James, Ida's ex-husband. Robert looked at Vera's sagging breast through her dress and the oddly rounded hips that sat next to him. She wasn't the prettiest catch in town, but she'd been there for him as far back as when he was picking cotton in Roanoke, Alabama. Vera turned around to see Robert staring at her body. Life had been hard on her. Her father had died after Robert left her and Alabama thirty years ago. She came to be with him later, only to find him married to another. Singing jazz was the only thing that saved her.

"Have you missed me that much, Bobby?" Vera faced Robert with her liquor-covered breath and kissed his lips. She could put em' away almost as fast as Robert.

"I just needed to get away tonight." Robert became anxious and looked around for Ming.

"Are you going to be with me all night?" Vera became happy a little too soon.

"Naw, I got a lot of things on my mind and I need to think them through," Robert felt relieved when he saw Ming coming toward their table with the drinks. He handed her a fifty-dollar bill.

"Keep the change, Ming," Robert said as he nodded his head to her. Ming smiled and nodded back to him. Vera got a little jealous whenever Robert gave Ming a big tip. As usual, she kept her envy inside. She clung onto his arm as he slung the bourbon down his throat.

"Come on, Bobby. Let's go home," Vera whispered in his ear. He hadn't made love to Indira in months, but Vera was filling the void.

"It's not my home, Vera." He massaged the back of his neck and closed his eyes.

"Here, baby, let me do that for you." Vera worked her hands on Robert's neck, enough to relax him. "Let's get out of here, Bobby."

Robert gave in to the relief of his tension and slid out of the corner booth.

"Good night, you two. I'll catch you later," Vera said as she wrapped her old coat over her shiny, red sequined dress and stumbled to her feet.

Robert led Vera out of the bar and into his car. He fumbled with the handle before getting in himself. Vera was proud to be with him. She had been with him for more than thirty years, but he had never made her his wife. She would do anything to stay with him. When Robert left Alabama, he had left Vera behind, but she had vowed to get him back someday. When he was married to Bridget, Vera was his woman and not his wife. Same with wife number two. Then he divorced her as promised. Next, while speaking at some college, he met wife number three, who was half Vera's age.

Vera stared at Robert with sour eyes, but what could she do? She was his. She'd given up everything for him. She never had children, had never been married, all for him. She slid next to Robert while he struggled to drive. She was his and no one else's. She didn't want anyone else. She took Robert anyway she could have him.

*****

Sydney was glad she only lived a couple of blocks away from Maxine. In no time, she and Jazzy were in their warm bed. Anthony had picked the apartment for them when Sydney found out she was pregnant. Anthony had predicted Sydney would get kicked out of the house, though Sydney never believed it would happen. She was almost in her second year at Wayne State University when it all came to a halt at the heartbeat of another human being.

Virginia wanted her daughter to grow up to be a success and nothing else. After Virginia's son Eric had died, Sydney became her main focus. When Sydney told her that she was pregnant, she went crazy. Though holier than thou, she told Sydney to get an abortion or get out. Sydney left. Virginia vowed to never speak to her again. Two years later, she still hadn't.

Jasmine yawned and turned on her side. Sydney was glad that she had Jasmine because she had become her reason for living.

"Would your daddy still be with me if I hadn't had you?" She rubbed Jasmine's hair lightly with the back of her hand. Sydney could only wonder what might have been, but in reality Anthony was gone and had been for a long time. Things had been real hard. They could barely take care of themselves, let alone a baby. Sydney couldn't work, so Anthony sold dope and worked a job. Things got harder each day and the dope game was bringing in more than his burger-flipping job. Along with the money came trouble. Anthony got caught up, so he left during her sixth month of pregnancy. Sydney was crushed, and still hadn't gotten over him.

But, he loved me so much, she mused.

Papa Joe had stepped in and helped his only daughter. He wanted to make up for the years he wasn't involved in her life. His only job was to provide for the family.

Sydney lay in bed and stared at the chipped paint on the ceiling. "If Anthony did really love me, he'd be with us now." Tears rolled off her face into her thick mane.

*****

It was late, but Maxine was still wide awake. She'd grown tired of her first choice and picked another book from her shelf. She tried to concentrate, but it was hopeless after the first page. She lay flat on her back searching her mind for answers.

"I don't understand what the problem is with these brothers. I think I'm an all right looking sister. They just don't know what they want." Maxine wasn't sure that she knew what she wanted in a man for that matter. Her past history didn't paint a perfect picture of bliss. None of her relationships had really led her anywhere.

"Where do you want to go Maxine? I don't know if I want to be some man's beckon call girl or wife." Maxine stood in front of the mirror and loosened her robe. She tried out her sexiest look against the mirror, and then sighed aloud.

"What do I want from this man?" Maxine hurriedly closed her robe and sat on the edge of the bed.

"For him to love me," she said decidedly. "I guess don't nobody want an old tar-baby like me, just like my mama used to say."

Maxine hurriedly closed her robe and sat on the edge of the bed. She felt a surge of emotion come over her. She hadn't thought about her mother in such a long time. She knew that she was still alive. That much she knew, thanks to Aunt Betsy. When Maxine was seven years old, her mother Maureen had brought her to live with her grandmother when she realized that she couldn't raise a child and do crack at the same time. From time to time Maureen would come by to see her only child until it seemed as if she'd completely forgotten that she had a daughter, and then she stopped coming by altogether.

She'll Learn

Maxine pulled her knees to her chest and rested her head on them.

"Here I am all alone, feeling sorry for myself. Again!" Maxine laughed in between the sudden rush of tears when she heard the phone ring. She picked it up in a hurry.

"Hello," Maxine sounded as if the world were going to end in a couple of seconds.

"What's wrong, Max?" Indira sounded concerned.

"Oh, nothing girl, I was just feeling a little down, that's all," Maxine wiped the remaining tears from her eyes and changed her tone. "Boy, this is a surprise. When was the last time you called me?" Maxine pulled herself up in the bed.

"Well you said if I needed someone to talk to, I could call." Indira didn't sound good either.

"Of course, Indi, I was just talking my usual shit. What's wrong?" Maxine was happy Indira turned to her for once. She and Sydney always had the better relationship than she and Indira.

"Lately, Robert has been getting worse than before and I don't know what to do. Everything and everybody says I should leave him, but I love him so much, Maxine."

Indira knew she loved him, but did he still love her?

"You know my answer to that, but I know it's not that easy," Maxine got quiet. Has he been hitting you again?"

"He got close when I came home tonight. He started accusing me of being with another man the minute I stepped through the door. I didn't know what else to do, but to reassure him that I didn't need another man." Indira held her face in her hands and talked.

"Did he believe you?" Maxine knew it was about time for Robert to flip his lid again.

"No, he looked at me for a long time, and then said he didn't need my love," Indira began to cry.

"He don't need your love, then whose love does he need?" Maxine had figured out a long time ago that Robert was seeing another woman. "Maybe that's why he's accusing you of being with another man."

"Gee thanks, Maxine. All I need is another woman in the picture," Indira fell quiet.

“I'm sorry, Indi. But if this is what's going on, you can't stand around and let him do it to you," Maxine was revved up now.

"Maxine, I wish I had your strength and backbone. Then I would have left him the first time he hit me," Indira felt stupid talking about this, but it was Maxine.

"Girl, I don't know what I would do in your situation. It's easy for me to just talk about it, but I'm not wearing your shoes," Maxine tried to make Indira feel a little better.

“I’m sorry about what I said earlier about your job. It was stupid.” Indira didn’t mean to hurt her friend’s feelings.

“That’s all right, I know your brain isn’t functioning right sometimes,” Maxine said jokingly, accepting Indira’s apology.

“Thanks for staying up with me, too, girl, I guess I better get some rest. I hope I’m good and asleep by the time Robert steps through the door." Indira cringed at the thought.

"Yeah, I've got a full lineup tomorrow. Take care and please don't ever think twice about calling me." Maxine knew that sometimes just talking was good enough. There wasn’t a solution to everything. "All right, girl, bye-bye."

“Bye.” Indira hung up the phone with Maxine and then sat hypnotized by a brief moment of peace. Things couldn't go on this way and Indira knew it. She had to help herself for a change. Maybe Robert didn't love her anymore, and what if he did have another woman somewhere? Indira looked over at the clock on the nightstand and saw that it was nearly twelve-thirty. Wherever Robert was, she knew he was drunk and probably not alone. Her husband hadn't so much as rubbed up against her in months, and she knew how much he enjoyed a woman's body.

*****

Robert cruised around his old neighborhood before heading to Vera’s. She sat damn near in his lap as he struggled to control his car. Everything had changed so much in the old hood. The streets seemed scarce with only the pet salon, the car wash, Esquire’s Deli and, of course, the Bottle and Barrel liquor store managed to survive the years. So much had changed inside of Robert over the years. Things were getting out of hand at home and Robert realized it. But what could he do? He thought he loved Indira, but he was entirely too jealous of her. He squint his eyes to get a better view of the road.

"What are you thinking about, baby?" Vera moved far enough away to look at Robert's face, which was covered with sweat. Robert never answered. He was sweating in nearly twenty-degree weather.

"What has she done to you now, Bobby?" Vera hated Indira, though she didn't even know her. She only knew of her. She hated her for being Robert's wife. She knew that woman had brought Robert nothing but grief.

"She hasn't done anything. It's me. I've been hitting on her again and I was mad enough to kill her tonight. Then I came to find you." Robert came to a complete stop in the middle of Fullerton, only three blocks away from Vera's.

Vera didn't want to hear any of that. She only wanted to hear him say he was leaving Indira.

"Bobby, please, she doesn't need you like I need you. She's got her art and her fancy friends. What would she need you for?" Vera spoke in a tone that cut through Robert like a knife.

Robert stomped his foot on the gas pedal then slammed on the brakes in front of Vera's rundown home. The house needed a good painting and the roof needed fixing, but Vera never asked Robert for anything. She wanted the entire package, not just his money.

"I'm the only one who'll ever love you, Bobby," Vera gave Robert a heartfelt look.

"Get out, Vera," Robert spoke in a low tone. Vera looked at Robert strangely, and then opened the door of the car. She staggered to her feet and turned to Robert.

"I'm sorry, Bobby if I said something I shouldn't have." Vera held her head low and swung her shoulders. "You know I talk too much sometimes and...."

Before Vera could look up, Robert had closed the car door and had driven off. Vera pulled her shawl onto her shoulders and marched to her door.

Robert came to a stop at a traffic light and laid his head on the steering wheel. "What does she need you for?" he repeated aloud.

Vera's sharp words were stinging his eardrums. Indira used to make him feel so young and full of life. Now she never had the time for him. Robert searched for his bottle of bourbon under the seat and missed the changing of the light to green. A police car cruised up to the side of the car and flashed Robert just as he sat up. The young police officer flashed Robert's face with his flashlight as if he were looking for someone else and then pulled off.

"Must've been a fan," Robert gleamed at the notion, though he knew it wasn't true.

*****

Indira lay in the dark room and stared out the window at the night sky. She knew a big change in her life was needed. She was still young and had a great career. She couldn't let some drunk ruin it for her, even if that drunk was her husband.

"He must be crazy if he thinks I'm going to let him continue to drag me down any further." Indira heard Robert's keys jingling in the keyhole of the door. She lay as still as she could and pretended to be asleep. She was surprised to see that her husband had beaten the sun. Robert let his trench coat fall to the floor and began his journey up the stairs.

"Indira, you asleep?" Robert was whispering the best anyone as drunk as he was possibly could. He tapped her bare shoulder with the hopes of getting some. Indira didn't move. She was frozen, she couldn't and wouldn't move. The smell of liquor and loud perfume announced his whereabouts.

Robert frowned and then began to get undressed. He took off his shirt and then nearly killed himself getting out of his pants. He turned to Indira to see if she had awakened. She hadn't. Indira lifted her eyes to see Robert banging his way into their bathroom. He came out and climbed into bed behind her. He wasn't going to give up that easily. He brushed his leg against her satiny gown and couldn't resist pulling his body close to hers. Indira opened her eyes wide when she felt Robert's hardness pressed to her backside. Robert began to slowly lift the gown off of Indira's legs before she suddenly moved away from him.

"What are you doing, Robert?" Indira sat up in their king-size bed and looked toward him.

She'll Learn

"I'm trying to fuck my wife," Robert spoke frankly and then sat up on his elbow.

"What! Why the need to touch me now. You haven't done that in months?" Indira tightened her grip on the sheets. She knew Robert was drunk and would go off on anything, but she had to tell him how she felt.

"You think I can't smell that cheap-ass perfume, besides the liquor coming through your skin?" Indira knew Robert had been with another woman and this was the end for her. Robert sat up on the side of the bed with his back to Indira. She was standing up to him in a way he was not in the mood for.

"What did you expect, Indira? You're never here." Robert never turned to look at her.

"And when I am here you're drunk!" Indira yelled.

Robert couldn't take hearing any more. Vera was right. She didn't need him anymore. He sat quietly for a few moments to calm himself before getting up to go sleep in the guest room; he closed the door behind him. Indira watched her husband leave their bedroom, knowing she'd hurt him badly, but only after she'd been hurt so many times.

CHAPTER THREE

Maxine rose out of bed at six a.m., like clockwork. She ran her slender fingers over the tight curls on her head as she sat on the edge of her bed. Though she was dead tired, she was determined to stay in shape. She changed into her running gear and hopped onto her treadmill. She had turned her Aunt Mary's old room into a mini gym. Neither one of her aunts could believe that Mable had left the house to Maxine, her granddaughter, and not one of her own children. Aunt Mary was the only one worrying about it. Aunt Betsy didn't care one way or the other. She had her own house.

Sweat trailed down the side of Maxine's face as the machine began to rise, pushing her to work harder. After forty minutes she slowed her pace and then finally came to a stop.

"Whew!" Maxine kicked her legs and tried to catch her breath. "Whew!" She learned to keep her legs from going weak by kicking them. It felt silly, but it worked.

"Way to go baby!" she shouted as she picked up her towel and dried her face and neck. She was sweating like a pig. She got that from her mama. Maxine grabbed her water bottle and took a few swallows.

"Much better," she said as she peeled out of her sweaty clothes and dropped them down the clothes chute. The pulsating water in the shower seemed to beat her skinny body back to life. She followed the same ritual every morning. First she ran for forty minutes, showered, rubbed her body down with Neutrogena Sesame oil, and then ate a light breakfast. Next came the trials of finding something to wear before going to open her salon. Today was no different as Maxine stood in her bra and panties searching through her closet. She decided on a velveteen pair of stretch pants and a matching black velveteen sweater.

Maxine pulled into the parking lot of Fashion Hair, and as usual, her receptionist Stephanie sat in her car awaiting her arrival. Maxine parked alongside Stephanie and then got out. Stephanie stood in front of her car with two boxes of doughnuts in her arms. She usually ate the majority of them before setting them out for clients.

She'll Learn

"How are you this morning?" Maxine spoke as she and Stephanie walked to the back door of the salon together. Maxine went through the door first to cut the alarm off.

"Girl, I am tired as I don't know what. I hung out all night at the Player's Lounge, it was ladies' night."

Stephanie hung out just about every night. Why not? She was twenty-two. Maxine loved to go out a lot when she was in her twenties, but things were different now. She still liked to go out, but now, she had a purpose. She was ready for something more. Maxine listened as her young colleague talked about her night while she struggled to remember the code.

Stephanie took both their coats and hung them in the closet near the front door. Maxine flicked on the lights and took a deep breath as she looked around. She was so proud of the place and she knew her grandmother was probably grinning from ear to ear in heaven. From the black couches to the metallic ceiling, Maxine pieced the place together with all she had. Her grandmother had turned the den of their home into a hair salon and had made her living in the back of the house, along with watching all the children she could.

Stephanie started the coffeemaker and then put the doughnuts on a tray for the customers. She picked up a chocolate doughnut and popped it into her mouth, just as Maxine turned to look at her.

Maxine put her hand on her hip and shook her head. "I thought you were supposed to be on a diet, Steph," she jokingly said to Stephanie who always seemed to be on some sort of diet.

"Well, God didn't mean for everybody to be stick people." Stephanie took another big bite of the doughnut to show Maxine just how much she cared about a diet.

Maxine continued to shake her head and walked into the room she shared with Dina. She put on her smock. She and Dina had started out together in beauty school and then they worked at the Foxy Lady Hair Salon under the tutelage of Mrs. Veronica Fox. When Maxine told Dina that she was branching off on her own, Dina was game for the opportunity to leave.

Dina came in through the door, unwinding her scarf from around her neck.

"Good morning, Stephanie." Dina, a petite woman, was tough and didn't take any mess from anybody.

Maxine stepped out into the hallway to greet her friend. "Good morning, Miss Thang." Maxine nicknamed her that because she harbored such an attitude.

"Mornin', Maxi pad," Dina hung up her coat and listened for Maxine to retaliate. Stephanie continued to eat doughnuts and laugh at the two.

"Keebler elf," Maxine turned and gave Stephanie a high 5.

"Girl, forget you. I quit." Dina put on her smock.

"Hey, everybody," Ficara, the nail technician, walked in dressed in her latest hoochie-mama apparel.

"What in the world have you got on?" Dina stood in front of Ficara and looked her up and down.

Ficara checked herself and then waved her fingers, flashing extra scary nails. "What is it this time little woman? Is it too short, too tight, what?" Ficara threw up her arms in disgust. Her dangling bangles sang a song.

"Nothing child, if you don't know, I ain't gonna' be the one to tell you."

The other hair technicians, Keith and Yolanda, strolled in a few minutes later. It wasn't long before the lobby began to fill. Everybody waited patiently on a turn for some special treatment. Maxine spoke to everyone then checked the log to see who her first appointment was. It was Sheila.

"Come on back, Sheila."

Sheila turned to her son before she left to get her hair done. "Now you sit your behind right here and don't you get up unless you ask Miss Stephanie."

He nodded okay as Sheila waved her thick finger at him.

"Yes, ma'am," the little boy replied obediently to his mother.

Maxine watched Sheila with her son. He usually did exactly what he was told. That was the kind of child she wanted; one who would listen to her. She knew that probably wouldn't happen since she raised so much hell as a child. What was she thinking? She didn't want anything to do with kids. At least not right now.

She'll Learn

She led Sheila back to her chair.

"What are you having done today?" Maxine took her eyes off Sheila and glanced at the little boy sitting quietly in the corner of the couch.

"I'm just getting a blow and go today, I've got to get to work." Sheila was always in a hurry. Maxine covered her with her leopard-print smock then quickly parted and scratched her scalp.

"Go on back to the bowls, I'll be right there." Maxine finished her coffee and then followed. "Let's go, baby," she said to herself as she tried to pump herself up for the day. She positioned Sheila's head in the neck rest.

"So how are things with you, Sheila?" Maxine ran the warm water over her hair to get it soaked. She knew just about everything about her customers. They all seemed to trust her and confide in her with all of their business.

"Girl, not good at all. That sorry ex-husband of mine still refuses to pay child support. I mean I don't see what his problem his. James Jr. and Shane are still his sons." Sheila folded her arms across her smock in dismay.

"Is he still working?" Maxine applied shampoo to Sheila's hair and began scrubbing. She was in and out of listening to Sheila. She couldn't take her mind off of Indira. Indira had told her that she was strong and had backbone. Maxine didn't feel that way. Sometimes she felt weak. When it came to men, she was extremely weak. Maxine finished shampooing Shelia's thick hair for a third time, and then rinsed.

"And now girl, guess what?" Sheila stopped talking; she really wanted her to guess.

"What, Sheila?" Maxine sat the woman up and towel dried her hair.

"He says he's getting married to that trick he left me for." Sheila let her head relax and flow as Maxine applied conditioner. "I can't believe his ass." Sheila was all wound up now.

"Girl, relax. He ain't even worth giving yourself a heart attack." Maxine slapped a plastic cap on the woman's head.

"I shall return, Sheila."

Sheila sat with her eyes closed rocking back and forth. Maxine called Tracey to her chair and permed her long tresses while Sheila's conditioner set.

"Your hair is growing so much, Tracey." Maxine knew it was because of her taking care of it and not Tracey.

"I know. It hasn't been this long since I was little." Tracey turned to watch Maxine in the mirror behind her.

"How's your mama doing?" Maxine went through the same routine everyday. She had known some of her customers practically all her life. Many of their mothers and grandmothers used to be the customer's of her grandmother.

"She said to tell you she is coming to get her hair done for Daddy's birthday party."

Maxine pushed lightly against the young girl's head to lower it. "Now your mama knows she's not coming to get her hair done. She has only been to this shop one time. And that was the grand opening!"

Maxine and Tracey laughed.

Maxine rinsed out Sheila's conditioner and put her under the dryer. "I'll see you in forty minutes," Maxine spoke under the hood for Sheila to hear. Sheila waved her hand okay.

After rinsing and applying setting lotion to Tracey's locks, Maxine wrapped it into a beehive and placed her under a dryer as well. She got started on Mrs. Mason's gray coif.

Sheila was curled and ready; she paid Maxine her fee.

"Thanks Maxine, I'll see you next Saturday." Sheila left as Tracey sat back down in her chair. Maxine combed down her wrap and styled it. After spraying oil sheen to bring out the shine, Tracey was on her way out the door, too.

Before she knew it, Maxine had finished three heads and was feeling the growl of her stomach. She took off her smock and exchanged it for her coat.

"I'm going next door to Ray's. Does anybody want something?" Maxine stood in front of the desk and announced her plans.

"I do, Max." Keith put down his clippers and reached into the pocket of his loose fitting Karl Kani jeans for some money. "Bring me back an order of beef fried rice, please." Keith handed Maxine a $10 bill.

“Girl, I was about to fall out from hunger,” he said exaggerating. Keith was such a flame, but he could cut some hair. Plus, he brought a lot of business to the shop.

"Anybody else?" Maxine heard no response, so she headed next door. The strip of businesses was an odd mix. There was her hair salon, a Chinese restaurant, a video store, and a nightclub. Maxine was a regular customer in the tiny restaurant, especially since it was so close.

The bell hanging over the door jingled as Maxine stepped inside.

"Hello, Maxine," Lan said as she stood in the doorway of the kitchen.

"How are you two doing today?" Maxine spoke to the owners Lan and Ray before checking out the buffet. It shined brightly in the dimly lit restaurant.

"I think I'll get the pepper steak and rice today." Maxine took in the heavenly aromas filling her nose. She would worry about smelling like garlic later on.

"You want egg roll too?" Ray scooped the rice onto the to-go tray, and then covered it with pepper steak. He began to look around in search of something.

"I come right back, I need to find baggy for egg roll." Ray was gone to the back before Maxine could object. He knew she didn't like the egg roll to get soggy.

The bell over the door jingled again as a tall man strolled in.

"Hello, sir. What can I get for you today?" Lan took over while Ray still remained in the back.

Maxine's nostrils filled with Tuscany. She knew it well since her ex-boyfriend Billy used to wear it faithfully. It had a different effect on her now.

Just as the man moved next to her to look over the buffet, Maxine lifted her eyes to see one of the finest black men in the city. The man looked up from the buffet and smiled at Maxine. She smiled back. His creamy mocha skin and his neat fade had Maxine feeling this man's presence.

"Hello," his deep voice rang out like a harmonious song.

She couldn't wait to hear him sing something else. She opened her mouth, but said nothing. She then swallowed and spoke.

"Hello." Her face was covered with embarrassment.

"Eat here often?" Bruce quickly became interested in the beautiful sister he was standing next to. She was just his type, chocolate.

"Maybe a little too often, I own the hair salon next door." Maxine had to put that out there.

Her inner voice began picking at her, "Dang, Maxine. He didn't ask you that." Maxine hoped he didn't think she was bragging; she was just proud.

Bruce loved confident women, maybe a little too much.

"Oh, that's great. By the way, I'm Bruce Washington." He extended his hand. Maxine shook the hand, and examined the smoothness and strength it possessed.

"I'm Maxine Harrell." She stared into his dark eyes.

"It's very nice to meet you, Maxine." Bruce stared at Maxine as she did him while they still held on to each other's hand.

Ray reappeared from the back.

"Here we are. I found baggy for eggroll." He wrapped the egg roll and slid the tray down to Lan at the register. Maxine and Bruce let go of their handshake.

Bruce began to order while Maxine handed Lan the money for her food. She looked Bruce over from head to toe as he stood only a few feet from her. He had a light mustache and gorgeous white teeth. Pretty teeth had always been a weakness for her. He had a nice husky build under his leather bomber jacket. Maxine was betting he had muscular legs like a running back. She loved a man with fine legs.

"Thank you, Maxine," Lan was handing Maxine's change out to her, but then noticed where her mind was.

"Very handsome," Lan whispered. Maxine continued to watch Bruce, and then turned her eyes to Lan who was grinning at her. They began to snicker like two schoolgirls.

"Sorry, Lan." Maxine grabbed her change. "Dammit, I forgot to get Keith's order."

Lan watched Maxine head back to the buffet line. She covered her mouth as she laughed again.

"Go get him, Maxine." Lan left the cash register and went into the back.

She'll Learn

Maxine slid behind Bruce who was leaning on the railing. Her chest brushed against the back of his jacket. "Excuse me," she said. She was now in line behind Bruce. Keith's order had earned her a few more minutes to watch this brother.

"Still hungry?" Bruce joked with her as he waited on Ray to complete his order. Maxine laughed inside as she thought about just how hungry she was for him.

"I forgot to get someone else's order," she coyly replied. She tried to keep her cool, but it was hard to do standing next to that six foot four inch man.

"Here you are, sir. Thank you and come again," Ray smiled and spoke at the same time.

Bruce turned his eyes to Ray and nodded to him.

"Thank you." He walked toward the cash register. Maxine placed Keith's order and tried not to look Bruce's way. Bruce paid Lan and walked out the door.

The bell over the door told Maxine to relax. He was gone. She had let another fine man slip through her fingers. Lan looked over at Maxine and shook her head. Maxine paid once again and left the restaurant with her tail between her legs.

To her surprise, Bruce was in front of the restaurant sitting on top of his Lexus 430.

"I was wondering if you'd mind me giving you a call sometime?" He reached in his jacket for one of his business cards and handed it to Maxine.

"I wouldn't mind that at all." Maxine opened her Coach purse and got out one of her own business cards for him; being able to do that always felt good to her. She smiled hard as she walked toward the shop.

"Would tonight be too soon to call?" Bruce slightly yelled for Maxine to hear him over the noisy street. Seven Mile Road was always busy with traffic.

Bruce looked so good sitting there against that car. How could she refuse?

"I look forward to it," Maxine waved to him then opened the main door to the salon. She buzzed for Stephanie to let her in. She was so excited she ran over to the couch and sat down between Kiara and Stacks to keep herself from fainting.

"Girl, I can't believe how cool I was." Maxine picked up a magazine from the coffee table and fanned herself.

"Cool where? What?" Stephanie leaned in closer from the desk.

Maxine stopped fanning and then looked at the young girls on either side of her.

"I just met one of the finest men in the entire city. He was a complete package." Maxine went on about Bruce and then got up from the couch.

"Thanks for getting out of the way girls," Maxine said as she made her way over to Stephanie at the desk.

"Did he give you a card or something?" Stephanie was being too nosey. Maxine reached in her pocket and retrieved his business card. Stephanie was dying to examine it for herself. She knew a fake when she saw one.

"Let me see the damn thing," Stephanie said as she held out her hand. Maxine reluctantly handed it to her.

"Looks legit to me," Stephanie continued on and read the card. Her eyes became wide with excitement. "Girl, do you know who this man you just met is?" Stephanie stared at Maxine and shook her head.

"No. Is he somebody important? He sure did look important." Maxine wanted to know all that the girl might know about the man. Stephanie didn't answer right away. Maxine was losing her patience.

"Girl, who is he?" Maxine yelled, causing heads to turn in the lobby.

"Okay, fool. Mr. Bruce Washington is a big boxing promoter. He owns that famous gym downtown where all those big-time boxers train. You know, he's the one who gets all those big fights at The Palace." Stephanie continued to study the card.

"How do you know all this?" Maxine took the card from Stephanie.

"Selena and I met him once at the Diamond Club." Stephanie turned her attention to the woman standing behind Maxine.

She'll Learn

"What can I do for you, Mrs. Russell?" Stephanie put on her customer service face. Maxine turned around to see the gray-haired woman in her late fifties; she quickly moved over.

"I would like for you to change my day to Wednesdays. I don't like coming on Saturdays anymore, just too many people." Mrs. Russell looked around the crowded lobby and sort of huffed.

"Sure thing, Mrs. Russell, I'll take care of it right away." Stephanie lowered her head into the schedule book and then looked up at Maxine and smirked. Maxine got the hint and went back to the task at hand, the bottom of the list.

*****

Indira sat at the kitchen table gazing out the window as she sipped her tea. Robert busied himself with the breakfast dishes. After a night of arguing and drinking, Robert always rose early and cooked Indira an apology breakfast. She was sick of the apologies because things weren't getting any better between them. She looked over her shoulder at her husband. He had changed in so many ways. He drank day and night. He stopped exercising. He hadn't finished a book in more than a year. And, he now slouched like an old man.

When she met Robert, he was so handsome, with a full head of naturally curly hair and the body of a twenty-year-old. It was obvious he worked out because of the way he chased her down on campus.

Robert turned around to see Indira staring at him, but not really seeing him. Things had gotten so bad between them. He knew she was thinking about him. He went back to his work. Indira snapped out of her daydream and scooted her chair away from the table. Robert stopped drying the dishes and turned to Indira.

"You leaving?" He promised himself last night that he would try with his young wife. The next step would be to leave her.

"Yes, I've got a lot of last minute things to take care of before the showing tonight." Indira stood up and pulled her robe together.

"Tonight?" Robert didn't know what was going on, he was totally in the dark about tonight.

"Don't tell me you forgot about the showing tonight at the gallery?" Indira put her hand on her hip and stared at Robert.

"No, no. I didn't forget. I just thought that, maybe, we could spend some quality time together today. That's all."

He had forgotten. Indira couldn't believe what she was hearing.

Quality time? she thought.

After everything he'd put her through the last couple of months. What made him think she'd want that?

"I'm sorry, Robert, but I can't today. I have been planning this event for months. I can't afford for anything to go wrong tonight." Indira brushed by him as she went upstairs to get dressed. He snatched the apron from around his waist and threw it down.

"The nerve of that son of a bitch," Indira said to herself as she slung off her robe and stepped into the shower. She closed her eyes and let the water beat across her face.

"Why would I want to spend some time with him?" She shook her head and put him in the back of her mind. She had better things to think about today. After pinning her hair up into a loose bun, Indira searched her vanity table for her bottle of Bvlgari and noticed the broken pieces of glass. She came to the conclusion that her husband had broken it in anger. She settled for Victoria Secret's Heavenly and sprayed it on.

After clearing the broken glass, she dressed in a pair of black slacks, a ruffled shirt, and her leather vest. Maxine told her that ruffles made up for a woman's lack of tits. Indira gave herself another once over in the mirror, grabbed her attaché case and headed down the stairs.

Robert stood at the bottom waiting for her.

"What time will you be back?" Robert tried to seem as genuine as possible.

"Probably just in time to get dressed for tonight. Oh, I laid your tux out on the bed."

Robert helped Indira with her leather swing coat. He went to kiss her glossy lips just as she turned her face, causing Robert to graze her cheek. Indira retrieved her purse from the couch.

"I'll see you later," she said as she opened the front door and rushed out of it. Standing on the other side of the door, Indira took the back of her hand and wiped Robert's kiss off her face. "Yuck!" She could faintly smell stale liquor.

She'll Learn

Robert walked from the hallway to his office in the den. He ran his fingers over the keyboard of his computer with which he hadn't been able to write anything in months, let alone another book. He was having one helluva writer's block. He wasn't worried, though. He had enough money from his five previous books to keep him comfortable. In the field of financial planning, he was well respected and highly praised for his work. But, what was happening to him was that he'd started drinking more and more and couldn't stop. He didn't want to stop. A picture of Indira and himself next to the terminal caught his eye. He picked it up.

"Indira," he said aloud. The bright smile that his wife had on the picture caused him to smile. "How in love we used to be." Robert put the picture back in its place.

"What have I been doing to you, Indira?" Robert thought back on the numerous times he'd hit her and taken his anger out on her.

Why she still loved him, he would never know.

CHAPTER FOUR

Indira opened the doors to the gallery to see everyone rushing around in a panic. “What in the world is going on?” Indira eyed Omari as he sauntered over to her. His face was pruned up tightly and was turning red.

“Thank goodness you’re here.” Omari took Indira by the arm and led her inside. He was so feminine when he wanted to be.

“What is it, Omari?” Indira pulled off her scarf and tuned in.

Omari put his hands on his hips and took in a deep breath. “The car I sent to pick up Eldridge Moss broke down on the highway and his plane lands in twenty minutes,” Omari looked his faithful assistant in the eyes.

“Where is your car this morning?” Indira rolled her eyes and turned toward the window, she knew one of Omari’s men had it.

“Well a friend of mine is borrowing it, but never mind that. What are we going to do?”

“No need to worry, I’ll just go and pick him up myself. Besides, it’ll seem more personable if one of us greets him at the airport.” Indira smiled at her boss of two years and then wrapped her scarf back around her neck. She had convinced Omari completely. She wasn’t quite up to being in a room full of panicky people anyway.

“I shall return.”

Omari and the rest of the staff began applauding as Indira left.

*****

Sydney Hastings had Jasmine in her arms and struggled up the steep stairs to her apartment. Though there was an elevator, it never worked. Sydney was getting a little too plump for walking the steps, so she sat down on the stairs of the second floor.

"Anthony, the things I did for you," she said to herself as she held onto Jasmine who looked up into her eyes. Jasmine looked so much like her daddy you'd think he was the one who had given birth to her.

"Don’t wanna walk, huh? You are getting too heavy." Sydney kissed her daughter on her forehead and then looked up when she heard a door close. It was Wayne, stepping out into the hallway. He didn't notice her on the stairs.

"Hey, Wayne." Sydney hadn't seen her friend in more than a month even though they were only two floors away from each other. Wayne could always cheer her up.

"Sydney." Wayne walked over to the stairs and gave her a hug. "Hello, Jasmine." He kissed Jasmine as he was glad to see them both. "What are you doing out here in this cold hallway?" He leaned against the banister with his arms folded tightly to keep warm.

"Taking a quick rest," Sydney was so beat she didn't want to move another inch with two more floors to go.

"I don't get to see you too often. What you been up to?" Wayne flashed a big smile and leaned in closer. He had been trying to get a date with her ever since Anthony had left, but she just wanted to be friends.

"Just working every day and taking care of Jazzy," Sydney replied.

"Can I hold Jazzy?" Wayne asked.

Sydney shifted Jasmine in her lap when Wayne reached for her. She handed her growing toddler to Wayne.

"Oh, she's getting so big," Wayne snuggled up to the baby as Sydney watched. She wished Anthony could have been more like Wayne—not really. She was attracted to thugs and roughnecks, Wayne didn't fit either of those categories, but he would have never left her.

Sydney was staring at the two, but she couldn't see them anymore. She could only see Anthony telling her that things had gotten too intense for him. Intense. She was in total shock from what she had heard.

"So, Sydney what do you two beautiful ladies have planned for tonight?" Wayne danced around with Jasmine and then noticed that Sydney hadn't answered him. She was sitting on the stairs with her arms on her knees staring just past him.

"Sydney."

Sydney heard Wayne and snapped out of her daydream. "Sorry, I got a little too deep into my thoughts." She turned her eyes back to Wayne.

"I was just wondering what two special ladies like you have planned for the night?" Wayne felt awkward as he stood staring at Sydney.

He had had his eye on her from the very first day she moved into the apartment. "I'm pretty sure you deserve it."

Sydney was hearing Wayne loud and clear, she did deserve it. Besides, what did she have to lose if she were to go out with Wayne? She could lose a good friend. He was the rock she had needed when Anthony packed up. She needed him, as well as Indira and Max.

"We do deserve a little special treatment, but not tonight," Sydney continued to smile as she rejected Wayne's offer, once again. She stood up from the stairs and took hold of Jasmine. "I already have plans for tonight and I've got to get started on the plans for this one's birthday party on Sunday."

"Oh, wow. She's turning two already!" Wayne seemed excited for the little girl.
"I'm going to have to go out and get you something precious." He bent over and tapped the baby's nose.

"You'll be able to come, won't you?" Sydney knew she sounded a little eager. "I mean, you don't have to work do you?"

Wayne stepped closer to Sydney and then reached beside her to grab the bags that rested on the stairs.

"No, I'm off on the weekends and I would love to come."

Sydney started up the stairs with Wayne following close behind. He watched Sydney as her hips swayed up the steep staircase with Jasmine hanging off her shoulder. Sydney was just his type.

After walking up two flights of stairs in silence, Sydney stood in front of her apartment. She opened the door for Wayne to put her bags in. She immediately caught a glimpse of his perfectly packed behind and nearly lost her breath as he bent over. Jasmine stepped down out of her mother's arms and climbed onto the couch. Sydney walked back to the door as Wayne waved goodbye to Jasmine. He stood only a few inches from Sydney, but it was enough for her to smell his aftershave lotion. She hadn't realized how long it had been since a man's aroma tickled her nose.

"Thank you for bringing the bags up," Sydney dropped her eyes to the floor. Wayne bent down until he reached her eyes and brought them back up to him.

"It was my pleasure, and I want you to think about that special evening." He reached for Sydney's hand and kissed it. Sydney felt herself become lightheaded.

"Oh, I promise I will."

Wayne nodded then headed down the stairs. Before Sydney could close the door, he was coming toward her again.

"Oh, I forgot to tell you, I sent my resumé to Channel 4 downtown and I have an interview next week."

He wasn't even going to apply until Sydney talked him into it.

"Well, good luck. I sure hope you get it."

Wayne smiled and then backed his way to the stairs. Sydney closed the door behind her and looked over at Jasmine.

"Baby, your mama has still got it; even though it ain't a size eight no more," Sydney laughed as she took off Jasmine's snowsuit.

*****

Maxine breezed through her long list of clients. Saturdays were the shop's busiest day and she knew how to get through it. Before calling for her next client, she picked up the phone to call Sydney. The phone rang nearly five times before she answered.

"Hello," Sydney sounded out of breath.

"What took you so long to answer the phone?"

"I was putting away these groceries and keeping my eye on Jazzy."

"Well I was just calling to tell you that I got one more head to do then I will be on my way."

"Sounds good to me, girl. Oh, I got something to tell you when you get here, too." Sydney couldn't wait to tell Maxine about Wayne.

"All right then I'll see you later. Bye." Maxine hung up the phone on the desk and checked the list for her last customer of the day.

"Lena, you can go on back to the bowl and I'll be there in just one minute." Maxine crossed off Lena's name and headed back to wash her hair.

*****

Indira swerved on the road as she tried to cleanup her car and drive at the same time, which was impossible for her to do. She found a half-eaten doughnut under the seat and tossed it out the window.

"Forgive me world." She looked up to see the traffic light turning red and stomped on her brakes, causing her tires to scream. She quickly bent over and gathered up the many papers that lived on the floor of her Mercedes, shoved them into the glove compartment and slammed it shut.

"I hope that doesn't blow just as he sits down in front of it."

She reached the airport in minutes and found a parking space. She began checking herself in the mirror. Indira often wondered about Eldridge Moss, the talented young man whom she'd never seen, and had only spoken to over the phone. Listening to his deep voice over the phone was enough to spark her interest in him.

After making a sign on the back of one of her leftover fliers, she strolled into the airport's baggage claim. The plane had landed fifteen minutes ago, and still no Eldridge. Indira was getting a little worried; she suddenly felt a hand on her shoulder. She turned with the sign still at her chest.

"That's me," the deep voice rang out like a love song.

The man mesmerized her. She snapped out of her gaze and extended her hand. "Eldridge, I'm Indira Carr."

The long, thick dreads that hung around his face caught her eye first, then the perfect white teeth that made up his smile, and then those remarkable eyes.

"Finally, I get to meet the sister with the calming voice." His eyes were so innocent. The compliment caused Indira to slightly blush, which was easy to see on her caramel skin. "No matter how bad things were, whenever I got your call, things seemed to get better." Eldridge towered over Indira.

"Thank you, Mr. Moss. I'm glad that I could be the one to make things better." She looked up into Eldridge's hazel eyes. There were those eyes again.

"Please call me El."

Indira could feel those eyes looking straight through her.

"Okay El, the car is just across the street." She reached for the suitcase that sat on the floor next to his leg. Eldridge took hold of her arm when she got near it. She looked up quickly.

"Now what kind of man would I be if I were to let you carry my bag for me?" He picked up his bag and smirked at Indira. She shrugged her shoulders and stepped out of the man's way. The wonderful smell of his cologne danced across her nose as he walked out the doors ahead of her. He was handsome, she had to admit, and he could dress—two more things she liked about him.

"I'm the cream sedan." Indira pushed her keypad to open the trunk. Eldridge nodded, giving his approval of her Mercedes.

Must be nice, he thought to himself.

"It was really nice of you to pick me up instead of some car service," Eldridge poured on the charm as he loaded his bags into the trunk.

"I wouldn't have had it any other way," Indira unlocked the doors and watched as Eldridge got into the car. She looked at her wedding ring in disgust and then got in.

Eldridge couldn't take his eyes off of Indira. He hadn't imagined her being so beautiful. He looked at her hands on the steering wheel and saw her wedding ring.

"There goes another one." He thought he was whispering.

"What was that Eldridge?" Indira turned to him with a slight smirk on her face.

"Nothing. I was thinking aloud." He turned and looked out the window.

"So, are you excited about tonight?" Indira broke the silence.

"I'm a little nervous, believe it or not," El was showing Indira his shy side. She was buying it.

"A talented man like you has nothing to worry about. Everything will be perfect."

Indira got on the expressway. On the ride to the hotel, the two got to know each other a little better and were comfortable with one another by the time they got there. Indira got out to confirm her reservations for Eldridge as he retrieved his bags from the trunk.

"Married!" Eldridge got loud just as Indira went inside the building. "The good ones are always taken." Eldridge headed over to the entrance with his bags.

"All right Eldridge, El, everything is taken care of," Indira handed him his key and glanced over at the bellhop loading El's luggage aboard his cart.

"I will see you at seven o'clock sharp." Indira flashed him a big smile. She almost felt like she knew him.

"So what are you saying? I won't be ready?" Eldridge began joking with her. He wasn't ready for her to leave just yet. But after a few moments of smiling at each other, Indira spoke up.

"I'd better get back to the gallery. There's a lot I still have to take care of. If you need anything, you can reach me at the gallery or just call my cell phone," Indira turned and walked to the door. She didn't want to seem interested.

Eldridge stood beside the bellhop as they both watched her walk away.

"See you tonight." He didn't speak loud enough to be heard by anyone but the bellhop.

"I wish I was seeing her tonight," the bellhop said as he shook his head and began pushing the cart to the elevator.

Eldridge waved to Indira when she looked back. She got into her car and stared at the steering wheel.

"What do you think you're doing, Indira Shay Carr?" She laughed and turned the key in the ignition. "He is mighty fine." She accidentally tapped her horn and pulled off.

*****

Maxine held the hot curling iron in Lena's blonde hair until it formed a perfect curl.

"All right, Lena. See how you like that," Maxine spun the chair around to the mirror for Lena to see her coif.

"Girl, this is sharp. Mark is going to love this," Lena examined her hair in the mirror.

"I knew you'd like this style," Maxine looked at her work with approval. Lena gave Maxine a tip and stepped out of her chair.

"Thank you, Lena. I'll see you next week." Maxine slid the money in the pocket of her smock and began sweeping up her area.

Dad walked by and noticed his boss. "I'll take care of that Maxine," Dad said as he took hold of the broom and began cleaning the hair from the floor.

"Thanks, Dad." Maxine was glad she had given Dad a chance. He used to hang outside her building and beg for money. One day she told him either to come in and cleanup or get from in front of her store. To her surprise, he came inside. Since he was a much older guy, everyone in the shop called him Dad. Nearly a year later, he had sobered up and become her full-time maintenance man.

Dina led her customer into the room and sat her down in her chair. She towel dried Mrs. Allen’s hair and then stepped over to Maxine.

"Girl I heard you met you a real one today," Dina was being all in Maxine’s business as usual.

"And what qualifies him to be a real one in your book?" Maxine stopped packing up her bag and turned to Dina.

"He's got a real job and seems to already have something. That makes him a real man in my book, honey." Dina snapped her fingers at Maxine and returned to her client. "Ain't that right, Mrs. Allen?" The woman lifted her head up from her slight nap and nodded in agreement with Dina.

Maxine zipped up her bag and got her coat out of the closet.

"You are really trippin’, girl."

Stephanie walked into the room from the lobby. "What y’all in here laughing about?"

Maxine slung her bag over her shoulder and brushed past Stephanie.

"All of you need to stop being so damn nosey! Oh, sorry, Mrs. Allen,” Maxine's grandmother had taught her to always respect her elders.

“That’s all right, baby; they’re picking on you.” The older woman folded her arms under her smock and closed her eyes again.

"You never did say when your date is?" Dina continued to pry.

"Don't worry about when my date is. Just remember to lock up everything before you go to happy hour." Maxine left her station and headed for the door, weaving around the couches that sat in the lobby.

Stephanie and Dina rushed to the door of the room.

"Yes, ma'am!" Dina replied.

Maxine stopped in her tracks and walked over to the stand that housed their stocking selection. She got two pairs for Sydney; she never had any stockings when she needed them.

"I'll see you tricks on Tuesday, I'm going to do Sydney's hair for her blind date tonight." Maxine buttoned up and got her car keys out of her pocket.

"Even Sydney's got a date?" Stephanie sarcastically asked as she and Dina looked at each other then at Maxine.

"Screw both of y'all," Maxine left out and closed the door behind her.

"I'll be real glad when she do get some. She ain't happy unless she's banging," Stephanie said before giving Dina a soft high 5. They cracked up with laughter then turned to see Mrs. Allen eyeballing them both.

"Sorry, Mrs. Allen," they said before returning to their designated places.

CHAPTER FIVE

Indira swerved into her driveway, nearly running down the lights that lined it. She had to get dressed fast and she was hoping that Robert was already dressed or at least halfway there. She opened the door quickly and rushed in.

"Robert, are you ready?" She stopped almost immediately when she noticed that the house was completely dark. Where was Robert? she wondered. She walked down the steps of the foyer into the living room. She peeked in every room and walked back to the den. There he was, lying flat on his face.

"Robert! Wake up!" Indira yelled to wake her husband. She pushed him harder when she saw the empty bottle of bourbon on the desk.

"Robert, how could you? You promised me!" Indira yelled and stormed out of the room. Robert groggily got to his feet and followed Indira the best he could up the stairs.

"Baby, I'm sorry. I got mad earlier then one glass led to another." He was trying to explain, but it was his routine performance. Indira became even more furious.

"You know how important this night is to me, but it doesn't matter to you." Indira took off her clothes in a hurry and slipped into her silk robe. Robert came into the bedroom and sat on the bed. Indira pinned up her hair, avoiding even looking at her husband and hurried into the bathroom. Robert fell back and laid his arm over his eyes to block the light.

Indira turned on the shower and stood in the mirror wiping off the makeup she had on.

"I can't believe that son of a bitch. Did it matter when I dropped everything to be at one of his book unveilings or his damn signings!" She dropped the ball of cotton in the wastebasket and looked at herself in the mirror. The steam from the shower caused strands of her long hair to fall. She opened the door of the steam-filled bathroom and walked over to the nightstand to get more hairpins. Robert was fast asleep on the king-size bed that they had shared for nearly six years.

"Some husband you turned out to be. After all you promised me. How stupid could I be to believe you?" Indira spoke her mind loudly and continued her search for hairpins in the drawer of the nightstand. She hadn't realized that her husband wasn't asleep. He reached out from the bed and grabbed her wrist tightly as she bent over the drawer.

"Robert," Indira whined as he tightened his grip.

"Is that what you think of me, Indira?" He pulled her toward the bed next to him.

"I'm nothing but an old drunk, a mean old man, what else do you say about me, Indira?" He shook her hard with his strong grip. "Do you say that to your friends or to your gay-ass boss?" He tightened his grip again.

"Let go of me, Robert." Her silk robe was beginning to slide off of her shoulder, exposing her breasts. She didn't want Robert to try anything, so she began to struggle to get loose.

"I'll let go of you when I am good and fucking ready." Robert got to his feet and pushed Indira onto the bed. He began to undo his belt then pulled his shirt over his head. Indira got up, but Robert caught her, throwing her back down on the bed. He then let his pants drop.

"Please, Robert. Don't do this to me tonight," Indira pleaded as Robert stood over her. He looked almost deranged and Indira was afraid of what was to come. He took off the remainder of his clothes and forced himself on top of his young wife.

"Is that all you're worried about Indira, that damned art gallery of yours?" Robert forced his mouth over Indira's. She could taste the liquor in his mouth and tried to push him off of her.

"You're not going to the gallery tonight, Indira. You're going to spend some time with your husband." He pushed down hard onto Indira's frail body and pulled her robe open. Just as Indira was about to yell, he covered her mouth with his hand. He moved his mouth onto Indira's breasts and began to suck them. Indira couldn't stand the feel of him touching her and had to do something. Robert eased his hand off of Indira's mouth. She opened her mouth and bit into his hand as hard as she could. He fell off of Indira and hit the floor.

Indira lifted herself off the bed, but Robert grabbed her leg before she could get up. "Bitch, is you crazy?" Robert got to his feet then slung his blood-covered hand, backslapping Indira across her face. She fell to the floor, hitting her head on the footstool that sat in the corner of their room.

"Robert, please." Indira rose up slowly off of the floor only to see Robert's hand just as it hit her again. The room went black.

*****

Sydney stood over the stove watching her dinner cook. She loved to cook just like her mother, but her mother didn't show her how to cook. Ms. Mable took all the credit for that. She would let her help with dinner and Sydney fell in love with cooking. Jasmine sat on the couch surrounded by stuffed animals, staring into the television. Sydney began washing a head of lettuce for a salad, when she heard a knock at the door. She turned off the water and wiped her hands on her sweatpants.

"Who is it?"

"You know who it is, open the door."

Sydney unhooked the chains that lined her door and opened it.

"Why is it so cold in this building?" Maxine stood shivering in the hallway. Sydney led her in then closed the door.

"Girl that heater in the hallway ain't worked since last winter," Sydney ran back over to the stove.

Maxine took off her coat and slung it over a chair. "Hey, fat girl." She bent over and kissed Jasmine on her forehead. "Hmmm, what's that your mama cooking?" Maxine sniffed at the aroma lingering in the air.

"Are you hungry, Maxine?" Sydney turned off the fire under the yams but let her ham continue to cook.

"Naw, I just had Chinese not too long ago." Maxine had set up a station to do Sydney's hair on the dining room table.

"Then you'll be hungry in a minute. Help yourself to it if you do get hungry. Papa Joe is usually starving when he gets here." Sydney could always depend on her father to keep Jasmine whenever she needed him. He loved Sydney no matter what she did, unlike her mother. Virginia had such high standards and Sydney couldn't live up to any of them.

"Hurry up, Sydney. I don't wanna be here all night," Maxine stood with her hand on her hip. "Go wash your hair and come on." Maxine sat down in the chair she had for Sydney.

"Mommy will be right back," Sydney said to her daughter. Jasmine barely noticed her against Elmo.

Sydney rushed out of the room to take a shower and wash her hair. Maxine plugged in her blow dryer and waited on her final client. Jasmine hadn't moved from in front of the TV since that red thing started singing. Maxine opened her bag and saw the card that Bruce had given her. She studied it closely and started to smile.

"Let's see what little game you have to play, Mr. Washington." Maxine tossed the card back into her bag when Sydney came out with a towel around her head. Maxine got up from the chair and let Sydney sit down. She dried Sydney's hair some with the towel, and then combed it down. Her thick mane would be enough to put Maxine over the top. She would be ready for the bed when she finally got home.

"So you're really not gonna go tonight, huh?" Sydney wanted Maxine to go also.

"No, Sydney, I'm not up to getting all dressed up for some snooty people lying to everybody about their lives." She clicked on the blow dryer and began working on Sydney's thick hair. Jasmine turned around with a frown when the noise interrupted her show.

“Make noise,” Jasmine waved her hand in disgust. Maxine and Sydney laughed.

“Auntie will go fast, okay?”

Jasmine hesitantly agreed, “Okay.”

After a few minutes, Maxine cut off the blow dryer.

"You should go tonight. You might meet somebody nice for a change," Sydney snickered at the last remark.

"Anyway, I did meet somebody nice today in the Chinese restaurant next door," Maxine was smiling through her words.

Sydney turned around abruptly. "And why are you just now telling me?"

Maxine turned Sydney's head back around.

"Jasmine, get that out of your mouth!” Sydney yelled. Jasmine dropped the ink pen she'd found in the couch when she heard her mother. Sydney continued, “Girl, what's he look like?"

"Girl, he was about six foot four inches and blackkk..." Maxine rubbed some moisturizer through Sydney's hair. "He smelled so good and he knew how to talk, just like I like ‘em. Literate."

"Don't even try it. You like men in general," Sydney started laughing. “Just need a pulse.”

"Yeah, we'll see what you do tonight with your date." Maxine began curling. “Wanna wear it up?” She tried to imagine a look for Sydney.

“Yeah, I guess.” Sydney hadn't picked out a dress yet.

"I hope you ain't set me up with no leach," Sydney watched Jasmine from where she sat.

"He can't be no worse than Anthony," Maxine knew that would shut Sydney up.

"Now don't even go there," Sydney fell quiet. After a few moments of silence, she started up again.

"You know that guy Wayne on the second floor?"

"Of course I know him. All those times he's helped you around here. What about him?" Maxine took a break from Sydney's hair.

"He asked me out on a date. Well, me and Jasmine."

"It's about damn time. As many times as he took out your trash or fixed your car, you should have asked him out," Maxine cracked up, causing Sydney to laugh.

"Why you trippin'?"

Maxine went back to work on her friend's coif.

*****

Robert gripped his hand in pain after hitting Indira. She saw the opportunity and squirmed into the bathroom, locking the door behind her. She leaned over the sink trying to catch her breath.

"He's gone fuckin' crazy! I can't let this shit keep happening."

Robert stumbled into the hallway and got a rag from the linen closet. He knew he had snapped. He could have killed her. He wrapped the towel around his hand and rushed back into the bedroom to get dressed.

Indira ran cold water over her face to wash away the blood from Robert's hand. She could still make the showing. She wasn't late yet. She stepped into the now cold shower and washed off her body. The cold water helped her shock subside. She couldn't help but think about what had just happened.

"He was going to rape me," Indira cut off the water and stood motionless, dripping wet.

Robert got dressed in a hurry. He had to get out of the house. He didn't want to be there when Indira came out of the bathroom. He had to find Vera. She could calm him down. He rushed down the stairs, nearly falling, and on out of the house.

"Oh, no. Please don't swell up," Indira leaned in closer to the full-size mirror to check her bruised cheek. The bathroom was too steamy to do her hair, so she decided to peek out the door. She opened the door slowly and looked around the room. Robert was gone. She breathed a sigh of relief and then checked the clock on the nightstand.

"Six-twenty!" Indira finished in the bathroom and began taking the hairpins out of her hair.

*****

Eldridge stood tall in the mirror tying the bow tie of his tuxedo. This was going to be one of the biggest nights of his career. He owed it all to one special lady, Indira. He hadn't stopped thinking about her since she had left the hotel. She would be the perfect woman for him, even though she was three years older.

"You would have to be married. Happily, I'm not so sure about," he thought. As beautiful as she was, she had to be, he figured. He finished with his tie and then checked himself one last time in the mirror.

"Sharp as a tack, as granddaddy would say."

*****

Indira walked over to the window to see that Robert's car was gone. She was in the clear for sure now. She sat down at her vanity and got to work on her face and her hair. Six forty-five was when she finished getting dressed, but she was now in search of her shawl. Finally, she looked under the bed to find it sitting next to yet another empty liquor bottle. She pushed it to the side and grabbed her shawl. Now she was ready. Indira had covered her bruised cheek the best she could and hoped it would work. Once downstairs, she slid into her leather swing coat and hurried out the door.

The streets were covered with rain and slush, but Indira blew through them anyway. It was now seven o'clock, and she was late picking up El. Robert had tried to ruin this night for her, but she wasn't going to let him succeed. A car pulled out of the alley just ahead of her, she slammed on her brakes with both feet and missed hitting the other car by an inch.

She'll Learn

She opened her eyes to see an old man waving apologetically from his car. She nodded with a forced smile, and then drove around him. At the traffic light ahead, she couldn't stop shaking. She had endured a little too much tonight. She took a couple of deep breaths and continued on to the hotel.

*****

Eldridge paced the floor of the lobby, checking his watch every few seconds. “Seven-fifteen! Hmph, seven o’clock sharp.” He went outside to see if he could see Indira’s car in the parking lot. “Where in the hell is she?” He put his hands deep into the pockets of his trench coat and waited a few more minutes in the cold.

“The most important night of my life, and I’m late.”

*****

Maxine packed up her things and wrapped her curling irons in towels to cool them off.

"Maxine, come in here for a second. I want you to pick out one of these dresses
for me," Sydney yelled from the bedroom where she and Jasmine were.

"What? Sydney. I am tired and I want to go home." Maxine picked up the irons and tapped them with her hand, "Still hot."

"Come on. I need some help," Sydney sounded desperate.

Maxine walked back to Sydney's bedroom where she had three brand new dresses laying across the bed.

"Okay, which one of these should I wear tonight?" Sydney stood looking at Maxine as she looked over the selection.

"I wouldn't be caught dead in none of these, personally," Maxine was joking.

"Forget you. You never have anything nice to say. Now which one should I wear?" Sydney rummaged through the dresser drawers searching for a pair of sheer black stockings. "Shit, shit, shit!" Sydney only cursed every blue moon. Maxine knew what the problem was before she asked.

"What's wrong with you, girl?" Maxine held the best of the three dresses in her arms.

"I don't have not one pair of stockings, let alone a black pair. I gotta go to the store." Sydney started searching around for her shoes. Maxine went back into the front room to retrieve her bag.

"Here, girl. You know I wouldn't forget." Maxine handed her friend the stockings.

"Girl, I don't know what I would do without you, sometimes." Sydney sat back down and started getting dressed. The doorbell rang.

"I'll get it." Maxine peeked through the peephole and saw Papa Joe standing in the hallway.

"Hurry up. It's cold as a coal miner's ass out here," Papa Joe complained as usual.

Maxine opened the door in a hurry, and the old man strolled in in his work boots and attire. "Nice to see ya, Papa Joe," Maxine stood to the side of the door.

“Hello, Maxine. Hadn't seen you in a while." He hugged Maxine and kissed her on the cheek. He saw Jasmine crawling toward them out of the corner of his eye. "There's my baby," Papa Joe let go of Maxine and went to pick up his only grandchild. "Give granddaddy some sugar." The old man bent down to kiss his granddaughter.

"Daddy, is that you?" Sydney yelled from the bedroom.

"Of course it's me, right on time as usual."

Maxine closed the door and put on her coat. “Now I know where she gets that from.”

Sydney finished dressing, and then sashayed into the front room to model her dress. "So how do I look?" She turned around slowly.

"That dress looks good on you. I told you I wouldn't wear it because I don't have no boobs." Maxine zipped up her bag and slung it over her shoulder.

"You oughta dress like that more often Syd. You too old to still be a tomboy," Papa Joe said as he started laughing while rubbing his beard.

"Oh leave me alone, Daddy."

Papa Joe strolled over to his daughter and kissed her before heading for the kitchen. "Ooh wee. What's smellin' so de-licious?" He opened the lid of the yams and sucked in the smell.

"Girl, am I free to go now?" Maxine looked dead tired.

"You mean to tell me you ain't going to stick around and see who or what it is you set me up with?" Sydney watched Maxine walk to the door.

"I don't wanna be here if he turns out to be ugly," Maxine started laughing and ran out the door. Papa Joe came out of the kitchen licking his fingers just as Sydney was closing the door.

"Where did Maxine run off to?" He searched around the room.

"She had a hot date with her bed."

"What?" Papa Joe looked at his daughter strangely.

"Never mind, Daddy. I cooked you some dinner just in case you were hungry."

"Now, I know all that ain't for me," Papa Joe sat down on the couch and pulled Jasmine onto his lap.

"No, Daddy. I cooked for tomorrow, too." She walked over to the mirror and checked herself again.

"You cook as good as your mother. Too bad she's too damned stubborn to come eat with you," Papa Joe shook his head at the thought of how his wife treated their daughter.

"Stubborn ain't the word. We haven't spoken in a year," Sydney turned when she heard a knock at the door.

Papa Joe sat the baby on the couch and got up to get the door.

"Who is it?" He squinted to see out the peephole.

"Be nice, Daddy," Sydney whispered to her father from the other side of the room.

"Zane Dupree."

"You don't have to tell me how to act," Papa Joe didn't hear the man in the hall the first time. "Who?"

"Zane Dupree," the voice proudly announced.

"I still don't know what the hell he said," Papa Joe turned and looked at Sydney.

"Just open the door, Daddy." Sydney was speaking higher than a whisper now.

Papa Joe opened the door and the man walked in. He was about five foot ten inches, a little shorter than Papa Joe, and light skinned.

"I'm Sydney's father, Joe Hastings," Papa Joe extended his hand to Zane.

"I'm Zane Dupree."

Sydney walked over to the two and immediately caught Zane's eye. "Hello, I'm Sydney Hastings."

Zane kept his eyes on Sydney and shook her hand. "Nice to meet you, Sydney. So are we ready to go?" Zane was anxious to get the date started. Sydney was much more than he'd expected.

"Yes, but I want you to meet my daughter, Jasmine."

He'd spoken too soon. Sydney led her date over to the couch.

"This is Jasmine." Jasmine looked up at the man with her big brown eyes and smiled. She was cute, but Christmas was too close for his taste. Zane was blown away. Derrick didn't tell him that he was setting him up with a ready-made family. Zane put on one of his fake smiles and bent down to the little girl. He was only in it for the pussy anyway. He had to admit, she was as pretty as her mother.

"Nice to meet you, Jasmine."

"Okay, now we're ready. Daddy, don't let Jazzy stay up too late and put the food up for me," Sydney gave her last instructions.

"You take care of my girl tonight, and don't make me have to come looking for you," Papa Joe put on a stern face to get his point across.

"No sir, no need to worry about that," Zane had already made up his mind that after tonight he didn't want anything else to do with this one. He walked out the door when Sydney opened it.

"See you later, Daddy. Bye, baby," Sydney kissed them both and then followed Zane out of the apartment. She watched him closely as he eased down the stairs. He was walking so light, the steps didn't even creak. He was so suave and handsome. He had honey colored skin and a full beard. Zane DuPree. What an extravagant name.

"I'm sorry about the long hike up and down the stairs. The elevator just went this morning," Sydney couldn't believe how quickly that lie flew out of her mouth. That old thing hadn't worked since the day she and Anthony moved into the place. Zane held the door of the apartment building for his date and showed her to his car.

Sydney could only stand with her mouth open when Zane opened the door of his Lexus for her. She'd never ridden in one before, and couldn't wait until she got to tell Maxine. Zane walked around the car thinking to himself that this was a lost cause for him. He just didn't want a ready-made family, even though she happened to be very pretty. Zane started the car then took another look at his date for the evening.

She'll Learn

"You look really nice tonight, Sydney." Maybe he was being a little too quick to make up his mind, he told himself.

"Thank you, Zane." Sydney was smiling from ear to ear and Zane could hear it in her words. He smiled back at her, and drove off.

CHAPTER SIX

Indira's Mercedes roared down the cold deserted streets like the wind. She was determined to make the showing on time.

"Oh, Lord, please help me. I can't let these things keep me from what I have to do." Indira took two deep breaths and continued on.

The hotel was only a couple of blocks away, so she took another deep breath and continued on. El came through the doors just as Indira pulled into the hotel parking lot. She pulled near him at the entrance and unlocked the door. He opened the door in a hurry and began questioning his escort.

"Where have you been? We're supposed to be at the gallery by now." He went on until he took a good look at Indira. She looked as if something had scared the life out of her.

"Are you all right, Indira?" He reached into the car to feel Indira's hands. She was shaking. "Get out of the car and come inside." He rushed around to her door and opened it. His hair was surrounding his face when he reached his hand out to her. Indira got out.

"No, Eldridge. We don't have any time." Indira knew she could use a good glass of wine to calm her nerves.

"There can't be a showing if I'm not there. So get out of the car. Please." Eldridge flashed a smile and motioned for her to get out of the car. Indira got out of the car and the valet took it away. Eldridge put his hand around her waist and led her into the hotel's lounge for a drink. Indira loved the way he was taking charge. Maybe he was even more mature than she was giving him credit for being. The bar had a small crowd, so Eldridge led Indira over to a table in the back of the room. The waitress saw the two from the corner of her eye and strolled over to them.

"What can I get you two tonight?"

El nodded to the woman and smiled, she returned the gesture. Indira could see that he was quite the ladies' man.

"I'll have a draft beer and the lady will have..." El looked to Indira who still seemed to be in sort of a daze. She snapped out of it and ordered.

"Oh, I'll have a white wine." She looked around the room and locked her gaze when she saw a couple at the bar. The gentleman seemed to be much older than the young woman. She began to wonder if they were married, or if she was his mistress.

Robert had a mistress and she now knew it for sure. She didn't notice when the waitress left the table, even when she walked through her view of the couple. Eldridge began to study Indira's face and noticed the small bruise forming on her cheek.

"What happened to your face, Indira?" Eldridge had a stern voice that immediately caught her attention. She turned around to see the concern in those beautiful brown eyes.

"Nothing, I...uh, I had an accident at home. I can be so clumsy sometimes." Indira smiled the best she could, and then dropped her eyes to the table. Eldridge reached across the table and rubbed his hand over her cheek gently. He knew she wasn't telling the truth. Indira lifted her eyes to meet his stare.

The waitress sat their drinks down hard on the table. Eldridge looked up at her with a puzzling glance.

"Thank you." He turned back to Indira and took a sip from his glass. "Indira, you don't have to lie to me." He took another swig of his beer as Indira watched him.

"And, why do I need to lie to you, Eldridge?" She was angry that he was prying so hard into her business. She drank some of her wine to calm herself.

"Does he do this to you often, Indira?" He wasn't letting up. He knew her husband was beating her. He could see Indira getting mad.

"You don't know what you're talking about. So why don't you just stay the fuck out of my business?" Indira drank the rest of her wine, and turned toward the television. She was so embarrassed. How could she sit there and defend that bastard for what he'd been doing to her. She slowly turned back to Eldridge's stare.

"No, I'm sorry, Indira. It's just hard for me to believe that a woman like you would let this man destroy your life," El sounded much wiser than his age told. He could feel himself developing much stronger feelings for her.

Indira couldn't believe how sensuous and caring he was. She smiled at him and then put her hand on top of his.

“Thank you, El, for being so sweet.” She began to run her index finger around the top of the empty wine glass and think about what was happening to her life. “My marriage has been falling apart for a little while now and things are finally coming to a halt. Alcohol and women have ruined my marriage,” Indira felt so hurt and ashamed, she wanted to cry.

Eldridge felt sorry for her. She wasn’t realizing that her husband was the one who had ruined their marriage.

“So he’s a drunk and he beats you?” Eldridge gulped down the remainder of his beer to conceal his growing anger. He was being so frank.

Indira couldn’t look at him, so she looked down at the table. “He’s been drinking a lot heavier ever since his last book didn’t do too well, and he was fired from the university,” Indira was defending Robert. Eldridge could see that she loved her husband even past his faults.

“That still doesn’t give him the right to hit you, or have you realized that?” Eldridge was so angry he could burst. It was happening to him all over again. He’d lost Iris, one of his dearest friends to the hands of her abusive husband and he couldn’t take that pain again. But it was too late. He already had feelings for the lovely woman who sat across from him.

“Yes I have realized that El, but I still love him and I can’t even understand why.” She dropped her head and then noticed the time on her watch.

“Neither can I,” El ran his hands over his thick dreads.

“We have to go. It’s nearly eight o’clock,” Indira rushed out of her seat and El threw a twenty-dollar bill onto the table and followed Indira out. The valet pulled the car up just as Eldridge reached the door. Indira jumped in, and then watched El closely as he slid into the car. She was happy that he had tried to pry into her business. Just as he closed the door, she pulled off.

*****

Zane and Sydney walked into the gallery arm in arm. Zane gave the hostess at the door their invitation and was directed to the coat check.

"Everything looks so beautiful. Indira really outdid herself this time." Sydney was feeling good tonight and she wanted to have a good time. She had the perfect date for the perfect evening.

She'll Learn

"Oh, so you've been here before?" Zane stared straight into Sydney's cleavage.

"Whenever I get the chance, I bring my daughter."

There was that word again. Every time Zane forgot about her, Sydney somehow fit her into the conversation.

"I would come here a lot myself if my friend were the curator," Zane handed the coat-check girl their coats and walked with Sydney into the main room. Zane hadn't been on a blind date in years, but it was about time he got out.

"I don't get to do much of anything as much as I'd like to. You know, working and taking care of the baby keeps me busy," Sydney continued to wear her smile and gaze around the room at some of the city's most famous people.

Baby. That last part stuck in Zane's head. Taking care of the baby. He wasn't even ready for that kind of shit. He knew this wasn't going to work out, so he decided to have a good time tonight only.

"Come on, Sydney. Let's walk around and check out this guy's work."

Sydney could feel something was wrong. Maybe she was talking too much or something. She didn't want to ruin the date this early.

"I wonder where Indira is?" She quickly tried to change the subject.

"She's probably busy greeting people. She'll find you."

"Yeah, you're right." Sydney held onto Zane's arm and strolled from painting to painting.

Omari paced the floor in a panic. Indira nor Eldridge had shown up yet and they were nearly an hour late. Omari's pale white skin had turned to the color of a Michigan apple. He saw Sydney and rushed across the room to her. Omari's young boyfriend followed closely behind him.

"Sydney, Sydney… have you seen Indira? She hasn't arrived yet with the guest of honor and I'm getting worried," Omari fanned himself with his hand. Jonathan, his close friend, as Omari called him, fanned him too.

"No, Omari, I haven't seen her. I hope nothing has happened. I'll call her to make sure she's not still at home." She opened her purse to search for her cell phone.

"Don't bother, Sydney, I already called; she wasn't there, and her cell phone went to voice mail." Omari turned to his companion in a panic.

“Oh, no. Where could she be?” Jonathan chimed in. He continued to console his now distraught friend.

"She'll be here soon. Maybe they had car trouble or something," Sydney soon realized that was not the thing to say.

"Thanks, Sydney. That was all I needed to hear."

The young man escorted Omari away from Sydney, rolling his eyes at her as he led him away.

The gallery was filled with art goers and celebrities from around the city. Indira felt proud when she saw how good everything looked from the outside. Her marriage was a flop, but this was the one thing she had to be proud of. She stopped just as she and Eldridge were about to reach the doors.

"Eldridge," Indira looked him in his eyes.

"El," he corrected playfully.

He was so caring, Indira felt loved in a weird way. "I didn't get a chance to thank you for everything you've done for me tonight. Sometimes I can be real naive to things." She lowered her head at the thought of her husband.

Eldridge lifted his hand to Indira's face and raised her chin. "You have nothing to be ashamed of Indira, your husband is the one who should feel ashamed." He smiled at Indira then lightly kissed her cheek. "Now let's go inside, I can't wait any longer."

He and Indira laughed and then escorted one another into the gallery. All eyes turned to them immediately. The many guests raised their glasses to Eldridge as he walked Indira down the center of the gallery.

*****

Omari paced the floors of the gallery frantically, with his companion following his every move. Omari came to an immediate halt when he heard the guests cheering on Eldridge as he strolled in.

"Thank goodness. They finally made it!" Omari made his way through the crowd to them. "Where in the world have you two been? I've been worried sick, haven't I Jonathan?" Omari turned to his young friend for assistance. He only shook his head in agreement. It seemed he agreed with everything Omari said.

She'll Learn

"Well, Omari, I..." Indira began to explain, but Eldridge cut her off.

"Actually, it's my fault that we're so late. I'm a very slow dresser and I can't tie a bow tie, but Indira was there to help." Eldridge gave Omari a phony smile and nodded to Indira.

"Eldridge, no need for an explanation. You're here now and that's all that matters." Omari put his arm on El's shoulders and led him into the crowd. Omari looked back at Indira and smiled. Eldridge winked to her just as he was being dragged away. Indira watched closely as Omari led Eldridge up to the platform in the center of the gallery. Omari clapped his hands to get everyone's attention.

"Can we stop the music for a moment, please," Omari waited for the singer and her trio to stop. "Everyone, I would like to introduce you to the man whose paintings you're all drooling over. Meet, Eldridge Moss," Omari began the round of applause that soon filled the room.

Indira clapped as hard as she could. She stopped when she realized how she had to be looking. She grabbed a glass of champagne from a passing waiter. She sipped from her glass, never taking her eyes off of Eldridge. He looked even more handsome standing up there on the platform. She was starting to feel a little awkward. This was a man she wanted for herself. How could she, when she belonged to someone else? She broke her gaze when she felt a pair of hands on her shoulders. She turned to see an old friend.

"Paul Henson," Indira said as she hugged her mentor. "What brings you to Detroit?" Indira stood in front of the tall, elegant man in his late fifties, with gray only near his sideburns.

"Business of course. I've been trying to get a hold of this kids' work for some time now," Paul stared admiringly at his old pupil. He was pleased at how well she was doing. He knew all about Robert and the changes he'd gone through. He didn't bother to ask about him. The two talked for a while when Indira began to search the room for Eldridge. She spotted him being introduced to the mayor and his wife. He looked up just as Indira had found him. Their eyes locked for a brief moment before El had to turn away to continue his small talk.

Indira turned back to Paul, who had noticed the two. Indira's face became flush when she realized that Paul was aware of her inability to keep her eyes off the handsome young man. He searched her face and slowly his lips turned to a knowing smile.

*****

After a much-deserved soak in the tub, Maxine lay across her bed with her nose in a romance novel. After forcing herself to read a few pages, she laid the book down on her dresser.

"If falling in love were this easy, every woman would have a man by now." She lay back on the bed and stared up at the ceiling. She glanced over at the business card that rested next to her book on her dresser. She hadn't had a good date in weeks, but there was Todd. They always had a good time together, plus he knew how to work that thang and exactly how to work her. Ralph wasn't really her type, but he was fun to go out with. There was Derrick, her Monday lover. He called every Monday, right after his late shift from work. Let's not forget Billy, the man who stole her heart then gave it to his wife. These weren't what Maxine called good dates. So what did she have to lose? She stared at the card for a few minutes then picked up the phone. Maxine scratched her head.

"It's now or never, Maxine." She started dialing the first number she saw on the card. There was no answer. "I can't believe he doesn't have an answering machine." She read the pager number, dialed it, and then sat waiting for her phone to ring. For some reason, the phone scared her when it started to ring.

"What the hell am I doing?" Maxine asked herself aloud, and then picked up the phone. "Hello."

"Hello, did someone just page this number?" He sounded so good. Maxine almost didn't reply, just to hear his deep voice again.

"Hi, Bruce. This is Maxine Harrell." She sounded nervous, so she sat up straight on the bed and took a quick breath.

"Hello, Ms. Harrell. I was waiting to hear from you," Bruce let out a cool sigh at the end of his words. That sound tickled Maxine's ear.

"I wasn't sure if you'd know who I was right away." She wrapped her long fingers through the phone cord.

"I don't give my number out to just anybody. Besides, how could I forget such a beautiful sister?" He continued to roll those words out of his mouth. She knew he was talking trash, but she was enjoying the flattery.

"What a nice thing to say, Bruce," Maxine was now twisting the curls atop her head.

"So, how soon can we get together? Tomorrow's good for me." Bruce knew he would be home alone this weekend since Erica and the kids were going to visit her family in Chicago.

"Isn't that a little soon?" Maxine wanted to see him right now, but she didn't want to seem too anxious.

"I don't think so. Why not get started and have a good time with me? I can promise you will," Bruce leaned back in his leather chair and kicked his feet up onto his desk. He eyed the pictures of boxers, old and young, crowding the walls of his office as he waited for Maxine's answer. He laid his free hand in his lap.

"You're right. I do deserve to have a good time. And I would love to spend it with you," Maxine wanted to play a little herself, so she added some flavor too.

"Good, good. Then…let's have lunch in Greektown somewhere, and we'll decide on the rest of our day from there. Sound okay?" Bruce glanced over at his wedding picture on his desk. Erica was beautiful and so in love with him then. Now she was only married to him because of the girls, and her share of the company.

"Sounds good to me." Maxine gave Bruce directions, and they chatted a little more then said goodbye. She was excited now. She flopped back on the bed and then looked toward the closet that was crowded with clothes she hated.

"Shit, now what am I going to wear?"

*****

Indira felt alone, even though surrounded by hundreds of well-dressed people. She spotted another waiter making his way through the crowd with a tray holding flutes of champagne. When he got close enough, she grabbed one from atop the tray and took a healthy drink. After all she'd been through tonight she needed a drink. Eldridge continued to work the room of potential buyers. He looked up and caught Indira's eye just as he was moving to another couple. She smiled and raised her glass to him.

"Indira!" Sydney yelled from across the room then rushed over to her. "Where in the world have you been? Omari was going crazy looking for you."

Zane was driving his eyes deep into Indira.

"I had a little problem at home earlier, but no need to worry. Everything's all right. Forget that, girl. I'm so glad you came," Indira put her arms around Sydney's shoulder and hugged her. "You look sharp, too."

"Thanks. You know I was coming. Oh, let me introduce you to my date." Sydney turned around to Zane. "This is Zane DuPree…Indira Carr," Sydney backed out of the way. Zane reached for Indira's hand and kissed it. Indira looked over at Sydney. Just what she needed, to be acquainted with yet another bullshitter.

"It is a pleasure to meet you, Ms. Carr," Zane held onto Indira's hand a little longer as he looked her up and down, and then dropped it.

"Mrs. Carr, and the pleasure is all mine," Indira gave him a false smile, and then turned back to Sydney.

"I have been meaning to come to the gallery before now, but I'll be back for sure." Zane was laying it on thick and Indira was reading through every line of it. Poor Sydney hadn't a clue as to what was going down.

"Well, the gallery is open to the public, so feel free to come and check it out," Indira continued to be civil.

"I've already checked out most things."

Indira watched as Zane's eyes dropped from hers to her breasts. She gave Zane a cold stare then grabbed her friend's arm.

"We'll be right back. We need to freshen up a little," Indira led Sydney to the ladies room. Sydney rushed over to the mirror.

"How do I look, Indira?" Sydney checked her teeth for lipstick.

Indira stood beside her and watched her in the mirror. "Girl, you look real good. You need to dress up more often." Indira began fiddling with her hair. She decided to forget telling Sydney about her date since she deserved to have a good time.

"So what do you think of Zane?" Sydney turned to Indira with anticipation. She had to ask.

"Oh, he seems like a real nice guy," Indira turned back to the mirror quickly.

She'll Learn

"Girl, don't you think he's fine?" Sydney couldn't see past his handsome face.

"He's nice looking," Indira never turned back to Sydney.

"Z-a-n-e...his name is real different, and I hope he is, too," Sydney straightened her dress then turned to Indira.

"Don't get your hopes up too high on this one. Just because his name sounds different, doesn't mean he is," Indira nodded to Sydney who shook her head in agreement.

"I know, but it's nice to think so. Come on, I want to get back out there," Sydney gave herself one more look, then left out of the lounge. "Girl, you haven't said anything about the fine man you strolled in here with, the man of the evening." Sydney pulled the back of Indira's dress slightly to adjust it.

"Stop it, girl. He's a client." Indira slapped at Sydney's hands. That had been Sydney's way of getting Maxine's attention ever since they were kids.

"You walk arm and arm with all your clients?" Sydney joked.

She and Indira stopped in front of the buffet. It was gorgeous; full of little sandwiches, an ice sculpture, and everything. Sydney fixed a small plate while Indira filled her in.

"His name is Eldridge Moss and he just helped me keep my head on straight tonight, that's all." Indira started on a small plate herself.

"That's all?" Sydney stopped in her tracks and looked at Indira.

"That's it, for now." Indira laughed and then Sydney caught the hint and joined in.

"Okay. I'd better get back to Zane before some rich woman steals him."

"I'll see you later, then." Indira watched Sydney through the crowd then moved to the other side of the gallery herself. She began making her final rounds to their guests. She stopped and talked to nearly everyone at the party. They all seemed to be having a good time. It seemed like the night had gone by so quick, or maybe she just wanted to be able to see Eldridge for as long as she could.

Mrs. Delaney trapped Eldridge. She was one of the wealthiest widows in the city of Detroit. She loved art and she especially loved young men. Indira caught sight of her trying to get her hooks into

Eldridge. Indira tried to ignore the sight of Madame Delaney and Eldridge, the man she could only wish to have.

"Everything turned out perfectly, my dear," Omari leaned over and kissed Indira on the cheek. "You've done a wonderful job, as usual. Didn't she, Jonathan?" Omari looked for the opinion of his partner.

"Everything was great, Indira," Jonathan spoke in compliance with Omari.

"Thanks, but I couldn't have done all of this without you," Indira touched Omari's hand.

"You didn't waste any time getting your hands on Eldridge," Omari joked with her, but she wasn't laughing. "This means she'll be spending a lot of that money she has," Omari laughed again, and then led Jonathan away.

"Right," Indira remembered sadly. She was jealous, but she had no reason to be. After all, El wasn't her man. She only wished he were. Indira realized right then that she was falling for him.

Mrs. Delaney held onto El's arm as he neared Indira. Indira retrieved that smile of hers again.

"I see you two have gotten to know each other." Indira wanted to choke that oversized woman in that too-small designer gown, but she continued to smile.

"We sure have, and I plan to get to know him a little better," Madame Delaney's mouth was watering now. "I will be contacting you about having a few of my hotels redecorated with Eldridge's work." Mrs. Delaney never looked Indira's way. She kept her eye on the young man.

"I will be looking forward to hearing from you, Mrs. Delaney," Indira rolled her eyes to Eldridge, and he knew the reason.

Just then, Omari reappeared. "I'm so glad you had a wonderful time, Amelia. Eldridge, they simply loved you. Believe me. Your future is set," Omari shook Eldridge's hand then pulled him closer to whisper in his ear. Eldridge only smiled and nodded to Omari.

Amelia spoke next. "We're going out for coffee. Would anyone like to join us?" She was only asking to be polite.

"Thank you, sweetheart, but no. I have plans tonight to celebrate. But I do have something for you in my office," Omari led Madame Delaney up the stairs to his office, leaving Indira and Eldridge behind.

Indira didn't know what to say to him, without sounding like a jealous girlfriend. So she said nothing.

"Everything turned out real well tonight, after all that happened," Eldridge smiled at Indira, but she didn't return the gesture. She felt guilty now, since she nearly ruined his evening.

"Almost everything," Indira was being cold, letting that slip out of her mouth. "Mrs. Delaney has taken a liking to you, I see." Indira folded her arms in front of her and stared at Eldridge.

"She's harmless, I'll humor her for a while then I'll go to my hotel and crash." Eldridge didn't seem to care too much about her. "Hey, will I get to see you tomorrow?" He seemed excited when he asked her. Indira was in total shock. She wanted to shout yes for everyone to hear, but she couldn't. There was Robert, her drunk of a husband who couldn't even come tonight for that reason.

"No, I don't think so, Eldridge." She felt renewed to find that he wanted to see her.

"El," he corrected Indira again.

"El, I can't. But I really appreciated your being there for me tonight." Indira wanted to hug him, but she only touched his hand.

"If you need anything or just want to talk, will you please call me at the hotel?" Eldridge was serious. He wanted to hear from her, no matter what the reason.

"Are you sure that's where you'll be?" Indira joked.

Mrs. Delaney, Omari, and Jonathan made there way down the stairs, and were headed toward them. Eldridge took another look at his date for the evening, and then answered Indira.

"Real funny. But I promise I will be in my room tonight." He laughed.

Madame Delaney strolled over to Eldridge and slid her arm through his.

"Good night, Indira. I hope your night will be as good as I'm expecting mines to be." Amelia turned to Eldridge and smiled.

"Good night," Indira said as she watched the two leave the gallery. Why was she so jealous? She knew exactly why. She wanted him for herself.

"Good riddance, bitch," Indira turned and walked up to her office.

*****

Sydney watched Zane closely as he opened the door of the car for her. She stepped out, using his strong hand as her guide. He seemed nearly perfect, but she knew something had to be wrong with him. She felt a little awkward as they passed Wayne's apartment on the way up to hers. He'd been so nice to her and she could tell that he really liked her. Zane put his hand on Sydney's back as if to move her on up the stairs. Sydney got her keys out of her purse and stood by the door.

"I had a real nice time tonight." She leaned against the door to her apartment. She was hoping he felt the same.

"Yeah. I had a real good time, too." Zane didn't want to get her hopes up. She was real nice, but he didn't want a ready-made family.

"Well, I would love to see you again." What am I doing? Sydney asked herself the moment after she said it. Zane came closer to her and gently kissed her mouth. She closed her eyes for that moment, and then quickly opened them. Yup, he's still here.

"I'll call you, okay?" Zane brushed her cheek with his hand and headed back down the stairs, not turning to look back. He reached the bottom of the stairs. "Too bad," he thought aloud.

Sydney on the other hand, continued to let the door hold her up while she tried to come off cloud nine. Papa Joe heard her at the door and opened it. Sydney went crashing to the floor, flat on her behind.

"What you doing leanin' against the door anyhow?" Papa Joe helped his daughter off the floor and into the recliner. Sydney could only laugh, because her father would never understand.

"I'm okay, Daddy." She got to her feet and took off her jacket. "Is Jazzy sleep?" She kicked off her high heels.

"Now you know I wasn't gonna let her stay up all night," Papa Joe bent over slowly to pick up some of Jazz's toys from the floor.

"Yeah, Poppy. Thanks for keeping her for me tonight. I don't know what I'd do without you," Sydney went over and kissed her father on the cheek.

"She's my grandbaby, ain't she? So don't thank me. Did you have fun with Zane? Who named that boy, I'd like to know." Papa Joe sat down on the couch.

She'll Learn

"Daddy, he was such a gentleman. He knew all about art and he was really nice," Sydney sat on the couch next to her father.

"Good, I'm too old to be hunting some grown man down like I promised," Papa Joe started laughing and patted Sydney on her leg.

"Oh, Papa. It's getting late. You'd better get home before Mama locks you out of the house," Sydney jumped off the couch, pulling her father up.

"I pay the bills in that house, and ain't nobody gon' lock me out. You got that?" Papa Joe griped as Sydney helped him put his coat on.

"Okay, Daddy. I love you, and be careful." Sydney watched her father down the stairs.

"I'll call tomorrow," Papa Joe yelled as he went down the stairs.

Sydney was still floating on air from her date, so she had to call somebody. She jumped out of her clothes, and then checked on Jazzy, who was snoring like an old woman. Papa Joe always wore her out with all his games and surprises. Sydney sat on her bed and dialed Maxine's number.

"Hello," Maxine said as she picked up the phone.

"Maxine, girl you set me up with one of the finest black men I have ever seen," Sydney tried to keep her voice down. Jasmine was a light sleeper like her daddy.

"For real? Um, I should have kept him for myself then," Maxine laughed out loud. She stood in her closet, tossing outfit after outfit onto the floor of her bedroom.

"Girl, he was all that and then some," Sydney got under the covers with the phone like she used to do when she was a teenager at home.

"Listen at you. He made a good impression on somebody," Maxine stopped what she was doing and listened to Sydney.

"The showing was real nice. Wasn't nothing but rich people there, though. Indira looked good as usual, but something was really bothering her. She said she had a problem at home, but that was it."

"You know what her problem was, that big mean-ass husband of hers." Maxine always got angry when she thought of Robert.

"Yeah, I know. Oh, but she came in on the arm of the guy who painted all those pictures." Sydney had forgotten to tell Maxine about him.

"What? I wonder how did that happen?" Maxine went back to searching for something to wear on her date. "I got a date tomorrow," Maxine was glad Sydney had called.

"I'm not surprised, you told me about Bruce when you were doing my hair." Sydney had heard her friend say those words many times over.

"Oh, yeah. Well, what should I wear then?" Maxine almost dropped the phone off her shoulder.

"All those clothes you got and you can't find nothing to wear?" Sydney turned off the lamp near her bed.

"I know. But I want to look good." Maxine pulled out a casual pair of blue slacks and her blue wool blazer. "I guess I could wear a body suit under this," Maxine was speaking aloud.

"Wear something nice," Sydney was yawning on the phone again. "I gotta start getting stuff for Jasmine's birthday party together. It's only a week away," Sydney kindly reminded Maxine.

"I've just decided on something to wear tomorrow. Hey, you better not fall asleep on this phone, either." Maxine knew how hard it was to wake up Sydney once she fell asleep.

"I guess I'd better get some sleep. Jazzy will be up before you know it. Plus, I don't wanna miss church. I'll talk to you later, bye."

"Bye, Sydney." Maxine hung up the phone and finalized her decision. "This looks okay for Mr. Washington." She hung up her outfit on the front of the closet door, and then got into her bed.

*****

Indira opened the front door of her house, expecting to see Robert sitting on the steps, but he wasn't there. She felt relieved. After fixing herself a cup of hot tea, she headed up to her bedroom to change her clothes. She slipped into her nightgown and clicked on the television with the remote. She was sort of getting used to being alone, because for the past few months Robert was barely at home, and she was glad. She sipped her tea and listened to the sad-ass news; she immediately changed the channel when she saw that someone had shot another black teenager.

"I'm already depressed, I don't need anymore sadness." Indira dripped a couple of drops of tea on her gown. She searched for something to dry it with. She looked in her small purse and pulled out a napkin from the hotel's restaurant. She thought about El and it brought a huge smile to her face, but then she thought about him being with Madame Delaney.

"I'll bet he's still with her right now, giving her the thrill of her life." Indira rolled over on her side.

"Maybe he is at his hotel. At least, I hope so." Indira switched off her lamp and went to sleep.

*****

Eldridge had finally made it to his hotel room after sitting in Amelia's stretch limousine for more than an hour. He talked her out of coming up to his room. He told her that he needed his rest and would be no good to her, even though he was lying. Eldridge knew that he would be too good to her. So good that he'd never be able to get rid of her. Amelia was disappointed, but she finally let him leave her car without her. She asked him to call her.

Eldridge couldn't take his mind off Indira. He wondered if she was all right. What kind of man would want to hurt something so beautiful? he wondered. Eldridge showered and then lay wrapped in a towel across his hotel bed. He began to wonder if he could ever have a chance with Indira; he would settle for just her friendship.

*****

Robert went to the bar looking for Vera, since she was who he needed now. After searching the cramped little room thoroughly, he looked over at the bar and saw Genie waving him over.

"What's goin' on tonight, Bobby?" Genie wiped down the bar for the fifth time and noticed Bobby's bloody hand; he eyed it curiously. Robert said nothing when he saw where Genie's eyes had landed. Genie caught the hint and fixed the usual for him. Robert gulped down the brown liquor and then tapped the glass against the counter for another. Genie fixed another glass right away.

"Vera hadn't been in here all night, if that's why you here." Genie leaned on the bar and towel dried a few shot glasses. He was always getting into other people's business as if it was his right being a bartender and all.

Robert finished his drink and then staggered to his feet.

"Mind your own damn business sometimes, Genie." Robert balled his fist up and put it against Genie's face. "One day you gonna say the wrong thing to me and I'm gonna knock the hell outta you." Robert stood up as straight as he could and walked out of the bar. Genie paid no attention to Robert. He had a threat for everybody. Genie only shook his head and watched him stumble away.

*****

Vera pulled her old terry cloth robe together when she heard the knock at the door. She looked through the peephole and saw that it was Robert. She couldn't believe it. She opened the door and wrapped her arms around his neck.

"Oh, Bobby, I'm so glad to see you," Vera looked down at Robert's hand and saw the bloody bandage.

"What happened to you, Bobby?" Vera let go of his neck and led him into the house. Robert sat down at the kitchen table and rested against it.

"Let me find some peroxide and some bandages. I'll be right back." Vera rushed around her house looking for what she needed. She loved Robert more than anything, and always had ever since she could remember. When the two were young, they were inseparable. Everybody thought they'd get married one day, and so did Vera. Robert had dreams of making it big as a writer and he knew he couldn't do it in Roanoke, Alabama. He planned on leaving when he turned eighteen and that's what he did. He wanted Vera to come with him, but her parents wouldn't allow her to leave unless they were married. Robert wasn't ready for her to be his wife, and he wasn't gonna let anybody force him to marry, so he left for Detroit alone. Vera loved Robert and told him that the minute she was old enough to leave, she would join him. In two years, Robert had written two best sellers and was on his way to the top.

Vera was eighteen years old then and was ready to join her true love in the big city, but her father became ill and she had to stay. Robert waited for Vera as long as he could. He grew lonelier every day and married his book editor. Vera was heartbroken, but she never blamed him for marrying someone else. Her father died after a long fight with throat cancer. She had faced more heartache than she could handle, so she packed her things and moved to Detroit to be near Robert.

She knew it was time for him to be here, with her.

*****

She’ll Learn

Indira awakened with Robert on her mind. She slid down into the covers. The bed felt so good. She sort of hoped Robert would never come home, but she knew he would. She glanced at the clock and began to wonder where he was.

“Don’t be stupid. You know where he is,” Indira spoke aloud to herself then rolled over to sleep. She knew it was time to stop fooling herself about her husband. Robert didn’t love her, he hated her. It felt like someone was poking a hot dagger through her chest. She felt stupid for still loving him, but she did. She wanted him to love her, but he couldn’t anymore.

*****

Vera switched on the light to her bedroom, exposing the pictures of her and Robert when they were young; pictures of her singing in smoky nightclubs, and a snapshot of her parents. She opened her dresser drawer and found the bandages. She rushed back into the kitchen to Robert.

"What did that bitch do to you this time?" Vera was angry. Nothing was ever Robert's fault in her eyes.

"We had another fight. That's all." Robert cringed at the stinging from the peroxide that Vera poured onto his wound.

"She really took a plug out of you," Vera continued to work on Robert.

"I could have killed her, Vera." Robert dropped his head and rubbed it with his free hand. "She had me so mad, I wanted to kill her." He knew it was time to leave her before he did. Vera finished wrapping Robert's hand then kissed it.

"Maybe it's about time you come to where you belong," Vera said. They were both getting old, and it was about time for them to be together. She had been waiting on the only man she had ever loved for nearly thirty years and three marriages. It was her turn. Robert lifted his head to look at Vera. Sometimes he could still see her as she was when she was sixteen. She was so beautiful and full of life. Now she was rundown, and as much an alcoholic as he was. But the two were made for each other.

"I think it's about time, too," Robert placed his hands on top of hers.

CHAPTER SEVEN

With each day's sunrise, Maxine was running on her treadmill, and this morning she was working extra hard. She wanted to look extra good for her date with Bruce. He seemed like an all right guy. He was polite and clean, and he had his own business.

"I hope he turns out to be the one for me. I don't know if I can take any less," she said aloud. Maxine pumped harder as the treadmill rose up a hill. The sweat beaded down her face and throat as she stepped off the machine. After taking a long hot shower, she covered herself in Victoria Secret's lotion.

She had a few hours until her date, so she lounged around the house in her robe and underwear. She thought about what Sydney had said to her, that she never gave herself a chance. She gave men what they wanted every time. If Bruce turned out to be Mr. Right, her days of being lonely would finally be over. This time was going to be different. She was going to write this script herself, and not be an extra.

"Sorry, Bruce. The game is on." Maxine rubbed her hand over her still cramping stomach. Her last day was as unpleasant as the first day of her period.

Maxine glanced over at the picture of her grandmother on the mantel.

"What do you think, Grandma? Is he the one?" Maxine smiled at the face on the picture then thought about what she would really say. "She wouldn't like him, no way," she concluded.

Her grandmother was a hard woman and didn't give much of a chance for anything. Her grandfather caught hell when he was alive. Maxine laughed some at the thought of her grandmother's ways. The big old house she had left Maxine could be real lonely sometimes.

"Damn, don't start getting all sad and shit before the damn date." Maxine jumped off of the couch and ran upstairs to start on her hair. Since it was so short, she didn't have to do much to it, but she had to do something. She rubbed moisturizer through her hair and then noticed that her stomach was still a little boated from her period.

"Thank, God this shit is almost over, I couldn't take much more of this. Well at least it will keep me from giving him some on the first date." Maxine started to crack up as she finished her hair.

*****

Indira tried to sleep in later than usual since Robert wasn't home. She usually went to the gallery on Sundays just to stay out of his reach, but not this Sunday. She wasn't going to step foot into the gallery. It was probably clean by now. The cleaning crew was booked for seven o'clock this morning. It was nearly eleven, and all she could think about was Eldridge.

"I wonder what he's doing right now?" She didn't really want to know that. She was starving, so she stepped out of her bed and headed downstairs to the fridge. There was nothing but containers filled with leftovers that never seemed to get eaten. She closed the refrigerator door and thought about calling El. She hesitated for a while, and then decided she should call him. Robert probably wasn't coming home anyway. At least, she hoped he wasn't.

Forget about Robert, she thought. Well, at least for the time being.

Indira reached for the telephone that hung near the doorway. "I hope the Madame isn't still lying in his arms."

*****

El was just coming out of the shower when he heard the telephone ring. He wrapped a towel around his waist and went to answer the phone. He knew it was one of two people, and he was hoping for Indira. It was.

"Hello, Indira, I am so glad you called me." He tucked the towel in the front and stood with a wide smile across his face. His chest was covered with water, so he retrieved the towel and dried off some.

"I am sitting in my kitchen practically starving to death and I started to wonder if you were feeling the same way," Indira felt a little corny after saying that, but it was over with now.

"Are you asking me out to lunch, Indira?" El stopped drying himself and took a minute to listen.

"Well I suppose I am." Indira heard a bump at the front door and jumped. It was just the paperboy throwing his bundle against her door. She took a deep breath. “Well, are you going to go or not?” She got her composure back.

“Of course, I accept. I wouldn’t turn you down for the world. You just surprised the hell out of me,” El stood naked with the towel slung over his shoulder.

“Give me an hour and I’ll be by to pick you up. Sound good?”

“Sounds real good.” El put on his underwear and let down his dreads. This was the chance he was asking for.

“See you then. Bye.” Indira hung up the phone and shook with excitement. She had to get out of there just in case Robert got home before she wanted him to. Robert. There she was thinking about him again.

“Where in the hell is he anyway?” Indira looked out the front door, and then walked up the stairs to her bedroom.

*****

Service was running a little long this morning. Reverend Givens was preaching hard. Sydney sat with Jasmine in her lap and listened to him closely.

“I know it’s gettin’ late, but I almost feel I need to be with you. There is a problem in our own home, people. We are not…do you hear me? Not, doing a good job on keeping our families together. You don’t have nothing if you don’t have your mother or your father, your son or your daughter, your husband or your wife. Please, and this is the last time I’m going to tell you, make amends, and get your families together. Amen, everybody. I’ll see you Wednesday night for bible study.”

The church began to empty quickly, but not before Sydney saw her mother standing in a crowd of women talking near the front of the church. Sydney wondered if she was even listening to the preacher. He was talking directly to her. Sydney stood with Jasmine in her arms, staring at the crowd of Sunday hats. She didn’t hear Lois come up to her.

“Sydney. Girl, wake up.” Lois went to high school with Sydney and was married to Reverend Givens’ oldest son, Eddie.

“Hey, Lois. I didn’t even hear you come up to me,” Sydney continued to watch her mother.

“I know,” Lois followed Sydney’s eyes to see that she was watching her mother.

"She still won't budge, huh?" Lois and the entire church knew about Virginia's stubbornness and there was nothing anyone could do about it.

"No, she won't even look our way. Right, Jazzy?" Sydney kissed Jasmine on the top of her head.

"She is so precious, Sydney." Lois played with Jazzy. "Don't worry, she'll come around soon. If she's as God-fearing as I think she is, she'll come around."

"Well we better get out of here, Lois," Sydney put her and Jasmine's coats on and waved bye to Lois.

"Keep praying about it, Sydney!" Lois yelled to her.

Jasmine was her only family now. Anthony was gone and her mother wanted nothing to do with her or her bastard baby. Sydney couldn't stop loving her, though. Papa Joe never cared what Sydney did, she was always going to be his little girl. Sydney cranked up Little Red and headed for home.

*****

Maxine got tired of checking herself in the mirror, so she went downstairs to wait for Bruce. She sat down on the couch, expecting to hear the doorbell ring any minute, but the phone rang instead. She hoped it wasn't him calling to cancel.

"Hello?" Maxine sounded unsure about the call.

"Hello, Maxi. What's wrong, baby?" It was Aunt Betsy. She always had the worst timing.

"Hi, Aunt Betsy. Nothing's wrong. I was just expecting someone," Maxine held the phone to her ear and stared out the window.

"You don't sound too glad to hear from me. Do you want me to call you back?"

"No, ma'am, it's okay. So how are you doing?" Maxine couldn't offend her favorite aunt, especially since she was always there when she needed her, unlike her own mother. Aunt Betsy talked for nearly thirty minutes before getting to what she wanted. Maxine hadn't thought much about Thanksgiving until her Aunt brought it up. From the look of things, she probably would be alone again, another round of holidays were approaching. Aunt Betsy continued to talk to herself in Maxine's ear.

*****

Indira slipped into a pair of tight fitting jeans and her blue cashmere sweater and rushed out the door to see El. She knew what she was doing was a little crazy, but if Robert could do it, so could she. In no time at all, she was pulling up in front of the hotel. El was standing in the lobby when he saw the car pull up. She wasn't late this time.

"Well, hello, lovely lady," El felt like he was seeing Indira for the first time again. She was beautiful.

"Hello, yourself. Come on. Let's go, I've got a lot of stuff to show you." Indira eyed El closely as he slid into the car. She couldn't take her eyes off his strong legs that pressed through his jeans. His cable knit sweater clung to the perfect curves of his chest and arms. She never realized how good a man could look with dreadlocks.

"Let's get out of here. I'm ready to see the Motor City," El said as he buckled his seat belt and reclined in the passenger seat. Indira flashed a bright smile at him, and then took off for downtown.

*****

It was almost one-thirty and still no Bruce.

"I can't believe this shit!"

And to think just a few hours ago, she was worried about marrying the guy. That was just like her, rushing into something.

"What did you just say, Maxine Harrell?" Aunt Betsy heard Maxine loud and clear.

"Oh, nothing, Aunt Betsy. I'm sorry, I was just thinking out loud," Maxine had completely forgotten about the phone resting on her shoulder.

"What's wrong with you, girl? You sound a little down." Aunt Betsy wasn't going to let this go anytime soon.

"Everything's fine," Maxine tried to put some cheerfulness in her voice to change her Aunt's observation.

"Well okay, but you know you can talk to me, baby. Right?"

"Yes, ma'am, I know." Maxine felt a change of heart. She needed to hear that someone cared for her, and her Aunt Betsy always had.

"Well let me know about Thanksgiving dinner. I don't want you having to eat junk on the holiday."

"I promise. I'm gonna see what Sydney and Indi have planned, then I'll call you." Maxine couldn't bear the thought of sitting around the great table in her aunt's house, listening to her six married cousin's question her life and tell her why she didn't have a husband. They were all experts on marriage and family.

"All right, baby. Take care of yourself and call me." Aunt Betsy was the hardest person to get off of the phone because she had to have the last word.

"Bye, Aunt Betsy," Maxine waited on her aunt's response.

"Okay, bye-bye."

Maxine hung up the phone and folded her arms across her chest. She looked at the clock on the wall and shook her head.

"I guess the son of a bitch is going to stand me up. What a fuckin' first date!"

Maxine sat back down on the couch and kicked off the hurting-ass shoes she promised herself she would never wear again, for any man.

"Oh, well. He missed out." Maxine put her feet up on the coffee table and closed her eyes.

*****

"So tell me something about yourself, Eldridge." Indira clutched the steering wheel a little tighter.

"What do you wanna know about me?" Eldridge turned and looked out the window. Indira was sort of turned on by his shyness.

"I don't know. Uh, where did you learn to paint?"

"I'd been painting since I was three, and then my mother put me in art school and here I am," El nodded and then sat quiet.

"So that's all to you, huh?" Indira was trying to start something.

"What do you mean by that?" Eldridge turned near her.

"I found a lot of interesting things about you in *Art* magazine," Indira was toying with Eldridge.

"Like what?" He wanted to know what she thought was so interesting about him.

"You know. You did the interview," Indira smiled jokingly then turned her eyes back on the road. "Let's see. You love to paint more than anything in the world. Your mother is your best friend. You have two German rottweilers, and you can't cook anything." Indira came to a stop at a red light and turned her brown eyes to Eldridge.

"So how about that?"

Eldridge just shrugged. "That was a real good summary of me. But I have a lot more to me than that." Eldridge was becoming even fonder of Indira, but he knew that it couldn't go anywhere, because of her husband.

Eldridge continued, "I can cook, but only for me. I wouldn't want to put anyone else at risk." He started to laugh, but then he stopped to watch Indira laugh. She was all he wanted in a woman. She loved art, she loved to laugh, and she was easy to get along with.

"All right, it's your turn. Tell me all about Indira Carr." Eldridge rested his elbow on the seat and opened his ears to Indira.

"There's really nothing this way," Indira shook her head.

"Let's play fair, now, I didn't get to do any research on you," Eldridge gave Indira a boyish smile.

"Well I've lived in Detroit all my life; I went to college in Atlanta. I have two best friends who I depend on dearly. I got married just after college. Real stupid, huh?" Eldridge said nothing but continued to listen. "I've been at the gallery for a little over two years now, and I finally feel like I'm accomplishing something."

Eldridge nearly melted when he saw Indira smile. She continued to talk.

"Look. This is downtown Detroit. There's Joe Louis' fist," Indira pointed as she drove.

"It's real funny that they made only his fist as the statue," Eldridge laughed a little.

"Hey, don't make fun of my home now. I guess that was all they needed," Indira tried playfully to defend her city. "This is the Renaissance Center, real nice restaurants and shops," Indira continued on with her tour.

"Hey. Let's get something to eat and go on that island," Eldridge suggested. He didn't know the name, but Indira knew what he was talking about.

"Who told you about Belle Isle?" Indira wondered what he'd heard about it.

"I used to have a roommate who said he practically lived there in the summertime. It was the place to be from what I hear." Eldridge watched the road as he talked.

"Yeah, it's sort of a pickup place. There are always plenty of women out there in the summer. I hadn't been on the island in a long time, though." Indira remembered that the last time she'd been she and Robert were having a picnic together. That must have been nearly two years ago. They were celebrating the anniversary of their first date. Indira was lost in the old memory of being happy with her husband.

"Indira," Eldridge called to her. He could see that she was somewhere else. "Indira," Eldridge put his hand on her shoulder, she looked at him.

"I'm sorry, El, I was just reminiscing a little." Indira straightened up again. "So where do you wanna get something to eat?" She had to get Robert out of her mind. Look at what she had right next to her, and all she could think about was Robert.

"There's a Wendy's. That'll be fine," Eldridge pointed to the restaurant across the street from the island entrance. "You don't mind if we eat in the car, do you?" He knew it was an expensive car, and didn't know how she felt about it.

"No, I don't mind at all." Indira wondered what was next.

"Good. We can eat and look out at the water." El seemed happy about his plans. He was hoping this would bring him and Indira even closer.

*****

Robert turned onto their street and was shocked to see that his wife's car wasn't in the driveway. He was a little relieved, but then he wondered where she was.

He searched his key ring for his house key, and then let himself in. After tossing his jacket across the couch, he stumbled up to their bedroom to take a shower and try to get his headache to subside. He stripped off his perfume-filled clothes and left them in a pile on the floor where he stood.

Though still slightly muscular, Robert didn't like what he was seeing in the mirror. He stared at himself and noticed everything he now hated about his appearance. His beard was almost completely gray, the hairs on his chest were gray, and his skin clung to him like an old suit. Growing old wasn't something Robert was looking forward to. He had always been proud of his looks, and now he didn't have much to be proud of. Out of the corner of his eye, he noticed a picture of Indira and himself on the dresser. He picked it up, and half-smiled at it.

"I really messed up things for us, didn't I, Indi? I never understood what you wanted with an old man like me anyway." He traced Indira's face with his finger. That only put his wife back into his mind.

"Where in the hell is she?" He tossed the picture onto the bed and stepped into the bathroom. He cringed as the water beat against his hand. It was only a reminder of how out of control he got when he drank.

*****

Indira drove across the long, narrow bridge to the island, while Eldridge gazed over the cold water below them.

"Pick a spot for us to park," he suggested.

Indira drove around until she found the perfect spot with a view, looking straight at Canada.

"This is perfect." Eldridge unbuckled his seat belt, and then reached for the door.

"Where are you going?" Indira wondered what he was planning in twenty-degree weather. "Do you think you can take the cold?" Indira smiled when she asked.

"I can take a little cold weather. What about you?" He opened the door and stepped out of the car. Indira watched him walk toward the edge of the bank and stare out at the water. She walked up behind him.

"I used to love to come here. I've got so many good memories from this place." Indira gazed at the water with a frozen smile on her face.

"I could get used to coming here." He turned to Indira. "Let's go eat before it gets too cold." Indira followed Eldridge back to the car.

"Could you cut some heat on in here?" Eldridge shivered in his seat.

"I thought you could take the cold." Indira started laughing, and then turned the ignition on to get some heat flowing.

*****

"Mr. Right! Was that what I was saying?" Maxine rested on the couch arguing with herself about the man she'd thought would be the one. She thought about the last time she'd been stood up as she moped up the staircase that seemed to go on forever. "Wendell, Wendell Johnson. Who could forget him?" Maxine didn't even want to go out with the guy. Then when she finally said yes, he didn't even bother to show up. She unfastened and unbuttoned and tossed her clothes across the room, landing them nowhere in particular. She slid into an oversize sweatshirt and her favorite pair of rundown blue jeans, holes courtesy of her garden out back.

"Well, another Sunday by myself and all the time in the world." Maxine threw up her hands and fell back onto the bed. She picked up the phone and dialed Sydney's number.

"She ought to be home from church by now." Maxine listened to the ringing.

"Hello," Sydney answered.

"Hey," Maxine sounded as pitiful as usual.

"Girl, what you doing at home? I thought you had a date with Mr. Right?" Sydney snickered under her breath.

"Mr. Wrong, honey. The bastard never showed up," Maxine sighed. "And he still ain't called with an explanation." Maxine was getting hot now.

"That's messed up. But since your day is shot anyhow, why don't you come and eat dinner with Jazzy and me? We ain't doing nothing." Sydney had cooked a big Sunday dinner as usual, with nobody to feed.

"I really don't feel like it, Sydney." Maxine thought about her empty refrigerator and got a sudden change of heart. "What you cook?"

"Does it matter? You gonna eat it anyway," Sydney joked.

"All right then, Miss Thang, I'm on my way." Maxine hung up the phone and grabbed her backpack. After running down the stairs to the door, she stopped to give the phone one last time to ring. It didn't. She buttoned her jacket and left the house.

*****

Erica led Chantel through each and every room of the house. She was proud of what she had, though it was all fake. She had her husband on paper only. He would never be hers.

"Now, this is my favorite place in the house. Bruce and I spend a lot of time in here." Erica loved to show off their huge home to her friends whenever she got the chance. When she got a call from one of her sorority sisters, she had canceled her trip to Chicago.

"I can see why you'd love this room." Chantel couldn't keep her eyes off her sorors handsome husband, though her own husband was with her.

"Come on, and let me show you the girls' room." Erica led Chantel up the stairs to the bedrooms.

Bruce sat in his leather recliner across from Chantel's husband, keeping him entertained with the Lions-Jets game. The one place he hadn't planned on being today was at home. His plan was to wine and dine Ms. Harrell. He looked at the silver Rolex that rested on his wrist, and saw that he was now three hours late for his date. Date? Who was he kidding?

"Say, man you want another beer?" Bruce towered over Ralph as he sat in the corner of the couch.

"Yes, I'll take another one. Thanks." Ralph sort of smiled to Bruce, and then turned his eyes back to the game. Bruce wasn't great company today. Things hadn't gone his way. Bruce got two beers out of the fridge and then popped the caps off, letting them fall onto the marble counter. He knew Maxine was probably on fire by now. He knew he'd have to play this real smooth to get back into the game. He laughed at the challenge and then went back into the den.

*****

Maxine hiked up the four flights of stairs to Sydney's.

"I wish they'd get that damn elevator fixed," she mumbled as she reached Sydney's apartment door and knocked a couple of times. Sydney opened the door.

"All of them people who live here need to get a petition going or something, and get that damn thing fixed," Maxine said as she pointed at the elevator, and then walked past Sydney.

"For what? The heat or the elevator?" Sydney asked as she closed the door. "Girl, you ought to see Papa Joe climbing those stairs." Sydney started laughing, and then sat back down next to Jasmine on the couch.

"Hey, Chubbs," Maxine reached over and tickled her play niece.

"So what do you think happened to the guy?" Sydney never turned to look at Maxine as she kept her eyes on the television.

"Hell if I know. He acted like he was so excited about it." Maxine leaned to the edge of the couch and picked up the *Ebony* magazine that lay on the coffee table.

"Maybe something really important came up," Sydney shrugged her shoulders at Maxine.

She'll Learn

"Damn. He could have still called me. Or was that asking too much?" Maxine huffed, and then fell back into the pillows on the couch.

Sydney got up and went into the kitchen to check on dinner. "Maybe he just changed his mind at the last minute," she yelled from the kitchen.

"Gee, thanks, Sydney. Am I that bad?" Maxine looked for an answer from Jasmine, who only smiled at her. Sydney came back into the room with two cups of hot cocoa and handed one to Maxine.

"Girl, be quiet, I'm just joking with you," Sydney said as she sat down, being careful not to spill the cocoa on her couch.

"Who knows what he was doing." Sydney raised her cup to Maxine.

"I let myself get all excited every time, and these niggas do the same shit to me every time. I don't know why I'm so surprised now." Maxine sipped her cocoa.

"Well I had a good time on my date last night," Sydney bragged.

"Girl, I forgot all about that. How'd it go?" Maxine was all ears.

"For one thing he was something to look at. He had muscles everywhere you could imagine. He was dressed to a tee, and was a total gentleman." Sydney took a sip from her cup and batted her eyes at Maxine.

"Shit, you doing better than me," Maxine rolled her eyes back at her. "So are you going out again?" Maxine wanted to hear some good news.

"He's supposed to call me today, but I haven't heard from him, yet," Sydney shrugged her shoulders again.

"Niggas. They don't know the shit they put us through." Maxine shook her head at the thought.

"Things were a lot easier with Anthony. I was comfortable with him." Sydney really missed him, and got sad whenever she talked about him.

"Forget about that punk. He wasn't too comfortable here with you." Maxine hated that Sydney still moaned and groaned over that man.

"You don't have to say that Maxine. I know," Sydney was nearly in tears.

"I'm sorry, girl. But I hate when you get all down and out over him." Maxine felt bad. "Come on, let's eat I'm starving."

Sydney put down her cup and walked over to the dinner table. "Yeah, I'm hungry too." She went into the kitchen and came back with two plates of collard greens, macaroni and cheese, cornbread, and a piece of roast.

"Dog, Sydney. Who you cooking all this food for?" Maxine looked at her filled plate.

"I don't know how to cook small." Sydney put Jasmine in her high chair at the table, and then went back for her plate.

"I wish Bruce would try and call me again, I'd give him hell, honey." Maxine dug into the cheesy macaroni that Sydney made from scratch. She was Ms. Mable's favorite pupil.

"Oh, I think he'll be calling you real soon," Sydney said as she sat down with her plate, and then began feeding Jasmine.

*****

After spending nearly two hours on Belle Island, Indira and Eldridge headed back downtown.

"Hey, would you mind if we stopped by the gallery so I can revel in my success?" El laughed at the thought.

"No, I don't mind at all. You should be proud. Everyone loved your paintings, especially me." Indira could feel El's eyes on her, she turned into their path. He was looking through her. She could tell he knew how she was feeling.

"It's nice to know that, Indira."

Indira turned into the parking lot of the gallery and the two got out of the car. She unlocked the doors and punched in the alarm code. El held the door for her to go in, and then locked it behind himself. Indira walked toward the stairs of her office then turned to see El gazing around the walls of the gallery filled with his work. He resembled a kid in a candy store where everything was free.

"How about giving the tour, sir?" Indira took off her coat and walked over to El. "I'd love to." He held out his arm for Indira and led her over to the paintings.

"I painted this after my father died. He loved the country, and he was happiest when he was there." He led Indira to the next painting.

She'll Learn

"This is one of my mother's favorites. She says it reminds her of the dances she used to go to as a young girl." El led Indira from one picture to the next, but Indira wasn't there anymore. She was lost in El's deep flowing voice and swimming in the fresh scent that surrounded him. El led Indira to a picture of a man and a woman in a tight embrace with lips pressed together. She walked close to the picture and stared.

"Do you like this one?" El leaned against the wall and watched Indira.

"I do… kind of… like this one," Indira held onto her coat and gazed at the picture. "Come on. Let me show you my favorite."

She led El up the stairs to her office. He watched Indira sway up the stairs in front of him, and he liked what he saw. She had done so much for his career. He was falling in love with her. A man like her husband didn't deserve such a woman, but he had her. Indira walked over to her desk and pointed at the painting of three little girls playing in a field of daisies. El couldn't believe this was the painting she chose for her office. It was one of his favorites.

"That's one of my best paintings," El folded his arms and looked over the framed picture. "I'm glad we came here, Indira. I can finally get the chance to thank you."

"Thank me for what?" She was looking into El's deep brown eyes.

"For what? If it weren't for you, none of this would be happening. I have been painting for years, and this is the first time I got to see how people felt about my art. Thank you."

El poured his heart out to Indira. He could only hope she would accept his feelings.

"You don't have to thank me. I just gave you a place to show your talent off." She turned her gaze back to the painting. She had to; she was getting a little too interested.

"But I am thanking you, Indira," El lightly rubbed his hand down her cheek. She felt herself shudder at his touch, and then lifted her eyes to him.

"You're quite welcome, El." Indira hadn't felt like this in such a long time, she wanted him to touch her again. This time he touched her with his lips. He put his hand around her neck and placed his fingers through her long hair. Indira graciously accepted his mouth onto hers. He stared into her eyes.

"Tomorrow's my last day in Detroit, but I don't want to lose touch with you. I know this is fast, but I've fallen in love with you, Indira. And believe me, I don't do that very easily." El slid his hand slowly from Indira's neck. "But I know you belong to someone else."

El walked away from her. She watched him in sadness, for she did belong to a man who didn't love her.

"I still want to keep in touch with you," Indira spoke almost in a whisper. El walked back over to her and put his hand into hers.

"I'll gladly welcome you as my friend," El said as he lifted her hand to his mouth and kissed it.

"It's getting sort of late. We need to be going." Indira slid away from his hand. El stood for a moment, and then followed Indira down the stairs.

CHAPTER EIGHT

Fifteen past seven, Indira was putting her key into the lock of the front door. She knew Robert would be on the other side waiting for her, and sure enough there he was. Robert took an obvious look at his watch, and then put his hard eyes back onto his wife.

"Hello, Robert." Indira tried to act normal and hung her coat on the rack behind the door. Robert continued staring at her when she went into the kitchen to start dinner. She could feel in her stomach that Robert wanted to fight, and he usually got what he wanted. She heard him come into the kitchen and pull out a chair from the table. He said nothing because he knew she'd been out all day and he'd been out all night. Indira tried to look busy as she washed a head of lettuce for a salad.

"So how was the showing last night?" Robert was right behind her at the sink. Indira stopped what she was doing and lifted her head in disbelief. She couldn't believe the nerve he had to even ask her about the showing. She took a deep breath to keep from saying anything that would start a fight.

"Everything turned out fine." She tore apart the lettuce into a bowl and began cutting tomatoes up into it. Robert could see that his young wife was trying to avoid him, so he got out of his chair to be near her.

"Don't you wanna know where I've been, Indira?" He stood behind her, pressing his body against hers. She could smell the stench of bourbon on his breath and shirt. She didn't know what to expect next, so she tried to keep busy with making a salad. Robert couldn't stand that Indira wasn't paying him much attention. She was showing how she really felt about him. He lifted his wife's long hair off her neck and kissed her roughly. Indira dropped the knife and the cucumbers in the sink.

"Please, Robert. Let me make dinner," Indira's voice cracked as she tried to anticipate Robert's next move. He continued to force himself on her neck and face. She pulled away from him completely.

"What is it, Indi? You don't like my touch anymore?" Robert walked over to her and grabbed her around the waist roughly.

"Stop it, Robert!" Indira yelled loudly. Robert let go of her quickly, and then sat back down in a chair. Indira watched him closely, and then eased her way back over to the sink. Why is this happening to me? Indira thought to herself, as smoldering tears began to fall from her eyes.

"Where were you today, Indira?" Robert rubbed his now throbbing hand. At first, there was silence. Then Indira finally answered.

"I had some work to take care of… at the gallery." Indira left the salad and stood with both her hands on the counter.

"I called the gallery today. No one answered the phone." Robert still sat in the chair. He was lying of course. He didn't even know the number to her job. Indira was at a loss for words because she was scared. "Where in the hell were you?" Robert pushed the table away from him.

Indira shook with fear from the loud bang. She stared out the window over the sink, then walked over to the refrigerator and opened a pack of chicken on the counter, never answering him.

Robert was so filled with anger he was nearly pulling his hair out as she ignored his questions.

"She won't even look at me," Robert mumbled to himself. Indira washed and seasoned the chicken, and then put it in a pan to bake. She was putting Robert out of her mind. For just one minute. That's when Robert rushed her against the sink, knocking the wind out of her. Indira gasped for air as he held his forearm forcefully against the back of her neck.

"Bitch, you gonna' tell me where you were today." Robert pushed down harder, lowering Indira's head into the sink. Indira, gasping for air, nearly passed out with her face pressed into the drain of the sink.

"Robert!" Indira whimpered and kicked her legs out, but Robert was nearly double her weight. He grabbed her hair and pulled her head out of the sink. Indira breathed in the air she needed. "Robert, please stop!" Indira screamed as he tightened his grip on her hair.

"Who were you with today?" Robert shook her head, and then put his finger in her face. "And don't you fuckin' say Maxine and Sydney." Robert had completely lost it.

"I was at the gallery and then I stepped out for some lunch," Indira spoke in a rough whisper followed by tears. Robert let go of Indira's mane and threw her to the side.

She'll Learn

"Lying, bitch. That's all you are." Robert wiped the sweat from his forehead and stumbled into the den, knocking over lamps, books, vases and anything else in his path.

Indira covered her face with her hands and cried harder than she ever had before because he had gone mad. This time she knew he was going to kill her. If not this time, then when. Indira stood in the center of the kitchen shaking.

*****

Maxine left Sydney's apartment before it got too late because she didn't like to be out on Dexter Avenue too late. When she got into her car, she saw that it needed gas.

"Damn, now I got to go to the gas station," Maxine said as she drove the icy streets and thought about Sydney and how much she missed Anthony. He had nearly ruined Sydney's life, but she still loved him more than anything. Maxine laughed aloud when she thought about what she'd said to Sydney about Bruce.

"I'd go out with that man in a heartbeat," she admitted to herself, as she pulled into the gas station. The usual gas station crowd was present. Two bums were near the cashier's window and at least two were by the pump. She assessed the situation and got out of the car. She was ready just in case anything jumped off. She didn't know what she'd do if anything ever did, but she'd at least be ready. She used her peripheral vision to keep watch on the two men who sat on the curb just a couple of feet away, and another man to her immediate left.

"Need some help pumping your gas, sistah?" The man kept himself at a respectful distance awaiting her response. Maxine finished paying for her gas before she turned to answer her pursuer. It was nearly below zero outside, so Maxine decided to give the guy a break, this time. Giving brothers a break wasn't a part of Maxine's routine.

"Thank you. I would appreciate some help." She rushed back to her car, unlocked the door and jumped in. After locking the doors, she watched the man from her rearview mirror. She was stern about her view of him, and he made eye contact with her in the mirror and smiled. She immediately smiled back, letting her previous thoughts about him subside.

She saw him walk toward her side of the car. She let the window down and handed him two dollars.

“Thank you, sistah, and have a happy holiday.”

“You do the same.” Maxine let her window up and pulled out into traffic. She thought about what had just happened.

Maybe I am too protective of myself, she thought as she contemplated if she was too hard on people by prejudging them without knowing anything about them. She looked out her driver side window at the streets of Dexter Avenue and realized she had to have that attitude in order to survive in her own community. She flicked on the lights in the living room, closing the door behind her. As she wrestled out of her leather coat, she saw the flashing red light of the answering machine.

“Bruce.” She would love to hear his dark-skinned tone right about now. She tossed her coat over the couch and hustled over to the device and hit the play button.

Beep.

Stephanie’s voice filled the room, announcing that she wouldn’t be in to work Tuesday, due to a dentist appointment.

“I thought she went to the dentist last week,” Maxine said aloud as she listened closely for the next message. It just had to be Bruce.

Beep.

“You haven’t gotten back with me about Thanksgiving dinner, baby.” Aunt Betsy would drive Maxine crazy if she didn’t call her back soon to say that she would be over for dinner. Just what she needed, dinner with the family…great. Maxine could see it now, sitting around the table filled with food and all her married with children cousins conveniently seated around it.

“Why aren’t you married yet, Maxi? When are you gonna start having some kids, Maxi?” Maxine trembled at the thought of the holidays.

“Maxi. It sounds like they’re all auditioning for a tampon commercial.” Maxine folded her arms and leaned against the back of the couch. “Ooh, yeah, I’m really looking forward to that.”

Beep.

Maxine began to laugh at herself, nearly missing the beginning of the third message. It was a man. He had that deep tone she loved. Maxine opened her ears wider to determine who the voice belonged to. Her heart was rooting for Bruce all the way.

"Hello, Maxine. Long time, no hear. Where have you been?" The voice took a long pause and then started up again. Maxine was intrigued now, but she couldn't put two and two together.

"I'm beginning to miss your fine chocolate self," the voice continued.

Maxine threw her arms up in the air in disgust. She wished she still didn't know who the voice belonged to. "Billy Gibson. What in the hell does he want after nearly two years?" she wondered aloud.

Maxine listened to the remainder of Billy's message and found that what he wanted was to see her again. Damn, they had had a good time together, all of seven months.

He could have been the one, but Billy wasn't quite ready to be anybody's one anything. Maxine thought back on those days with Billy. The one thing she could say about him was that he loved to please a woman, but on the other hand, that was also his problem. Forget that, she didn't have time to think about Billy right now. Her mind was set on having Mr. Bruce Washington. He was what she wanted, but he wasn't the man who called.

"What is it, Bruce? What do I have to do to make you a little more eager to see me?" Maxine stood over the answering machine in deep thought. She had to do something if she wanted this man.

"Well, Mr. Washington, if that's the game we're playing, I'm in." Maxine liked a good challenge every now and then herself.

*****

Indira stood over the sink running cold water over her face. It was all she could do for the moment to calm herself. She hoped Robert was tucked away in his den, not to return. Her body ached as she tried to make her way out of the kitchen. From her neck to the back of her thighs, she was throbbing. She had to get into some hot water before the pain got worse.

The soothing warm water was exactly what she needed. Indira lifted the washcloth from the water and let it roll off her neck down to her back. This was where she did all of her thinking, in the tub.

"This is it. I can't take anymore of this," she said aloud as she repeated her ritual with the water. "Lord, give me the strength to carry through this time. I don't want to be like my mother." She had made up her mind. She was going to end this abusive marriage. As a child, she watched her father paint her mother's face and body black and blue every day, until she died. There was still one thing different in her situation. She was going to make the decision and go through with it.

Robert sat slouched down in his recliner with his glass of bourbon in hand. He never meant for things to get this out of hand. He loved Indira at one time, but now he had nearly no love for her. He spun around in his chair to face the window. He would draw the line since she wouldn't. Either he had to leave her, or he would end up killing her.

"Guess I'll be leaving." Robert turned back to his desk and reached for a pen and paper.

Dear Indira,

Robert stopped writing and filled his glass to the rim once again. He was leaving his wife of five years. He had no other choice, in his mind. He had written nearly two paragraphs when he ended with, *Thank you.* After folding the letter, he put it into an envelope and addressed it to his wife. "I'm so sorry, Indira," Robert mumbled under his voice then slid the letter to the corner of his desk out of his sight.

"Vera Carr sounds okay to me." Robert gulped down the remaining liquor in his glass.

*****

Monday morning… back to work. Sydney wasn't quite ready for it just yet. She lifted Jasmine out of the tub and dried her tiny body off real good, and then doused her with baby powder. Jasmine clapped her hands as the white stuff fell around her.

"Come on, Jazzy let's hurry up and get dressed so mommy can get to work on time." Sydney laid her little girl down in the middle of the queen-size bed and put a fresh diaper on her bottom. "Now it's my turn," Sydney said as she let her robe drop to the floor as she sprayed perfume onto her bare body, and then stepped into her panties. Bloomers are what Maxine called them. Sydney finished dressing Jasmine, and then herself, and began her daily search for her car keys.

She'll Learn

"Oh, Jasmine, where are my keys?" Sydney was looking high and low. "I know you were the last one with them."

Jasmine was cracking up because she thought this was fun. Sydney lifted a towel from the dinner table and found them.

"Okay, Jazzy, let's get outta here." Sydney was cutting it a little close today. The clock read 8:15 and she had to walk through Telecom's doors at 9:00 a.m. sharp. She'd been working for the telemarketing company for nearly a year now and had probably been late only once. She liked the place, especially since they were the only company in town that would hire a pregnant woman. Sydney grabbed her purse, Jasmine's bag, her car keys, and finally Jasmine, and then stepped out the door. The two flights up to Miss Lee's apartment seemed to be getting harder and harder with each passing day. She huffed and puffed all the way to the old woman's door.

"Let me help you, baby," Miss Lee came to Sydney's rescue by taking hold of her twenty-pound daughter. "Hello, precious." Miss Lee carried Jasmine into the apartment.

"Thank you, Miss Lee. Those steps are killing me." Sydney leaned against the door.

"It's because you've gained so much weight, child." Miss Lee never held her tongue for anybody.

"I know, Miss Lee. But I swear I don't eat much of nothing." Sydney noticed a pretty Mexican girl sitting on the floor. "Whose little doll is this?" Sydney waved playfully to the little girl.

"That's Maria's daughter."

Sydney couldn't place the face.

"You know, the pretty Mexican girl on the second floor." Miss Lee put Jasmine on the floor next to her.

"Oh, Maria. I know who you're talking about now." Sydney didn't know where her mind was. Maria was the woman who tried to set her boyfriend on fire last year.

"I didn't know she had any kids." Sydney remained in the doorway.

"Me neither, until she asked me to watch her while she worked. She's a sweet baby."

Miss Lee loved children, though she never had any of her own. The old woman was a godsend for Sydney. She didn't know what she would have done without her. She was there for Sydney when she needed help the most.

"Well, Miss Lee, I have got to go before I'm late. Bye, Jasmine." Sydney bent down and kissed her baby's cheek. "I'll see you around six, Miss Lee. Thanks."

Miss Lee waved bye to Sydney as she rushed back down the stairs. It was now 8:26. Sydney reached the first floor in no time so she could still make it through the double glass doors of Telecom before nine o'clock. With car keys in hand, she reached the front doors where she could see the thick white snow on the ground through the narrow glass.

"Sydney!" Someone was calling her name, but she didn't have time to stop now, she was going to be late for the first time in nearly a year. She was brought up to always be on time.

"Sydney, wait!" She couldn't ignore that voice anymore, she knew it was Wayne. She stopped just inside the front door of the apartment building. "Sydney," Wayne saw Sydney stop at the doors. "I was yelling your name all down the hallway," Wayne bent over to catch his breath.

"Sorry, Wayne, but I'm about to be late for work," Sydney sort of smiled when Wayne lifted his hazel eyes to hers.

"I got some good news to tell you." Wayne still hadn't caught his breath all the way.

"Maybe you need to start exercising a little more," Sydney put her hand on his shoulder.

"I got the job at Channel 4, Sydney. I got the job." Wayne was smiling from ear to ear.

"You got it! Oh I'm so glad for you," Sydney wrapped her arms around Wayne's neck and hugged him. She was glad that something good finally happened to someone so nice. When Anthony left her, Wayne was there for her whenever she needed him. He took out her trash, fixed her car, and even took care of Jasmine once.

"Wayne, that's great." She was still holding onto him when their eyes met again. Sydney felt a little awkward so she pulled away from him, blushing.

"Sydney, I wasn't going to even send a resumé, until you forced me to. I owe it all to you." Wayne leaned over and kissed her on the cheek. He wished it could be more, but Sydney would never give him the chance. She was still hung up on Anthony. Wayne didn't want to let this chance slip by him, so he prepared himself for rejection once again.

"Sydney, why don't you celebrate with me tonight? It'll just be dinner, for three, Jasmine's invited, too." Wayne drilled his big beautiful eyes into hers, daring her to turn him down. How could she resist? She was so happy for him. She gave him an answer before she could think about it.

"Yes, I would love to celebrate with you. This is reason to celebrate." Sydney stood nonchalantly at the door as if she had nowhere to go.

"Well, I'll see you and Jasmine tonight around seven o'clock." Wayne couldn't believe it, she finally said yes. Sydney caught a glimpse of the old, dust covered clock hanging above the out of order elevator.

"Oh, God, eight forty-five! I'm going to lose my job," Sydney ran out the door without saying another word and hopped into her car. She knew her car didn't like it very much when she just took off without letting her warm-up. Today she would just have to be pissed.

*****

Billie Holiday's sultry voice floated throughout the room as Maxine climbed higher and higher up her treadmill. *Good mornin', heartache, sit down*," Maxine huffed out the words. She knew exactly what Billie was talkin' about. When her four miles were completed, she started to clean up the pigsty she referred to as her bedroom. She had a bad habit of never hanging up her clothes, which left the closet near empty most of the time. Now her clothes were hung up, her shoes were in their designated place, her dresser was neatly organized, and most of all, her bed was made. Her grandmother used to never let her get away without making her bed first, but she wasn't around anymore to get on her about stuff like that. Maxine gave her room the once over.

"Now that looks like a bedroom should look." She sat on the corner of her king-size bed to catch her breath.

Ding! Dong!

Maxine lifted her head quickly at the sound of the doorbell.

Ding! Dong!

"Who in the hell could that be? It's eleven o'clock." Maxine poked her lip out and headed down the stairs to the front door.

Ding! Dong!

"Okay, okay, I'm coming." Maxine reached the door and then hesitated when she saw the huge shadow that filled her doorway.

Bruce? Naw, he wouldn't just come over to my house. Maxine looked through the fogged glass again. "Who is it?" Maxine had a touch of sarcasm in her voice.

Bruce didn't have time to call. When Erica announced that she was going to see her father in the hospital in Chicago, he was as good as out the door.

"It's Bruce."

Maxine's heart was beating so hard, it felt like it could leap out any minute. This was too much excitement. She was in shock, she didn't see Bruce as the type of guy who would just pop over at your door unannounced, especially after he stood her up yesterday. Silence fell between the door and Bruce when she remembered yesterday.

He knew this wasn't going to be easy.

"I know you're mad, Maxine. But I promise you, I'll make it up to you." Bruce was keeping it together. He hadn't planned on begging. Maxine was upset, but she wasn't stupid. He could beg for her forgiveness inside the house. She wiped her sweaty hands against her spandex shorts and turned the doorknob. A cold breeze blew around Bruce as he stood in the doorway. Maxine stood aside, allowing him to step inside. She closed the door. She stayed with her back turned for a moment.

Take the oath, she said to herself. After just seeing Bruce, she knew she'd better take it. Bruce studied Maxine's perfectly fit frame. His eyes were glued to her muscular thighs when she turned around to face him. She was glad he liked what he was seeing, but there was no time for that just yet. He was dressed to a tee. From his Cole Hahn boots to the midnight blue Armani suit, to the diamond that lived on his pinky up to his silver satin tie. She was immediately hooked.

"Can I take your coat?" Maxine watched Bruce slide out of his leather trench, and then his suit jacket. She hung his things in the hall closet. He looked around the house and was impressed. Bruce sat down on the couch and watched Maxine take a seat in the recliner across from him. Wise choice, no matter how horny she was, she'd taken the oath. She couldn't give him any, especially after he stood her up.

She'll Learn

"Damn, Maxine, you look like you could outrun Jackie Joyner Kersey." Bruce's eyes were stuck again. Maxine didn't flinch. She remembered how she was feeling yesterday. "This is a very nice house you have. I grew up in a house just like this." Bruce began to get up then stopped. "You mind if I look around?" Maxine slowly unfolded her arms and took the evil look off of her face. Bruce knew exactly what he was doing. He had to break this thick piece of ice.

"Where'd you grow up?" Maxine was beginning to relax some.

"I grew up in Cleveland." A small-framed picture caught Bruce's eye. "Is this you?" He leaned in a little closer. Maxine felt a rush that nearly knocked her down. Bruce was looking at a picture of her mother. Though this was her house now, it was once her grandmother's and she loved all her children, so the picture stayed. Maxine didn't want to make her business known already, so she kept her composure.

"That's my mother… Maureen," Maxine let the name fall off of her tongue instead of roll.

"A very beautiful lady, I can truly see the resemblance."

Maxine gave him a turned up smile at the compliment.

"Follow me, please." Maxine turned and led Bruce down the hallway and into the kitchen. "I recently had the kitchen remodeled. My grandmother hated the old kitchen." She moved into the living room and then into the den. "This is the shop, my grandmother used to fix hair in this room."

There were lots of pictures of women, kids, and a few men who had graced Mable's chair.

"Now this is you. Am I right or wrong?" Bruce pulled away from the picture and smiled widely. Maxine looked at the picture, and then began to blush.

"You're right. That is me." Maxine took a gander at the picture herself. "And that's my ganny."

Bruce could read Maxine's feelings for her grandmother all over her face. "You really miss her, don't you?"

Maxine slowly turned to Bruce and nodded, "She was a very special lady."

Bruce continued to examine the many pictures and question Maxine about them. She enjoyed his questions and was now completely relaxed. Bruce was in the clear now. He could see that Maxine was loosening up to him. That was exactly what he wanted.

"You were a very beautiful child." Bruce turned to Maxine and stared into her almond-shaped eyes, "You are very beautiful now." He eased his hand around her waist and pulled her against his body. His thick lips were covering her mouth with a wet kiss. She usually didn't like wet, sloppy kisses, but this time was completely different. Maxine gave in wholeheartedly to his kiss.

"Remember the plan," Maxine's inner voice was speaking loud and clear. She eased herself out of Bruce's hold. She couldn't let this man get in that easily. "He stood me up, and don't no man get away with that," Maxine's voice was now drowning Bruce completely out. Bruce knew this wasn't going to be a piece of cake. Maxine led Bruce back into the living room and motioned for him to sit on the couch. Bruce knew what was coming next and he was trapped. Maxine stood over him with her arms crossed, like a hawk seeking its prey, she honed in on him.

"What happened to you yesterday?"

Before Bruce could think of his answer, she continued.

"You seem to be thinking that this is our first date." Maxine burned her eyes into him. Now they looked like two fireballs to him, instead of almonds.

Bruce took a little while to answer, and then after throwing up his hands, he was ready.

"Look, Maxine. I'm sorry about yesterday and I'm sorry about any other dates I mess up with you in the future." He eyed Maxine as she stood over him. Her crossed arms began to loosen. For him to say something like that was enough to melt Maxine right then and there. Instead, she kept a hold on herself for not to attack his body.

"I accept your apology, Bruce." Maxine dropped her arms completely and sat down on the couch next to him.

"You see, I'm a promoter and I have to keep a close eye on my gym. So that takes up a lot of my time." Bruce wanted her to know that he worked every day.

"Even on Sundays?" Maxine was playing with him now. She leaned nearer to Bruce to plead her case better. Her glowing dark skin mesmerized him.

"What? Were you just working out or something? Your skin looks so good." Bruce had a real thing for dark-skinned women. He loved to touch. He reached his hand toward Max's face. She stopped his hand in mid air.

"Don't change the subject," Maxine jokingly moved back away from him.

"I thought you already accepted my apology." Bruce looked like a spoiled little boy not getting his way now. Maxine caught a chuckle from the sight of him.

"I have accepted your apology, Bruce. But I still deserve an explanation, don't I?" She folded her arms across her chest again.

"Yes, you do. I was extremely busy yesterday and I completely forgot about our date." Bruce looked a little disgusted. "Now, are you happy? I didn't want to tell you that I forgot all about you." Bruce sat up on the couch rubbing his hands together. Maxine said nothing, but only watched him closely. He was so handsome sitting there and so full of shit, but she was loving every minute of it.

"I'll bet you smooth talk your way out of practically everything, or practically into everything," Maxine started to laugh, and then she couldn't stop laughing. Bruce didn't find anything amusing at first, but watching her laugh all by herself sort of made him start laughing.

"I'm sorry, Bruce. I just wanted to know why you stood me up. That's all," Maxine wiped the tears of laughter from her face.

"Well are we through with all of that now?" He was still sort of laughing.

"Yes. We can start from scratch now."

Bruce reached over to Maxine and slid her body next to him and then onto his lap. He touched her face with his hand and then slid it around to the back of her neck. Her warm lips were what he wanted. He let his hands roam freely over Maxine's butter-soft legs as his tongue did the same to her neck and mouth. Maxine's eyes were beginning to roll to the back of her head, a sure sign that she was losing it.

"Remember the plan, Max!" Her inner voice never let up.

Bruce eased his hand under the tiny tube top that Maxine wore and found his way to her nipples. They peaked with excitement, but Maxine knew she was enjoying this a little too much. She hadn't had a man touch her like this in nearly a month.

"Forget about that girl. You don't know him!" Her inner voice was right, she'd just met him. Maxine pulled her mouth away from Bruce without any warning.

"Hold up a minute," Maxine eased herself off Bruce's lap. Finally, she was getting a hold on herself again.

"What's wrong, Max?" Bruce was loosening the satin tie he wore from his neck. He was ready and he wanted her real bad. He and Erica didn't make love much. She didn't care for sex at all.

"This is only the second time I'm seeing you, Bruce. Things have changed a little too much for me just to give it up like that." Maxine was finally learning. She had to sooner or later. She'd had this same situation in her life a dozen times and each time it ended the wrong way.

"You're right. You're right. I can understand that nowadays, but I couldn't help myself." Bruce looked Maxine up and down, as if he could eat her up. "Look at you. You look like you on the Olympic track team. I mean, damn."

Bruce pushed down the lion that had grown in his pants.

"You do understand, don't you?" Maxine sort of felt guilty for playing the tease game, when she already decided not to give him any.

"Baby, we've got plenty of time for that. Run upstairs and put some clothes on, and we'll go have lunch or something." Bruce straightened his shirt and tie. Maxine was still looking a little puzzled.

"Go on, plenty of time." Bruce reluctantly waved for Maxine to get dressed. He slapped her across her ass when she went by him. She was glad he reacted that way. Most of the time if you told a brotha' some stuff like that, nine times out of ten he was gonna think something was wrong with you.

"I'm going up. I'll be down in fifteen minutes."

Bruce watched Maxine as she ran up the stairs. He sat on the couch shaking his head. Who was he kidding about having all the time in the world? Erica would be back from Chicago in two days.

*****

It was already going on eleven o'clock and El's plane was leaving at one o'clock. Indira didn't care what she had to do to get out of the house, but she had to see Eldridge before he left. Indira said nothing as she put on her coat. Robert sat at the kitchen table staring out the window. He didn't care too much about where she was going. But, you could never tell with him. Indira slid her purse strap onto her shoulder and grabbed her keys and briefcase.

"I'm leaving now, Robert. I'll see you later." Indira stood frozen when she saw Robert walking toward her. He cupped her face lightly with his hands and kissed her softly.

"Goodbye, Indira." He let go of her face and walked back into the kitchen. Indira was at a loss for words.

"Goodbye," she whispered under her breath, watching her husband walk away. What in the hell is up with him? she wondered.

Indira had no time to figure Robert out right now. It was what she'd been doing all along, trying to figure out her husband. What did he want from her? It was too late now. She was tired of trying. Indira closed the door softly behind her.

Robert didn't give his wife time to get out of the driveway before he was in his office positioning his goodbye letter…his goodbye letter. He couldn't believe he was doing this to Indira. He couldn't believe he was beating her, either. He hurried up the stairs to the bedroom they shared and gathered some of his things. He wasn't concerned about the rest of his things because Indira wasn't the type of woman who would do anything rash, like burn his remaining things. After checking the house for anything important, he poured himself a drink. This would be his final drink in this house. His new home would be with Vera.

*****

"I don't get downtown too often. So I haven't had the pleasure of eating here before," Maxine said as she looked around the busy walls of the restaurant. They were crowded with autographed pictures of some of Detroit's famous and there were plenty of sports paraphernalia everywhere. Bruce watched Maxine as she turned to take in all she could. This was perfect. The restaurant was dimly lit, and not too many people were in there yet.

It was a Monday afternoon and an hour past the lunch rush.

"I usually bring investors here from time to time. It's a pretty relaxed place."

"What can I get you to drink?" The waitress stood before the couple with her tray resting on her hip.

"Would you like some wine?" Bruce and the waitress turned to Maxine.

"Yes. White wine, please," Maxine closed the menu and held on to it.

"We'll have a carafe of White Zinfandel and I'll have…"

Maxine watched Bruce order his food and got lost somewhere in his words. She wasn't hearing a thing anymore. She had changed the entire scenario completely. She was hearing him speak to her...

"I am the man for you, Maxine. No need to search any further." Maxine leaned in closer to his voice. "I'm what you're looking for. I'm nothing like anyone you've had in the past."

Maxine woke up from her dream sharply. She was putting too much in too early and she knew it.

"Oh, and I'll have an order of red beans and rice with that." Bruce closed the menu and handed it to the waitress.

"And what will you be having?" The waitress stood at attention with her readied pen.

Maxine ordered with the same hidden pressure on her. Bruce's scenario was a lot different than Maxine's. He saw the two of them wrapped up tightly in an embrace trying to swallow each other's tongue. He was looking forward to this fantasy coming true. Fantasizing was a part of his daily life. Living with Erica wasn't much of a fantasy. Maxine could be more to him than another piece. He wanted her to be more.

Bruce eyed Maxine carefully as she ordered her meal. She was a smart businesswoman, in shape, plus she knew who she was.

"What are you staring at?" Maxine sat with a cute smirk on her face. Bruce was reveling in this.

"Nothing. I was just checking you out, that's all." Bruce never took his eyes off of her.

"Checking me out?" Maxine gave Bruce a puzzled look.

"You know. Listening to how you ordered, watching your lips and mouth form each word. Seeing your eyes light up when you found something you liked." Bruce gave her an approving nod. "Yes, just checking you out." He let his eyes off of Maxine and examined his surroundings.

Maxine began to confess, "I checked you out the first day I met you. The bell over the door rang and in stepped this stranger. His Indiana Jones hat pulled tightly over his head to shield the wind, the full-length leather trench coat that swayed with each move he made. Once in the light of the buffet, I saw the creamy black skin on your face, the strength in your arms, down to your manicured nails; one of the finest men around." Maxine knew she was teasing him now, but he did start this game. "Oh, did I check you out."

Bruce looked as if he could eat her up right now.

"You really did check me out. Glad I passed." He knew this was going to be something special. He and Maxine were gonna have a great time together.

*****

Indira took the elevator up to the fifth floor of the hotel. El's room number was 520. She was being quite bold just coming straight up to his room like this, but she had to do something.

"520." Indira stood at the door. She straightened her clothes, rubbed her frosted lips together, and then knocked on the door.

"Who is it?" Eldridge was squeezing the remainder of his things into his suitcase. No one responded.

"Who is it?" El sounded upset now. Indira couldn't open her mouth. The door opened up slowly.

"Surprise," Indira tried to smile. She was nervous and hadn't the slightest idea why.

"Indira," El quickly wrapped his arms around her neck and hugged her. "I'm glad to see you. Are you taking me to the airport? I wasn't looking forward to Omari and Jonathan." El led Indira into the room and closed the door behind her. Indira looked around the room. It smelled so manly, steam drifted out of the bathroom, and El smelled divine. She was in his room. Her eyes locked on the unmade bed. The rustled sheets threw her into a fantasy. She hadn't been with another man in nearly six years.

"Six years," she mumbled aloud. Indira sat down on the chair next to the window.

"What was that, Indira?" El rushed around the room getting his things together. He glanced over to Indira staring at the bed.

"Nearly six years since I've been with another man." Indira took her eyes off the bed and locked them onto Eldridge. "I have wasted so many years with him, and for what?" Indira's eyes began to water.

Eldridge could see there was more to this, so he walked over to her. "You're talking like your life is over, Indira. Life is more than just a happy marriage. You've got so much time ahead of you, ahead of us." He was stroking her long and lightly. Indira let the tears swelling in her eyes fall. He was making so much sense to her. Her marriage was everything to her. She wanted it to work no matter what.

"It's over, Eldridge. I know it is." She turned around to Eldridge, who stood behind her. "The sad thing is I don't want it to be over." Indira stood up. "I know you're thinking, how can she want to be with this man? The very man who beats her black and blue like a stranger on the street." Indira was letting the tears flow and her feelings out.
"The same man who drinks himself into such a coma, he can't fuck."

Eldridge felt so bad for his new friend, she was in so much pain. He didn't want to stop her. If he missed his flight, so what? He couldn't leave her like this.

"What's wrong with me, El? What the fuck is wrong with me?" Indira had tired herself out and fell onto the bed. El sat down on the bed next to her. Indira couldn't stop crying because she was finally letting it out. Somebody had to know what was happening to her. Maxine and Sydney didn't even know; her two best friends. She was too embarrassed to tell them. Indira could feel El's hands rubbing her back and shoulders. She was more embarrassed now. She had made a complete ass of herself in front of a man she'd only known for a few days. She wiped her face with her hands and sat up on the bed next to him.

"I'm so sorry, El. I did it to you again. I'm laying all this shit on you," Indira sort of laughed at herself. El put his arm around her shoulders and kissed her cheek. "I just needed someone to talk to I guess." Indira started to cry again. El got off the bed and went into the bathroom to get some tissue. He gave the tissues to Indira.

"It's okay, Indira. I told you last night to call if you needed to talk or something." He took one of the tissues from Indira and wiped her eyes.

She'll Learn

"I can't leave here until I know you're all right. I mean that." He stared into Indira's red eyes. It was now twelve-fifteen. El gently placed his hands around Indira's face. The sadness in her eyes was tearing at his heart. He couldn't believe he was letting himself fall for this woman. She belonged to another man, yet he wanted her for himself. El continued his gaze into Indira's eyes. She was lost in his gaze and didn't want to lose this moment. El pulled her mouth to his and kissed her. He let his fingers roam through her long strands of hair. Indira let go and accepted his kiss openly and wantonly. They slowly pulled away from one another and dropped their heads like two teenagers. They made eyes again and started to laugh.

"You all right, Indira Carr."

*****

Robert used his key to let himself into Vera's. This is where he belonged, with Vera. She loved him unconditionally and that's what he needed, a woman who didn't need to change him or straighten him up. Robert tossed his bags onto the worn chair that sat near the door. The place could use some brightening up. Maybe he and Vera could do it together. This was another chance for Robert. He could wipe his slate clean of Bridget, Cynthia, and Indira. His focus would only be on Vera and himself.

With the hope of a new start, Robert headed to the kitchen to fix a drink. He began to cough uncontrollably and rushed the liquor into his mouth. Vera would be so surprised when she got home. Robert smirked at the thought. He was what she'd always wanted and now she had him. Robert stood over the sink and gulped down another shot of bourbon. He checked the clock on the chipped and stained wall. It read 1:25. Robert still had a couple of hours before Vera came home. She cleaned houses for white folks. She was still living in the past. There was no reason nowadays to be cleaning nobody's house, but your own. Robert began to think of Indira, his young wife of five years. It was over. He wondered if she'd found his letter yet.

"I couldn't go on like that, Indira. I hope you understand." Robert sat his glass carefully into the sink and walked into the living room. After finding some comfort in the rundown sofa, he dozed off.

*****

"So where to now, Ms. Harrell?" Bruce grabbed a mint just before opening the door for Maxine.

"I don't know, Mr. Washington. What do you suggest we do now?" Maxine was ready to forget the oath completely. She wanted this man and wanted him badly. Bruce closed the door of his Tahoe behind his date and hopped in the truck himself. He didn't give any suggestions. He only stared at Maxine as she sat next to him.

"You smell so good. What is that?" Bruce continued to take in her aroma.

"Pear Glaze," Maxine leaned in closer for him to get a good whiff. Bruce lightly kissed her smooth neck. She sat back in her seat in a state of shock.

"I'm sorry, but your neck was looking so tasty and smelling so good." Bruce shrugged his shoulders and smiled. Maxine knew exactly where she wanted to go now.

"How about we go to my house for some wine," Maxine couldn't wait any longer. Forget the damned oath.

"I would love a glass of wine." Bruce started the ignition and pulled out of the blanketed lot. "To Max's, we go." Bruce was glad she'd said that. He didn't want to pressure her. He didn't have much time, but he wanted to get the ball rolling.

"Ooh girl, you smell good!" Bruce reached over and touched Maxine's hand on the seat.

I could get used to this man. He is fun to be with. I'm comfortable with him, Maxine mused as she sat silently and stared out the window as the wheels turned in her mind. He even knows how to eat in a restaurant. But what would I expect from a man of his status?

Maxine turned her eyes slightly to glance at Bruce—manicured nails, creamy black skin, and a beautiful set of teeth. Maxine couldn't take her eyes off him. She unbuckled her seatbelt and slid over closer to Bruce. She flashed a girlish smile at him and he wrapped his arm around her shoulders. Sydney was going to kill her if she found out.

At least, I'll die happy, Maxine thought.

*****

Indira slowly pulled into her driveway, relieved that her husband's car was nowhere in sight. At 2:30 p.m., it was too early for even Robert to hang out at the bar. Not thinking another thought about him, she hurried out of the cold air and into the house. It was a beautiful house, and you would think that a happy family lived there. There were pictures of Indira and Robert, her sister Clarissa, Robert's three children, and even a picture of Indira's mother and father. It was all fake. Everything represented nothing but sadness. That sadness was beginning to consume Indira.

She retrieved the mail, uninterested in what it had to offer until she saw a card from her sister. She quickly tore it open. The card announced that she would be coming to stay with her for a week during Christmas. Indira couldn't wait to see her. They hadn't seen each other in nearly a year. Clarissa was going to use her usual travel provider, Greyhound.

Indira had promised herself that once she could afford it, she would never ride that thing again. Strange people sat next to you, and some of them stunk like hell. The best thing to do was act crazy or pretend to be asleep. People knew something was wrong with you if you went to sleep on the bus.

Clarissa didn't have it like her sister. She was struggling in D.C. She went to school in the daytime and shook her ass throughout the night. Her money was tight, but she didn't know what to do. There were so many things she wanted to do with her sister, she didn't know where to start. Maxine and Sydney would be so glad to see her. She was like their sister, too.

The card that Clarissa sent was in the spirit of Christmas, so Indira placed it neatly on the mantel of the fireplace in the living room. Indira felt better now that she had gotten some of her problems off her chest to El, her newly found friend. Her baby sister was coming to visit her, the sweet kiss from El, and Robert nowhere to be found. She couldn't ask for anything else.

"Maybe I should get started on my own Christmas cards." Indira strolled down the hallway and into Robert's office. She kept her stash of Christmas cards in the file cabinet near the window. She pulled open the drawer in search of her cards. She had so many people to send cards to. She would do the gallery's clients next week. Indira stopped searching when she noticed an envelope carefully placed in the center of the desk. Her name on the front immediately caught her eye. Robert had written her a letter. It was probably just another one of his apologies. Indira grabbed the envelope and unfolded the letter inside.

She read the first line, anticipating something mushy to make her forgive him quickly. Instead, she continued reading, and then sat down in the chair behind the desk. Indira let go of the letter, letting it slowly float to the floor. She couldn't believe what she had just read. Robert was gone for good.

"The son of a bitch left me." Indira slammed her fists hard on the desk, and then began to cry. She wasn't prepared for this. She frantically looked around the room. He never went anywhere without his laptop computer. It was gone. Indira felt sick inside. He wasn't supposed to leave her. She was supposed to have left him.

"I don't believe this shit. What a damn fool I was for staying. " Indira, in a rage, slid everything off of the desk to the floor. She refused to believe that Robert had left her. After five years of abuse, physical and verbal, the drinking, and the other women, he left her. She felt like a fool. She was the fool.

*****

Maxine opened the front door of her house with Bruce following closely behind her. Once in the door, Bruce grabbed her around her waist and turned her to him.

"I didn't really come here for any wine." Bruce pulled her to him and kissed her hard. She didn't have a chance to react, only to go along with the flow.

The two began grabbing at each other roughly. Maxine pulled Bruce's coat off his strong arms and started at his satin tie. They were picking up where they left off earlier. Letting his coat drop to the floor, Bruce began undressing his prey. He wanted her so badly he nearly ripped off her blouse. Maxine pulled her top over her head, exposing her breasts, to keep him from tearing her good blouse. They made their way over to the couch and fell onto it. Bruce lay on top of Maxine, grinding his groin into her. She could only imagine what he'd have done if his pants weren't still on. Maxine freed his belt and unsnapped his pants, letting his shirt out. She continued to kiss his mouth and neck while she let him devour her.

She'll Learn

"Let's go upstairs to my bedroom." Maxine couldn't take it anymore. Fuck the oath. Her eyes began to roll to the back of her head as Bruce nibbled at her breasts.

"Wait just a minute, baby. I can't stop now." Bruce lifted her on top of him as he slid under her on the couch. Maxine worked her body against his when she began to feel a strange vibration against her thigh. She tried to ignore it, but it wouldn't stop. It was his pager. Bruce stopped caressing her back and reached for his pager. Maxine lifted off of him and fell to the couch. His attention was solely on finding out who had paged him. Maxine covered herself with one of the throw pillows.

"Ooh baby, I have got to go. This is something I really have to take care of." Bruce dressed in a few seconds flat and was headed out the door before Maxine could get two words in. She still sat curled up on the couch with a pillow covering her tiny breasts.

"Where are you going, Bruce?" Maxine had to say something before he ran out the door.

"I promise I'll make it up to you, baby." He grabbed his coat off the floor, and put his hat on his head.

"I don't think you can make this up, Bruce." Maxine was trying to act hard. She wanted him to know that she wouldn't tolerate this shit. Bruce walked over to her, got on his knees and put his mouth on hers. He kissed her for a good couple of minutes, and then pulled away. Maxine was beaten. He had her just where he wanted her.

"Will you go to this cocktail party with me tonight? I don't have a date." Bruce got up and headed toward the door. Maxine couldn't speak so she just nodded yes.

"I'll be back around 8:30 to pick you up." Bruce was out the door. Maxine remained balled up in the corner of the couch covering herself with the pillows.

"I guess the oath remains good."

*****

The floor was mopped, and the dishes were washed, dried, and put away. Now all that was left to do was to get her pay for the day. Vera walked through the extravagant house to the sunroom where her employer sat reading.

"I'm finished with everything, Mrs. Mancuso. There's dinner for you in the oven and your dessert is in the refrigerator.

It was one old woman taking care of another old woman. Mrs. Mancuso was nearly seventy and had no one, but Vera. She'd become bitter after her husband died five years ago. Vera was all she had, though she would never consider her a friend, only her help. Vera didn't want to grow old alone like Mrs. Mancuso. She didn't want to die alone, as she thought she was destined to do.

The woman only stared out the window while Vera spoke to her, and then she turned her eyes to her.

"Your money is on the dining room table."

Finding her money was always a game to Vera. Mrs. Mancuso never handed her money to her directly. She placed it elsewhere every day.

"I hope that the kitchen is satisfactory, Vera." She watched as Vera walked toward the door. "I'll be checking."

Vera stopped in her tracks the minute she heard the old woman's voice. "Yes, ma'am," Vera replied. She never turned around to the woman; she only left through the door. She had worked there for nearly fifteen years and there weren't too many occasions where Mrs. Mancuso had a kind word for her. Vera hated working there, but she was getting too old to be out looking for a job. Plus, this was an easy gig. That old bitch was too stiff and blind to ever check behind her like she threatened.

Vera tied her scarf around her head and put on her coat. She found her pay on the dining room table and headed to the bus stop. The same routine had been haunting her life for so long. Time was running out for her and she could feel it deep inside her bones. The many years of drinking hard liquor and smoking cigarettes were finally taking their toll. Robert was her reason for living. She'd loved that man ever since the first day she laid her eyes on him. She'd been waiting so long to be with him, she hoped she wasn't waiting in vain. He'd made many choices other than her, but she knew he loved her and that was all that mattered to her.

The bus came up the street rocking side to side slightly from all the weight it had to bring up the hill. The doors opened and Vera stepped on. The bus was crowded, and there weren't any seats left. She grabbed hold of the rail and took a deep breath.

She'll Learn

"Would you like to sit down?"

Vera lifted her tired eyes to see a handsome young man standing and offering his seat to her. As tired as she was, there was no way she was turning him down.

"Thank you." Vera slid by the man, careful not to touch him, and eased into the now available seat. The man took hold of the railing over her.

"You sort of remind me of my aunt. She wore her scarf just like yours. I hadn't thought about her in years, until I saw you." The man seemed to be feeling guilty about not thinking of his aunt.

"It's so easy to let things slip away from your mind," Vera acknowledged.

The man looked down at her and smiled. Vera knew better than anyone, how easy it was to forget. She'd put her whole past behind her. She had to, or it would have consumed her entirely. The pain of being alone and not having anyone left in the world was damn near unbearable. She knew, all too well, how to forget. All she had was Robert, and one day, he would be hers. Vera reached up and pulled the bell when she got to her destination. She had two blocks to walk, and then she could finally rest her feet.

*****

Indira left the mess in the office and went into the kitchen for a cup of tea to calm her nerves. She was completely shocked by what had just happened. Just like that, her life had taken a sharp left turn. She sat down at the table and sipped her tea. Her eyes begin to wander around the kitchen. She noticed bottle after bottle of liquor on the counters, on top of the cabinets, and under things. She put down her tea and slowly walked over to the counter and grabbed two bottles of bourbon. She unscrewed the tops and began pouring the liquid down the sink. She grabbed another bottle and poured it down the sink. The kitchen had filled with the sour stench of liquor. She felt like she was pouring her life down the drain. She continued to pour until the kitchen was filled with empty bottles.

There were nearly ten empty bottles scattered around the place. Indira slid the trash can over and tossed them in one by one. Why stop here? Indira stormed out of the smelly kitchen and rushed up the stairs to the bedroom she and Robert once shared. If he was leaving, he would need all of his things. Indira opened the closet and began snatching things off hangers and pulling down boxes. There was shit everywhere. She had cleared his closet except for a couple of boxes at the top. She would come back to those later, after she packed up all that belonged to him. She knew he would be back sooner or later to retrieve his things.

*****

Vera was coming near the end of her two block journey home. She made her usual stop at the liquor store for a fifth and a pack of Newport's. With her head hanging low, Vera neared her home. She was so out of it, she didn't even notice Robert's car in the driveway. She reached into her ragged coat pocket and retrieved her door key and let herself in. Pulling the scarf off of her head and letting her coat fall to the floor all came in one motion. The only thing she wanted to do was kick her feet up, pour herself a drink, and blaze one up.

Vera pulled a chair from the dining table and sat down to take off her shoes. The old things looked as worn out as she did. Her tired feet went up on the table. Vera lit her cigarette and took a long pull. She nearly choked when she heard a loud noise coming from the other room. She let her feet down off the table quietly, and eased into the living room where she heard the noise. She couldn't believe her eyes. It was Robert stretched out across her couch. Was he here to stay or just visiting? she wondered.

However it was, he had arrived at her doorstep, she wouldn't be turning him away. Suddenly she had energy again. She turned and tiptoed out of the room not to wake her man. Her man, damn that sounded good. She would cook him a good home-cooked dinner and hope he was staying the night. Vera was so excited she didn't notice the small duffel bag in the corner of the room.

Vera started pulling out pots and pans as quietly as she could. Robert woke up groggily, holding his heavy head in his hands.

"What in the hell is going on?" Robert got to his feet and stumbled his way into the kitchen. Vera was busy at the stove frying and stirring away before she realized that Robert was behind her.

"Oh, baby, I'm so glad to see you." Vera wiped her hands on a towel then quickly wrapped her arms around the man she loved. "Are you with me for the night?"

Robert put his arms around Vera's waist and pulled her body close to his. "I'm here for good, Vera." Robert was serious as he stared into her tired eyes. "This is where I belong. I've been a damn fool not to be with you all these years, I'm sorry Vera."

Robert damn near fell on her. Vera pulled strength from deep within her frail body and held her man up. Was he for real or was she hearing things?

"What did you say, Bobby?" Vera helped Robert sit down at the dining room table.

"I said I love you, Vera, and I want to be with you for the rest of my life." For however long that may be, he thought. Robert took hold of Vera's tired hand as she stood over him. His words forced her legs to grow weaker and she sat down at the table. "Are you okay, honey?" Robert could see that Vera was in some sort of a state of shock.

"Oh yes, Bobby, I'm fine. I've been waiting nearly half my life for you to say those words to me. It was all worth it Bobby." Vera took hold of Robert's hand. "You were worth the wait."

*****

Sydney got home from work and felt like she could collapse right there when she got a glimpse of the many flights of stairs she had to climb.

"Ms. Lee would live on the sixth floor," she uttered. After finally reaching her destination, she picked up Jasmine and headed down the stairs to her little home. A smile came to her face as she closed the door behind her. She had made it through another day, she was home. Sydney held onto her daughter and eased down on the couch. She was beat, and only wanted to relax in front of the TV with Jasmine, when it hit her like a bolt of lightning, "My date with Wayne." She took a long sigh then turned her little girl to face her.

"What do you think Jazzy, should we go?" Sydney looked into her eyes in search of an answer, but what answer would a one-year-old have for her? Jasmine answered with a smile.

After that and some thought, Sydney decided not to disappoint her friend. She got off the couch and changed her clothes, nothing spectacular, only a pair of stretch pants and a Michigan sweatshirt. She wasn't trying to impress him or anything.

Wayne on the other hand, was trying to impress Sydney. He opened the door to his apartment with a handful of flowers for Sydney and one flower for Jasmine. "Please come in, my two beautiful guests for the evening." Wayne stepped to the side and let the two inside.

"Wow, Wayne, I wasn't expecting all of this. I just thought..." Sydney saw how nice the table had been set and candles were lit all over the place. The place looked…romantic.

"You weren't expecting what?" Wayne pulled out a chair from the table for Sydney. "You weren't expecting me to go this far for you?" He retrieved the bottle of wine chilling on ice on the table and poured two glasses.

"I haven't forgotten you, Jasmine," Wayne said as he came back from the kitchen with a chilled bottle of apple juice for the baby. "I hope she likes it."

Jasmine took the bottle with the biggest smile that warmed Wayne and Sydney's hearts.

"She's easier to please than you are, Sydney."

Sydney became relaxed from seeing this side of Wayne. She knew he was a special guy, but not this special. "What do you mean by that?" Sydney awaited Wayne's response.

"I just mean that you are hard to get close to. It's taken me nearly a whole year to start speaking to you, let alone ask you out," Wayne turned shyly to Sydney.

"That's so sweet, but we are all past that now. Here we are," Sydney smiled at Wayne.

"Yes we are. I hope you like Italian food." Wayne served dinner to Sydney and took care of her every need. They ate, talked about any and everything, including Anthony and how much he'd changed her life. Wayne listened so intently, Sydney was letting it all out. Wayne didn't mind one bit, he was just glad she was there with him now.

CHAPTER NINE

Maxine oiled her legs good and slipped into her sheers. She wanted to knock Bruce and his friends off their feet tonight. The sequined mini dress she found at Shay's Boutique on 10 Mile would definitely do the trick.

"Yeah, Maxine, this little number will turn some heads," she said as she checked herself out in the mirror.

Ring! Ring!

"This better not be Bruce." Maxine answered the phone, "Hello."

The voice of her Aunt Betsy was immediately recognized.

"Hello, Maxine and how are you doing?"

Maxine really wasn't in the mood to talk right now.

"Fine, I'm just getting ready to go out, Aunt Betsy."

"Well, good for you, baby, I just wanted to call and tell you that I bumped into Maureen earlier this week. Maxine almost dropped the phone. She hadn't seen her mother in years. Grandma had forbidden her from coming around as long as she was on drugs. She didn't even go to grandma's funeral.

"Maxine, are you there honey?"

Maxine sat silently and held the phone.

"Yes, I'm here. I just wasn't expecting to hear her name that's all."

Aunt Betsy didn't want to hear that from her niece.

"She is your mother, Maxine, and remember, God only gave you one."

Maxine twisted her hair in deep thought.

"Yes, ma'am, I know." She still said nothing.

"Well, what about Thanksgiving, honey? I didn't get your answer."

Maxine knew what would get her aunt off of the phone.

"Yes. I will make it over for the holiday." It was too late to turn back now.

"Beautiful, we will all be so glad to see you. I'll call you again soon, okay?" She stopped talking to hear Maxine.

"Okay, Aunt Betsy, I'll see you then." Maybe this wasn't such a good plan after all.

"And remember what I said about your mother, goodbye."

Maxine put the phone on the receiver. Thinking about her mother only brought pain to her heart. Maxine was a strong woman, but that pain never went away.

*****

Bruce didn't want to be late so he rushed around the big empty house getting ready. He remembered the food that Erica left in the refrigerator for him to eat. He took the plate out and poured it into Sam's bowl on the kitchen floor. He would enjoy it more than Bruce ever would.

Bruce was at Maxine's in no time. She came out of the house looking straight off the cover of *Essence* magazine. Bruce jumped out the car to open the car door for her.

"You look good enough to eat." Bruce took a quick peck on Maxine's bare neck.

She was hoping she wouldn't catch pneumonia out there; she was just looking too fine tonight to wear a heavy coat.

"Wait until after the party tonight, as a matter of fact, let's say forget the party," Bruce suggested. He started the car.

"Oh, no, I didn't put this dress on for nothing. We're going to this party." Maxine didn't want to give Bruce the chance to miss showing her off to some of his friends. She really didn't want to miss meeting any of them.

*****

Indira pulled the footstool over to the closet then pulled the size twelve shoebox down from the back of Robert's closet. After lugging all the bags filled with his things down the stairs, she was ready to now see what was inside the box. She blew the thick coat of dust from the top, nearly choking herself. She took a deep breath and pulled the lid off. Indira couldn't believe her eyes. There were tons of pictures, letters, postcards, announcements, and stacks of newspaper clippings.

"The son of a bitch was human after all," she said as she pulled out a picture of a woman on stage singing. She was gorgeous and looked to be really singing her heart out. She sort of reminded her of Billie Holiday. Indira turned the picture over and read the back.

To Bobby,

The one real thing in my life, I love you more than the stage. Someday soon we'll be together. I'll be here when you come for me.

Love, Vera

This wasn't the only picture of Vera in the box. There were black-and-white pictures of the two when they were young. They looked as if they were meant to be together. Indira took hold of the tattered picture and stared into it. Who was this woman? And why wasn't he with her? Indira smiled as a reaction to the happiness in the photo. Robert seemed to be a totally different person then, it was evident in his smile. His smile, she hadn't seen that in so long she could barely remember it, until now. She wondered if this was the woman he really loved. Was this the one person who could make him happy? Tears began to stream down Indira's face, her marriage was truly over and she knew it. Indira kept rumbling through the box and came across a stack of doctor's prescriptions and paperwork. She began to read through the documents; her eyes stopped abruptly—cancer.

Indira felt her stomach drop. "Oh, God, he's dying." She held the paper close to her heart.

*****

Bruce pulled up to the front of the extravagant house where two young valets were waiting eagerly. The door opened and Maxine was helped out by one young man as the other traded places with Bruce. Bruce met Maxine with his hand out and led her to the door. Maxine was overwhelmed once the front door was opened.

"Bruce, glad you could make it." A strikingly handsome man gave Bruce a strong hug then quickly turned his eyes to Maxine. She usually didn't give white men that much credit, but he deserved it.

"And who is this fine woman you have with you?" The man never took his eyes off Maxine, making her feel somewhat like a piece of meat on a hot grill.

"Maxine Harrell, meet Jameson White, one of the state's best and biggest investors I know."

Jameson wasted no time; he reached for Maxine's hand and slowly kissed it.

"Pleased to meet you Jameson," Maxine watched as her hand was being molested, she eased it away politely.

"The pleasure is all mine." Jameson left them and got back to his other guests. Bruce nodded and pointed to others he knew at the party, finally finding two seats at the bar.

So, these were the friends I so desperately wanted to meet, Maxine thought.

Bruce ordered, "Scotch on ice and white wine."

Maxine caught him eyeing her legs as she climbed onto the barstool.

"And what are you looking at?" Maxine asked jokingly.

"I'm really wishing I would have skipped this and took you right into the house." Bruce gulped down his drink never taking those hungry eyes off of Maxine. He really knew how to make her feel as if she were the only woman in the room.

"Well, we don't have to stay long if you're that anxious. I just wasn't getting all dressed up for nothing." Maxine took a sip of her wine and gazed around the room at all the people, the sharp furniture, and paintings that surrounded the place.

"This is one special place Jameson has here," Maxine said as she continued to check out the scenery, but Bruce had seen it all before, he was only interested in her.

"That bastard ought to have a nice ass house as paid as he is." Bruce finished off his drink and caught the eye of the bartender for another. "Plus, he's made a lot of other people rich." Bruce took a gulp from his drink.

"Are you one of those people, Bruce?" Maxine leaned in closer to Bruce playfully.

"Let's just say we've helped each other out along the way.

"Bruce! How in the hell are you?"

Maxine and Bruce both turned around.

"Jack, you old dog, where have you been hiding?" Bruce reached around and shook the older man's hand.

"Oh, here and there, you know I can't stay in one place too long."

Maxine smiled as eye contact was made.

"Jack Wheeler, this is Maxine Harrell. Jack and I go way back."

Maxine shook hands lightly with the man.

"Very nice to meet you, Maxine." Jack looked to be in his early fifties, but in tip-top shape. His many days in the tanning salons were taking a toll on his skin. He was nearly as dark as Maxine. Jack ordered a drink and eased over to Bruce's free ear.

"What ever happened to that beautiful wife of yours?" Jack had a slight snicker in his voice.

"Well, you know, I don't have to explain the game to you."

Jack and Bruce toasted glasses and enjoyed a quick laugh.

"I'll see you later Bruce, and it was nice meeting you, Maxine." Jack disappeared into the crowd. After a couple of hours, Bruce was tired of the party scene and was desperate to leave.

"I think I've had enough, sweetheart, let's get out of here." Bruce gave his nods and shouts to his cohorts and led her to the door. The valet rushed to get the car Bruce had driven that night, his BMW 750. The valet had it before them in seconds flat.

"I just remembered I need to stop by the gym for a minute and check on some things, do you mind?"

Maxine shook her head no, but she really did mind. "You won't be long will you?" Maxine seductively eased over to Bruce and kissed his ear. "Your place is our next stop right?" Maxine whispered in his ear.

"Yes," Bruce said as he sped off.

Bruce pulled in front of the small building labeled Buster's and cut the ignition. "Well this is the place, my life." Bruce eyed Maxine as she stared out the window.

"Buster's?" Maxine looked puzzled.

"Come in with me, I wanna show you something." Bruce escorted Maxine to the door. She could see that he was excited to show her the gym. He leaned against the door and shoved it open, nearly falling in.

"Welcome to Buster's." Bruce closed the door behind them and stood next to Maxine. To her surprise, she was beginning to feel a little excited herself. The place was just like in the movies—the punching bags, the equipment, the pictures of past greats along the walls, and the ring.

"This is great, Bruce," Maxine walked toward the ring.

"This ring has seen the likes of some great boxers." Bruce put up a finger. "Wait right here, I'll be right back." He disappeared into the darkness and returned with a pair of boxing gloves.

"And what are you planning on doing with those?" Maxine covered her bare shoulders with her arms as she felt a damp breeze whisk by her.

"Come on, Max let me show you a few thangs about boxing." Bruce had taken off his shoes and was now inside the ring dancing around.

"You want me to get in there?" Maxine looked around for witnesses, there weren't any.

"Come on, Max. You scared?" Bruce was badly impersonating Muhammad Ali.

Maxine thought what the hell. "All right, I'm coming."

Bruce held a section of the ropes open for her to climb through.

"You know I'm not quite dressed for this."

Bruce let the rope go and slipped out of his jacket. "This will be fun. Here, put this glove on." Bruce handed Maxine a single glove.

"You sure you wanna do this, Bruce?" Maxine smiled and began taking her high heels off.

"Oh, I'm sure." He slapped his glove with his free hand to show his readiness. "Come on," Bruce danced around.

"Where's the bell?" Maxine began to dance around herself.

"Ding Ding, baby."

The two touched gloves and rushed to each other.

"Wait, wait no low blows." Before Bruce could say another word Maxine had punched him in the stomach, "Owww." Bruce was holding his stomach.

"That was for standing me up." Maxine put up her guard as Bruce lifted his eyes to her out of breath.

"So you wanna play like that, huh?" Bruce picked himself up and came at Maxine. He punched her softly on her butt. Maxine didn't like that and retaliated quickly with a combo.

"Whoa, Maxine you're getting a little serious," Bruce got his composure only to see Maxine coming again. This time Bruce caught Maxine's thin frame with his free hand and pulled her toward him tightly.

She'll Learn

"I thought you wanted to fight?" Maxine stopped her slight struggle for freedom.

"I just wanted to play a little. You were trying to kick my ass." Bruce eased his gloved arm around Maxine. "Weren't you?" Bruce was now looking into Maxine's eyes.

"I was just going along with the game. What are you talking about?" Maxine relaxed in Bruce's strong arms.

"You know what I'm talking about." He pressed his mouth into her lips and pulled her closer. He wasn't planning on stopping, he wanted Maxine. She was feeling the same and returned blow for blow whatever Bruce laid on her. Bruce untied the glove with his teeth as Maxine helped with her free hand. Now free, Bruce worked his way under Maxine's tiny dress. Her head was totally gone.

I can't believe I'm about to fuck in a boxing ring, Maxine thought, and sort of laughed a little before losing herself in Bruce's touch.

Bruce was seeing all the right signs, he was going to do what he wanted. Maxine wasn't stopping him so the light must be green. That was all he needed to know. He unbuttoned his pants and let them fall to his knees. Maxine said nothing, but plagued his neck with wet kisses. Bruce lifted her onto him and began to make love to her. Maxine wrapped her long legs around him.

"What in the hell am I doing?" Maxine heard her conscience as she pushed her breasts into Bruce's face. "Being a total slut fucking in a boxing ring. And I mean…" Maxine was forced back to reality. Bruce began to shake real hard and grabbed onto Maxine tightly.

"Ooh, I couldn't hold it any longer. Whoa." Bruce leaned back against the ropes and kissed Maxine on the cheek. "We must have looked like two fools standing here with our asses showing. I'm glad the place is empty." Bruce let Maxine down and pulled his pants up.

"Glad. This place had better be empty." Maxine felt a little odd, no a lot odd. What in the hell did he mean by that shit? Maxine thought to herself. As if he was living out some sort of fuckin' fantasy. She was becoming a little ticked now. But soon she would be lying in her man's arms for the night. After coming to grips with this decision, she straightened her clothes and turned to Bruce.

"Do you wanna get something to eat before we get to my house?" she asked. Bruce began buckling his belt and shook his head.

"Maxi, I can't stay the night. I've got to fly to Philly in the morning." He eased out of the ring as Maxine gave him a cold look.

"Baby, I thought I told you. I'm sorry." Bruce slipped into his jacket. "I was planning on packing and going to bed," he lied. He got what he wanted, now he could go home.

"Damn, Bruce. Do you know how that makes me feel?"

He gave her a puzzled look.

"Like a ho', Bruce, like a real ho'."

Bruce laughed and put his arms around Maxine. "Stop it before you go any further," he said.

Maxine was really p-o-ed now. "No, you stop. What is this shit you're trying to pull, Bruce?" Maxine frantically stepped out of the ring without any assistance.

"I will make it up to you when I get back, I promise." Bruce kissed Maxine before she could say a word.

"Come on, I'll take you home."

Maxine felt like a first-class ho'. Well, maybe second class. A first-class ho' would have at least been in a hotel.

"I can't believe I let this man fuck me in a nasty, sweaty, stinking boxing ring. What in the hell was I thinking?" Maxine continued to mumble angrily as she followed Bruce to the door, barely in her heels good. Bruce stopped at the light switch, not making eye contact as Maxine passed him out the door. He flipped the light switch and slammed the door closed. Nearly breaking her ankle on some rocks, Maxine made it to the car. Bruce roared out of the parking lot.

At home, Maxine closed her front door behind her and watched the headlights of Bruce's car turn away from her house.

"Oh, Maxine what have you done now? What does he think of you?" Maxine cut the lights off and headed up the stairs to her bedroom. She flipped her shoes across the room, knocking her Millennium Barbie off the nightstand and onto the floor. She took off her dress and stood in front of the mirror.

"Where's your money, Maxine? You forgot, a first-class ho' gets paid, too." Maxine shrugged her shoulders. "This deserves a joint." After taking a long, hot shower, she slipped into her nightgown and sat on the edge of the bed. She kept a light stash of weed for hard times in a shoebox under her bed. She had never totally stopped smoking. She'd been off and on since high school. While lighting her remedy, she dialed Sydney's number. The phone rang a few times; Maxine looked over at the clock. It was twelve thirty. Sydney must be sleep.

"Wake your ass up, Sydney I need to talk," she uttered to herself. Maxine knew that when Sydney was real tired she cut the ringer off on the phone to not wake Jasmine.

"Damn, Sydney." Maxine took a long pull and hung the phone up. She didn't want to try Indira's and chance having to speak to Robert, so she put out her joint and went to sleep.

*****

Robert was dying. Indira couldn't get the thought out of her mind. Robert knew he was dying. The pain he must have been going through all this time, she thought. The doctor's note was from nearly a year ago.

"Why didn't you tell me, Robert? You knew how much I loved you. I could have helped you through this." Indira looked around the room and decided to come back to this task later. She put the documents back in their place and placed them in the closet just as he'd had them. She stopped suddenly in her tracks.

He didn't want my help, she thought. Indira knew this was too much for one person to take. First, Robert wrote a letter saying he'd left her, and now she found out that the man she'd loved so hard was dying. Indira had to swallow her feelings and realize that Robert didn't love her anymore and didn't want to spend his remaining time with her. Being alone at this point in her life was going to be hard. She would be thirty-two in a few short months and her clock was ticking in stereo.

"For once in my life I'm not prepared," she said aloud. Indira could see her hopes and dreams of having a family slowly slipping out of her control. She was feeling so low, but there was no one for her to turn to. Indira could think of nothing else to do, but what Ms. Mable had taught her as well as, Maxine, and Sydney. Indira reached for her bible in the dresser drawer and began to read aloud.

CHAPTER TEN

Vera was awakened by the loud noises coming from the bathroom. She slipped into her robe and opened the door to the bathroom. Robert was on his knees throwing up blood into the toilet.

"Bobby, what's wrong? There's blood coming out of your mouth. Do you want me to call an ambulance?" Vera was nearly panicking. Robert lifted his head from the bowl. Vera wet the nearest towel and placed it on Robert's sweat covered face and head. She knelt down on the floor with him.

"What is it Bobby, what's wrong?" Vera held onto Robert tightly as he held himself up against the toilet.

"I have cancer, Vera." Robert was nearly out of breath when he spoke in a low mellow tone.

"Cancer?" Vera lifted off of Robert and turned his face to hers. "Oh no, Bobby, is it terminal?"

Robert nodded yes to Vera. Vera wrapped her arms around Robert and held him close to her. "Yes it is, and I don't know how much time I have left, but I want to spend it all with you." Robert began to cough roughly and had to rush back onto the bowl.

"I'm calling an ambulance."

Robert grabbed Vera's hand. "No. I don't want any damn ambulance, I know I'm dying so what can they do for me?" Robert let go of Vera's hand. He could see the fear in her eyes, she was afraid for him. Vera kept silent and watched Robert pull himself to his feet. She could remember like it was yesterday how strong and how beautiful he was. She began to reminisce.

All the girls in our town were so jealous of me. I had the finest man around. Time has done a number on both of us, but we are finally together again, no matter what.

Vera helped Robert back into bed then lay down beside him. She had so many plans for them growing up and she kept them in her heart always. She hadn't missed a day of work in almost two years of working for Mrs. Mancuso. Today would be the first of many. She had Robert to take care of now, and she wouldn't leave him for anything.

She'll Learn

"How are you feeling, Bobby?" Vera could see that Robert was falling in and out of sleep. She used her hand to wipe the sweat from his brow.

"I love you so much, Bobby. I knew this day would come, I prayed for it. I'll make the most out of the time we have together." Vera got quiet and listened to the sounds of the neighborhood beginning to awake and start their day.

"I'd dreamed of us being married and sharing our lives together." Vera began to lightly rub Robert's chest. The room fell silent.

"I want to marry you, Vera." Robert was listening to Vera the whole time. He put his hand on top of hers and held it close to him. "I love you, Vera and I want us to get married."

Vera leaned over and kissed him. "I would be proud to be your wife, Bobby." Vera had a smile on her face so big she closed her eyes and went to sleep.

"Don't you worry, Vera we'll be married in no time, I promise." Robert made plans to call his lawyer later that day and arrange everything.

*****

After a couple of days of crying, soul searching, and getting some much needed rest, Indira returned to work in control of her feelings. There was no way she could have made it in to work the past two days. But now she was feeling much better. She was showing a potential buyer around the gallery when a young man entered through the glass doors. He began looking around the gallery. Indira turned her attention back to her customer. Mrs. Loretta Young owned two upscale restaurants and wanted to furnish her bare walls with works from the gallery. Her mind was made up about the gallery before she arrived.

"I have another appointment so I must be leaving, Indira." The well-dressed older woman offered her hand in thanks.

"I hope everything was to your satisfaction, Mrs. Young." Indira kept her eye on the young man strolling around the gallery.

"Goodbye, Indira. I'll be in touch soon." Mrs. Young left out the doors. Indira watched Mrs. Young beyond the doors then she turned to see the young man standing before her.

"Indira Carr?" The young man had an expressionless face.

"Yes, I'm Indira Carr." Indira watched as the man retrieved a paper from his jacket.

"You've been served."

Before Indira could get the letter open, the young man was walking out the doors. "Served?" Indira tore open the letter to see that it was a petition for divorce. She nearly fainted. Luckily the wall was close by. Omari saw everything and rushed to Indira's side, he glanced at the letter in Indira's hand.

"Honey, I am so sorry," Omari put his arms around her shoulders and helped her up the stairs to their office. Indira sat down at her desk and began to sob quietly. It was all happening so fast. In a matter of one short week, Indira's life had been turned upside down.

"Here, honey, drink this." Omari handed Indira a cup of tea.

Indira took a small sip. "Whoa, what's in this?" Indira took another whiff of the brew.

"Believe me, honey you could use more than what I gave you, but that'll do." Omari had poured a little of his private stock of bourbon into the tea.

"Thanks, but I'll pass on the tea." Indira didn't feel like drinking right now. She wanted her mind to be clear.

"Then you won't mind me having it then."

Indira slid the cup over to Omari who had pulled up a chair to her desk.

"Be my guest."

Omari reached over and wiped Indira's cheek with his handkerchief then gave it to her. "You know, Indira when I opened this gallery nearly ten years ago, I had no idea it would still be around today and doing so well." Omari moved his chair closer to the desk. "I opened this place not because it was my own dream, but the dream of my partner. He died of AIDS in 1987. Eric was a painter, he loved it first then me."

Indira was barely listening to Omari, but she knew he was only trying to help.

"Eric always wanted to open a place where people like him could show off their work and not be judged for what he was." Omari rubbed his head roughly and shivered. "I miss him so much. I still get so sad just talking about him." Omari took hold of his shoulders to warm himself.

"Well, the reason I'm telling you this is so you'll know that you do go on, Indira." Omari had grown to love Indira like the daughter he had never had. Indira took Omari's words to heart.

"Thanks, Omari."

Omari winked at her and left her desk. Indira heard the bell acknowledging that a customer had entered the gallery. Omari sashayed toward the stairs.

"You stay here, I'll take this one," Omari whispered to her. He was in his early fifties, gay, and had done so many great things in his life. Indira was glad to have a friend like him in her life.

The phone rang, nearly scaring the life out of Indira. She picked it up, "Indira Carr."

"Hello, Indira, it's Eldridge."

Indira began to feel better already. El was just what she needed. "Hello, El, how are you?" Her voice picked up.

"Are you okay, Indira you sounded a little down before?" El hoped it wasn't anything to do with her husband.

"I got an awful surprise today, that's all. I'll be fine." Indira knew that wouldn't be enough for her new friend.

"What news, Indira?" He sounded as if he could come through the phone.

"Robert left me and I just received a petition for a divorce from him."

El fell silent. He was at a loss for words. "Damn, I guess you have had a helluva day."

Indira sort of laughed at his response. El could hear her laughter.

"You always know how to bring a smile to my face," Indira said as she wiped her eyes and smiled. "Now, to what do I owe this phone call to?"

El's concern turned to cheerfulness easily. "I was calling to tell you that when I got home I had a message on my machine from Paul Henson. He wants to fill his private office building with my paintings." El was so excited; this would be a big sell for him, for them both.

"That's wonderful, El. I'm so happy for you," Indira wished inside that El were there with her. She could use his strong shoulder to lean on.

"And hey, if this is any consolation, I'll be back in Detroit New Year's Eve, I've been invited to an elaborate party for the governor." El couldn't wait to see Indira again, this time there would be no husband in the way at home.

"Great, El, I can't wait to see you." If only she knew how much he'd wanted to see her. "Thanks for calling to tell me the good news. You were right on time as usual."

El waited for her to finish then asked, "Will you go out with me New Year's Eve night, Indira?"

Indira wasn't expecting that question. It was yet another surprise for her.

"Eldridge," Indira was back to calling him Eldridge. "With so much going on, I don't want to answer that right now."

El stopped her. "I totally understand, take some time to think about it and call me. I would love to hear from you."

Indira listened and began to smile. "Thanks, El. I'll call you soon. Bye." Indira listened for his response and hung up the phone. Just hearing El's voice made everything better. After work, she would go to the mall to get her niece a gift for her second birthday. She also had a couple of things to get for the party on Saturday at Maxine's. That would take her mind off some of the drama in her life.

*****

Without even a thought as to whether Maxine was still mad at him for leaving town, Bruce called up to the shop and left a message for her with Stephanie. He said he would be by after the boxing match up in Flint. It would be late, so he wanted her to stay up. Maxine was dead tired. She'd done at least eleven heads that day. She was looking forward to seeing her comfy king-size bed. It was almost eight o'clock when Maxine stopped at the front desk to give her receipts to Stephanie. Maxine was the owner of the shop, but Stephanie assisted her with the books.

"Oh, Maxine, I forgot to tell you that Bruce called and said he'll be by after the boxing match up in Flint. It'll be late, so stay up." Stephanie went back to adding up the receipts for the day. She could feel Maxine's cold stare on her head. Her intuitions were right. "What's wrong?" Stephanie didn't know what was going on.

She'll Learn

"What time did Bruce leave this message?" Maxine took off her smock and laid it on the front desk.

"I guess around two o'clock." Stephanie quickly caught on to what was happening. Maxine was too tired to fight, but if she was pushed a little harder...

"Two o'clock! Girl..." Maxine tried to keep her composure, "Don't you know that if I knew this bit of information earlier, I wouldn't have kept on accepting walk-ins like there was no tomorrow? I am tired. Do you hear me, Stephanie? Tired." Maxine needed some rest plus she would have a house full of children tomorrow for Jazz's birthday party. But did she need some dick more? It'd only been five days, but it seemed like a lifetime. Maxine realized she was upset for nothing.

"I'm sorry, Maxine, but we were so busy I totally forgot. With that lady acting all crazy, you know, Dina's customer," Stephanie couldn't remember the woman's name. "It just slipped my mind." Stephanie was really sorry. It had been a crazy day around there.

"Yeah, I know Stephanie. I'm sorry too." Maxine went to her station and got her purse. "Well, I'm going home to get ready. I don't know where I'm gonna find the strength."

Dina walked out from the back. "Damn, you need that much strength for him?" Dina stood and waited for an answer from Maxine.

"Believe me, he gives me a real workout." Maxine didn't want to say anymore. Women only need one good reason to seek out your man. "You lock up and call me when you get home." Maxine headed toward the door.

"Don't forget I'll be out tomorrow for Jasmine's birthday party, and tell Dad to mop out the basement for us." Maxine did her usual 10-minute goodbye full of last minute things to do, before actually making it out the door.

"Will you please leave? Go home. I already know all of these things you are telling me," Stephanie said. She laughed and shook her head when Maxine peeked back through the window and waved to her.

*****

Saturday morning Sydney was so excited about her baby turning two years old. She couldn't wait for the big party. She jumped out of bed and got showered and dressed, then got the birthday girl dressed in one of her new birthday outfits.

"Happy Birthday, Chubbs."

Jasmine looked at her mommy's big smile and laughed.

"You're so pretty. You should be on a Gap commercial." Sydney covered her daughter's face with kisses. The phone rang.

"Hello."

It was Indira. "Hi, Indi. Say happy birthday to Jazzy." Sydney put the phone to the baby's ear. Indira sang to her. "Hey, Jazzy, it's your birthday, it's your birthday." Indira was as glad as Sydney was for this day. All their lives changed when Jasmine was born. They were like sisters and were all a part of Jazz's little life. When Anthony left Sydney, she needed the girls more than she'd ever had. And they were there for her.

"Okay, what's up Indi?" Sydney brushed Jasmine's hair lightly into little ponytails.

"I was just calling to see when you wanted me over to Maxine's."

Sydney tied the ribbons while holding the phone with her shoulder. "You know we are going to have to cleanup. She's a slob, remember." The phone slipped from Sydney's shoulder, slinging across the room. Sydney held onto the baby as she retrieved the phone. "My fault, girl, the phone dropped." Sydney put the baby back between her legs.

"When are you going to get you a cordless phone?" Indira should have been used to this by now.

"When I can afford one, rich lady," Sydney joked with Indira.

"I can't take it no more, that's what I'm going to get you for Christmas."

Jasmine held onto her bottle tightly and seemed to drift off to sleep.

"Aww, now you ruined my surprise. You know I like to be surprised."

"Girl, shut up. I will meet you over at Maxine's at eleven o'clock, okay?" Indira laughed at her friend.

"Okay, but I'm on my way over there now." Sydney couldn't wait until eleven o'clock.

She'll Learn

"Don't you think it's still a little early, especially for Maxine? After a Friday night at the shop, she's probably out like a light still." Indira didn't want Sydney to just drop in on Maxine that early in the morning.

"Yeah, I guess you're right. I'll give her another hour."

Indira laughed again. "It would still be only nine o'clock."

"She'll be up." Sydney was going regardless.

"Okay, I'll see you later. Bye."

Sydney hung up the phone and went to pack Jasmine's baby bag for the day. She didn't want to forget anything, although she and Maxine just lived two blocks away from one another.

It was nine fifteen in the morning and Sydney was at Maxine's front door. Bruce lay in bed next to Maxine with his strong arm across her breasts.

Ding-Dong! Ding-Dong!

He awoke, startled by the doorbell. He was out of it. He had to remember where he was. Bruce glanced at the clock, it read nine twenty.

"Let me get out of here." Bruce knew his wife would be expecting him this morning. "Maxine, wake up. Somebody is ringing your doorbell."

Maxine looked at Bruce with one eye then fell back to sleep.

"Maxine, wake up." Bruce gently shook her. She sat up sleepily in the bed and checked the clock. She didn't have to think twice.

"It's Sydney."

Bruce began getting dressed as Maxine groggily walked down the steps to open the door for Sydney.

Ding-Dong! Ding-Dong!

"Sydney, if you don't stop ringing that damn doorbell, I'll break your finger." Maxine opened the door angrily and stood in the way.

"Good morning, Maxine." Sydney eased past Maxine carrying baby, groceries, and a lot of other stuff. "I see you're in a good mood already." Before Sydney could say another word, she noticed a handsome man rushing down the staircase. Maxine followed Sydney's eyes over to Bruce.

"Oh, leaving so soon?" Maxine watched as Bruce hurriedly got his things on. Maxine stood in the hallway in her tiny nightgown as Sydney watched.

"Yeah, I have to go. I have some things to do today, but I'll call you tonight." Bruce walked over to Maxine and kissed her. What could she do, beg him to stay? No, she couldn't do that. Instead, she braced herself for the wind that would accompany the opening of the door.

"I'll give you a call later," Bruce repeated himself to reassure her. He caught Sydney's eye.

"Hello, I'm Bruce. Need some help?"

Sydney shook her head as Bruce grabbed some of the many bags she'd brought in. "I'm Sydney and this is Jasmine."

Bruce nodded his head and took the bags into the kitchen for her.

"So that's, Bruce, huh?" Sydney hushed quickly as Bruce walked back into the room.

"Nice to have met you, Sydney…and, Jasmine," Bruce winked at Maxine and left out the door.

"I'll have dinner ready around nine." Maxine couldn't just let him leave without saying something.

"Thank you!" Sydney yelled out the door and then closed it. She stood looking at Maxine in her skimpy gown.

"Don't say shit to me." Maxine pointed at Sydney to be quiet.

"What? I didn't know you cooked."

Maxine started up the stairs.

"At least you won't be so damn evil today," Sydney had to say something.

"I said don't say shit."

Sydney chuckled as Maxine slapped her ass for her. Sydney laid Jasmine down on the couch as she slept then went to retrieve the rest of the things from her car. "This party is gonna be great."

*****

Bruce watched the clock on his dashboard all the way home until he was pulling into the driveway of his suburban home. It was almost noon. He knew he would have a fight on his hands, or maybe she wouldn't say anything to him. Who knew? These days their relationship was anything but a marriage. Bruce was hoping for the latter. He opened the front door to a dimly lit hallway then his eyes fixed on a shadow of something. It was Erica.

"Hello, honey."

She'll Learn

Bruce wasn't prepared for this. Erica stood totally naked in front of the blazing fireplace.

"Erica, what are you doing?" He watched his wife closely as she sexily made her way over to him. He hadn't seen his wife's body in months, maybe an entire year. She looked beautiful. Two children had done nothing to tarnish her beauty. Erica helped Bruce take off his coat.

"I'm just trying to give you what you've been wanting, baby." Erica wanted things to change between the two of them. Their marriage was never ordinary from the start. Erica was in love with Bruce and Bruce was in love with boxing. Her father owned world-renowned gyms that produced champion boxers all over the country. In Bruce's eyes he was bigger than Don King. Bruce would have done anything to be a part of that world. He started dating Erica after meeting her father, Buster Maddox, at a boxing match. Buster took him under his wing and during that time, his daughter fell in love with his young protégé. It'd been nearly ten years since Buster made Bruce an offer he couldn't refuse.

"If you marry my daughter I will give you complete control of my promotion company and my boxing organization." The words were still clear in Bruce's mind. He accepted.

"I thought that if I were to be the slut you want you'd stay your ass at home a little more." Erica dropped to her knees in front of Bruce and began working on the zipper of his pants. Bruce moved back away from his wife.

"C'mon, Bruce. Don't tell me this isn't what you've been wanting."

Bruce stood frozen as Erica crawled on her hands and knees to him again. "Erica, you don't have to do this." Bruce zipped his pants back up and made his way over to the stairs. Erica sat up on her knees. She was embarrassed. She snatched the leopard print throw from the couch and covered her body.

"Fuck you, Bruce. If you don't want this marriage to work then you walk back out that fuckin' door," Erica pushed her way past Bruce on the stairs. Bruce knew that he didn't have a choice. He couldn't and he wouldn't give up the boxing game. He was the man he was today because of Buster. He'd lose everything if he left Erica. The old man would have had him cut off in the blink of an eye.

"Wait, Erica." Bruce caught his wife's hand before she got too far away from him. He knew he had to do something. Erica's eyes began to soften as Bruce held her hand.

"I do want us to work, baby," Bruce spoke in a low tone.

"Then show me." Erica led Bruce to their bedroom.

CHAPTER ELEVEN

When Maxine finally made her way back down the stairs, Sydney and Indira were busy hanging up decorations in the dining room.

"Well, hello, Maxine," Indira smiled at Maxine and held up a handful of pink and white balloons. "Start blowing, or are your jaws too tired?"

Sydney busted out laughing, nearly tumbling off the step stool.

"Shut up, Indira." Maxine snatched the balloons from her.

"You missed a good looking man, Indi," Sydney sounded as if she were describing some sort of dish.

"He's that fine, huh?" Indira stopped what she was doing and turned to Maxine. At first Maxine just stared back at her longtime friend.

"Yes, girl, he is all that and a dime sack," Maxine joined in with a high 5 to Sydney.

"What?" That flew completely over Indira's head.

"He's got it going on," Sydney filled Indira in on the slang. Indira looked at how excited Maxine had become.

"You've fallen for this man, haven't you?" Indira walked over to Maxine.

"Is it that obvious?" Maxine began blowing up a balloon.

Indira looked over toward Sydney. "Hell yeah, girl. You look happy. I'm glad for you. "

Sydney stepped down off the stool and checked out the banner hanging over the doorway.

"Me too. The only happiness in my life is my baby," Sydney peeked in the other room at Jasmine, still asleep on the couch. She felt blessed to have such a beautiful daughter and have the chance to raise her. She wanted to do her best for her. She was all she had.

"Well, I have to admit it. I am in love and I hate myself for it," Maxine stopped blowing for a minute and sat down at the table. "I can't figure this one out. Bruce is a damn mystery to me." Maxine knew she was in love with Bruce, but she didn't know how he felt. He treated her like a queen, when he was with her.

"What is your problem, Maxine? You are always crying about not having a man and when you finally get one you nitpick at everything,"

Sydney said as she spread the tablecloth that Ms. Mable had given her. She used it whenever she was having something special. This was a special day for Sydney. Indira tied a string on the end of her fully blown balloon and watched it float to the ceiling.

"Sometimes it's hard not to nitpick at everything. You worry about it every day.
Is this person for real or is this all some sort of game?"

The room fell quiet.

"My marriage was just a game."

Maxine and Sydney gave each other a puzzled look and turned their ears to Indira. Sydney sat down next to Maxine.

"I gave my all to Robert and he just played with it. I let myself become lost in him then he let me go," Indira had to get this impossible load off of her chest. She needed to tell her friends.

"He let you go?" Maxine wanted to know what Indira was getting at.

"He left me a couple of days ago. He wrote me a letter instead of telling me to my face like a real man." Indira now had burning tears trickling down her face.

"Oh no, Indira," Sydney rushed over to hug her. "I'm so sorry." Sydney knew what she was feeling. She'd been there herself. Anthony wasn't man enough for the task either. He called her from the bus station before he left her and Detroit.

"That old-ass bastard left you? I can't believe that shit. He was lucky to have you," Maxine became upset over Indira's sudden news.

"I thought he loved me, but he couldn't stand my ass." Indira used one of the Teletubbies napkins to wipe her eyes dry. "I was too embarrassed to tell you two this. He was beating my ass at least twice a week."

Sydney turned to Maxine suddenly, as if to acknowledge her notion.

"I knew it!" Maxine yelled out. Sydney gave her a mean look.

"You win again," Indira was obviously hurt by Maxine's outburst.

"I didn't mean it like that, Indi. It's just that we could see that something was seriously wrong, but we didn't want to make you tell us anything. When you felt comfortable enough, you would tell us." Maxine got up from the chair and walked over to Indira. "Just know that you ain't gotta be by yourself. You have us." Maxine touched Indira's hand, and then went into the kitchen.

"I'm sort of glad he left." Sydney waited on her friend to respond.

"Why, Sydney?" Indira knew that both Maxine and even Sydney hated her husband all along.

"I was so afraid that he was going to take you away from us. He's a mean man and I just couldn't see someone as sweet as you surviving that situation." Sydney turned her eyes away from her friend. "Please don't ever feel too embarrassed to tell me anything. I am your sister. You and Maxine have been like sisters to me all of my life."

Maxine, overhearing Sydney, came back into the room with the punch bowl.

"Ms. Mable loved us and taught us to love each other," Maxine felt a lump coming in her throat. Sydney looked over to her other sister. "We are a family and nothing could ever come between us."

That did it. All three women were in tears now. They hugged each other, with an extra tight squeeze from Maxine.

"Little Sydney, the baby of the bunch is a grown woman. I love you broads, you two fucked-up broads. Look at me, I don't have anyone left. After grandma died that was the end of the family chain in my eyes," Maxine said as she looked over to Sydney. "My mother has her own problems, too, and I stopped letting her problems dictate my life years ago."

Indira felt closer than ever to her friends. She would be fine. She wasn't alone. "I love you, too, Maxine and you, too, Sydney. This day is special to me also, and I wanted to be here for my niece and for my family." Indira smiled and wiped the tears from her face.

"Okay. Let's stop this shit. We look like the Joy Luck Club. Come on. Let's get ready for the little rugrats that will be here in less than two hours," Maxine clapped her hands together loudly for Sydney and Indira to get to work.

"Shhhh!" Sydney held her finger to her mouth. The girls laughed and hopped to their feet. Everyone stopped when they heard Jasmine yell.

"Be back in a minute." Sydney rushed out the dining room and up to the guestroom where Jasmine was sleeping.

"Hey, start putting those cookie trays in the oven for me," Sydney hollered over the landing at Maxine and Indira.

"Okay," Indira yelled back. Maxine followed Indira into the kitchen. Indira walked over to the stove and placed two baking sheets of chocolate chip cookies into the oven. "I was at the gallery showing this woman around and I saw this young guy come in. I was watching him the whole time I was with her." Indira set the timer on the stove. "After the woman left the gallery, the man I had been watching walked up to me," Indira began taking the other things out of the bags on the counter.

"Damn this is getting a little eerie," Maxine leaned against the doorway and listened to Indira.

"I know, right? But then, we were face to face." Indira slid the cake out of another bag. "Oh, this is so gorgeous."

Maxine rushed over to see the cake.

"Jazzy is gonna love this. Sydney went all out. It looks just like her," Indira said as she and Maxine stood admiring the cake created in Jasmine's image.

"What a beautiful cake." Maxine suddenly remembered where they'd left off. "Now finish telling me about the guy in the gallery. Was he fine, crazy or what?" Maxine sat down at the kitchen table. Indira put the cover back on the cake.

"He asked me, are you Indira Carr? I hesitantly said yes. Then I watched him pull something out of his pocket. He handed it to me and said, you've been served, and walked out the door."

Maxine knew where this story was heading.

"He had handed me a petition of divorce from Robert," Indira bogged her eyes out to Maxine in disbelief.

"You are joking," Maxine stood away from the wall. "The old dog has some balls on him. I gotta give him that. I probably would have bopped the delivery man, too." Maxine shook her head.

"Girl, that man knew how to do his job. By the time I lifted my eyes off the paper, his little ass was out the door."

Maxine covered her mouth and laughed. The room was silent as the two began making finger sandwiches the old-fashioned way—make a sandwich however you want it then cut it in fours, without the crust.

She'll Learn

Sydney wasn't about to let any grocery store do what she could do better than anybody; cook.

"That is a trip, Indi. He didn't waste any time did he?" Maxine poured jellybeans into her grandmother's crystal bowls.

"He doesn't have much time," Indira never stopped making the sandwiches.

"Much time for what?" Maxine prepared party bags of candy.

"I found some doctor reports when I was in his closet. He's got colon cancer and he's dying." Indira dropped the knife on the cutting board and wiped her hands on the apron she wore. "Let's make the daiquiris. I think I'm going to need a drink real soon." Indira retrieved the blender from the pantry.

"I know you do need a drink. All this in what…three days?" Maxine looked at her friend in disbelief. "You need a strong drink." Maxine got the ice and the drink mix. "Are you all right, Indira?" Maxine asked in a concerned tone. Indira turned and smiled at her.

"I am now."

Ding Dong!

"I'll get it. Let's get this party started," Sydney said as she hurried to the door.

"Hello, Papa," Sydney opened the door wide for her father, who had an arm full of bags.

"Hello, baby," Papa Joe made his way into the house and kissed his daughter. "The house looks beautiful." Papa Joe took off his leather cap and began to search the room with his eyes. Sydney knew what her father was doing.

"She's asleep, Daddy. The princess must get her rest."

Papa Joe placed the bags on the sofa table as Maxine strolled out of the kitchen.

"Hello, Slim," Papa Joe stretched out his arms to Maxine.

"Nice to see you, Papa Joe," Maxine gave the old man a huge hug.

"This was nice of you to let Jasmine have her birthday party in this house. This is a special place. Your grandmother was a good woman, and this house was always full of love." Papa Joe stood and took a good look at the house. It brought back memories of better days for him and Virginia. His words brought a smile to Maxine's face. Everyone loved her grandmother, and it felt good for her to get a compliment in the same breath as her.

"You don't have to thank me, Papa Joe. I love that baby like she was my own." Maxine fluffed the pillows on the couch. She'd put up most of her crystal trinkets and things for fear of little hands.

"Hi, Papa Joe," Indira rushed over to his waiting arms.

"Hello, beautiful. You look lovelier each time I see you."

Sydney and Maxine glanced at each other.

"Why thank you, Papa," Indira gave him a kiss on the cheek.

"Now why did she get all that extra stuff?" Maxine turned to the old man with her hand on her hip.

"Girl, you know he has always been partial to Indira," Sydney said as she grabbed the bags her father brought in and took them into the kitchen.

"I know, I remember all the times she got to ride in the front seat. I just thought things might have changed some."

Indira sat down on the couch and began blowing up more balloons. "Jealous, that's all," Indira said just under her breath.

"I heard that," Maxine walked over to Indira and playfully pulled at her half-blown balloon.

"I love seeing you girls together. You've been friends nearly all your lives and you're still friends. That's a blessing for each of you, a friend," Papa Joe said.

"It sure is, Papa Joe," Maxine said.

Indira shook her head in agreement as Maxine walked away.

Sydney came out of the kitchen with a tray full of ice-cream toppings and whipped cream.

"Kids love whipped cream," she said happily. She was so excited about today. She wanted everyone to enjoy him or herself. "I'd better start getting Jasmine ready. The kids will start getting here soon," Sydney placed the tray on the dining table and untied the apron from her waist.

"Finish filling those bowls on the counter with potato chips, please," Sydney said as she held the apron out for Maxine to take it from her. Maxine grabbed it after a few moments.

"Do what, now?" Maxine hesitantly tied the apron around her waist. She headed into the kitchen as ordered.

She'll Learn

"You heard me. Come on now. Hop to it, girl." Sydney hustled up the stairs to Maxine's room to get her daughter. Indira began tying her blown up balloons to the goody bags Sydney had prepared for the kids.

"Here, Papa Joe. Start putting these on the tables," Indira said.

Sydney did a great job of rearranging the front room so the card tables would sit perfectly.

"Sydney sure did go all out for this party. I hope she didn't spend all her money," Papa Joe said.

Indira put the last bag on the table.

"We all chipped in, so hopefully she didn't go beyond that. But knowing, Sydney..."

Papa Joe and Indira looked around the room at the beautiful cakes, the food trays, the tablecloths, and the Teletubbie matching napkins and cups.

"She did," they said.

*****

Bruce had planned on being with Maxine tonight, but he knew that was out now. This was where he was going to be. He was motionless as he thought about Maxine.

"Are you all right, baby?" Erica was on her knees facing the headboard. She had turned around to see why Bruce had ceased their lovemaking. "Don't stop, Bruce."

Those were the magic words. He snapped out of his thoughts and began pumping furiously until his wife's face was buried in the pillows once again.

"I'm just fine, baby." Without missing a beat, Bruce wiped the sweat beginning to cover his forehead. He placed his hands on his wife's shapely hips to balance himself.

She's gonna be pissed off, Bruce thought as he could only imagine how upset Maxine was going to be tonight when he didn't show up for dinner.

"Ooh Bruce, I've missed you so much," Erica moaned and groaned as Bruce continued his pounding to her petite body. She was loving every minute of it. Reality had set in once again for Bruce. Things were starting to go a little too deep. He was going to have to stop seeing Maxine. He couldn't take his mind off of her and that was a very bad thing for a deeply attached man. Bruce eased his wife over onto her back and planted himself between her thighs.

Erica moaned with delight since Bruce hadn't touched her in months. She thought about how she should have done this a long time ago. Whoever the other woman was, she was gone now. Erica had always known about the other women. She would sometimes feel like she was married to a politician or some famous athlete. She was always waiting for the next challenger to surface, but none of them would ever have him. Erica knew that Bruce had someone else, and that he was falling for her. She couldn't and wouldn't let that happen. She had what he wanted and he would never give that up—boxing. Bruce lifted his wife's legs onto his shoulders and looked into her eyes.

"I want us to start over, Erica." He let her strong legs fall to his arms as he slowed his movements. "I want us to be a family again. I want us to be together again." He stopped and laid his sweaty face on his wife's flat stomach. He had given in. There was no need in trying. He would never leave her. Erica put her hands lovingly on her husband's head. She'd won, again.

"I want that for us too, baby." Erica caressed his head softly against her body.

Bruce knew what he had to do now, but it wouldn't be easy.

*****

Ding Dong!

"Come on in, Ms. Lee. Thank you for coming over," Sydney helped Ms. Lee take off her coat.

"I wouldn't miss my girl's birthday party. She's such a sweet baby." Ms. Lee put her gift on the already filled table and found Jasmine in her high chair surrounded by children. Now it was time to cut the cake. Jasmine looked so happy. She acted as if she knew that the party was for her. The lights went out, and then suddenly the room was lit up by candlelight. Sydney was doing such a great job at being a mother. She had grown up so fast. Papa Joe was glad that the lights were out, so no one could see the tears flowing from his eyes. He only wished that his wife would come to her senses and join in on her daughter and granddaughter's lives.

She'll Learn

"Okay, everybody, let's sing Happy Birthday to Jazzy," Sydney said happily.

Indira placed her hand adoringly onto Papa Joe's shoulder and begin to sing. His tears weren't his secret after all. Without words, the old man admitted his feelings to her then kissed Indira's hand.

"*Happy Birthday...Jasmine Elise Hastings,*" Sydney added a little extra to the traditional song.

"*Happy Birthday to you*!" Everybody yelled and clapped their hands as Jasmine laughed and smiled along with them. Maxine flicked the lights back on at Sydney's cue. She had everything planned to a tee. The party was perfect, and everyone was having a great time, even the adults.

"I can't believe I'm having such a good time." Maxine was enjoying watching all the smiling faces of the kids. The little girls were dressed so pretty. She could see the care that the mother's had put into their children.

"Oh, my God. What am I doing?" Maxine put her hand on her forehead. Indira, sort of laughing, walked over to her.

"What's up with you, girl?" Indira changed her tone after she saw that Maxine wasn't laughing.

"Girl, nothing. Just losing my mind that's all," Maxine went into the kitchen with Indira following behind her.

"I was standing there watching all those kids laughing and singing," Maxine dropped her head. "I got a little sad in a way. I feel like I'm missing out on some big secret. Sydney looks so happy. We thought that her getting pregnant was the worst thing that could happen to her, but look at her. She's happy."

Indira didn't know what to say. She could understand all too clearly what Maxine was feeling. Indira got closer to her.

"I had planned to have two children by now; two children," Indira said as she held up two fingers. Maxine nodded her head to acknowledge them. "I wanted to be happy just like she is now, but I have one big obstacle," Indira walked away angrily, and then turned around to Maxine whose attention she fully had. "Do you know what that obstacle is? Miss Feeling Sorry For Your Damn Self."

Maxine could see what Indira was getting at now. She was being extremely selfish.

"All right, Indira. I get your damn point," Maxine folded her arms across her chest. She could see that Indira wasn't going to quit that easily.

"No. You don't get the point, Max. My life is fuck'd up too, right now. But I am so happy and proud of that girl in there. Sydney did what we thought none of us could do, especially Sydney."

Maxine dropped her head again. Indira could always bring her down a peg or two whenever she needed it.

"And I know you're proud of her, so don't ruin this day for us, too. We are damn good aunts, if I may say so myself." Indira stopped and waited on Maxine to respond.

"Yes, I am proud, but I just wanna be happy, too." Maxine was pouting like a baby.

Indira jokingly put her arm around Maxine's shoulders. "Happiness is coming, I can feel it. I'm feeling happier, already." Indira pushed Maxine lightly and went back into the living room.

That bitch is crazy. Maxine laughed to herself then caught a glimpse of the clock on the stove. Five o'clock. She would have to get started soon. She was going to cook a fabulous dinner and get some fabulous sex. That was exactly what she needed.

Wayne had finally gotten Sydney to sit down next to him and take a break. She'd been running at full speed all day.

"The party was cool," Wayne looked at Sydney and smiled.

"I'm glad you enjoyed yourself. I was sort of surprised to see you at a kiddy party," Sydney sort of laughed.

"I didn't come here for the party. I came to see you."

Sydney looked surprised, as if she didn't know that Wayne really liked her. She was starting to like him, too.

"Oh, yeah?" Sydney slid back on the couch.

"Oh, yeah," Wayne laughed back to Sydney. "Ever since that night the three of us had dinner, I can't stop thinking about you."

Sydney began noticing that she and Wayne had the attention of the party. Wayne looked up at them and nodded his head.

"What's up?" Wayne whispered to Sydney. "Can I come by later, to talk?"

Sydney shuttered a little with anticipation as Wayne's soft breath filled her ear. Sydney said nothing, but nodded her head yes.

"Okay," Wayne said as he lifted off of the couch and then extended his hand out for Sydney. She walked him to the door.

"I'll see you later, then," Wayne opened the door and stepped out.

"See you later," Sydney closed the door behind him and turned to see that all eyes were on her again.

"Dang, Sydney, macking out at your daughter's kiddy party." Cherita always had a joke.

"It's about time. She should have been macking a long time ago," another woman said. All the women agreed and joked as they buttoned up their children's coats.

"Thank you, Miss Sydney. I had fun," Rick said. He lived in the apartment two doors down with his father.

"You are so welcome, Rick. Did you get some cake for your daddy?"

Rick lifted his cake to prove it to Sydney.

"Thanks for coming everyone," Indira held Jasmine as she tried to wave to her departing guests.

"Goodbye, everybody. It was fun," Maxine was glad things had wrapped up because it was 5:30 and Bruce would be on his way soon. Sydney closed the door.

"Hold on, Sydney. I'm gonna get on outta here too," Papa Joe kissed his granddaughter. "Happy Birthday, Jasmine. I hope I get to see many more of them with you." Papa Joe made his way to the door.

"Oh, Daddy, you'll be around for plenty more," Sydney hugged her father at the door.

"Goodbye, girls. I'll call you, Sydney."

The girls said goodbye in unison.

"Whoa!" Sydney rushed over to the couch and fell onto it. "The party went off without a hitch!" Sydney clapped her hands at her success, careful not to be too loud. Jasmine was starting to drift off in Indira's arms.

"You did a wonderful job, Sydney. I even enjoyed it myself." Indira kissed the baby's cheek, "You are getting to be such a big girl."

Maxine began cleaning right away. She folded the table and chairs in seconds flat. Sydney and Indira watched in amazement.

"Let's put all this food up. I have some containers in the cabinet," Maxine said as she walked through the kitchen door. She immediately came back through when she noticed that Sydney and Indira were not behind her.

"Come on, y'all," Maxine was trying to motivate her friends to get a move on.

Indira laughed and then looked to Sydney. "I think she's trying to rush us."

Sydney kicked off her shoes and put her feet on the coffee table. "I just know she isn't trying to put me out. I had planned on having another glass of wine before I headed home."

Maxine put her hands on her hips and stared in silence at the two women.

"Okay, okay, okay! I have a date tonight with Bruce. He's coming over around 8:30," Maxine bent down and picked up a crumpled napkin from the floor.

"Girl, you've got plenty of time. It's only 5:50 and she's trying to put us out," Indira was starting to raise her voice, and then she remembered the sleeping baby in her arms.

"Sit down, Maxine. We'll be out of here before your man gets here," Sydney patted the seat next to her on the couch.

"All right, I just need some and I'm getting all excited about it," Maxine rubbed her hands together playfully and turned to a smirking Sydney.

"Girl, you are crazy."

Maxine gave her a high 5, "Crazy about dick."

Indira nearly choked.

"What's wrong with that? That's my problem for real. I am crazy about dick and it gets me into trouble every time."

Indira was laughing as quietly as she could without waking Jasmine. "I wouldn't know what to do with one, anymore. I haven't seen one in so long."

Sydney put her hands to her mouth and burst out laughing.

"Once you know how, you just never forget how to love. That's Luther." Maxine loved Luther Vandross, the old and the new.

She'll Learn

"Uh, uh, Maxine, it is the year 2001. Please stop quoting Luther Vandross's songs," Indira shook her head in disgust.

"Ooh, I just remembered something. I'll be right back." Maxine dashed up the stairs to her bedroom and returned holding up something in her hand.

"Guess what I've got?" Maxine danced around with the mysterious object hidden in her hand.

"What is it, Maxine?" Indira tried to get a glimpse, but Maxine put her hand behind her back.

"Lay Jasmine down in the den so we can hear her if she wakes up."

Indira did as Maxine suggested and came back to her chair.

"What's behind your back?" Sydney was too tired to play games.

Maxine pulled her hand from behind her back. "Ta da!" Maxine held a tightly rolled joint in the palm of her hand. "I know this is gonna seem strange coming from me, but I have been craving a fat joint ever since all this stuff started."

The girls looked at each other, and then burst out into laughter.

"Well, fire it up, then. I'm game," Indira said.

The girls eagerly huddled closer together as Maxine sparked the joint and pulled it.

"Oh, I forgot to say that Clarissa will be here for Christmas. She's going to stay a week with me."

Sydney pulled twice, and then passed it to Indira.

"That's good, Indira," Sydney choked her words out through the smoke.

"We haven't seen Clarissa in a few years. Is she still dancing in D.C.?" Maxine felt relaxed now. She fell back into the couch. Indira was pulling smoke as Maxine asked the question. After a couple of moments, Indira exhaled the smoke as well as her response.

"She's still dancing, and that so called boyfriend of hers is really her pimp." Indira thought about her baby sister, and thought about how their situations were very similar. They were both being abused by the men they loved and they both took it.

"I can't wait until tonight. I can't wait to wrap my legs around that strong body," Maxine pulled the smoke in and fantasized as she let it out.

"No need to make us jealous over here. Right about now, Sydney and I are looking like two re-born virgins."

Sydney smoked instead of responding. It was pretty much true. She hadn't made love to anyone else since Anthony had left.

"You may be alone real soon, Indira," Sydney eventually uttered.

Both Maxine and Indira turned their attention to Sydney.

"What you talkin' 'bout, Willis?" Maxine did her Gary Coleman imitation.

"Oh yeah, you're high," Indira pointed to Maxine and began to chuckle.

"Wayne asked if he could come by later on tonight to talk." Sydney threw her hands up into the air in triumph.

"I saw you two all over here whispering to each other," Indira turned her tone to concern. "That's all your behind better be doing, is talking."

Sydney rolled her eyes and laughed. "Can you hit this? I know you don't wanna burn your nails." Indira shrugged her shoulders and took hold of the small roach between her fingers and pulled like a pro.

"Once you know how, you just never forget." Maxine was at it again, she and those damned Luther Vandross songs.

"Make her stop, please," Indira begged. The girls started laughing for no apparent reason, and then looked at one another and burst out with laughter again.

"That was some fire, Max," Indira stretched her legs out from the chair and relaxed.

"Don't start getting all sleepy and shit," Maxine leaped off the couch. "I don't care where you go, but you gotta get the hell up outta here."

Indira got up slowly and headed toward the bathroom.

"You should fix Bruce a plate of food before we put it all away," Sydney yawned and took a good hard stretch.

"I had planned on cooking for him tonight."

Everything got quiet. The girls could not believe their ears. Indira sat slouched down in her chair.

"Did I hear you say that you were going to cook dinner for this man?" Indira sat up in the chair.

She'll Learn

"I can cook. I don't know what the hell y'all trippin' about," Maxine became offended by the sly remarks.

"Like I said, maybe you'd better fix him a plate before we put the food up," Sydney laughed as Indira gave her a high 5 for a change.

"Oh, you are too funny." Maxine started picking up around the house again. "On second thought, I will make him a plate. That will give me more time to get ready."

Indira continued to laugh at Maxine.

"Then you can put up the food" Sydney said to Maxine as she lifted slowly off the couch and took a good stretch before retrieving Jasmine from the den. "Well, I guess we should get going. Jazzy and I have had one busy day." Sydney put her coat on and searched her pockets for her car keys. "I'm going outside to warm up Little Red so she'll be good and ready to go."

Maxine began bringing out boxes and bags full of gifts and decorations from the kitchen.

"What time is your man coming over, Maxine?" Indira asked again.

Maxine was wrapping the last of the birthday cake in Saran wrap. "He said he would be here around eight thirty," Maxine began to snicker. "I can't wait."

Indira just watched and said nothing. Sydney made her way back into the house, leaving the door ajar.

"Girl, it is too cold out there." Sydney picked up another box that Maxine had managed to pack up and took it to the car. Indira heard Jasmine starting to wake up and went to get her. Indira picked up the baby and went back into the living room with Jazzy fast asleep on her shoulder. "I hope you had a good birthday, Jazzy." Indira kissed Jasmine lightly on her cheek. "You got such nice things," Indira rubbed the baby's back lightly as she slept. Sydney came back into the house stomping the snow off her shoes at the door.

"Oh, did I wake you up, Jazzy? Mommy's sorry," Sydney kissed her daughter's forehead, and then retrieved the final box from the floor. Maxine came out of the kitchen with two more bags in her hand.

"The birthday girl is worn out," Maxine touched Jasmine's hair with her hand. "C'mon, Sydney. Let's get this shit out of here," Maxine yelled to Sydney as she came in the door.

"All right, stop yelling," Sydney picked up the bags. "She must be horny or something." Sydney walked right back out the door. Indira laughed quietly, so as not to wake the baby.

"What are you smiling about?" Maxine sat down on the couch and stretched her feet out.

"Nothing. I was just thinking about something." Indira began putting on Jasmine's hat and snowsuit for Sydney. She had enough to do already. Indira loved to help out with Jasmine. She wanted her own children someday. With Robert gone, her hopes of having children anytime soon would have to be delayed. Sydney came in stomping her feet once again.

"Keep the snow on that rug, will you?" Maxine inspected the snow on the floor.

"Oh, thank you, Indira, for getting her ready. I am beat." Sydney took hold of Jasmine all bundled up. "Oops, I'm forgetting her baby bag." Sydney searched around for the bag.

"Here it is." Indira found the bag on the side of the couch. Sydney made her way to the door carrying the baby, her bag, her purse, and yet another bag of something.

"Okay, ladies we are out of here. Thanks for everything. I feel so blessed to have two special friends like you and I love y'all." Sydney and Indira were both on the verge of tears already.

"Sydney, please!" Maxine interrupted her heartfelt speech. She jumped off the couch and hugged Sydney, and then kissed Jasmine before opening the door wide.

"Goodbye, Indira and thanks." Sydney said her final goodbye as Maxine pushed her out the door.

"I'll call you tomorrow," Maxine closed the door as Sydney pulled off, waving to her from the car. Maxine turned her eyes to Indira, who was still relaxing on the couch. Indira's shoeless feet caught her attention.

"Don't tell me you don't have your shoes on yet," Maxine looked at the clock on the wall. It read six eighteen.

"I guess I'll get ready to go too, since you're putting people out."

Maxine was starting to feel a little guilty when she noticed how slow Indira was moving. She probably wasn't ready to go home. She didn't need to be alone right now.

"On second thought, let's have a glass of wine."

Indira immediately looked up from her shoes.

"I thought you were putting me out?"

Maxine put her hand on her hip. "Stop saying that. I just get so anxious when it comes to Bruce. That's all." Maxine walked into the kitchen and returned with two glasses of white wine.

"I didn't really feel like going home just yet. Robert wasn't much to go home to, but at least someone was there." Indira took a sip of her wine. "I'll be out of here long before Bruce arrives."

Maxine took a sip from her glass. "Don't worry about him, he's never on time," she said as she took another sip.

*****

Sydney unpacked the car and started her journey up the stairs to her apartment. She turned around when she heard a door opening. It was Wayne.

"Why didn't you call and say that you were gonna need some help?" Wayne rushed over to Sydney and took hold of all but Jasmine for her.

"You are my hero. Thank you, I was going to have to make at least three trips." Sydney headed up to her apartment to put her daughter down to sleep. By the time she made it to the fifth floor, Wayne was on his way back up the stairs with the rest of the things from the party.

"I locked the car."

Sydney unlocked the door and went inside.

Wayne sat the bags down on the floor and stood in the doorway. "Are we still on for later?" Wayne didn't want to seem anxious because he knew Sydney was tired.

"Yes, we're still on. Give me about half an hour to get Jazzy in the bed and come on up." Sydney closed the door slowly as Wayne looked on.

"Okay." Wayne rushed down the stairs to his apartment to get ready.

*****

Lying in bed smoking a cigarette with Erica fast asleep in his armpit, the ceiling served as a screen as Bruce reminisced about Maxine and himself. He enjoyed being with her and the sex was all that.

Only if I wasn't in this situation, things could be different, Bruce thought as he moved the hair from his wife's face. But I am in this situation. Bruce let his thoughts of Maxine and a different life fade away as he slid his body closer to his wife of eleven years and closed his eyes.

*****

The minute Indira walked out the door, Maxine began her final cleanup of her house and finally all was back in its place. The candles were lit, Carl Thomas was singing softly through the speakers and Maxine was as hot as a Roman candle on the Fourth of July. All she needed now was Bruce to set her off. It was just now eight o'clock. Maxine decided that she had time to have another glass of wine and relax a little before Bruce arrived. She clicked the television on and flicked quickly through the channels. She stopped on the Lifetime network. *The Other Woman* or something like that was just coming on.

"I'll check this out for a little while," Maxine said as she tied the robe of her leopard print loungewear and let her feet rest on the edge of the couch. She admired the work of Ficara on her toes. She dressed hoochie, but she knew her craft. Maxine sipped her glass of wine and focused her attention on the movie. The movie opened up with a middle-aged white man and a young white woman in a hotel room. The man seemed to be in a rush.

"I'll call you this weekend and don't worry I'll be there." The half-dressed man kissed the woman still lying in bed, and then left the hotel room. The woman said nothing, only turned over as he left the room. The camera zoomed in on the face of the woman as tears began to roll down her cheeks.

"I guess she's okay with that." Maxine got a little more comfortable on the couch, putting two pillows behind her head. She yawned, and then turned her eyes to the clock on the mantle piece. It was eight-twenty.

"Come on, Bruce." Maxine turned her now tired eyes back to the movie on television. The next scene showed the man at home with his wife and kids having breakfast. Things seemed to be fine between them.

Why was the husband cheating on his wife? Maxine stretched out some more on the couch as she continued to watch. The phone rang. The husband looked a little shaken as the wife answered it.

"Hello," the wife answered cheerily. "He-ll-oo," the wife continued to greet the caller. "Oh well, I guess they hung up." The wife hung up the phone and returned to the kitchen. The man was relieved and turned his attention back to the newspaper he was reading. Maxine began to think about the movie. She wondered if she would ever know if she was the other woman and how she would feel if she was. She let out a long, drawn-out yawn this time. She looked at the clock again. It read eight thirty-five.

"Please don't let me fall asleep on this couch." After just barely watching a few more minutes of the movie, Maxine lay fast asleep.

*****

Knock, knock.

Sydney checked herself in the mirror and opened the door.

"Hi, come on in." She opened the door wide enough for Wayne to come in. The apartment was quiet and dimly lit.

"Is Jasmine sleep?" Wayne sat down on the couch.

"Yeah, I didn't have to do anything because she was tired." Sydney sat down in the chair next to Wayne. The two got quiet. "Would you like something to drink? I've got a lot of soda left from the party," Sydney gestured like she was ready to go and retrieve whatever he needed.

"No, I'm fine. Thanks." Wayne smiled, and then turned his eyes to the television that brightened the entire room. This moment had finally come. Wayne was alone with Sydney, but now he couldn't think of one thing to say to her.

"So are you liking your new job?" Sydney thought she had better break the ice a little.

"It's cool. I have to do a lot more around the station, but it's cool." Wayne was beginning to feel uncomfortable. "I think I will have something to drink." He tried to loosen up some while Sydney was in the kitchen. Don't blow this Wayne, he thought to himself.

Sydney returned with a glass of soda and handed it to him.

"Thanks." Wayne watched Sydney as she sat back down in the chair. "The party was great today. All of those kids running around and yelling. They were having a good time," Wayne took a drink from his glass.

"Did you see how happy Jazzy was looking?" Sydney leaned back in the chair. "I wish her daddy would have been around to see her today."

It was too late. Sydney realized that she was talking about her old boyfriend, her baby daddy, to another man. "I'm sorry, Wayne. I didn't mean to start talking about Anthony."

"That's okay. I mean, he is Jasmine's father."

Sydney was glad to hear that. She got up from the chair and sat down next to Wayne on the couch.

"Thanks. It's hard not to talk about him, sometimes," Sydney handed Wayne the remote to the television, and then snuggled up closer to him.

"I understand," Wayne hesitated, and then put his arm around Sydney as she leaned against him.

"Thanks for coming to the party today. It was nice to see you there," Sydney lifted her eyes to Wayne. Her huge brown eyes mesmerized him.

"I would like to be around a lot more, if you let me," Wayne couldn't wait any longer. He touched Sydney's cheek then softly kissed her lips. Sydney closed her eyes and accepted his kiss.

"I'd like that." Sydney let Wayne kiss her again, but this time there was much more intensity behind it. Wayne held Sydney's face in his hands.

"I've been waiting in the background for a long time and I want us to be together now," Wayne planted his wet lips onto Sydney's once more. Sydney was at a loss for words. She wrapped her arms around Wayne's neck and let her mouth and tongue explore his. Wayne lay back on the couch and pulled Sydney on top of him. Sydney hadn't had a man touch her like this in months, damn near an entire year. She had become a born again virgin. She was enjoying this, maybe a little too much. Wayne's strong hands made their way up Sydney's back under her shirt. He massaged her skin gently as he traveled up her neck with his mouth. Sydney couldn't help grinding her hips into Wayne's. She began to feel him harden beneath her. Wayne let his hands migrate south to Sydney's butt. He felt her hips press a little harder against him. He was turning her on easily. He knew things were moving too quickly. Wayne valued his friendship with Sydney and didn't want to ruin it by moving too fast, so he brought his hands north.

Sydney hadn't made love in such a long time, not since Anthony. There had only been two men in her life, sexually. Her first love was Deon and her second and last love was Anthony. She loved both of them with everything she had. Sydney loved Anthony even harder than that. She began to let her mind wander as Wayne continued to kiss her neck and collarbone.

What am I doing? Get out of my head, Anthony, Sydney thought.

Wayne wanted Sydney so badly, but he would only move on her call. Sydney decided to forget about Anthony and move ahead. She needed this. She deserved to feel wanted and desired. She was missing a man's touch, the feeling that a man and a woman share. She missed Anthony. She began to feel lightheaded, so she lifted herself off of Wayne and sat on the couch. It felt like her head was spinning around in circles. Wayne could see that something was wrong with her.

"You okay, Syd?"

The sandwiches, the cake, the daiquiris, everything came crashing in Sydney's stomach all at once. Wayne lifted up and let Sydney lean against his shoulder.

"I think I'm gonna throw up."

Wayne helped her off the couch as he searched the apartment for the bathroom. How could he miss the bright yellow room? He led her directly to the toilet bowl. His eyes began to get lost in the walls and forget where he was.

"This is a great bathroom."

There were smiling suns and daisies all over the walls. The yellow and orange candles and towels matched perfectly. It was happy, like Sydney. Wayne snapped out of his haze as he heard Sydney let her lunch go into the toilet. He took hold of her long brown hair and held it out of the line of fire.

"Are you better now?"

Sydney was too embarrassed to answer him. She just wanted him to leave her alone.

"Yeah, I'm okay." Sydney crawled to the tub and drowned her face under the cool running water. Wayne continued to be the perfect gentleman and hold her hair. This was too much for Sydney right now. She turned to Wayne and gave him a look that let him know to release her hair.

"Sorry," he whispered. He could see that he should leave now.

"Can you give me a minute alone please?" Sydney wasn't feeling much for closeness right about now. She was feeling extremely uncomfortable. Wayne left the bathroom. Sydney pushed herself up from the tub and wearily lifted her eyes to see herself in the mirror.

"You just couldn't let it happen. You had to start thinking about Anthony," she said to herself. Sydney turned the faucet on and let the water run. She reached for her face cloth and soaked it. "He's never coming back. Get it through your head girl." Sydney began to feel the tears roll down her face. She saw them in the mirror, and then quickly wiped them away with her towel. "Am I ever going to be able to get over him?"

Wayne didn't know what to do. He knew this probably wouldn't be a good time to hang around, so he left the apartment. Sydney heard the door close as she turned off the faucet. She came out of the bathroom and let herself fall over the arm of the chair.

"I blew it." Sydney looked over to the telephone and then at the clock. It was five after ten.

"I'll bet Maxine has her legs high in the air by now." Sydney grabbed the television remote and switched it off then went to bed.

*****

The sounds of police sirens and horns blared from the television awaking Maxine. She lifted off the couch and grabbed her aching neck.

"Damn my neck hurts." She rolled her neck around, and then took a deep breath and straightened it.

"Shit, I hate when I do this." Maxine saw that another movie had started on the tube. "What time is it?" Maxine focused her eyes to see the clock. "Ten thirty? That son of a bitch never showed up." Maxine ran her fingers through her cropped hair roughly.

"Damn, Bruce. Back to your games again I see." Maxine knew something was wrong. "Why now? Why start playing this damn game again now?" Maxine rose off the couch angrily and paced the floor letting the robe to her pajamas fly open.

"I keep denying the shit, but something is wrong here. Something is definitely wrong." Maxine flopped back down on the couch. "This is so fucked up." She flung her arms into the air. "Fucked up!" Maxine yelled through her empty house. The phone rang, startling her. She laughed then calmed herself. She didn't want to let him know that he'd made her upset, just yet. The phone rang again.

"Hello," Maxine waited on the caller to answer.

"You don't sound too out of breath."

Maxine relaxed. It was Indira. "What do you want, Indira?" Maxine pounced down on the couch.

"I just thought I'd call you. I'd forgotten about you having company until the phone was already ringing," Indira sounded drunk.

"Are you drunk, Indira? You sound real fucked up to me," Maxine turned the volume of the television down.

"So what if I am drunk. I'm at home, in my own house minding my own damn business."

"Indira, I don't feel like this shit. That black-ass dog didn't show up. He didn't even call me. I just woke up on the damn couch with a fuckin' crook in my neck, so don't start no shit with me," Maxine had sent herself into a frenzy on her friend. Silence took over the conversation. After a few more seconds, Maxine heard whimpering on the phone. Indira was boo-hooing.

"Damn, Indira, I'm sorry. I'm not mad at you. I'm upset with that, never mind."

Indira continued to cry. It wasn't about Maxine losing her temper, but about all the things that had gone wrong in her life. "No, I'm sorry. I just can't believe all this shit is happening to me," Indira slurred her words out to Maxine, who was hearing her loud and clear.

"I just turned thirty and my clock is ticking so damn loud, I can't hear the rest of the world sometimes." Indira dropped the phone and blew her nose. Maxine sort of laughed at her friend, who couldn't handle two wine coolers. Indira picked the phone back up.

"Maxine!" Indira yelled into the phone.

"Yes, girl, I'm here." Maxine felt sorry for Indira. She didn't deserve this. She gave Robert her all. "You are going to have to let that jackass go, honey. He has done everything to prove to you that he wasn't the man for you. No matter how long your damn clock was ticking." Maxine knew that this wasn't what her friend wanted to hear right now, but she was going to tell her anyway.

"I know, Max. But I love him so much and it just irks the shit out of me that he had the gall to leave me. I should have left his ass. I feel so damn stupid." Indira got quiet.

"Don't think I don't know about that. I feel extra stupid right now. We are in the same boat, girl, sinking fast," Maxine was upset.

"I hate this. What am I gonna do?" Indira was letting her drunkenness take over again.

"I hate it, too," Maxine replied.

Maxine and Indira fell quiet. Neither woman said anything for a long time until finally Maxine spoke up.

"Indira."

She didn't answer.

"Indira," Maxine sung Indira's name to her, then she yelled. "Indira!"

Indira had fallen asleep on the phone.

"What, what?" Indira began to snore.

"Indira! If you don't get your ass off this phone and take your ass to bed," Maxine yelled through the phone.

"Okay, dammit. Stop yelling at me," Indira hung up the phone so fast Maxine jumped at the loud click that rang in her eardrum.

"Drunk, bitch," Maxine announced under her breath.

She'll Learn

CHAPTER TWELVE

Monday afternoon, the week of Thanksgiving, Maxine and Indira decided to have lunch together at Bennucci's and shop for shoes to cheer themselves up. Maxine stepped through the yellow doors of the restaurant and looked around the room for Indira. They loved this place because it was gorgeous—the ceiling that looked to be floating and the colorful accents throughout the place. But the best thing was the theatre-style open kitchen. She and Indira found the place years ago while they were shopping for shoes for Indira's wedding.

Maxine spotted Indira sitting at a cozy table near the window. The place was crowded as usual. The atmosphere was always good. Maxine nodded to the waiter who stood to the side as she passed him. Maxine knew she was looking extra special today and liked to see the men's heads turn.

"Hey, girl," Indira stood up from her chair and hugged Maxine around her neck.

"What's up, girl?" Maxine took off her coat, and then sat down in a chair across from her friend. Maxine was somewhat disappointed to see that Indira wasn't up to their traditional game of "who can out-dress who" today. She was dressed in a plain old tank and cardigan with a pair of old jeans. Maxine had wasted her brand new BeBe sweater and her wool pants. Maxine knew it was silly, but it had been like a game to them for years now.

"I'm so glad you came, Maxine. I didn't feel like going to work today, and I know this is your day off, but I promise you some fun." Indira tried to sound excited, though Maxine didn't seem too excited about giving up her off day.

"It's cool, Indi. I wasn't doing anything no way," Maxine sipped from her glass of water. "I haven't even heard from Bruce in two days." Maxine displayed her "got the nerve" lips.

"What is his problem?" Indira was upset for Maxine.

"I don't know what his problem is. One minute things are all lovey-dovey, and then the next minute I can't find his ass." Maxine angrily took another sip from her glass of water, and then noticed the waiter walking toward their table.

"Are you ladies ready to order?" The young Latin waiter smiled as he held his pen and notepad at attention.

"I guess we're ready to order," Maxine said. Indira nodded her head in agreement. "Let's see. I'll start with a bowl of potato soup, and then I'll be having the Mediterranean chicken," Maxine smiled hungrily at the handsome boy.

"And, for you?"

Indira searched the menu once again for her final decision.

"I'll also start with a bowl of potato soup and I'll have the spaghetti and meatballs dinner."

The waiter eagerly jotted down the order. "And something to drink?" He turned back to Maxine who was in the middle of giving him the once over, but in her case the twice over.

"I'll have a strawberry margarita," Maxine said.

He turned to Indira, who was staring at Maxine. She couldn't forget her pounding headache from her drinking excursion two nights ago.

"I'll have lemonade, thank you." Indira handed the waiter her menu, as well as Maxine's. The waiter strolled away to the kitchen with Maxine's eyes burning his backside.

"He was too cute," Maxine acknowledged as Indira watched her and shook her head in disgust.

"He was all right, I guess."

Maxine was now staring at Indira.

"You know you're gonna have to get back out there someday. Why wait?" Maxine leaned closer to the table.

"I don't think so! I'm going be spending a little time getting to know myself again," Indira rolled her eyes and slumped down in her chair. "I don't really feel like rearranging my life for another asshole, just yet." Indira couldn't sit still in her chair. "He would have to be one helluva a man for me to get with him right about now."

Maxine laughed as she watched Indira get some of that stress off of her chest. "I hear you, girl. You are right. After all that shit Robert put you through, I would need a vacation from men myself."

Indira knew that wasn't true, Maxine couldn't take a vacation from men if she wanted to. It would be just too hard for her. Maxine eyed the waiter as he delivered their salad and soup. The waiter flirted back with Maxine, as he tossed the salad between them.

"Toss it up," Maxine joked. Indira hated that she could be so ghetto sometimes. There were no limits for her when it came to men.

"Would you like pepper?"

Indira nodded yes to the waiter. He and Maxine were at it again, smiling away at each other. Indira couldn't stand it anymore. She was becoming quite annoyed with Maxine's behavior. She held up her hand to stop José from loading her salad with pepper. He turned to Maxine with the pepper cracker.

"Oh, you know I want some." Maxine stopped him prematurely. "That's good. Thank you." She noticed the sour look on Indira's face.

"What's your malfunction?" Maxine asked, but she really didn't care.

"Why are you acting so silly for that little boy? He couldn't even crack my pepper right. Look at this." Indira pointed to her salad that was covered in cracked pepper. Indira tightened her lips again and waited for Maxine to cut her up with insults. To her surprise, Maxine didn't retaliate.

"You're right, Indi. But I can't help myself. I have always been that way and you know it." Maxine dropped her head. Indira began to snicker.

"You know you love some men, Maxine. Black, White…Latino, don't make no difference does it?" Indira looked to Maxine and smiled.

"Not really."

The two women cracked up with laughter, and then started eating their soup. The waiter returned with their entrees and left smiling from ear to ear all the way back to the kitchen. Maxine felt embarrassed now, and then covered her plate in Parmesan cheese.

"I think I'm obsessed with dick."

Indira dropped her fork on the floor. "What?" She retrieved it. The waiter who couldn't take his eyes off of Maxine rushed to Indira's aid with a fresh one.

"Thank you, José." Indira waited until the waiter was gone. "What did you say?"

Maxine looked at her friend with a straight face. “I truly think I’m obsessed with dick.” Maxine cut her chicken, and then stopped. “Well, good dick.”

Indira shook her head and ate her food. “I thought that’s what you said,” Indira buried herself in her meal, trying to ignore Maxine.

“I can drop a bad dick in a snap,” Maxine snapped her fingers.

Indira looked up in shock. “You know you are crazy.” Indira got back to her spaghetti and meatballs because she hated cold food.

“Don’t lie, Indira. You know you can get over a little dick man in no time,” Maxine took a bite of her chicken. “I can’t remember one time crying my eyes out over some little dick man.”

Indira dropped her fork in her plate. She was about to burst with laughter, she used her napkin to cover her mouth.

“Admit it, Indi.” Maxine ate and preached her gospel to Indira.

“You are so right. That is so true.”

Maxine took a swallow of her drink that was nearly gone. “It’s so funny to me how that works.” Maxine held up her glass to alert José that she needed another drink.

“How what works?” Indira continued to eat and listen to Max.

“The little dick men love your draws and want to be that one for you, but you just can’t imagine yourself laying next to Pee-wee for the rest of your life.” Maxine finished her drink just as José brought her another. Indira said nothing, but only laughed.

“Then on the other hand, the men who have it going on and really know how to put it down, treat you like shit, and then fuck your brains out.”

This was too much for Indira to take. She was laughing so hard. This was exactly what she needed; Maxine always knew how to cheer her up.

“Maxine, your butt is too funny, but you are so right. I rarely shed a tear over a guy with a small dick,” Indira laughed and held up her pinky.

Maxine and Indira ate their food silently, and then Maxine stopped.

“I hope I don’t have to shed no tears this time.”

Indira knew for sure that her friend had fallen in love.

"You don't have to do anything," Indira touched Maxine's hand to reassure her. "Let's hurry up and finish. I'm ready to spend Robert's money." Indira was making Maxine laugh this time.

"It's just burning a big ole hole in your purse ain't it?" Maxine joked with Indira.

"You damn skippy it is."

Maxine took another sip of her drink and caught the waiter. "We'd like our check, please."

*****

Robert woke up in a cold sweat, shaking non-stop. Vera rushed to his side and covered his forehead with a cool washcloth.

"Oh, baby, please. Let's call the doctor." Vera felt Robert's body shaking violently against her own body.

"No, I don't want all those damn people probing over me when I know that there is nothing they can do for me," Robert tried to talk between shaking.

"Lord, please watch over my man and help him pull through this sickness." Vera lifted her eyes to the ceiling and spoke to God, the only way she knew how. Robert wrapped his arms around Vera's tiny waist and held her close to him. He wondered if he was too late to be calling on God for help. Did he deserve what was happening to him? he thought.

"Payback," Robert whispered under his breath as Vera prayed to the heavens on his behalf. His heart ached from all the pain he'd caused his first wife Bridget and their children, his second wife Cynthia, then Indira, and worst of all, Vera. Robert pulled his medication out from his pocket and popped the top. He swallowed three pain pills without water and rested his head on Vera's leg.

"Oh, Robert, is that why you think you're sick?" Vera caressed her man's head, which rested upon her. "This isn't payback, Bobby. God is a forgiving man. He doesn't do payback. It's never too late to come to the Lord." Vera looked into Robert's watery eyes. "It's never too late."

Vera eased Robert's head off of her leg and got on her knees next to him. Robert watched Vera closely as he lay on the bed. Vera put her hands together, closed her eyes and began to pray. Robert watched intently, and then he pulled himself to his knees next to Vera. "It's never too late to come to the Lord," she repeated.

Robert bowed his head on his hands and prayed to God for forgiveness. Tears ran uncontrollably down his face. He hadn't cried in more than thirty years. Vera lifted herself off her knees and sat on the edge of the bed next to Robert. He then placed his head in her lap.

"Do you think God will forgive me for all the horrible things I've done in my life?" Robert was feeling low. He knew he didn't have much time to fix things, only time to ask for forgiveness.

"If you really mean what you are saying. He'll forgive you." Vera stood and helped Robert to his feet and back into bed.

"I'll be right back, baby." Vera remembered that she hadn't called Mrs. Mancuso, and it was nearly two o'clock in the afternoon. Vera found her employer's phone number on the door of the refrigerator. She'd rarely used it since she hadn't missed a day of work in almost fifteen years. The phone was on its third ring.

"Hello," the voice sounded weak and afraid, unlike the old woman she knew.

"Hello, Mrs. Mancuso," Vera spoke loudly so the aging woman could hear her clearly.

"Is that you, Vera? Where are you?" Mrs. Mancuso began to sound frantic. Vera was all she had left. She'd outlived her husband and her three children.

"Yes, ma'am, it's me." Vera took a deep breath to get some composure. She was nervous now. "I am calling to tell you that I won't be returning to work. I quit."

Mrs. Mancuso became silent, and then cleared her throat to speak, "Ohh," the woman didn't have anything else to say.

"I'm sorry, Mrs. Mancuso, but I will send Ora in my place. She's great and will help you with everything you need." Vera could tell that her now former employer was hurt, but there was nothing she could do about it. She had to take care of Robert.

"Thank you, Vera."

Vera was frozen. In all of the years that she had worked for Mrs. Mancuso, she'd never had one kind word to say to her. Vera began to feel guilty, but she wouldn't let that deter her from her man.

"You are so welcome, ma'am, and I thank you for having me for all these years." Vera heard the old woman hang the phone up.

She'll Learn

"Goodbye." Vera held the receiver down with her finger to clear the call before dialing Ora's number. She was going to be thrilled to hear of a job opening. Her nanny position had just ended with the Richmond family, and she was in need of a job after seven years. Vera dialed the phone number from memory.

"Hello." The phone rang only once.

"Hi, Ora. It's Vera," Vera tried to sound upbeat so Ora would be lured to listen.

"Oh hey, Vera. What's going on?" Ora relaxed her tone. She was expecting a bill collector.

"I have a job for you," Vera put some pep into her voice to intrigue Ora. Vera peeked around the corner to see Robert lying in the bed staring up at the ceiling.

"A job? You know I just lost my nanny job." Ora didn't give Vera a chance to get a word in, as usual.

"Yes, honey. I just quit my job with Mrs. Mancuso and she'll be needing somebody right away."

Ora began to recall all the bad days Vera had spoken of with that woman. "You talking about that mean old lady you've been with for damn near fifteen years?"

Vera knew her employer's reputation would soon surface in this conversation. Mrs. Mancuso was known throughout their net of nannies and housekeepers for being notoriously cruel and nasty to her employees.

"Yes, and she's not that bad," Vera tried to sound convincing.

"Then, why are you leaving?"

Vera knew that her answer would determine whether or not Ora would take her place or not.

"Bobby has come home to stay," Vera was pleased to announce this news to her friend. Ora really didn't believe her friend. Ever since she had known Vera, Robert had been in and out of her life like changing seasons.

"Get out of here, Vera. Robert really is there?" Ora hated that Vera had wasted her life waiting on that man, but it was her own choice.

"Yes, my man is home to stay," Vera tried to keep her excitement to a minimum so as not to wake Robert. Vera sounded so happy. Ora had no choice but to be happy for her.

"Well if he can come home after all these years, then I guess I can help you out."

Vera nearly dropped the phone. "Oh, thank you, Ora, I knew I could count on you."

Though Mrs. Mancuso wasn't very nice, Vera didn't want to leave her without someone to care for her.

"The money is real good and just ignore the old broad when she starts running off at the mouth." Vera gave Ora her last minute instructions. "And please, Ora, don't be late. She will be expecting you at nine o'clock sharp." Vera didn't want her friend to get cursed out the minute she got in the door.

"Okay, okay. I'll be on time, besides I need the job anyway. Thanks a lot, girl."

Vera knew Ora all too well, and knew that her instructions went in one ear and straight through the other one. "I'll talk to you later then, bye." Vera hung up the phone. She was relieved that she had found a replacement right away. Mrs. Mancuso was so mean, but only because she was lonely. Vera understood her situation all too well. She was lonely herself.

"Not anymore. My man is home now," Vera smiled, and then quickly began to frown. "But, for how long?" Vera looked up to God for her answer.

*****

"That man has stood me up more than once." Maxine modeled the Kenneth Cole loafer in the shoe store's mirror.

"Oh, yeah?" Indira sat and observed Maxine in the mirror.

"I don't know what to make of this man. We've been together almost a month, granted. But I still don't feel like we're a real couple." Maxine pointed at the shoes and waited for Indira's approval.

"Why not? Oh, they look good." Indira sat back and listened to her friend.

"He's always busy and he never stays the night. Girl, I don't even have the man's home phone number."

Indira opened her eyes wide with surprise. "Are you for real, Maxine?"

She'll Learn

Maxine took the shoes up to the cash register with Indira following close behind.

"I hate to admit it, but yes. I guess I'm in some sort of denial shit."

The sales clerk laughed as he listened to the two women. They both turned to him immediately with looks of stone on their faces.

"Out of one hundred, here's $28.60. Thank you."

Without saying a word, Maxine took hold of her bag and rolled her eyes at the sales clerk as they left the store.

"As I was saying, I don't know the man. I've been screwing a man for damn near a month and I don't know shit about him," Maxine threw her hands up.

"Well, Maxine, I know you don't wanna hear this, but you hadn't been very candid with me so...I think he's married." Indira stopped Maxine dead in her tracks.

Maxine's lip dropped, nearly hitting the floor. "Please don't say that shit, man." Maxine pouted through the hallway of the shopping mall.

"Don't say that?" Indira was correct. Maxine didn't want to hear what she thought. "Maxine, please. Any man that only gives you his pager number is flashing the first red light right then. Do you have his cell phone number?"

Maxine hesitated then shook her head from left to right.

"No. I can't believe you, Max. You really don't know shit about this man," Indira was becoming upset herself.

Maxine began to feel dizzy and searched for a place to sit down.

"What's wrong, Maxine?" Indira helped her friend sit down near the fountain.

"Ooh, I don't know. I felt like I was about to fall out." Maxine put her hand on her head and took a deep breath.

"Fall out!" Indira took a step back and looked Maxine over. "You're not pregnant are you?" Indira held onto their bags with one hand and the other was placed on her hip.

"Hell naw, I am not pregnant." Maxine lifted herself up slowly. "Let's go. I don't feel like shopping no more." Maxine angrily walked away from Indira. "Am I pregnant? What the hell is wrong with her?" Maxine slowed down her pace and waited for Indira to catch up.

"Why are you running away from me? I just asked a question, that's all," Indira shrugged her shoulders.

"That shit wasn't funny, Indira. First you say I'm fucking a married man. Now all of a sudden, I'm pregnant—not funny, Indira." Maxine put on a forced grin and led Indira out the door to the parking lot.

"Well, I'm sorry, but you asked what I thought." Indira spotted her Benz and headed over toward it.

"And for the record, I didn't ask what you thought."

Indira unlocked the car doors with her remote, snickering as she sat down behind the driver's seat. Maxine caught her in the act, before she could stop. Indira started the ignition. She knew that Maxine was upset, but she was her best friend and if she didn't tell her, who would? Jill Scott crooned her mellow tones through the radio before Indira turned it down.

"Let's face it, Max. You and I have been had. I've wasted five years of my life on a man who didn't really love me. I was stupid, not him. And you, you're in denial. The man you've fallen in love with is married. He belongs to another woman, another sister." Indira looked into Maxine's saddened eyes.

"We can do much better than this, girl. I know we can." Maxine began to smile.

"You are something."

Maxine shook her head and laughed.

"Ever since we were kids you've always been right and you're right this time," Maxine sighed and then looked out her window at the people strolling to their parked cars. "I know it's true. I feel it deep inside me. My gut is telling me that Bruce is married." Maxine let her eyes journey back to Indira's.

"What are you gonna do?"

Maxine stared at her shoes. "I'm gonna give him a chance to tell me the truth, and if he's married, which I'm hoping he's not..." Maxine turned to Indira. "I'll have to stop seeing him. Damn that was nasty." Maxine tightened her lips up as if the words put an awful taste in her mouth.

Indira laughed at Maxine and pulled out of the parking lot.

"You are a fool, Max."

Maxine smiled and then turned the radio back up and began to clap her hands to Mary J. Blige.

*****

Sydney pulled in front of her building to the usual crowd of men that hung around it. The bums were an awful sight sometimes, but on bad days, they were like security.

"Hey, Sydney," Sydney turned toward the voice and saw Joe waving from the corner as he walked over to join the others. He had known Sydney since she was a baby and he was once her father's good friend, until his wife died and he let everything slip away from him. Sydney smiled and waved back to him, and then walked to the entrance.

"Hey, everybody," Sydney spoke to the entourage as she did every day.

"Hello, Ms. Sydney."

Sydney nodded her head and walked through the doors. The heat reached her face and relaxed it. She unbuttoned her coat and looked toward the stairs.

"Damn, seems like I would have lost ten or fifteen pounds by now," Sydney started up the stairs.

"Hey, Sydney," Wayne was standing outside of his apartment.

"Well hello, Wayne," Sydney came back down the stairs. Wayne met Sydney at the bottom stair with a sweet kiss. Sydney accepted it, wholeheartedly.

"What was that for?" Sydney was smiling from ear to ear. They were growing closer and closer with each passing day. Wayne had fallen head over heels in love with Sydney, and he was feeling better than he'd felt in years.

"I have a surprise for you," Wayne reached behind his back and handed her a small box.

"Oh, Wayne. What is it?" Sydney opened the lid of the tiny box. "It's Jasmine's birthstone. It's beautiful, Wayne."

Wayne remembered seeing Sydney admiring the charm as they shopped for Jasmine's birthday gift. Sydney put her arms around his neck and gave him a deep, long kiss.

"Thank you so much, Wayne. This is so sweet of you," Sydney stared at the citrine stone nested in a gold oval.

"These past few weeks with you and Jazzy have been so great for me. I just wanted to do something for you."

Sydney was seeing Wayne clearer than ever. He was in love with her. There was one problem for Sydney. She wasn't in love with him. She was about to speak, just as Wayne put his finger to her lips.

"I know you're not ready to have a relationship right now, but you do have a friend," Wayne moved his finger slowly.

"Thanks. I'd better go and get Jasmine. Ms. Lee hates it when I'm late." Sydney started up the stairs again. "I'll see you later, okay? And, thanks again." Sydney could feel Wayne watching her as she made her way up the narrow stairs. She didn't look back until she made it to Ms. Lee's apartment on the fifth floor. After regaining her breath, she knocked on the door. Ms. Lee opened it, holding Jasmine on her hip.

"Hello, baby," Ms. Lee greeted.

Sydney stepped inside and closed the door behind her. The air was filled with the aroma of collard greens coming from the kitchen.

"I'll send you some greens when they get done, and some cornbread." Ms. Lee gathered up all of Jasmine's things while Sydney buttoned Jasmine's sweater.

"You know I was smelling them at the door."

Ms. Lee came back into the front room with Jasmine's baby bag and her bottle in hand. "She wore herself out today. She and little Maria played all day. They like to watch Barney and do whatever he tells them to do." Ms. Lee laughed and waved her hand, "You ought to see 'em."

Sydney stood up with Jasmine hanging over her shoulder. Jasmine woke up briefly to see her mother's face. Ms. Lee handed Sydney the bag and kissed Jasmine's hand.

"She's such a sweet baby. I'll see you two in the morning." Ms. Lee clung to her tattered housedress as she opened the door for Sydney. "Are you ready for Thanksgiving yet? I know you cooking for your nice daddy."

Sydney laughed at the old woman who wore bright red lipstick every day of her life. "Yes. I'm cooking for my daddy and for Indira and Maxine, too. I've got one more day to get myself together," Sydney said as she stood outside the door.

"Well I might drop by to say hello to your father," Ms. Lee began to laugh at her own audacity.

"You know that you are always welcome." Sydney headed down the stairs to her apartment.

"I'll see you tomorrow," Ms. Lee said as she closed her door.

CHAPTER THIRTEEN

The loud screeching of tires startled the passengers of the Greyhound bus as they arrived at the bus depot. Everyone jumped out of his or her seats trying to be the first to get off and get to the luggage. Anthony remained in his seat and stared out the window at the street. He was back. Back to the place he ran away from just over a year ago. Things would be different this time. He had a plan. First, he would check out the job that his sister lined up for him and get some change in his pocket. Then, he would go and get his family back. He hadn't had a choice in leaving because he was in too deep. The dope game had taken over his life and had gotten inside his head. Then Sydney's brother Eric overdosed on the dope he'd sold him. It had all been too much.

Anthony got out of his seat dressed in a Karl Kani blue jean suit, dry clean creased, and a pair of deep brown Timberlands. Two young girls took notice as they flirted and giggled behind him. Anthony gave the girls a smile and stepped off the bus. He looked around at the tall buildings, which surrounded the tiny station.

"Back up in this motha'. Anthony nodded his head with confidence at the city that nearly defeated him.

"But I'm ready for you this time." He picked up his duffel bag from under the bus and headed inside the bus station. Valerie held Sukia close to her as she watched for her younger brother to walk through the terminal. She was so glad he was coming back home. She'd missed having him around.

"Val," Anthony spotted his sister and niece.

"Alabama must have been treating you well. You look good," Valerie gave her brother a strong hug.

"What's up, Sukia? You done shot up on me."

The little girl he knew before he left had blossomed into a young lady. "Hey, Uncle Tony," Sukia buried her face into her uncle's chest as she hugged him.

"Y'all must have missed me or something?" Anthony joked and threw his duffel bag over his shoulder.

"Boy, you know we missed your crazy self," Valerie squeezed his hand.

"Let's get up outta here. A brother like me is starving."

"Don't worry. I got you covered. And we are going to throw down Thursday."

Anthony had picked the perfect time to come home—the holidays. Valerie knew what she was doing in the kitchen and Anthony had missed that just as much.

"I wanna go see about that job tomorrow," Anthony tossed his bag into the back of his sister's Chevy Tahoe that sat illegally parked in front of the station.

"That's cool. It's all set up. Just call the office in the morning."

Sukia hopped into the truck and closed her door.

"You always been lucky," Anthony said as he closed his door and smiled to Valerie as she sat down behind the wheel.

"What are you talking about?" Valerie started the SUV and pulled into traffic without so much as a glance over her shoulder.

"You was all parked illegally, and shit," Anthony shook his head from left to right. "If that was me, I would be laying on the ground with guns pointed at me."

Valerie turned up her mouth, "Boy, shut up. I didn't get no ticket, did I?"

Anthony threw up his hands. "See what I mean?"

Sukia laughed as Anthony turned to her.

"I sure have missed you two," Anthony turned his eyes back to the road and tried to prepare himself for the adventure ahead of him.

*****

Maxine waved goodbye to Indira once she got her front door open. The dimly lit house seemed solemn and quiet. It seemed a bit lonely. Maxine noticed the red light flashing on her answering machine.

"I'll bet Bruce found time to call me while I was out." She pushed the play button on the machine. Beep! Maxine took off her leather jacket and hung it in the hall closet.

"Hello, Maxine. It's Bruce. I want to apologize for not showing up for dinner the other night and for not calling you. I've got a lot of things on my mind right now. I want to…" Beep! The answering machine cut Bruce's message short.

"Dammit! You want to what?" Maxine was standing over the small contraption awaiting the next message for part two of Bruce. Beep!

"Hello, baby. Everything is all set and ready for Thursday. We can't wait to see you."

Maxine's heart dropped when she heard the dry voice of her Aunt Betsy.

"You don't have to bring nothing but yourself. Happy Thanksgiving, bye."

Maxine wasn't ready to spend the day with her family—the black Brady Bunch. Maureen with one child, Maxine; Betsy Ann married twice, with six children; James, the father of eleven children, never having married; and Natalie Marie, the youngest of Mable's four children, was a college professor in Atlanta who had never been married and had no children. The family rarely heard from her, except on the holidays.

Aunt Betsy's bunch was the worst of all her cousins. They were all do-gooders and braggers. All six of her children went to college and had successful jobs. Aunt Betsy didn't have time to stop bragging, and neither did they. Maxine grew up the only child with a crackhead for a mother. If it weren't for her grandmother she wouldn't have survived.

Beep! Maxine had gotten so worked up, she'd forgotten about the machine.

"I'll be there at seven o'clock," Bruce said.

Maxine didn't know what to think. She'd heard that before.

"I'll be there at seven. We'll see if you can get your black ass here at seven." Things were different this time. Maxine flicked on the television and flopped down on the couch.

"No candles, no sexy clothes, and no food. My feelings are on the line here." Maxine kicked off her shoes and watched the six o'clock news.

*****

Indira took the liberty of using Robert's off-limit office, since he wasn't there anymore. Her feet dressed in her new Prada heels rested comfortably on his handcrafted mahogany desk imported from Africa. His antique phone was nestled up to her ear.

"I can't wait to see you. It'll be just like old times. I hope you can stay longer this time. We didn't get to do anything the last time you were here," Indira needed the company and her sister would be perfect. With

Robert gone, she could be free around her sister without upsetting the drunk.

"Yeah, I can't wait to get there. I really need a break from all this shit," Clarissa sat at the desk of her sleazy boss dressed in her skimpy cowgirl costume. BJ had the perfect view of the stage from his office. Lit up with florescent lights and shining poles where the girls sold themselves to the hungry wolves, he could see everything that went down in his club from there. Where he couldn't see, there were cameras. He didn't miss a thing.

"I need a real break," Clarissa stressed again. Suddenly, showing her pussy for a living wasn't too appealing to her anymore. She'd made a mistake that had changed everything for her.

"Then stay for as long as you like, Clarissa. I would love for you to come home to stay. That damn club isn't going anywhere and it won't crumble without you in it."

Clarissa dropped her head when BJ stepped through the door of his office.

"I have to get to work now. I'll talk to you later." Clarissa hung up the phone and eased out of BJ's chair. He touched her back lightly with his hand as she passed him.

"I need you strictly in the private VIP room tonight. You were requested for a private party tonight for five gentlemen," BJ smacked Clarissa on her ass. "Make that money, girl." He laughed as she made her way to the stairs. "Oh, Cocoa, I expect to see you tonight. You know our little arrangement is working out real good for me."

Clarissa made her way down the stairs to the dressing room. The other girls were all getting dressed and taking their hits of cocaine or doing whatever they had to do to get on the stage.

"Cocoa, you don' messed up this time, getting in with BJ," Jill said. Jill was a freshly turned nineteen-year old who got caught up in the game the same way Clarissa did. She fell in love with a smooth man who said all the right things to her and somewhere in there she ended up dancing. He taught her everything she needed to know. How to make money for him, and how not to be afraid to show her body. Just about every girl in there had that same weakness. Before they knew it, they were in so deep they were gasping for air to stay alive.

"I know, Jill. But, it's a little too late now to rethink some shit, ain't it?"

Clarissa began putting on her lipstick. Nobody had to tell her that borrowing money from BJ was the worst thing she could do, but she needed the money. Indira was having problems of her own with Robert and she didn't want to ask her for money to pay her dealer.

"Have you told him about Christmas?" Jill spoke in a normal tone as if they were at a real job with real vacation time.

"Will you shut up, Jill?" Clarissa looked around the room, but no one seemed to hear her. "I don't want none of these crabs to know my business." Clarissa swallowed a shot of whiskey, and then stood up to adjust her tightly squeezed breasts in the mirror. "I'll be just fine. Don't you worry about me, worry about yourself." The music was bumping loudly upstairs to let the girls know that it was time to get to work. They crowded the stairs like a herd of cattle being rustled up from the field.

"It's all about the money." Clarissa made her way onto the floor filled with men from wall to wall.

*****

Bruce pulled in front of Maxine's house and cut the ignition. It was six-fifty. He was early.

"All right, Bruce. This is it," he said to himself. He checked himself in the rearview mirror. "The pussy was good, but I got to let her go. Damn I hate to let it go." Bruce opened the car door and stepped out onto the snow covered ground. He pulled his coat together and walked to the front door.

Get somebody to shovel some of this shit, he thought. He rang the doorbell and waited. Maxine lifted off the couch in shock. It was six fifty-eight.

"Damn. Something must be wrong." Maxine rushed to the front door and opened it quickly. Bruce stepped into the warm house and removed his hat.

"Hi, baby." He kissed Maxine's cheek. She helped him out of his coat and tried to take it.

"I'll keep it with me."

Maxine stood in disbelief as Bruce walked over to the couch. He had something up his sleeve, and he wasn't staying very long. She folded her arms across her chest and sat down next to him on the couch. She could see that he was not his usual cool as ice self. He seemed apprehensive.

"Would you like something to drink?" Maxine asked. Something was definitely wrong. The two were being as formal as if they'd just met. Maxine stepped into the kitchen to open a bottle of wine.

"You were right, Indira, he's married and he's about to break it off," Maxine said to herself as she slammed the drawer hard after retrieving the corkscrew. "Fuck this. I ought to just stick him with this right now," Maxine acted out the stabbing of Bruce with the corkscrew. She put it down fast on the counter. Bruce watched the television to pass the time. Maxine walked back into the living room carrying two glasses of white wine. Let's get this shit over with, she thought.

Bruce took his glass from Maxine. "Thanks."

Maxine sat down next to him and sipped her wine as he guzzled his. "Are you all right, Bruce? You seem a little shaken or something."

Bruce swallowed the last of his wine. "I've just been having a lot of things on my mind. I have some things I need to tell you." Bruce was a bold and confident man. This wasn't the first time he'd had to give this speech. Maxine was different from all the others, but he was the same. Maxine focused her attention on him as he placed the flute on the coffee table.

"I haven't been totally honest with you, Maxine. But I wasn't lying when I said I'd fallen in love with you. There's just one problem, I'm married."

Maxine jumped to her feet and moved away from Bruce. She didn't want to be near him just in case she did snap.

"You see, Bruce, this is exactly what I was talking about. Just lying all the damn time, not caring who gets hurt by the lies, just as long as you have a good time." Maxine began to pace her Asian rug. She'd planned to keep her cool. But when he said some shit like that, the plan fell through. "Is that supposed to be some sort of conciliation prize or something?" Maxine stopped her pacing and came toward Bruce.

"Am I supposed to be happy that you're in love with me? Bruce you just told me after nearly one month that you're married. That's fucked up."

Bruce reached for his coat on the arm of the couch.

Maxine continued, “I thought about sticking you with that fuckin’ corkscrew in the kitchen. I should have done it.”

Bruce put on his coat without any worry of harm coming to him. He knew she wasn’t stupid.

“You need to tone down your language. You sound like a sailor,” Bruce put on his scarf, and made his way to the door.

“You didn’t mind it when I was riding your tired ass.”

Bruce laughed and shook his head. “I’ll be leaving now. I’m sorry we had to end like this. I wanted us to keep in touch.”

Maxine opened the door wide for Bruce.

“I don’t need any friends like you. Oh, sorry, like your ass.”

Bruce made it out the door just as it was closing behind him. Maxine leaned on the back of the closed door.

“Damn, I knew it was coming and it still hurt.” Maxine poured another glass of wine for herself.

“Why didn’t I know he was married sooner?” She took a swallow of her wine.

“Maybe I just didn’t want to know he was married.” She stared into the air and thought about what had just happened.

“Who is he to tell me I need to tone down? He was just trying to hurt my feelings. Forget his ass.” Maxine took her glass into the living room, and relaxed on the couch. It was too early to head upstairs to bed.

*****

Sydney rose out of bed bright and early to get her sweet potato pies into the oven. She’d been cooking all night and still wasn’t done. There were only a few more things left to do before the meal could be complete. She pulled down a crystal platter from the top of the cabinets, another gift Ms. Mable bestowed upon her.

“After I finish the deviled eggs, I will make the punch and take a shower before Jasmine gets up.” Sydney wiped her hands on the apron she wore over her pajamas and began setting the dining table.

“Let’s see, Indira, Papa Joe, Maxine, Wayne, Ms. Lee, and me.” Sydney placed her fine china on the table in between the perfectly aligned silverware.

"My table looks as good as yours, Martha," she said proudly. She'd even put a setting on Jasmine's high chair. Sydney checked the clock to see that she had plenty of time. It was just eight thirty. She could get some rest before her company arrived. She set her alarm clock so she wouldn't let the pies burn up. Sleep didn't seem to be coming Sydney's way as she lay in her bed. As she closed her eyes, her mind began to find another place to be. She dreamed of days like this, preparing Thanksgiving dinner for Indira, Papa Joe, Maxine, Wayne, Ms. Lee, Mama, and Anthony—her family, the whole family, sitting around her table enjoying her food and each other.

Sydney wanted her family back more than anything. She needed her mother more than she ever imagined she could. But her mother couldn't forgive her. Why couldn't Virginia forgive her only daughter? Her only living child. It wasn't Sydney's fault that Eric was hooked on dope, but Sydney had introduced him to her boyfriend Anthony. Sydney kept her eyes closed as she journeyed back to her brother's life. Eric started buying his dope from Anthony. Virginia blamed Sydney for his addiction, for bringing it into her home, and eventually for his death. When Sydney told her mother that she was pregnant, Virginia kicked her out of the house.

Sydney held her head and opened her eyes as tears filled them. She was in love with a drug dealer, a menace to society, and a young man.

"I'm sorry, Eric," she said aloud.

When Anthony left the city for good, Sydney knew her brother's death was not her fault. Eric had started using drugs to escape his life and his failures in it. He flunked out of college and couldn't hold a job.

Sydney sat up on her bed just as the alarm clock sounded. She hadn't slept at all. She only thought about the past. She wiped the tears from her face and got up to turn off the stove and sit the pies out to cool.

Virginia was a part of this, too, if I'm to blame, Sydney thought as she peeked in on Jasmine, who was still asleep. She stayed up a little too late last night.

Sydney lathered her body with her Calgon body wash as the water beat down against it. She knew that things would have been much different if Anthony hadn't left her. He sold drugs on the corner all day and all through the night. When the two of them got together, Sydney was vulnerable and lonely. Indira had gone off to art school in Atlanta, and Maxine didn't have much time for her anymore since she had opened her hair salon. Home wasn't the place to be either. Her mother was struggling to keep her family away from the streets and she was losing her mind as well as the battle.

Hanging out on the streets of Dexter with Anthony filled the void in Sydney's life. There was an awful price to pay for dealing drugs. Your back was never safe. Anthony was coming up strong, and making all the money he could to the dismay of the rival dealers.

Sydney remembered back to one of the hottest days of that year. Steam hovered just above the black pavement. The tension had gotten so thick in the neighborhood. Crack had destroyed the community and the people who lived in it. The fond memories of boys playing on the same little league football teams had vanished. Those same boys were now drug dealers on different teams. The rumor on the streets was that Anthony had been picked up by the police and had to give up some names to be let go.

Sydney and Eric had been sitting on the front porch of their home and had watched Anthony and his crew posted up on the corner. That particular day just wasn't right to Sydney. She was feeling sick to her stomach. She blamed it on the heat, and turned her attention back to her boyfriend. Jerome had joined the boys on the corner. Sydney could see that he was upset and shouting to Anthony about something. He was in Anthony's face arguing with him.

"What now?" Sydney had wondered as she stepped off of the porch with her arms folded across her chest. Eric followed her with their mother watching closely from behind the screened door. Virginia didn't like what was happening to their neighborhood, and she didn't like her daughter messing around with the cause.

Sydney stayed in front of the house as Eric made his way over to the corner. Anthony pushed Jerome to the ground, and then turned to give Eric a pound, as if nothing had happened. Jerome hurried to his feet and tried to rush Anthony. Eric warned him in time enough for him to beat Jerome until he was black and blue. Anthony kicked Jerome with his fresh Air Jordan's and walked away from him. Sydney watched Anthony beat Jerome like some sort of mad man. She threw up in the yard and was close to falling out. Jerome pulled himself up off the ground vowing to return for Anthony. Eric and Anthony walked over to Sydney.

"Are you all right, baby?" Anthony helped Sydney onto the porch.

"I saw you fighting Jerome, and the next thing I knew I was throwing up." Sydney turned quickly as her mother opened the door.

"What is he doing on my porch, Sydney?" Virginia knew what Anthony was about, and didn't want her children to have anything to do with him.

"He was just helping me onto the porch, Mama."

Eric slipped by his mother at the door and eased into his bedroom with his package. Anthony stood up slowly, and stepped down the steps. He waved and kept talking to Sydney, though her mother had come outside to confront him.

"Get from in front of my house before I call the police on you."

Anthony blew a kiss to Virginia out of disrespect to her and began heading back to his trap.

"Are you that stupid, Sydney? Can't you see that boy ain't nothing but trouble?" Virginia's words were in and out of Sydney's ears. Before Sydney could answer her mother, she heard the screeching of car tires coming fast up the street toward Anthony. Sydney yelled at the top of her lungs.

"Anthony!"

Bullets rang out on the street as the boys ran in every direction. The car disappeared into a cloud of smoke. Sydney ran off of the porch with her mother screaming behind her. There were two bodies that remained on the ground as Anthony got up dusting his clothes off. Sirens could be heard getting closer to the street. Anthony waved to Sydney and took off.

The shower began turning colder as Sydney stood in deep thought under its rain. "Damn." She hurriedly shut the water off and wrapped a towel around her body. That day had been burned into Sydney's brain forever. It was the last time she saw Anthony and the last time she saw her brother alive. He overdosed in his bedroom that same night on the dope that he'd bought from Anthony.

Sydney flushed her face with cold water, and then stared deeply into the mirror.

"Snap out of it, girl and forget about him for one day." Sydney took a deep breath and started getting herself together.

"Jasmine will be up in no time."

CHAPTER FOURTEEN

Maxine arrived early at her aunt's house with the hopes of missing her many cousins. She didn't. All six of them were already there, along with their families.

"Hey, everybody," Maxine stepped into the kitchen and hugged her aunt.

"Well hello, Maxine." The women were all crowded into the kitchen watching Aunt Betsy as if she were putting on some sort of play or something. Her cousin Bonnie spoke first, and then the others followed.

"I'm so glad you could make it, baby," Aunt Betsy tried to keep the family together like her mother asked her to do. Maxine was her only niece and she didn't want to lose her, too. Eddie Jr. was the oldest, and then there was Edmond and Erica—the "E's." Her aunt's first three children's names all started with an "E," after their father. Then there were the "B's"—Bonnie, Bonita and Bertice, the youngest of the bunch. Maxine hadn't been very close to her family since her grandmother died. They were always jealous of her for being grandma's favorite. Maxine followed the rest of the family to the table, and found her name tag next to her cousin Eddie Jr. He was always pretty cool with her. He was older than all of them, so he tried to act like he had some sense.

"How have you been, Max?" Eddie asked, as his wife Monique looked dead into her mouth awaiting an answer.

"I've been busy at the salon, and that's about it." Maxine could see that she had the attention of the entire table.

"I've been meaning to stop by. I pass it on my way to work," Edmund's wife Neico eased her way into the conversation.

"Me too, Maxine. I could use a new look," said Bonita.

Maxine knew it wouldn't be long before her archenemy since birth, Bonita, joined in. The same age, born only two days apart, they were destined to be in competition with one another. Maxine had a successful business, but Bonita had a husband who adored her, and two beautiful daughters. She was in the lead by a landslide right now.

"You're welcome to come on in anytime," Maxine was trying to be cordial. She couldn't relax because they were all being so plastic.

"Still looking for Mr. Right?" Bonita turned and laughed with Bertice.

"Am I what?" Maxine caught her tongue as Aunt Betsy made her grand entrance from the kitchen with the beautifully browned turkey. Maxine would be on her treadmill for sure in the morning. Between her aunt's and Sydney's cooking, she was guaranteed to put on at least six pounds.

"That looks fabulous, Mama," Bonita said.

Betsy sat the bird on the table next to a great assortment of dishes. She could feel the tension in the room. Nothing had changed in more than twenty years. It was obvious that Maxine still didn't get along with her cousins. She and the boys had always gotten along fine, but those cats on the other hand were something else. Maxine never got over the numerous pranks that the quartet of sisters played upon her, time after time.

"All right, everybody. Everything is on the table, and I am ready to eat," Edmond said as he stood and held out a chair for his mother at the head of the table. She'd taken over the seat after Eddie Sr. died. It was rightfully hers to begin with.

"Me, too. I don't get cooking like this at home very often," Lawrence looked to Bonnie and smirked. She didn't find his comment very funny, especially not in front of her sisters. Maxine laughed some, as Eddie nudged her to look at her cousin checking her husband with her eyes.

"Carl. Would you say the blessing, please?" Aunt Betsy asked.

Erica had married herself a big time preacher. He had his own television show and all. She told Maxine once, that being married to a preacher was like being married to an athlete. He had plenty of groupies, too. On top of that, he had the nerve to be extremely fine and charming.

"Yes ma'am. I would be honored." Carl lifted out of his chair, holding his tie to his chest. "Let's all bow our heads and hold hands."

Thanks to Aunt Betsy's seating chart I was safely holding hands with Neico. The many grandchildren sat in the adjoining room at their designated tables doing the same.

"Lord, thank you for this beautiful day and the gathering of this family. Thank you for the abundance of food and love amongst us. We give all praises and glory to you, Lord. Amen," Carl sat back down in his chair.

"Amen." Erica hugged Carl's arm, but he didn't seem affected.

"Then, let's get started," Aunt Betsy winked to her niece and began passing dishes around the table. Maxine took a light helping of everything. She had to leave room for Sydney's food, too. Her feelings got hurt if you didn't eat her food.

*****

Indira pulled her sweater over her head, and checked herself once again in the mirror. For the first time in six years she was going to be without Robert for the holidays. It was not as if he'd been such great company, even then. But, at least he was there.

He was there. Don't I sound stupid? she thought.

Indira loved Robert, but why did she stay and take his abuse? Indira fluffed her long tresses in the mirror and thought to herself. Was it that she loved the thought of being married?

"Yes, and I will never make that mistake again." She had come to grips with reality, Robert was gone and he wasn't coming back. The phone rang just as she started applying her lipstick.

"Hello," Indira continued her task, unconcerned with who was on the other line.

"Hello, Indira. It's Eldridge."

Indira dropped her lipstick on her vanity table when she heard his deep voice.

"El, what a surprise!"

Eldridge was glad to hear Indira sound so happy to hear from him. He didn't want to seem like he was pestering her or something.

"Well, Happy Thanksgiving." He knew he sounded corny, but being in love made people do that. He knew he'd fallen in love with Indira the minute he stepped on the plane to leave her.

"The same to you. So what have you been up to, superstar?"

Eldridge laughed at Indira. "Nothing really. I just wanted to let you know that I will be in town the week of Christmas." He paused for a moment, "I would like to see you again, Indira."

Indira reveled over her smile in the mirror at the thought.

"I would love to see you, El."

Eldridge was relieved to hear Indira's answer. With everything that had happened to her in the past few weeks, he didn't know what to expect. "That's great. I will call you soon and let you know my plans."

Indira felt good about her relationship with Eldridge, and began to look forward to seeing him already.

"Have a Happy Thanksgiving and don't eat too much," he said.

Indira was smiling from ear to ear. "I'll talk to you soon. Bye." She hung up the phone and patted herself on the back.

"Bravo. Only days after being served your divorce papers, you, Indira Carr, are back in the game," Indira clapped her hands together and cheered. She grabbed her purse and coat and headed over to Sydney's.

*****

The family seemed to be growing larger and larger with the passing years, causing the food to disappear faster than ever before. The table was nearly empty on the first go round, and you could see it on the faces around the table. There was never a lot of food in the house because too many people lived there. Maxine wasn't worried. She would get her fill at Sydney's.

"So, Maxine, are you still with Billy?"

Maxine recognized the voice right away and turned to Bonita sitting on the other side of the table. Good move on her aunt's part, Maxine thought.

"No. I'm not with Billy anymore, Bonita," Maxine smiled and went back to her candied yams.

"Well, don't you think you'd better get started looking again?" Bonita continued her attack.

Why is this bitch starting with me? Maxine questioned herself.

"That's right. Your clock ought to be clicking loud in your ears by now," Bertice added her jokes and pointed to her sister.

Maxine had to cut them down quick.

"Well, I just didn't want to marry any old lame for the sake of saying I'm married. No pun intended," Maxine smirked to her opponents.

"Good come back," Eddie Jr. whispered in her ear.

The girls just turned their mouths up and glanced at their husbands who fit her description to a tee. Aunt Betsy slammed her fork and knife on the table loudly, grabbing the attention of the entire room.

She'll Learn

"I am so sick and tired of listening to you put down one another with all these smart remarks and going-ons. Why in the world can't you all be nice to each other sometimes?" Aunt Betsy shook her head as she eyed her daughters and her niece.

"Don't you girls…I'm sorry…women know what's more important than all this pettiness?"

Maxine felt like a child being scolded for being bad, but she was right. They were behaving like children. Maxine hadn't seen her aunt that upset in years, and from the looks of things, neither had her cousins.

Aunt Betsy continued, "Your family and your circle of friends are the most important things in life. We all need some place to belong, especially women. We need to connect to something and be able to go to that place whenever we need to. Togetherness offers women a time to vent, to give and receive support, express themselves, and to comfort one another through the trials and tribulations of life."

The entire room was focused on the words of wisdom that flowed out of Aunt Betsy's mouth. Maxine was seeing her aunt for the first time. Her words were attaching to her brain and making sense right away. She was right. Maxine needed her family and her friends.

"Women aren't looking for solutions to their problems, only friendship," Aunt Betsy looked into the eyes of all the women sitting around her table. Each of her daughters was on the brink of tears. They were hearing her loud and clear, too. The room fell silent. "We are a family, and I want to see you act like one. That's all I have to say." Aunt Betsy went back to eating her dinner without so much as looking up from her plate again.

"I'm sorry, Aunt Betsy," Maxine spoke softly. Aunt Betsy looked up and nodded to her as an acceptance of her apology. The green-eyed bandits lingered on the fact that Maxine apologized first.

"We're all sorry, too, mother," Bonnie spoke for all her sisters. They couldn't fool the pro, Aunt Betsy knew her words had vanished in the air before reaching them. Maxine checked the grandfather clock that stood in the hallway. It was after two o'clock. She would head over to Sydney's soon to get out of this soap opera. After a few moments of silence, forks and knives began clinking noisily again as everyone served themselves the dessert and coffee that was on the table. Aunt Betsy excused herself from the table with Maxine watching her. Maxine knew what was next—the bathroom session. Growing up in her grandmother's house, there was never any privacy. Even the bathroom served as a place for discussion.

"Maxine!" Aunt Betsy was yelling her name from the bathroom down the hall. With the envious eyes of her cousins on her, Maxine got up from the table. Slowly, she opened the door to the bathroom to see her aunt sitting on the toilet. All of their talks usually took place in there.

"Yes, ma'am," Maxine leaned against the sink and checked herself in the mirror to avoid looking directly at her aunt. She didn't have to look. She could feel her.

"I've been thinking about you a lot lately, Maxine. I want to tell you that God has blessed you in so many ways and I want you to turn all your woes over to him," Aunt Betsy paused in her speech for a moment of struggle. Maxine was now staring at her aunt on the toilet.

"Are you okay?" Maxine asked, though she knew it was just part of the procedure. Maxine ignored the stench that was growing stronger in her nostrils.

"Yes, baby. I'm fine. It's you that I'm worried about."

"I'm fine, Aunt Betsy. I have good and bad days like everyone else," Maxine turned back to her reflection in the mirror.

"Me and your Uncle Eddie were married for 35 years before he died, and I miss him something terrible sometimes. I get lonely sometimes, too."

"I'm not lonely, Aunt Betsy. I have the salon and I've got my girls." Her reflection didn't lie. The truth was in her eyes. She was lonely. Maxine turned away quickly.

"I spoke with your mother again, Maxine."

Maxine nearly swallowed her tongue. Her mother served as a sore spot for her heart.

"She asked about you."

Maxine dropped her eyes to the floor. She didn't know what to feel about her mother. She was filled with discontent for her. Though Maxine's grandmother never spoke ill of her mother, Maxine never forgave her for leaving her.

She'll Learn

"What did she want?" Maxine couldn't hide the anger in her voice. Betsy recognized it right away, as she washed her hands.

"She's not doing well, Maxine." Betsy hoped this conversation with her niece could be a little easier. "She's got AIDS, and she doesn't have long to live." Betsy towel dried her hands and spoke without ever looking Maxine's way.

"Oh, my God," Maxine uttered as she sort of fell against the towel rack. She never forgave her mother for leaving her, but she wouldn't wish the disease on her worst enemies.

"I've known for a while now, but I wanted to tell you face to face." Betsy could see that her niece didn't know how she should really feel. "There's one more thing, Maxine."

Maxine turned her eyes to her aunt.

"She wants to see you," Betsy watched as Maxine dropped her eyes back to the floor.

"I don't know about that, Aunt Betsy. It's taken all these years for me to get over her leaving, and now I'm supposed to want to see her?" Maxine threw her hands up in disgust.

"I know it's something hard for you, but there are a lot of bumps on the road of life." Betsy sat down on the chair of her vanity table given to her last Mother's Day by her oldest son. Maxine stared at the floor in silence.

"She'll be staying here with me."

Maxine lifted her eyes from the floor.

"I'm alone here in this house so I can take care of my big sister. She took care of me." Betsy reached out her hand for Maxine. "Please, Maxine. Just think about it."

Maxine took hold of her aunt's hand and then hugged her. "I will."

*****

Indira stared out the window at the falling snow. It snowed just about every Thanksgiving Day in Detroit from as far back as she could remember. The turkey day football games wouldn't be right without it, even though the Lions played inside of a dome. Indira couldn't take her mind off of Robert. Finding out that Robert was dying had put Indira in a state of unease. She wondered how long he had known and why he didn't want her to know. She asked these same questions over and over in her head. Her eyes began to fill with water. She fell back to reality just as Jasmine slammed into her legs.

"Hold me," Jasmine stood all dressed up in her dark green velveteen dress with her arms stretched out to Indira. She looked like an expensive doll.

"Okay, big girl," Indira picked the two year old up, nearly dropping her.

"You've been eating too much of your mama's cooking, Pudgy."

Jasmine made herself comfortable on Indira's lap.

"What are you two in here doing?" Sydney noticed Jasmine half-asleep on Indira's lap, giving her the opportunity to find out how her friend was doing.

"Jasmine is trying to get a little nap," Indira rubbed her back lightly, and then smiled at Sydney.

"You're a natural, Indira," Sydney walked over to the window and looked out to the street. "Maxine will be here in a little while. I'd better put up a custard for her. I don't feel like getting cursed out."

Wayne watched Sydney instead of the football game playing on the small television set. Sydney noticed his eyes on her and smiled to him, giving him all the satisfaction he needed. He couldn't remember when exactly, but he'd fallen in love with her. He knew deep inside that this wasn't a good thing for him. During their entire relationship, Sydney had continuously stressed to him that she only wanted to be friends. As he watched her bending over to talk with Indira, he could only hope things would change.

*****

Maxine subconsciously drove the slick streets. Her eyes were on the road, but her mind was on her mother. Her mother…that concept had evaded her thoughts for many years. She had taught herself to think of her mother as dead. Now, she had AIDS and was going to die. Maxine stopped suddenly at a red light. After nearly ten years, her mother wanted to see her. Maxine gripped the steering wheel of her truck tightly as her heart began to rise.

"Why now, Mama?" Maxine's heart was hurting from Bruce's footprints, and now this.

Bomp! Bomp!

She'll Learn

Maxine looked in her rearview mirror to see an old man becoming frantic with his horn. The light had turned green without Maxine knowing. She saw the light as it turned yellow, and then punched the gas pedal of her SUV. The light turned red, stranding the other car. Maxine looked back sympathetically at the man and continued on to Sydney's.

Maxine climbed the steep stairwell, which seemed to never end, up to Sydney's apartment. Before she could lift her tired fist to knock on the door, Sydney opened it, greeting her with a smile.

"Happy Thanksgiving, Maxine," Sydney was full of holiday cheer. These were the types of days she lived for.

"Yeah, yeah. Happy Thanksgiving," Maxine felt her spirit pick up as she watched Jasmine blowing bubbles to Papa Joe.

"Hey, woman," Indira hugged Maxine. Maxine was glad to see that Indira was looking much better.

"Hey, Indira. You're looking good today." Maxine and Indira walked into the dining room shoulder to shoulder.

"I'm doing good, that's why." Indira smiled and joined Jasmine in her bubble play.

"Hello, Papa Joe…Wayne," Maxine touched the man's shoulder.

"Brown Sugar," Papa Joe jumped with surprise, and then rose out of his chair to hug Maxine. "You are just in time for the second go-round." Papa Joe pulled out the chair next to him for Maxine to sit down.

"Thanks." Maxine smiled to Wayne jokingly.

"Max," Jasmine stopped blowing bubbles to acknowledge her.

"Hey, Pudgy. You look so pretty, all dressed up."

Jasmine nodded her head in agreement. Sydney sat down at the wooden dining table she'd found while out thrift store shopping with Papa Joe.

"I put you a sweet potato pie to the side, for later," Sydney told Maxine.

Papa Joe and Wayne were working on fresh plates of food.

"Thank you. It's nice to know that I'm loved by somebody." Maxine's plate was full, her mental plate. The news of her drug addict mother having AIDS pushed her breakup with Bruce to the edge.

"Uh, oh," Sydney looked to Indira who met her eyes with worried ones of her own. "What are you talking about, Maxine?"

Indira sat next to Jasmine playing with her ice-cream dessert. Maxine's emotions were in a bundle and she didn't know what she was feeling. This wasn't something she wanted to keep inside.

"Maureen has AIDS."

Papa Joe and Wayne simultaneously put their forks down. Indira covered her mouth.

"Oh, my God, Maxine…that's terrible. How did you find out?" Sydney came to Maxine's side.

"Aunt Betsy gave me one of her famous bathroom talks and told me," Maxine sort of laughed as she spoke, and then took a sip of water designated for anyone dining at the setting. Sydney made sure that everything was perfect and in its place.

"That's not all. She wants to see me," Maxine looked to Indira with a knowing smile.

"Are you going to see her, Maxine?" Indira spoke up quickly, but in a soothing voice. The entire room was awaiting Maxine's response. Even Jasmine had stopped playing in her ice-cream to listen to the grown-up conversation.

"I don't know. I just haven't had time to think. It's been so long since I've even seen Maureen." Maxine folded her hands high on the table and rested her heavy head on them.

"I can remember back when Maureen was going to high school over here at uh…uh," Papa Joe looked to anyone in the room for a jump-start to his memory, "Central High School," Papa Joe snapped his fingers. "I still got it. Anyway, your mother was so full of life back then. She was kind and real sweet to everybody, just like your grandmother. Unlike Mable, her oldest daughter was very naïve."

Sydney sat back down at the table to finish listening to her father's memories.

"Your mother and me had just moved to the neighborhood. I don't think we'd been there a good month before Maureen started hanging around these two thugs."

Maxine listened closely. There were so many things she didn't know about her mother. She needed to know about her now, more than ever before.

"What thugs?" Maxine asked eagerly.

"Larry and Snipes. They caused a lot of problems in the neighborhood and nobody ever understood how she got mixed up with them." Papa Joe loved a crowd. He had everyone's attention. But, this time his story wasn't for the attention. It was for Maxine. The old man took a swig of his beer.

Jasmine yawned loudly, catching the story's brief intermission. "Hold me, mommy."

Sydney rushed over to her daughter and picked her up.

"My juice," Jasmine whined, her habit when overcome by sleep. Sydney retrieved Jasmine's sippy cup, and then hurriedly sat back down as if she were holding up the story. Indira watched Jasmine curl up in her mother's arms and close her eyes.

"They bought her things and took her places. She was young and pretty. Those two turned your mother on to heroine." Papa Joe was leaning closer to Maxine. He was speaking directly to her.

"Your grandmother did all she could for your mother, but it was too much for her to bear. She still had to take care of her kids. Maureen ran away with Larry and Snipes, not to be heard from in two or three years." Papa Joe looked around the room as he spoke. "When she came back home, she was beaten up and rundown. And she was pregnant with you."

Maxine jumped back when Papa Joe pointed his slender wrinkled finger at her.

"Mable had given her burden to God long before Maureen came back, so she was ready for her when she returned. Maureen cleaned herself up for a while, and then she started to drift back to her old ways. Crack was the new thing in the streets and Maureen became one of the many that got immediately hooked on its power. That shit ruined everything around here. Dexter hasn't been able to hold its head up high in a long while," Papa Joe stopped talking and shook his head. Indira looked to Sydney for an answer. Maxine still watched the balding man sitting next to her. Her grandmother always had good things to say about him, but not his wife.

"Are you telling me that one of these men could be my father?" Maxine anxiously awaited Papa Joe's answer. She never knew of her father. That subject was never encouraged around the house.

"Nobody ever knew, because you looked just like your mother."

Damn, when it rained it poured, Maxine thought. Her plate runneth over.

"This is too much for me to handle right now. I've got plenty of other shit on my mind." Maxine sat back in her chair roughly.

"You have to go see her, Maxine, if you ever want to know anything about your mother, about yourself, for that matter." Indira was uncharacteristically peeved. "Stop being so damn selfish for once, and talk to your mother." Indira had spoken without thinking. Sydney prepared herself for Maxine's wrath. To their surprise, there was nothing. Maxine only stared at the lace tablecloth that once belonged to her grandmother.

"I don't feel so good." Maxine rushed up from the table and dashed into the bathroom, letting out her entire meal from her aunt's house. She lifted her head out of the toilet to see Indira standing at the sink. "Those greens didn't taste right from the beginning," Maxine blamed her sickness on her Aunt Betsy's cooking.

"Are you sure that's it? You and Bruce have been romping around quite a bit. You can tell me," Indira kneeled down to Maxine and wiped her face with a wet towel. Maxine accepted the cool sensation on her forehead.

"We broke up last night," Maxine dropped her head back into the toilet and threw up again.

"Oh shit, Maxine. Why didn't you tell me? I'm sorry." Indira rubbed the damp cloth on the back of Maxine's neck. "Damn. I guess we're both single women again." Indira sort of laughed as Maxine pulled herself off the floor. Sydney stepped in through the door.

"What's up with you? What did you eat over at Aunt Betsy's? She didn't catch on to the cooking thing too well, huh?" Sydney put her hand on Maxine's shoulder as she splashed her face with cold water.

"Maxine and Bruce broke up last night." Indira filled Sydney in on the news before she could put her foot into her mouth like she had.

"What? Damn. Is it possible for anybody to be happy anymore?" Sydney sat down on the edge of the tub.

"What happened?" Indira asked as she flushed the toilet and then rested on the closed lid.

"Remember when we were at lunch talking about married men? Well he's one of them." Maxine lifted her face slowly from the sink then dried it lightly with a towel. "Sydney, it is entirely too bright in here. This shit would drive me crazy every morning. You went too damn far with the sunshine theme." Maxine straightened herself up in the mirror. Then she reached for the bottle of mouthwash on the shelf.

"I like it. Sometimes it picks me up just when I need it the most," Sydney ignored Maxine's comments. This was her favorite room.

Indira read the affirmations that hung along the wall above the towel rack. The words inside a yellow frame caught her eye.

"Love and honor thy mother and father," Indira glanced over to Maxine coyly.

"You never let up, do you? I said I'll think about it." Maxine opened the door quickly and made her way to the couch. Indira and Sydney lagged behind her.

"The sun is right up on you in there," Indira said as she playfully squeezed her friend's shoulders as they walked into the living room where Maxine was residing.

Knock. Knock.

The light rapping on the door caught everyone off guard. Sydney had sat down already, so Indira headed toward the door.

"Who is it?" Indira placed her ear near the door. After a few silent moments, a man's voice responded. Anthony was unsure of what he was doing there. He never completed his plan in his mind. He swallowed hard.

"Is Sydney here?"

Indira leaned closer to the door. "Can I say who's asking?" Indira turned to Sydney in the living room. She was busy carrying Jasmine to her room.

Papa Joe had turned around in his chair to investigate what was going on for himself. Wayne had a clear view of the door from his chair. Anthony took a deep breath and held his head high.

"An old friend."

As the locks on the door became free, Anthony prepared himself for whatever was to come next. He wanted his family back, by whatever means necessary. Indira opened the door slightly to a pair of deep brown Timberland boots. Her eyes skipped the tour and rose to full view.

"An old friend, huh?" Indira slowly let the door open wider.

Anthony stepped into the apartment, hesitantly. He knew it well. Maxine lifted up from the couch to get the shock of her life.

"Well ain't this a bitch?"

"Hello to you too, Maxine," Anthony stood in the middle of the apartment and let his eyes roam his old crib. The memories of the place flooded his mind so quickly he didn't see Sydney walk out of the bedroom they used to share.

"Anthony," Sydney gasped for air loudly when she saw her lost love standing in her living room. Anthony let his eyes take their time finding Sydney. He had been waiting to see her for so long, he wanted it to be the same. He was pleasantly surprised to see that Sydney was the same beautiful girl he'd fallen in love with years ago. Sydney ran over to Anthony without thinking, and wrapped her arms around his neck.

"Sydney."

The two held each other in a long embrace. It seemed even longer to Wayne. He had a front-row seat to the end of his happiness. The man Sydney loved had returned. Wayne felt his chest tighten. Sydney pushed herself away from Anthony. The pain and hurt he'd caused her rushed back into her body.

"Wait, Sydney. I came to say I'm sorry and to…" Anthony was losing his confidence. His chest began to drop from that level he had placed it on in the hallway.

"And to what, Anthony? See your daughter, whose birthday, by the way was last weekend?" Maxine wasn't sick anymore. She felt good enough to cut into Anthony, knowing that Sydney wouldn't. She'd been praying for the son of a bitch to come back since the day he left.

That did it. His chest was back to normal. Maxine always had that affect on him. Her tongue cut like a knife and he'd been sliced before. He looked past Maxine and walked over to Sydney.

"Look, Sydney. Can I talk to you, alone? Please."

Those hazel eyes she'd missed so much were pleading with her. They still spoke to her without him ever saying a word. Wayne looked on quietly. He knew it wasn't his place to say anything.

"Hell, no, you can't talk to her alone. Sydney can listen to your shit right here in front of us," Maxine made her way off of the couch and into the living room. Her voice had become loud and violent. Sydney was calm and poised. There was no need to yell and scream just yet.

"Okay. Let's go into the back," Sydney told Anthony.

Maxine could see that Sydney was in a haze already. She should've been tearing into him, right then, but she wasn't.

"What? Go in the back?" Maxine got louder as she questioned Sydney.

"Stay out of it, Maxine," Papa Joe spoke up from the dining room. Anthony turned his eyes to that familiar voice. He nodded after hearing Papa Joe speak. He never gave Anthony any problems. Virginia was enough of a headache for anybody. Plus, Papa Joe knew that Sydney loved him. Anthony walked over to the old man as Maxine reluctantly backed down. Indira motioned for her to come and sit by her on the couch.

"Sit down, and shut up," Indira whispered to Maxine.

"You shut up. Who does he think he is?" Maxine eyed her enemy shaking Papa Joe's hand then following Sydney into the kitchen. The sliding door was shut for privacy. Sydney took a deep breath, and then turned around to face Anthony. He was still fine as hell and still dressed like he was rapping on stage. She couldn't let that deter her right now. Right now, she had to be strong and let him know how she felt inside.

"Sydney, I…"

Sydney put her index finger on his lips. Her touch awakened his body simultaneously.

"You missed your daughter's second birthday by one week and two years. Oh, but you've never even seen your daughter," Sydney tried to keep her voice calm.

"Sydney, I feel so damn bad, man. I love you and I have never stopped loving you," Anthony turned his back to her and stepped toward the stove. "Everything was happening so fast. I'm so sorry I left you, Sydney." Anthony made his way over to her and cupped her face in his hands lovingly. "I made the biggest mistake of my life."

Sydney's eyes had filled with painful tears, but she stood strong.

"You sure did, Anthony." Sydney removed his hands from her face. They were rough and callous, unlike the days of easy money.

"You left me when I was pregnant, Anthony. My brother died that night. I died that night." The tears rolled down her cheeks as Anthony watched in dismay. Anthony was someone new. Sydney had grown up and became a woman when he wasn't looking. She couldn't change her toothpaste without Anthony knowing, when they were together. Now, he didn't know her at all.

"Sorry just won't get it this time, Anthony," Sydney let the tears pour as she stood before him.

"Can I see my daughter?" Anthony had not once ever seen his only child. He hoped she looked just like her mother. Sydney wiped her eyes, and then shook her head yes.

The sliding door came apart slowly as all eyes watched Sydney and Anthony come out of the kitchen and walk to the bedroom. Sydney never looked at anyone. She only led Anthony to see his daughter.

"I hope she knows what she's doing," Maxine folded her arms in disgust.

"And, you do?" Indira replied sarcastically.

Maxine smacked her lips loudly. She turned her attention back to the two, just as the bedroom door closed softly.

"I think I'm going to go on and get out of here," Wayne said as he slid away from the table.

"All right now, Wayne." Papa Joe watched Wayne walk to the door with his heart dragging far behind him.

"Hey, there," Papa Joe called out to the young man. "Don't give up too easily. You never know what the divine plan may be."

Wayne nodded his head, and then slipped out the front door. He didn't bother to say goodbye to Indira and Maxine.

"Well. No need in just waiting by the door. Let's start cleaning up," Indira said as she leaped off the couch, pulling on Maxine's arm.

"I'm sick, Indira, remember?" Maxine was on her feet.

"Come on. You can tell me what you can do for my hair. I need a new look," Indira touched Papa Joe's shoulder as she passed his chair to the kitchen.

CHAPTER FIFTEEN

Jasmine lay spread out in the center of the queen-size bed, the same bed that she was conceived in. Anthony was smiling from ear to ear. His daughter. He'd wondered what she looked like. She was beautiful. She seemed to have split them straight down the middle.

"She has my eyes, and your nose and mouth," Anthony got down on one knee beside the bed, "and your beautiful hair." He touched his daughter's head, and then looked up at Sydney. Sydney stood smiling at him. She stopped suddenly.

"You've done so good, Sydney. She's looks so healthy." Anthony didn't feel like a man, right now. He felt like a weakling. Sydney proved she could do whatever was necessary to raise their daughter. He wanted his chance to prove that he could do the same. He closed his eyes and thought about his child and the woman standing before him.

"Baby, I am so sorry for leaving you. I was afraid and I ran away," Anthony said to Sydney as he kissed Jasmine's cheek, and then got to his feet. Sydney was beginning to loosen up. She could see that Anthony's feelings were genuine.

"I know you were scared, Anthony, but so was I." Sydney sat down on the edge of the bed. "I loved you with all my heart. You were the last person that I thought would ever abandon me." Sydney let her head drop.

Anthony didn't know where to go next. He knew things would take time. He moved close to Sydney and took a knee in front of her.

"I never stopped loving you, Sydney. You're my boo, and now I've got a baby boo."

Sydney laughed halfheartedly, and then turned to look at their daughter.

"All I need is a chance, Sydney. A chance for me to prove that I can take care of my family," Anthony turned her face to him with his hands. Sydney stared into his eyes. Loving Anthony had been the hardest thing she'd ever done. His love brought heartache and pain, more than she wanted to handle.

"I don't know, Anthony. You just walked your ass back through that front door after two years, as if you had gone out to the store. You are more than just a little late." Sydney moved Anthony's hands from her face once again.

"Whatever you want, Sydney, I'm willing to do it. I want my family back." Anthony had begged enough for one day. His pride was now on his sleeve. It was obvious that Sydney wasn't just going to take him back today.

"I know you need time to think, so I'm gonna go. I'm staying at my sister's if you want to talk. But I'm not giving up baby, I'll be back." Anthony opened the bedroom door and stepped out into the hallway. Maxine and Indira came out of the kitchen to help him out the door.

"I hope she kicked your ass out and told you to never come back," Maxine was talking loud with her hand on her hip.

"Maxine, stop it." Indira walked toward the door behind Anthony.

"I'll be back. You can bet on that," Anthony said back to Maxine, and then eased out the front door.

Maxine bit her tongue. There was nothing for her to say. Sydney was still in the bedroom. Papa Joe opened the door quietly and then sat down next to his daughter on the bed. Papa Joe had seen this look of confusion on his daughter's face before. He put his arm around Sydney's shoulders.

"Is he gone, Daddy?" Sydney rested her spinning head on her father's arm. She could always find comfort there.

"Yeah, he's gone, and so is your friend."

With that realization Sydney lifted her head. "I can't believe I totally forgot about Wayne," Sydney put her head in her hands. "You see, Daddy. That boy just waltzed back into my life and messed things up that quickly." Sydney threw her hands up in disgust.

"We had some drama around here. I didn't think Anthony would ever come back. He's a better man than I thought he was." Papa Joe held onto his leather cap as he scratched his balding head.

"I hate to admit it, Daddy, but I still love Anthony more than any other man. But, I can't just let him step in and out of our lives whenever he gets ready. It's been two years, Daddy."

Jasmine was still sound asleep, so Sydney tried to keep her voice down.

Papa Joe said nothing and watched his daughter pace the floor of her bedroom.

"Your friend seemed hurt when he left."

Sydney stopped her pacing. "I didn't mean to hurt him, but what was I supposed to do? Not let the man see his daughter?" Sydney sat back down on the bed next to her father.

"No, you were right."

"That's the type of affect Anthony has on me. I didn't even realize that Wayne was gone." Sydney dropped her head again.

"We all have someone who does things to us. It's your mother, for me."

Sydney sort of laughed at that understatement. Her mother had more than just some affect on her father. She had him wrapped around her finger.

"Yeah, I know, Daddy." Sydney rubbed her father's leg sympathetically. Papa Joe eased himself off of the bed slowly, thanks to his ailing joints.

"I'm going on home now. Your mother fed the homeless today. She should be on her way home by now."

Sydney always thought her mother was a work of art. She loved the church more than life itself. Virginia cared and gave all her time to strangers, leaving her family to find their own sources of love. Sydney walked her father to the front door.

"Good night, girls. Y'all be careful going home tonight." Papa Joe placed his signature cap on top of his head.

"Good night, Papa Joe," Indira and Maxine sang in unison.

"Thanks for everything, Daddy," Sydney kissed her father's cheek, and then closed the door once he made it to the stairs. Sydney took her time with the door, because she could almost feel the eyes of two nosey women buried into her back like nails.

"All right. Bring it on," Sydney turned to face Indira and Maxine, who were not behind her after all. The two women had positioned themselves on the couch and chair. Sydney was sort of ticked by that move. Why weren't they interested in what happened? She stood over the women with her arms folded.

"What's up with you two?"

Maxine looked at Indira and smiled. "What? What's wrong?" Maxine was going along with Indira's game. Indira thought that some laughter might lighten the load on Sydney's shoulders.

"What's wrong, Syd?" Indira shrugged her shoulders. Sydney flopped down next to Indira on the verge of tears. Maxine rose from the chair.

"Girl, we just bullshittin' with you. We thought you might need to laugh some after that nigga showed up." Maxine placed her narrow frame on the arm of the couch.

"I'm sorry. We were just playing. You had one hell of a surprise tonight, girl," Indira playfully touched Sydney's leg.

"You ain't lying. I thought I would never have to see that face again," Maxine spoke frankly then nonchalantly got off of the arm of the couch.

"Hold up, Max. You don't have any right to talk about Anthony like that. He is Jasmine's father whether you like it or not," Sydney was staring coldly at her friend.

"I like it just fine. I was trying to look out for your ass. He left you two years ago, not me," Maxine let her emotions attack her friend prematurely. Sydney didn't deserve the lashing she had given her, but she was there.

Jasmine was calling for her mother just as Maxine caught Sydney's glare. In silence, Sydney went to her daughter in her bedroom. Indira sat with her mouth wide open.

"What the fuck is wrong with you, Max? Why did you go off on Sydney like that?" Indira had the stern voice of her mother. Maxine knew she had messed up and responded to it.

She ran her hands roughly over her crop and sat down in the recliner.

"I am going fucking crazy, Indira. So much has been going on. Of course your ass had to be right. Bruce is married with two daughters. We argued last night when I confronted him about it. That bastard's gone." Maxine closed her eyes and placed her hand over them. Sydney walked back into the room with Jasmine lying on her shoulder. Indira smiled to her reassuringly as she sat down.

Maxine continued, "And my mama is dying." Maxine felt a sharp sting in her heart. Her mother abandoned her. How could she be feeling anything for her?

"Maxine, you have to go see her. I mean you may never get a chance to again," Indira sat back into the couch with Jasmine. Arnelle lived a hard life, but she always had the love of her daughters.

Indira and Clarissa loved their mother more than life itself, but were pained to see the life beaten out of her by their father. Maxine held her face in her hands.

"Indira's right, Max. If my mother was sick, I would be by her side no matter what." The door to Sydney's emotions was unlocked, and Virginia and Anthony each had a set of keys.

"Why should I be by her side? She was never by mines?" Maxine reached for her wine glass on the table, and was angered by its emptiness. "Damn."

"Come on, Maxine, you don't hate your mother. You never did. You said it yourself that her leaving you with Ms. Mable was the best thing she could have ever done for you," Indira said as she placed Jasmine on the pillow next to her and covered her with the blanket.

"It was the best thing for all of us. None of our mothers are or were perfect, but they are still our mothers. Look at Virginia. She ain't so much as waved at my ass since God knows when. And we sit four pews behind each other in church every Sunday," Sydney nearly leaped out of her chair as she spoke. "But if her mean ass was sick, I'd still be there for her."

"I mean y'all can say that. Your mothers at least kept you with them. They didn't just drop your asses off somewhere and never came back. That bitch did. She fuckin' left me."

"Chill, Maxine," Sydney hated to see her friend upset like this. Even when they were kids, if Maxine was upset, Sydney was upset. "God only gonna gives you one mother, man." Sydney had been taught to honor her parents and love them. She knew someday those words would serve her well.

Maxine grabbed the thick twisted locks of hair on her head.

"I get so mad sometimes when I think about her. Maybe this is what she deserves to have happen to her ass. Fuck her." Maxine rose out of the chair and headed toward the kitchen where there was one more bottle of white wine in the fridge.

"No, Maxine. Don't say that. You don't mean that shit," Indira pleaded. Maxine didn't glance at her or Sydney. Indira's eyes stared into Maxine's back as she walked away.

"This is one fucked up Thanksgiving. First, Anthony nonchalantly waltzes his black ass up in here and now this. What kind of holiday is this? And damn, did I mess it up with Wayne or what?" Sydney vented.

Maxine returned with a freshly opened bottle of wine and began filling all of their glasses, spilling wine around them and onto the table. "Yeah, honey. You can count him out," Maxine said, agreeing.

Sydney watched in amazement as Maxine carelessly poured the wine. If it was her spotless castle, they would have all been put out by now.

"Slow up Maxine, I ain't trying to get drunk up in here," Indira held her hand out to stop her from pouring any wine into her glass. Maxine rolled her eyes at her.

"Why not? You ain't got nothing to rush home to. You can sit your ass right there all night if you want to and can't nobody do shit," Maxine sort of stumbled as she stood, telling Indira off. She was drunk two glasses ago. Indira was at a loss for words. She couldn't tell between Maxine being drunk and Maxine just being Maxine. The sport of throwing harsh words was their game of choice.

"Shut up, Max. You drunk as hell and don't need to pour nobody none. As a matter of fact, sit your drunk-ass down," Sydney had reached her limit. She wasn't up to hearing Maxine's act tonight.

"I guess I will sit my ass down. If I've made Sydney curse me out, something is wrong," Maxine knew she had gone too far and sat down.

"Thank you, Maxine. Too much stuff has gone on tonight and I can't take anymore of this shit," Sydney said as she began to cry. Indira put her arm around Sydney's shoulder.

"What are you going to do, Sydney? Your prayers have finally been answered. Anthony's back, now what?" Indira waited for Sydney's eyes to reach hers.

"I don't know, Indira. How do I know what comes next? I don't really know what to expect from him anymore. It's been so long." Sydney gazed over at her daughter asleep on the couch. "I have to do what's best for Jazzy."

"Yeah, you do, but you don't have to make the dumbest mistake of your life in the process," Maxine could barely hold her head up as she spoke.

"What mistake?"

"If you let that bastard come back up in here like he left two days ago and not two
years ago," Maxine was losing her buzz the more she thought about Sydney's love life.

Her words reached out and grabbed her… Sydney's love life, not mine.

Maxine knew it was more than the liquor talking. Indira kept her mouth closed. It was late and things were starting to unravel.

Sydney spoke up again, "Bastard. Maxine, you didn't even have to go there. Whatever decision I make will be my decision, and not yours." She tightened her mouth up and rolled her eyes at Maxine.

"Well, so much for this shit. I'd rather go home to nothing than watch you two fight," Indira quickly rose from her seat and started toward the closet to retrieve her coat. Sydney watched Indira in silence. She could only hope that Maxine would follow suit.
Indira walked back into the room, putting her arm into her coat.

"Well, good night girls. I'll talk to you two later," Indira bent over and kissed Jasmine's forehead. "Good night, Pudgy and take care of your mama. She's gonna need you." Indira was closing the front door just as Sydney said goodbye.

"Good riddance," Maxine muttered.

Sydney looked over to Maxine making herself comfortable in the chair. "Maybe you should take your drunk-ass home too, Maxine." Sydney gathered the empty glasses from the table and took them into the kitchen. When she returned, she carefully lifted Jasmine off the couch and carried her into her bedroom.

Maxine sat up on the edge of the chair and rubbed her hand over her hair. "Damn, let me go home." In reality, she was the one with no one to go home to. She slipped into her leather jacket and eased out the front door. As she made her way down the flights of stairs, she began feeling guilty about meddling in Sydney's business when she had enough business of her own to handle. Maxine put her hand on her stomach. She told her friends everything that was going on in her life, but left out one thing—the news of her pregnancy by a married man.

The frosty wind sobered Maxine up all too fast. She really felt bad now. After Monday, she could start her life over.

*****

Maxine pulled up in front of a house hidden away from the main street.

"This looks like a spooky house." Maxine searched the mistreated landscape until she found an address. "541. Damn, this is it." She got her purse and cut the ignition to her Explorer. Just as she was reaching for the door to get out, she stopped herself.

"Lord, I'm sorry, but I am not at all ready to be somebody's mother. Please be with me and let me know that I am making the right decision." Maxine took a deep breath and then opened the car door.

"All right, here we go, Maxine. Damn. Why did I come here by myself?" Maxine fought her way through the rugged bushes to the steps of the old house, "because I was too fuckin' stupid to tell my own friends. I could die in this bitch, and nobody would know it." Maxine pulled open the stained-glass door. She could feel her knees beginning to buckle under her. The nurse's desk sat to the far end of the room behind a thick glass.

"Damn. They need all that?" Maxine suddenly had the realization of where she was. She was at an abortion clinic, preparing to kill her baby. Of course they needed all of that. Maxine suddenly lost her breath and looked to the thick glass at the far end of the hall.

"Shit. I gotta sit down before I fall down." Maxine made her way over to the chairs to the left of her. She was completely out of breath. She led her eyes around the mustard-colored walls of the perfectly square room. The place had a weird calming affect on her. The soft colored walls and the thick carpet on the floors gave the place a homey-like feel. Maxine regained her breath and then headed for the nurse's desk once again. The two women sitting behind the glass pane gave Maxine a sympathetic look.

"Are you okay, ma'am?" The first woman spoke through the speaker in the glass.

Maxine stared at them behind the glass pane. They weren't much older than she was. Maxine wondered if they had ever been in this situation before, or was she the only completely stupid woman in the entire city of Detroit.

"Yes, I'm fine. I have an eight o'clock appointment," Maxine's mouth was working on its own. She was in two places at the same time—the abortion clinic, and hell.

"Your name?" the second nurse never looked up, only watched her clipboard.

"Maxine Davis." Too ashamed to use her real name in case the files ever got into the wrong hands—it was an abortion clinic.

"Yes, Ms. Davis. You can come on back." The second nurse buzzed the door for Maxine to come to the other side. Maxine laughed slightly.

"Who am I? The President? Nobody gives a shit about me being here, especially this baby's daddy." Maxine reached for the door without actually realizing her own movements. The door closed behind her lightly. Maxine was almost glad to see that she wasn't the only stupid woman in the city of Detroit, after all. The exclusive waiting room was packed with pregnant women. Older women who didn't want any more children, teenage girls who didn't need any children, and the others were probably just like her. Sleeping with a married man and got pregnant.

"How could I be so stupid?" Maxine frowned upon an apparent businesswoman who was sitting only a couple of feet away from a young girl who was sitting alone. The businesswoman was talking loudly on her cellular phone without a care in the world, business as usual. She wasn't worried. It was probably her third or fourth time.

Maxine stood near the door placing judgment upon the room. On the other hand, that young girl looked as if she'd seen a ghost.

We're all pregnant and here to kill our babies, she thought. Maxine felt her legs beginning to weaken again, at the same time her stomach jumped. She snapped out of her gaze when she was greeted by a heavyset woman dressed in a nice suit. Armani in an abortion clinic? What next? Maxine didn't have the energy to turn her nose up at the woman right then. She was in need of a seat herself.

"Hello. I'm Gladys King." The woman extended her hand to Maxine who accepted it unknowingly.

"If you will wait here, I'll get the other ladies." The woman went to the lobby and gathered up its occupants. Each woman made her way over to where Maxine stood at the head of an endless hallway. They looked like a herd of cattle on their way to the slaughterhouse. Maxine felt like the head cow.

"If you ladies would follow me, please." The suit fit the woman leading the group like a glove. The walls were filled with pictures of mothers holding their babies and of kids playing in the park.

Was this some sort of reverse psychology or what? Maxine thought.

"Take a seat and try and get comfortable." The woman watched the group sitting down in the cushion-filled chairs and couches, and then she closed the door. Maxine couldn't help staring at the pregnant woman sitting on the couch. She looked to be ready to deliver. She can't be here to have "it" done. The word brought strong emotions to Maxine, so she resorted to just not saying the word "abortion."

"You ladies will be spending the next two hours with me. I am a counselor here at Women's Choice, and I am here to help answer any questions you might have and help you make sure that you are making the right decision for yourselves."

Most of the women smacked their lips loudly in disgust. They must have wanted to get it over as soon as possible.

Maxine's mind was made up. She couldn't have the baby. Bruce was fucking married, her mind screamed out. Her stomach rumbled softly.

"I want to help you ladies in any way I can, so please don't hesitate to ask me any questions."

Maxine got comfortable in the recliner as Gladys took her place at the front of the room. Suddenly, Maxine sat up to the attention of nausea. She was about to blow any minute. With her hand over her mouth, she ran out of the classroom in search of a bathroom. The growing baby inside her was making itself known.

Maxine blindly opened a door to see a young woman on a table with her legs spread wide apart and a doctor strategically standing between them. She was in the operating room. This was where it all happened. Maxine ignored the rants for her to leave the room, but her gaze was stuck on the contents in the huge jars on the countertop. Upon the realization that she was looking at fetuses in the jars, Maxine threw up on the floor of the operating room.

"Get her out of here!" the doctor yelled angrily to the nurses that stood by and watched her drop to the floor. "Everything's fine, ma'am, just lay back and relax," the doctor tried to assure the young woman on his surgical table that nothing was wrong.

Maxine woke up on a bed. When she opened her eyes, she saw other women lying on cots all around her.

What's happened? How long have I been here? Maxine sat up in the cot. She felt fine, plus she was fully clothed. She checked between her legs just in case.

"Thank, God," Maxine said under her breath.

"Are you feeling better, Ms. Davis?" A nurse was walking toward Maxine.

Maxine lifted the covers off of her and put her feet on the floor. "Where are my shoes?" Maxine hopped down off the bed and followed the nurse's finger pointing at her shoes under the bed. "Thanks." Maxine slipped them on and stood before the nurse.

"I've changed my mind. I'm not going to go through with this. I can't even say the damn word." Maxine retrieved her purse from the table next to the bed.

"I wish you all the luck, Ms. Davis." The nurse started turning down the bed that Maxine had used.

"The name's Maxine Harrell. I'm not ashamed anymore," Maxine said proudly.

"Then good luck, Ms. Harrell." The nurse smiled, and then watched Maxine leave the recovery room. Maxine noticed a couple of the women from her group resting comfortably on the cots after having "it" taken care of. Their faces loomed with confusion and sadness as they watched her walk by them. No words spoken. Only eyes connected. Maxine left out through the front doors the same way she came in. She boldly strolled to her truck parked in front of the house.

"Lord, if this is what is to be, then so be it!" Maxine screamed to the sky, and then got into her truck. She sat staring at the steering wheel. She didn't feel like going to work and home wasn't too enticing either.

"Oh well. I'm pregnant, so I'll eat my sorrows away." Maxine looked around the street to notice a café within walking distance of the clinic. She opened the door and slid down out of her SUV.

Inside the café, Billie Holiday was playing low in the background, putting Maxine on good terms with the place. She smiled to the bartender as he watched her enter. Maxine took a seat at the bar because she never liked to eat alone.

"How can I help you?" the hefty man, with a white apron tied around his waist, said through a smile.

"I would like a slice of apple pie and a cup of hot chocolate." Maxine licked her lips. For the moment, she would enjoy her pie, and then worry about what to do next. She stared at the many liquor bottles that lined the far wall of the bar, and then noticed her reflection in the mirror between them.

"No more White Zinfandel for you, young lady. I'll miss you, my friend," Maxine laughed, and then looked at her reflection again. This time there was someone different staring back at her.

"I'm going to be someone's mother," Maxine laid her head down in her hands on the bar. The door opened, letting a cool draft run free through the tiny spot. Through the mirror, Maxine eyed a nice looking man making his way over to the bar. She knew the man from someplace, but couldn't remember. She turned her head to the bartender as he placed her pie down in front of her.

"Would you like some whipped cream on that?" The man stood ready with the spray nozzle in his hand.

"Yes, I would. Thank you." Maxine forgot all about the man sitting only three stools down from her at the sight of her pie. She hungrily ate then noticed the man coming toward her.

"I can't quite seem to remember when, but you and I have met somewhere before," the middle-age black man said as he sat down on the stool next to her.

Maxine obliged. "You do look familiar to me." She patted the corners of her mouth with the napkin.

"Dammit, I hate when I can't remember things. I'm getting old," the man said as he smiled at Maxine and laughed. She laughed back.

"You don't look old." Maxine sipped her hot chocolate, which was now sort-of hot chocolate.

"Now I know. We met at John's party. I'm Gerald. I own the gas stations." The man tried to give Maxine a hint to help her memory, as well.

"Oh yes. I do remember now… Maxine," she nodded her head to greet him formerly as she reintroduced herself.

"You were looking fabulous in that sequined dress." The man's eyes began to twinkle at his recollection of her that night.

"You didn't seem to have any problem remembering all of that." Maxine ate the last of her slice of apple pie with Gerald watching her open her mouth to eat the last bite. He seemed satisfied by the result.

"I also remember that you were with Bruce Washington that night." Gerald put up his finger for the bartender, his shot of bourbon arrived. He threw it down his throat.

"That night? How do you know we're not still together?" Maxine questioned the man.

"Let's just say I know his wife doesn't like to share." Gerald wasn't sparing any feelings.

Maxine felt the knife that was thrown at her, but she couldn't retaliate. "Well, I've got to be going now." Maxine hopped down from the stool and quickly put on her jacket. She pulled five dollars out of her pocket and left it on the bar. Gerald put his hand on top of hers with the five under them.

"I'll take care of it." He lifted his hand off of Maxine's. Instead of cursing him out, she forced a smile.

"Thank you."

Maxine stood outside of the doors. "Lord, help me."

*****

Jasmine playfully splashed water on Anthony as he sat by the tub and watched Sydney give their daughter a bath.

"She's so happy. I can tell she didn't miss me," Anthony let his head lay against the wall.

"She missed you, whether she knew it or not. She still needs you, Anthony." Sydney lifted Jasmine out of the water as she kicked her legs. Anthony sat up and wrapped the towel around his daughter. He still couldn't believe he was somebody's father.

"What him name?" Jasmine spoke in her deep voice to her mother.

Sydney smiled and turned to Anthony. Sydney and Anthony had talked every day on the phone ever since he had come back. She was glad she let him come over this morning. She'd never called in sick to work, so it was no problem.

"My name is Daddy," Anthony said proudly. Jasmine looked to her mother. Sydney smiled at her baby. She was two years old going on five.

"Okay, my name Jasmine," Jasmine held her towel around her and headed to the door.

Anthony and Sydney sat on the floor watching their daughter.

"Come on," Jasmine stood at the brightly painted yellow door.

"Okay, little girl, I'm coming," Sydney followed Jasmine out of the bathroom and into the bedroom. Anthony sat on the floor of the bright yellow bathroom in amazement at how much his daughter had grown. He was glad to be home. Now he had to get Sydney to let him come back for good. He got up from the floor and joined Sydney and Jasmine in the kitchen. They were eating toast and fruit at the table. He sat down next to Jasmine in her booster seat. She laughed.

"Hi, Daddy," Jasmine held the peeled banana in her hand. Anthony was shocked at the sound of those words. He jumped back with delight. Sydney could see the surprise in his eyes. She couldn't be happier than at this very moment. Nothing really mattered anymore. It was up to her now.

"Hey, Jasmine," Anthony replied.

Jasmine yawned loudly. Sydney checked the clock on the wall and knew it had to be close to her naptime.

"She usually takes a nap around twelve-thirty," Sydney let Anthony in on his daughter's routine.

"Yeah, she do look sleepy."

Jasmine continued to eat her banana until she was too tired to hold her head up at the table.

"I seepy, Mommy," Jasmine put down the remainder of her banana.

"Okay, bug. Let's go and take a nap." Sydney picked Jasmine up from her chair and lifted her onto her hip, "I'll be right back."

Anthony watched Sydney walk away. She had put on some weight, but it was in all the right places.

"Bye, Daddy," Jasmine waved as Sydney took her to her bedroom.

Anthony was a hard man, but he was on the verge of tears.

"Bye."

Jasmine fell fast asleep just after hitting her Winnie-the-Pooh pillow. Sydney closed the door behind her, only to see Anthony staring at her. A huge smile came to her face, and she was damn near blushing.

"Do you like what you see?" Sydney acted as if she were on the catwalk, spinning in front of Anthony.

"Yeah, girl," Anthony followed Sydney's hips closely. She didn't have those the last time he saw her.

"I know I put on some weight, but I'm not worried about it." Sydney stood in front of Anthony as he sat down in the chair at the table.

"I ain't worried about it, if you ain't worried about it." Anthony wrapped his arms around Sydney's waist and held her close to his face. He was that same thug she loved back when. He was all that and some.

"Baby, I am so sorry," Sydney said as she stood with her elbows up, not returning his show of affection.

"I'm sorry, Sydney, for everything."

Sydney couldn't hold out any longer, she let her hands rest on top of Anthony's head. He held her tighter, burying his face into her stomach. The tab of her jeans pressed against his cheek. Anthony started to cry and held her against him so she couldn't see his face.

"I know, Anthony. I know." Sydney could hear his tears and then she let her hands lift his face up. Her prayers had been answered. The man she loved was home. She wiped the tears from his face and softly kissed his mouth. She closed her eyes from the sheer pleasure of it. Two years had gone by and their kisses were still brand new.

Anthony gripped Sydney's full hips as their lips connected. He pulled at her shirt with his mouth until it fell out of her jeans. Sydney sat down on Anthony's lap, grazing the desire he possessed for her in his loose fitting jeans. She straddled Anthony, fully wrapping her arms around his neck, as they covered each other with old and new kisses.

"Can I stay the night, Sydney?" Anthony was massaging her back. She was loving every minute of it and could not refuse him. She never could.

"Yes. Stay with me tonight."

That was all Anthony needed to hear. He lifted Sydney up and carried her into the bedroom they once shared.

CHAPTER SIXTEEN

So much had gone on in the past couple of weeks that the conversation at Maxine's salon would probably prove to be very eventful. Indira finished dressing after thoroughly gathering up all of Robert's things and placing them in his old office. The house was spotless, as if she had tried to clean all of Robert completely out of it. She couldn't stay there if she had to think about all the things he'd done to her. The phone rang as Indira pulled her snug-fitting cable knit sweater over her head.

"Hello," Indira said as she pulled her hair out of the sweater and then placed her ear closer to the phone. "Hello," she sang again.

"Hello, Indira?" El sounded nervous. He was nervous. Indira stirred up emotions and feelings inside of him that he'd never wanted to admit he even had.

"El, it's so nice to hear your voice. How are you?" Indira sat down in the recliner at Robert's desk. She was glad to hear from El. He'd proven that he could be there for her, and she truly appreciated that quality in him.

"I didn't catch you at a bad time did I?" El had been thinking of Indira each and every day they'd been apart. His heart felt heavy and weak, but he was painting the best stuff of his life.

"No. I've always got time to talk to you. I'll be on my way over to Maxine's in about an hour." Indira sat back in the chair and put her feet up on the mahogany desk.

She didn't know what to expect, but she was getting stronger with each day and was ready for just about anything.

"Ah, yes. Thursday's at Maxine's."

Indira was sort of surprised that El even remembered her telling him that.

"Well, I was calling to tell you that I will be in town the week of Christmas, and I'd like to see you." El didn't want to rush Indira into something that she might regret later, but his feelings for her had grown strong.

"I would really like that, El. I don't want to sound corny or anything, but I've sort of missed you and those gorgeous locks," Indira giggled at her newly found boldness.

"Oh you like the locks, for real?" El was smiling through his words and Indira could hear it.

"Yeah, I like the locks. I think they're sexy," Indira laughed again, and this time with El joining in.

"I can't wait to see you, girl." El's deep voice sent a thrill through Indira's body.

"Will you be here Christmas Day?" Indira put her pinky finger playfully into her mouth.

"I had planned to spend it with my mother and my sister. But, if something else is going on, I'm there." El jumped full speed ahead.

"No, not really, I was just asking. My sister will be in town that week, too. I'm going to be spending most of my time with her."

Indira let her eyes roam the contents of Robert's desk. The picture of the two of them in front of the house put her in another place. She could remember that day so clearly. It was the first day she saw the house that Robert had bought for them, without her. They looked so happy on the picture. But, in reality, when she questioned him about buying the house without her, he busted her bottom lip with a backslap.

"I look forward to us getting together, Indira. But I'm gonna get off of this phone now. I'm not exactly rich just yet, but I'm on my way," El let out a deep laugh.

Just as Indira was about to speak, the doorbell rang.

"Someone's at my door. Hey, call me when you get here, or call me whenever." Indira made her way out of the recliner, still holding the cordless phone.

"I'll do that. Goodbye," El said with sincerity, and then hung up the phone. Indira put the phone on the receiver and stepped into the hallway.

"Who is it?" Indira asked as she walked toward the door.

"It's Robert. I don't have my keys." Robert could barely stand up straight. His body had become so weak. He'd lost a significant amount of weight since he'd left. Indira froze in her steps. Was he coming back? No. He can't come back. Indira took a deep breath to calm down.

"Just a minute," After fluffing her hair—no need for him to see how badly she'd been doing—she unlocked the door and pulled it open slowly. Robert stood on the front stoop of the house. No words were exchanged. Indira opened the door wider for him to come inside. He stepped in without looking at her. Just before Indira closed the door, she noticed a woman sitting in Robert's car in the driveway. It was her. She'd finally gotten what she'd been waiting her whole life for, Robert. Indira looked her husband up and down. He looked awful. It was true he was sick. Indira put her hand over her mouth, as Robert could barely stand up before her.

"Indira, I came here to tell you that I'm sorry. I know I went about things the wrong way and I want to apologize to you," Robert turned his eyes to the couch in the living room, and then made his way over to it. Indira sat down in the chair across from him.

"Is that all you're apologizing for Robert? What about the other things Robert or have you forgotten about them already?" Indira felt no mercy for her dying husband. What nerve he possessed to bring his woman to their home.

"No. I can't forget, Indira. And, that's why I'm here." He pulled himself up from the couch and walked over to his office to notice huge garbage bags on the floor. He turned to Indira for an explanation.

"I'm pretty sure you were not planning on coming back, so I got your things together for you."

Robert now realized that Indira had seen Vera waiting in the car.

"I'm not here to fight, Indira. Hell, I can't fight." Robert ran his hand over his thinning hair. "I came to get my things. That's all." Robert came out of his office and started up the stairs.

"I guess you couldn't wait for the divorce hearing to get them," Indira stood with her arms folded and her mouth tight.

Robert made it to the third step and stopped. He knew his secret was out; Indira had to know he was sick if she had packed his things. His box was what he came to retrieve. It was all he had left to remind him of the life he was leaving.

"So I guess you know I've got cancer." Robert disregarded his young wife's sly remarks and remained calm. He sat his tired body down on a stair.

"Yes. I found your box when I was clearing out your closet," Indira came over to the staircase near Robert. Her emotions were roaring like a lion inside her. She could feel a sense of strength over him. She knew her strength came too late. Robert was too weak to even defend himself. “So, are you finally going to make her your wife?” Indira stood just below Robert. He sort of laughed at his young wife. He deserved that after all he’d put them both through.

Indira continued, “Was she who you went to whenever you left here?” She couldn’t keep her arms folded any longer. She had her hand on the curtain peeking out to the driveway. She could feel an intense heat growing inside her now. Even sick, he was an asshole.

Robert didn’t give her the decency of supplying an answer. He said nothing, only sat with his head down. Indira began to pace the small space of the staircase.

“I just don’t understand it, Robert. I tried to be everything you wanted me to be.” Indira continued to argue at her husband. “I lived for your ass, Robert. I went to all those damned book shows and conferences and wherever else you needed me to be.”

Robert could hear the tears in her words, and then lifted his head to see her. She wiped them quickly as they rolled down her cheeks.

“We could have been happy, Robert. But, you were too much of a coward to change,” Indira’s words hurt Robert because they were true. He had been a coward all those years. Now he was afraid to die.

“Why, Robert? I should be the one leaving your ass,” Indira was flinging her hands with the intensity of each word she spoke.

“I know that, Indira,” Robert spoke the words nonchalantly. Indira looked into his eyes strangely. She heard no remorse in those words for what he’d put her through.

“Is that all you have to say to me?” Indira leaped from the first step and let loose on Robert with her fists. She beat his face and head uncontrollably. She attacked him before he could realize what was even going on. After a thorough assault, Robert grabbed Indira’s wrists with what little strength he had. He stopped her.

Indira cried out, “I hate you, motherfucker!” She sobbed harder, as Robert tightened his grip. Robert let his tongue explore his lip to feel that it was cut. He squeezed her wrists tighter and stared into her hurt eyes. His temper eased, seeing the pain in them; the same eyes that used to hold the key to his heart. Robert loosened his grip.

“I’m sorry, Indira. I know I hurt you, but this can’t go on. I don’t want to go on hurting you any longer,” his voice was trembling and his hands were sweaty. Indira let the tears flow as she pulled away from him.

"Do you hear me, Indira? I had to stop this. I could have killed you." Robert dabbed his mouth, lifting himself from the stair with the help of the railing. Indira stood against the wall watching him. His words had backed her against it.

"Please, Indira. I only came here to get my things. I'll get them, and then I'll leave." Robert used his handkerchief to wipe the blood that trickled down his face.

Flashbacks of Floyd beating Arnelle interrupted her view of Robert. She slowly nodded her head in agreement, watching Robert make his way up the remaining stairs.

Indira eased down the stairs into the front room. She sat down quietly. He was right. He could have killed her. This was the end of her life as she now knew it.

*****

Sydney was feeling like she was on top of the world. For the past six or seven days, she and Anthony had been making up for lost time.

Maxine seemed all too annoyed that Sydney was in such a good mood. Her emotions were raging out of control, and watching Sydney gloat about having her so-called man back wasn't helping any. There wasn't much for Maxine to be excited about. First Bruce dropped her like a hot pan of grease, and then she found out she was pregnant with his baby. She hadn't quite come to terms with the situation that she was in.

Sydney took the liberty of putting on some music. She had brought Anthony's CD case with her. Somebody named Jay-Z was cursing loud and fast over a headache-pounding beat.

"Girl, if you don't get that shit off of my stereo, I'll throw it at you." Maxine put her hand over her forehead, and then sat down on the couch. She wanted a glass of wine so badly it was killing her.

"Damn. What's up with you tonight?" Sydney stopped the CD player, and joined Maxine in the living room. "Where are the wine glasses?" Sydney looked to Maxine for an answer.

"Oh, they're in the kitchen. I don't feel much like drinking tonight." Maxine tried not to make eye contact with Sydney. What difference did that make? Sydney put her hand on her hip.

"That's all," Maxine said loudly.

"That's all, huh? If you ain't drinking, then something is going on." Sydney got up from the recliner and sat down next to Maxine. Maxine continued to stare straight ahead. "Is there something you're not telling me? Are you feeling okay?" Sydney was becoming concerned now since Maxine hadn't answered her. Just then, the phone rang.

"Let me get the phone," Maxine bolted off the couch to answer it. Sydney watched her closely.

"Hello," Maxine picked up the phone on the second ring. The voice on the phone was deep and mysterious. It felt familiar to Maxine, but distant. It was Anthony. At this realization, Maxine removed the cordless phone from her ear without hearing another word out of the runaway's mouth.

"It's your man." Maxine dropped the phone in Sydney's lap with much attitude. Sydney was eyeing her with such vigor that Maxine could feel it on her back. Maxine knew she was wrong for doing that.

Damn why did I do that? Maxine thought as she nestled back into the couch. Its cushions seemed to be soothing her newly found back pain.

Sydney rolled her eyes at Maxine and then waited until she was all the way out of the living room before she started talking.

"Hey, baby. How's Jasmine?" The tone in her voice sounded as if she were smiling from ear to ear. Maxine could tell, already, that this was going to be a long night. No wine and no weed for her meant no fun. She closed her eyes and put her hand on her stomach. She tried to concentrate on the baby growing inside her, but was soon interrupted by the green-eyed monster. She could hear Sydney whispering to Anthony on the phone.

How can she take him back after all this time? Maxine thought as she rubbed her hand around in circles on her belly. She has got to be stupid. Maxine continued to bitch and rub her belly. "Stupid," she said aloud.

"Listen to my ass calling somebody else stupid," Maxine sat up on the couch and began to laugh. "I let this happen to me. I let Bruce, the married motherfucker, get me pregnant."

Maxine tried to force more laughter, but to no avail. "I'm the stupid bitch." She stopped laughing and started crying. She was crying so hard that Sydney, though pissed off at her, looked in on her from the hall.

She'll Learn

Sydney rushed Anthony off of the phone. She sat down next to Maxine and put her arms around her shoulders.

"What's wrong, Max? I knew something was wrong with your ass, girl."

Maxine let her head rest on Sydney's shoulder. The secret had to come out. Maxine didn't have a choice. The only family she truly had was Sydney and Indira. If she couldn't talk to them, who could she talk to?

Maxine wiped the tears from her face and took a couple of deep breaths. Sydney watched her in wonderment.

"Damn. What is it?"

Maxine sort of laughed, and then smiled at Sydney. "I'm pregnant," Maxine let the words blurt out of her mouth before she had a chance to retrieve them.

"Damn," Sydney said sharply. It was all she could say.

"Yeah, man. It's Bruce's, and get this," Maxine began, as she ran her fingers through her hair. Sydney became more interested. "He's married with two daughters. Ha!" Maxine screamed and clapped her hands loudly. Sydney shook her head empathetically. None of that even mattered anymore. What mattered was her unborn child.

"Maxine's gonna have a baby," Sydney sang, and then hugged Maxine tightly.

"Thanks, Sydney, and I'm sorry for being such a bitch." She hugged Sydney back, squeezing her neck and then letting her go.

"That's all right. You've been a bitch most of your life," Sydney burst out into a heaping laugh. The doorbell rang as Maxine wiped the tears from her eyes. Sydney continued laughing and went for the door. She stood aside as Indira walked in.

"Indira, girl, have we got some news for you!" Sydney had a huge smile across her face as Indira looked like her life was over. She didn't even react to Sydney as she passed her and headed toward the couch. Sydney closed the door and followed her into the living room.

"Are you okay, Indira?" Sydney sat down next to her friend on the couch.

Now she was comforting her as well. No one would really care that she and Anthony were back together. Indira gathered herself and took a deep breath.

"Robert came home and got the rest of his things tonight. He had the nerve to bring his woman with him." Indira slid out of her coat and laid it on the arm of the couch. She turned her eyes back to her two friends to see that she had their undivided attention.

"What? He brought his woman to y'all house?" Maxine sat up in the chair. After hearing that, she couldn't keep her body still. "He brought his bitch to your house?" Maxine grabbed her hair angrily with her hands. Sydney watched Maxine. It was evident that she was hurt, too, and was for once in a predicament that she couldn't make her way out of.

"Yes, girl. He brought his bitch to my house," Indira was becoming more and more upset along with Maxine, "my damn house." Indira was pointing to her chest with her finger. Her true colors were beginning to show up her unshakable elegance. She and Robert had shared that house for nearly five years, and he had the audacity to bring his side woman to it. Sydney watched in disbelief as Maxine and Indira hyped each other up more.

"See what I mean? What the fuck makes men think they can get away with shit like that?" Maxine stood up and slapped her hands against her thighs.

"Calm down, y'all. He ain't even worth all of this. Is he Indira?" Sydney needed to be the strength tonight. Things were looking up for her, but her two best friends were going through their worst.

"Robert had the biggest set of balls in the world. He knew he could do it to me, Maxine. He didn't have to show me any respect. I never made him." The tears made their way into her words. Indira was crying hard, and then buried her face in her hands. Sydney put her arms around Indira. She thought about the good news she had come to Maxine's with tonight. She and Anthony had decided to give it another try, but she knew that this wasn't the time or the place to bring up her man.

"You right, Indira. You did let his old ass treat you like shit." Maxine felt dizzy, so she sat back down in the chair. Indira lifted her eyes to Maxine.

"I know what went on, Maxine. I was there. You don't have to remind me of any damn thing, okay?" Indira got up with a snap from the couch and went into the bathroom. Sydney hadn't so much as said two words after Indira's vent.

She'll Learn

"Maxine. Why do you always have to be so damn evil?" Sydney folded her arms across her chest and fell back into the cushions of the couch. Maxine looked at Sydney, and then shrugged her shoulders in a sarcastic manner. "You gonna have to stop that shit, or your baby will come out the same way."

Sydney and Maxine realized at the same time what she was saying.

"Baby," the girls said in unison, and then playfully touched hands across the coffee table. Maxine and Sydney laughed and saw that someone was missing. They both rushed into the bathroom to Indira, who was sitting on the edge of the bathtub crying.

"Girl, get your ass out of here. If you can't take my shit by now, then we need to end this." Maxine stood at the sink and Sydney sat down on the closed lid of the toilet.

"I ain't even thinking about your dumb ass, I'm so pissed off at myself. I let that son of a bitch dog me out for at least four of the years we were married." Indira wiped her eyes with a crumpled piece of tissue. "And I know better. I know better than anybody." Indira dabbed her eyes again as the tears fell faster down her face. "I watched Floyd, my daddy, beat the shit out of my mother. Then, I get away from them, to let Robert beat the shit out of me." Indira's heart and her pride were both shattered.

"Look, Indira. You are going to have to chalk this shit up to the game," Maxine sat down on the tub next to Indira, who looked puzzled.

"What game?" Indira looked to Sydney who shook her head in dismay.

"The game of love, life, whatever," Maxine took a deep breath of her own, and put her hands on her stomach.

"Oh. That game." Indira dropped her head low.

"You live and learn every day that you're here. The men who come into our lives bring new lessons. Sometimes they are good lessons. Most of the time, they are fucked up lessons. But you learn from them, Indira." Maxine had tears rolling down her cheeks. Bruce had taught her the biggest lesson of all—to leave married men with their wives where they belong.

"Believe me," she continued, "I'm going to learn from this one."

Sydney felt left out and joined the girls on the last bit of space left on the edge of the old, lion pawed tub.

"I just loved him so much." Indira sat up quickly and wiped the tears from her face. "I wanted us to have this fairy tale marriage like I'd dreamed of like a dummy while growing up. So it was my fault, too."

Sydney nudged Indira with her shoulder.

"Are you crazy, girl? It's not your fault you married a nut. He had us all fooled." Sydney smiled to Indira.

"Uh uh, not me. I knew he wasn't shit from the beginning. He was too damn old for you five years ago," Maxine said.

The girls remained in the tight space in the dimly lit bathroom.

"Can you ever say anything nice to me? Does it make you feel better to make me out to be stupid?" Indira said as she got up from the tub and stood in front of the mirror of the podium like sink.

"I don't think you're stupid, Indira, I'm the stupid one. I've been dumber than all of us have ever been," Maxine replied.

Indira ran cool water over her face without regard for her makeup. She wasn't up to impressing anyone right now. She eyed Maxine's reflection in the mirror.

"I'm pregnant, Indira." Maxine stared into Indira's reflection as well. Indira dried her face and turned around. Maxine waited for the cruel comeback from her worst critic and best friend.

"Maxine. I'm so happy for you. Everything will be fine." Indira leaned down in front of Maxine and wrapped her arms around her neck. Pleasantly surprised by Indira's reaction, Maxine began laughing and crying all at once. Sydney laughed at the two hugging, as tears rolled from her eyes.

"I'm happy, too." Maxine held on to Indira tightly. She then reached out for Sydney's hand next to her. She squeezed it to let her know how much she meant to her.

The girls let go of their embrace and wiped the tears from their faces. Indira stood up erect and straightened her blouse.

"Who's the father?"

"Here she goes again," Maxine said as she started laughing with Sydney.

CHAPTER SEVENTEEN

The plant was steamy and filled with men and women on the assembly line, putting cars together. Anthony stepped back from his duties and took in the feeling of being a part of something. He was glad to have the chance to even be here. His sister came through for real this time. She promised to get him a job and she did. Anthony shook his head with a pleasing smile as he got back to work.

"Hey, Banks! Let me talk to you for a minute." The short, chubby Italian man stood just outside of the door to his office. Anthony turned quickly and headed toward the aisle of steel to his new foreman's office. He slowed his pace at the thought of receiving bad news. What if Gus was calling him into his office to fire him? Anthony moved even slower with the realization that he wouldn't have much to offer Sydney if he didn't have a job. He had never been happier in his life than he was right now. Sydney had been slowly letting him back into her life, and spending time with Jasmine was unbelievable.

He had never stopped loving Sydney, but much had gone on back then, he had to leave. He had to do what was right for him and his life. It would probably haunt him for the rest of his life.

Anthony didn't feel he had had much choice in the matter when it came time to take revenge on the fools who shot up their spot. He shook his head as he remembered Sydney crying and begging him not to go with his boys that night. But it wasn't enough to stop him. With the rage of the streets deep inside his belly, he had retrieved his .38 handgun from under the bed and rushed out the door, brushing Sydney's chest as he passed her. After getting in an old Chevy with two of his so-called closest boys, he knew he had made the wrong choice. The car slowed and KeJuan cut the lights.

They spotted two of the niggas that was busting caps at them the week before. That old Chevy was as quiet as it had ever been, and Anthony could hear his heart beating loudly in his ears. So loud, he didn't hear when the shots started firing. He saw one guy fall to the ground, and then another. KeJuan yelled out, holding his neck and dropping to the floor of the Chevy. The last standing man on the playground had shot him.

Anthony couldn't move. He sat erect in the back seat of the car as the bullets poured past him. He could see KeJuan's mouth moving violently, but he could only hear his own pounding heart. KeJuan became angered with Anthony for freezing up and turned the gun on him. Anthony simply closed his eyes. Suddenly his ears came back to life from the loud blast of two gunshots. He opened his eyes to see KeJuan lying face-down dead with half his head blown out against the steering wheel of that old beat up Chevy he loved so much. His killer lay dead on the black tarp of the playground. Anthony had climbed out of the back seat of the car and ran away as fast as he could without ever looking back.

He was determined to do everything right this time. Anthony finally reached the outside wall of Gus's office. He looked to his right to see the others hard at work on the assembly line. Only a few eyes turned to meet his in wonderment since he had been called to the office. Anthony closed his eyes and prayed to God.

"Father in heaven, please give me this chance. I promise to make good on it. Amen." Anthony stepped into the office, towering over Gus seated at his makeshift desk covered with unimportant papers.

"Hey there, Banks. What took you so long? I thought you got lost," Gus laughed at his joke, forcing Anthony to smile.

"Sit down. Sit down. You've been working like a madman this whole month."

Anthony pulled up a chair in front of the desk.

"Before you sit down, would you mind closing the door?" Gus held out his hand, and watched Anthony close the door as he sort of pimped back to the chair and stood beside it. Gus laid his hand easily over his other hand, which rested on the desk, to look professional.

"We can't have every Tom, Dick, and LaQuita knowing our business," Gus nodded his round head, which was covered with a hint of gray hair. He eyed Anthony, reassuring him. Anthony popped his chin upward in agreement. He lifted the crotch of his oversize work pants and took a seat in the chair.

"What is it you wanted to talk to me about, Gus?" Anthony spread his legs wide and slouched down into the tiny metal chair. He was not at all anxious to know what the topic of conversation would be.

Gus unfolded his hands and pushed back from his desk, bumping against the wall.

She'll Learn

"You got over eighty hours this pay period, and we don't like to pay overtime too often. So you got the next two days off." Gus threw up his hands. Anthony felt his burden of worry lift off of his shoulders. He now had a smile for his foreman.

"Thursday and Friday. Thanks, Gus," Anthony stood up and shook Gus's chubby hand.

"Ah, get out of here. You earned it." Gus folded his hands behind his head and watched Anthony walk out the door of his office.

I hope he shows up next week, Gus thought to himself as he rolled up to his desk and started on his paperwork.

Anthony kept his emotions intact, knowing good and well he wanted to yell for his stroke of luck, but he didn't need anybody in his business.

We can be like a barrel of crabs all clawing to get to the top while holding down another sometimes, he thought to himself. He didn't need Gus to tell him that.

Anthony started up his sister's souped up Buick Regal and sat back as the car warmed up. It wouldn't be long now before he could buy Sydney a ring and ask her to marry him. He wanted to come correct to her and not look like a buster off the street when he asked for her hand in marriage. He wanted his family back and he was willing to do all that it took to have that again. Anthony put the car in reverse and backed out of the space near the entrance of the plant. He reached the guard tower and waved to the bearded man sitting inside as he passed. He looked at the clock on the dash to see that it was still early.

"All this free time, and I don't know what to do with it." Anthony turned left onto the expressway. Without thinking, he was heading toward Sydney's apartment, his old crib.

"Guess I'll pick up my baby from Miss Lee's today." Anthony turned up the latest 2Pac song on the radio, rocking his head to the beat.

"Even dead, his shit is still bangin'." Anthony tapped the steering as he drove.

*****

Indira lifted one hand from the steering wheel and touched Clarissa's hand lovingly.

"I'm so glad you came home for Christmas, Clarissa." Indira kept her eyes on the road while her younger sister kept her eyes on her. Indira would never know how glad she was to be home; glad that she had a home to go home to.

"Nobody's called me Clarissa in so long, I almost didn't know it." Clarissa turned her eyes back out the window to the familiar streets of Detroit. She closed her eyes for a moment, and thought about the club. She knew BJ was probably still cursing her out. She failed to inform him that his headliner was leaving and never coming back. She clutched her bosom where she held the money she took from BJ as her final payment.

I wish Mama was here to see us two together right now, Indira thought, and then turned to her sister who seemed to be in another place.

"Is everything okay with you, Claire? Indira glanced back and forth from the road to her sister.

"Huh?" Clarissa left the club and came back to the ride with Indira. "Yeah, yeah, I'm fine. I was just thinking about a few things I left in D.C." Clarissa sat up in the seat of the car.

"Don't worry. If you need anything while you're here, I'll get it for you. I'm so happy you're here with me." Indira needed her sister now more than ever. Maxine and Sydney were her sisters in friendship, but Clarissa was her sister by blood.

"Thanks, Indi and believe me, I'm glad to be home." Clarissa turned and smiled at her big sister.

"There's something I haven't told you, and I didn't because I was too embarrassed. But I'm not, anymore," Indira admitted. She never took her eyes off the road as she spoke. Clarissa was staring at Indira's beautiful skin and her gorgeous hair. She thought about Indira's perfect man.

What in the hell could be wrong in her world? She'd always had it all, Clarissa thought to herself.

"I never told you that Robert was beating my ass all these years, and sleeping with other women." Indira kept her eyes on the road. She was almost to her street. Clarissa sort of gasped unexpectedly. Indira stopped at the stop sign inside of the subdivision and turned to Clarissa.

"He left me three weeks ago, and now I'm all alone." Indira pulled off, and then slowed down as she neared the house. Clarissa was in a state of shock. She couldn't believe that her perfect sister didn't have the perfect life after all. She dropped her head in sadness. The thought of them both going down the same path as their mother, hurt Clarissa's heart. Indira pulled into the driveway just as Clarissa began to cry.

"This is too fucked up, Indira. We are both so fucked up. I thought you were here living the life in your big fancy house with your husband, when all along you were going through the same shit that I was," Clarissa watched the tears that were also streaming down her sister's cheeks.

"I was living the life, all right," Indira began. Clarissa wiped her sister's tears with her hand, "the life of a stupid-ass woman who let it happen to her." Indira cut the ignition of the car and wrapped her arms around the steering wheel.

"I'm that stupid-ass woman, too," Clarissa replied.

Indira lifted her head and turned her eyes to her sister.

Poor Clarissa, she thought. So much had gone on in her life of twenty-two years, enough to fill a lifetime. Their father's advances toward them as girls, and then watching him punish their mother for his mistakes opened their eyes to the violence they would later face in their adult years. They needed each other more than they had ever imagined they would. Indira reached out and hugged Clarissa tightly from across the seat of the car. After a few moments, the two let go of their embrace.

"Damn. It's cold out here," Indira said as she pulled her keys out of the ignition. "My feet are getting numb. Let's go in the house."

Clarissa opened the door of the car and leaped out.

"Pop the trunk," Clarissa said as she scoped out the size of the house while making her way to the trunk of the car. "Damn. At least, you got something in return." Clarissa got her two suitcases and duffel bag out of the trunk. Indira took hold of the duffel bag and opened the front door. Clarissa put her bags down at the door.

"This might have been worth a few ass whoopings," Clarissa said as she laughed and then walked into the huge living room.

"Not funny, Clarissa," Indira struggled with the duffel bag that felt like it weighed a ton. "What in the world do you have in this bag?" Indira slung it onto the floor, near the staircase. "This is way more than a week's worth of clothes." Indira straightened her back to see Clarissa staring at her with the disappointment of her life in her eyes.

"That's because it is. I'm not going back to D.C." Clarissa stood in front of the mirror along the wall of the hallway. Indira watched her younger sister, feeling her pain as if it were her own. Too many things had gone wrong in both their lives and it was time for a change.

Clarissa continued, “I ain’t trying to move into the big house or nothing. I’m going to look for a place to stay while I’m here with you. Then, I’m out.” She took one more look at her reflection in the mirror then turned to Indira. Clarissa felt her heart fall to her stomach when she saw the tears rolling down Indira’s face. Clarissa walked over to her and put her arms around her.

“What is it, Indira?” Clarissa led Indira to the leather couch in the living room and eased her down, never letting go of her. Indira wiped her face dry with her hands.

“I want you to live here with me, Clarissa. I want us to be sisters again.” Indira was trying to be as sincere as she could. She knew that she and Clarissa had always had their differences. Indira went away to college, Clarissa ran away from home. Indira married a rich man; Clarissa fell for a strip club owner in Washington, D.C. They were very different from one another, but they shared one commonality. Indira and Clarissa were both abused by men for the better part of their adult lives. It was definitely time for a change.

“Are you sure about this, Indira? I don’t want you to be feeling sorry for me.” Clarissa removed her arm from around Indira’s shoulders.

“Yes. I’m sure, Clarissa. You and I are all the family we have left, and I need you now more than ever.”

Clarissa let her eyes roam the walls decorated with paintings of black children playing in a field. Indira had decided to take home the paintings that Eldridge had given to her so they would bring a smile to her face.

“These paintings are beautiful. They kind of remind me of when we were all little and stuff.”

Indira followed her sister’s eyes to her favorite of the trio of paintings. “A friend of mine gave those to me just when everything came crashing to the ground.”

Clarissa let Indira’s words digest in her mind, “Male friend, right?”

Indira nodded to her sister.

“They make the best kind of friends,” Clarissa said as she sort of laughed. Indira was right. Clarissa came home because she needed a change and what better place to do that than with her sister.

"I'll stay here with you on one condition," Clarissa snapped out of her gaze and faced her sister.

"Condition?" Indira put her hand on her hip slightly as she sat on the couch.

"On the condition that you treat me like an adult and not like your child," Clarissa put her hand on her hip as well. Indira paused for a long time without saying a word while looking at her sister. Clarissa had grown up, and she'd missed it. Thank God for a chance for them to start over again.

"I can do that as long as you act like an adult."

Clarissa looked down at the floor. Her mind raced back to the club, the place where she wasn't acting like an adult. She acted like a silly child letting just about anything happen to her. She didn't want to go back there.

"I think I can handle that part." Clarissa shook her head as she smiled. Indira put her arm around her shoulders and squeezed.

*****

Maxine put her hand on the counter of her station to keep from falling. She was dead tired and the end of her client list was nowhere in sight. After she finished with Lisa, she could take a break for some food. Dina walked into the room the two shared, eyeing Maxine in the mirror on the wall.

"How are you feeling? If you don't mind me saying so, you look like death warmed over." Dina shook her head and sat down in her empty chair. Her next client was running late and with all the snow, who knew when she'd get there.

"I do mind your saying so, and forget you," Maxine tugged at Lisa's hair when she snickered at Dina's wise cracks.

"Maybe you should take a break or something." Dina was primping in the mirror, her favorite place to be.

"Just as soon as I get Lisa out of my chair, I will." Maxine spritzed and curled with a rhythmic motion, giving Lisa a flawless look. She spun Lisa around to the big mirror on the wall.

"That is on, Max." Lisa admired her hair in the mirror as she reached into her pocket for her money. She handed her a crisp fifty-dollar bill without taking her eyes off of the mirror. "Now I need to get my eyebrows arched." Lisa eased out of Maxine's chair, just missing her.

"Ficara can hook you up. She's in the back," Maxine pointed to the end of the hallway.

Ficara had the last room of the hallway all to herself. She was the head manicurist and did eyebrow arching. Sometimes the line resembled the line at the club. It seemed you would never get in.

"Let me pull my ass out of this chair and go get something to eat before Miss Tina and her daughter get here," Maxine said as she took off her smock and checked herself in the mirror.

"What you doing all that for? You don't need nobody to be looking at your ass now," Dina whispered to Maxine, and then laughed hard.

"See. I knew I shouldn't have told you shit." Maxine shook her head and left the room. Stephanie had the phone up to her ear and her hand on the appointment book. Maxine passed her receipt and money to Stephanie to be recorded, and then pointed to her mouth. Stephanie nodded her head. Maxine managed to find her coat in the cramped closet at the door and put it on. Even though she was only going next door, it was cold enough to freeze you up whole. She made her way through the clients who seemed to be everywhere. During the week, women came to get their hair done after work with their kids, no matter the number, to get the only source of pampering they had access to.

Maxine took a deep breath once she made it outside. It wasn't so bad outside. After all, the night air seemed to help relax her tense nerves. Ever since she found out she was pregnant, she'd been on edge. Way on the edge, and hanging on by her nails. Maxine had always hated not having a solution or being in a situation she couldn't handle. It was becoming obvious that she was pregnant. Her stomach used to be as flat as a board. With her tall and slender frame, she was either pregnant or had a beer belly. Maxine glanced at the cars speeding up the busy street, and then walked to Ray's. She would make this a quick stop since she didn't want to get all mushy and start thinking about Bruce. After all, it was her place first. The bell over the door clanged as Maxine walked through the door's entrance.

"Hello, Maxine," Ray spoke cheerfully as he rang up a customer. Maxine slowly walked up the buffet line.

She'll Learn

"Hi, Ray." She watched for the curtain covering the entrance of the backroom to open, but it never did. "Where's Lan?" Maxine felt concern for Lan, she never knew she had any for her. Ray completed his transaction with the last customer in line.

"Thank you, sir and come again." Ray made his way toward Maxine behind the buffet counter. "Her mother sick, so she go home to see her." He grabbed a to-go tray from the stack that stood unbalanced against the wall.

"She went all the way to China to see her mother?" Maxine asked in a surprised manner. Ray looked at her strangely, as he put her usual order of sesame chicken and rice on the tray.

"You got mother, Maxine?" Ray looked at her over the buffet counter. Maxine didn't expect that question, so she hesitated to answer.

"Yes, I have a mother." She forced her mouth to say it, but without any feeling. She couldn't hide it from Ray. He could see that this was a touchy subject for his neighbor.

"Wouldn't you go all the way to China if she sick?" Ray turned his eyes from Maxine to greet a customer entering the restaurant. "Hello, sir. How are you, today?" Ray sang his greeting song and handed Maxine her order.

Maxine stood still. Ray struck a chord in her mind that wouldn't let go. The answer was no. She wouldn't go to China to see Maureen if she was sick. Maxine carried her container to the cash register. She suddenly felt sad because she knew her feelings for her mother were wrong. It wasn't how she was feeling at all. Maxine had loved Maureen all her life and had never stopped loving her deep down. Growing up without her, Maxine had to force herself to believe that she didn't love her mother in order to go on. She stood at the register, becoming impatient with Ray, who continued to help his new customer. Ray turned his eyes to notice Maxine at the register with a look of anger on her face.

"It's on me tonight, Maxine. Take care of yourself." Ray smiled to her from the distance, and then turned his attention back to his customer.

Maxine knew that she must have been looking pretty pitiful for Ray to give away anything. She waved goodbye to him as she left out of the door. Confused by his reasons, but enlightened by his words, Maxine made it back to the shop.

*****

Miss Lee watched Anthony carefully put his daughter's coat on her arms. She could tell that he hadn't done this many times before.

"Are you sure Sydney is okay with this? I don't want no trouble with her," Miss Lee held her housedress together with her hands.

"Yes, ma'am. She told me that I could get my daughter anytime I want," Anthony reassured thc old woman for the fifth time.

"I want hat," Jasmine stood with her lip poked out. Miss Lee passed Jasmine's knit cap to Anthony.

"Here you go, baby girl," Anthony pulled the hat down snugly onto his daughter's head. She was the spitting image of her mother, but she was his color. Anthony took hold of the car seat that sat at the front door. Sydney left it there just in case Anthony did come by to get Jasmine.

Some time ago, a person couldn't get Anthony to lift two fingers to do much of nothing. Anthony knew that picking his daughter up would prove to Sydney that he had changed for the good. Miss Lee continued to hold her housedress closed as if Anthony was going to try and sneak a peek.

"You be careful with that baby, now. Sydney is testing you."

Anthony nodded to the elderly woman, knowingly, and then opened the door of the tiny apartment.

"I know, Miss Lee. But I'm gonna' pass this time." Anthony smiled and then headed down the staircase. He held Jasmine up high in his arms. He couldn't believe how much his daughter had grown.

"You gon' be tall and skinny, just like your daddy." Anthony squeezed his daughter tightly, and then tickled her. The two were laughing and playing so much, Anthony didn't notice Wayne standing at the entrance of the building. He stopped laughing at the sight of him blocking the entrance. Wayne looked serious as he stared at the pair. Anthony didn't know how to take it exactly. Was Wayne trying to punk him out or what? Anthony got near the door, noticing that Wayne didn't seem to be moving out of his way. Enough trouble had come Anthony's way in the last few years and he didn't need any new additions. He calmed himself mentally, even before he could get riled up. He did learn something from his Uncle Junior during his stint in the country.

"What's up, Wayne?" Anthony popped his chin, speaking in a low tone, and then brushed Wayne's shoulder as he passed him. Jasmine watched Wayne from her daddy's shoulder and waved to him. He waved back to her like she was leaving him for good. In a way, she and her mother had left him for good. Wayne let his chest down and watched Anthony take Jasmine out the door. He wanted to let Anthony know right away that he wasn't a punk. Even though Anthony was Jasmine's biological father, he thought Sydney was making a bad decision bringing him back into her life.

"Sydney's baby daddy. Damn," Wayne shook his head as he stared out the window at Anthony and Jasmine driving off. Whose car did he steal? he wondered.

CHAPTER EIGHTEEN

Anthony pulled up and parked on the street in front of an old brick house hidden by tall frostbitten hedges and plastic covered flower bushes. He felt deep inside that he had to make things right between Virginia and Sydney or things could never be right for the three of them.

"We're here, baby girl. This here is your grandparent's house." Anthony turned around to Jasmine who was strapped securely in her car seat, holding her sippy cup tightly.

"Who Daddy?" the light voice flowed out the tiny body, magically. Anthony sort of jumped back when he heard his daughter call him Daddy. He hadn't gotten used to playing that role yet, but the fact was he wanted the part. Anthony was on the verge of tears when he caught himself and fought them all the way back into his head. He was too hard to let his daughter see him cry. He suddenly realized that Jasmine probably had never been to see her grandmother. He was about to change that.

"That's right, baby girl. I'm your daddy." Anthony reached back to the seat and put his hand up to his daughter, "Gimme five, baby girl."

Jasmine put down her cup and slapped Anthony's hand with her smaller one.

"Yayyy!" Jasmine cheered.

"This is Papa Joe's house." Anthony lowered his head to look at the house. This was the Hastings' second house. After Eric died, Virginia insisted on moving out of the old neighborhood. She was hoping that it would get Sydney away from Anthony. Her plan didn't work, but ironically, Anthony left anyway.

"Come on, baby girl. Let's go in and meet your grandma Virginia. She won't be glad to see me, but she will be glad to see you." Anthony stepped out of the car into the sharp breeze, and then opened the back door to get Jasmine out. He made sure to cover her face with her scarf to keep the wind off of her. He nearly melted when he stared into his daughter's big brown eyes, her small nose peeking out above the crocheted scarf across her face.

"You so pretty, just like your mama." Anthony closed the car door and made his way up the walkway of the house. He now stood at the front door with Jasmine watching him closely.

She'll Learn

"Take a deep breath, baby girl. I don't know what's gonna' happen next." Anthony rang the doorbell and stepped in front of the screened door. He shifted Jasmine in his arms, waiting for the door to open. Instead, he saw the curtain in the window pull back. He let Jasmine block the view of the person in the window. He couldn't see her, but he knew it was Virginia. Anthony turned his eyes back to the door when he heard the locks being undone from the inside. He and Jasmine eyed the door closely as it slowly opened.

"Can I help you with something?" A sharp voice came through the thick screen door at the two. Anthony would know her voice anywhere. He'd heard it screaming at him plenty of times.

"Hello, Mrs. Hastings. It's me. Anthony," he spoke in a calm and soothing manner. He didn't want to cause Virginia to be afraid in anyway. He moved closer to the door to give Virginia a better view of her granddaughter. Virginia locked her eyes on the beautiful baby sitting proudly in Anthony's arms. She didn't care anymore why he was there. She only wanted to see her grandbaby. Virginia opened the screen door and stepped out, holding the door with her body.

"Hello, Jasmine. Can grandma hold you?" Virginia never once laid eyes on Anthony. She quickly reached for Jasmine, who openly moved into her grandmother's arms. Virginia turned and walked into the house letting the screen door slam shut in front of Anthony. He shook his head and sort of laughed.

"Lord, give me the strength to handle myself and do the right thing. All right? Amen." Anthony wiped his feet on the mat, and then opened the door and stepped inside of the house. He looked up to God for reassurance once again, and then closed the door behind him.

Virginia disappeared into the kitchen with Jasmine on her hip. Anthony took a seat on the plastic covered couch. His leather jacket wasn't agreeing with the fabric so he moved to the edge. Anthony looked around at the pictures of Eric and Sydney all over the walls of the living room. He smiled when his eyes ran across his and Sydney's prom picture. It brought back memories of worry-free days and extra long nights. Those days were long gone. Now he had a daughter to think about.

Virginia returned with Jasmine walking along side her with one hand gripping Virginia's, and the other holding a pudding snack. Virginia sat down in the recliner directly across from Anthony.

"Want to sit with grandma and eat your pudding?" she asked Jasmine.

Anthony watched Virginia as she took off Jasmine's hat, scarf, and coat. He was happy to see Virginia smiling and enjoying her.

"So, what brings you back to town?" Virginia laid her eyes on Anthony like a ton of bricks. Anthony could feel the load behind them.

"You holding my reason. And Sydney of course."

The couch made strange noises as Anthony adjusted his body on it. Jasmine laughed loudly.

"Daddy make noise," Jasmine laughed some more, and then filled her mouth with chocolate pudding that was changing the color of her cheeks.

"I'm glad it only took you two years, instead of ten. I didn't think you had it in you to come back here." Virginia wiped Jasmine's cheeks clean with the paper towel.

"Oh, I was coming back. But I had to get some thangs right, first." Anthony tried to relax, causing the plastic covers to speak louder. Jasmine laughed, and Virginia laughed slightly. Anthony knew that it was now or never. Jasmine had Virginia in the best mood she'd ever been in with him around her.

"Virginia. The reason I came over here today is to apologize for all the things I've ever put you and your family through," Anthony spoke with such sincerity. He could see that Virginia was hearing him. "I know you blame me for Eric dying, but I need you to know I didn't cause Eric to die." Anthony put his hands together. Virginia put Jasmine on the floor and let Anthony go on.

"I came back to Detroit to get my family back." Anthony glanced back and forth from his daughter's eyes to Virginia's eyes. "And that family includes you and Papa Joe." Anthony sat silently as he watched Virginia staring at the coffee table as if she were in deep thought about something.

"It took me some time to realize that it wasn't your fault that my son died. But, it's taken until now for me to forgive you." Virginia took her eyes off of the coffee table and put them on him. "I want my family back too, Anthony. I miss my daughter, my only living child." Virginia's eyes filled up with tears. The pain of not having any of her children in her life had become unbearable. "I don't want to miss out on my grandbaby's life. She sure did split you and Sydney down the middle. Jasmine looks just like both of you." Virginia sat back in the Queen Anne chair and lifted Jasmine onto her lap. "Yes, Sugar. Grandma wants to be there for you." Virginia squeezed her only grandchild close to her face and landed a big kiss on her.

Anthony smirked at the sight of the two. Half of his mission had been completed without any problems. He hadn't anticipated things would go so well. Now all he had to do was get Sydney to believe that he was for real, and to ask her to marry him.

"I want Sydney and me to get married," Anthony let Virginia in on his plan.

"You should get married. You are Jasmine's father," Virginia said matter of factly.

"But I need your help, Virginia." Anthony leaned forward on the couch and crossed his hands.

"What can I do? Sydney and I haven't so much as said hello to one another in over a year." Virginia shook her head at the thought of their situation. "I know I've been stubborn, but Sydney doesn't even try anymore. I guess she didn't need me after all." Virginia wiped the slow rolling tears from her face.

"You're wrong about that, Virginia. I've been wrong, too. Sydney needs both of us. She needs us both to be there for her. I didn't know how much I needed her until I left and didn't have her." Anthony let his hands drop and rubbed them over his freshly faded hair.

"I've been so wrong to stay out of Syd's life. I need her, too. If you haven't noticed, I'm getting pretty old and so is Joseph," Virginia gave a glance to Anthony for his reaction. She had aged, but she'd aged well. She was the meanest lady on the block, and one of the finest back then.

"You still look good, Mrs. Hastings. All the fellows in the hood knew you were mean as hell, but we said you was still fine." Anthony was doing all he could to make his future mother-in-law feel better about herself. It was working.

"Thank you, Anthony. I needed that." Virginia noticed Jasmine yawning as she downed the chocolate pudding. "You sleepy, Sugar?"

Virginia let Jasmine lay against her chest. She quickly closed her eyes and fell asleep.

"I miss my baby, and I'm going to let her know it," Virginia said as she nodded her head to Anthony, "thank you for coming here today."

Anthony stood up walked over to where Virginia was sitting. Virginia touched Anthony's hand.

"Thank you," he replied as he squeezed her hand back. It was a step in the right direction for both of them and Sydney. "We'd better get going. Sydney will be home soon." Anthony felt pleased with himself that things were finally beginning to fall in place for him.

*****

Ella Fitzgerald sang in a whisper through the speaker with Vera singing along as she lay next to Robert.

"*April in Paris*," Vera said as she ran her tired brown hand over her man's hair. "Now, who can I run to?"

There was nowhere for Vera to run. Robert had become so weak. Too weak to even do anything, Vera thought. The walls in her bedroom seemed so different now to her. They seemed lifeless and dull. There was no sign of life smiling upon them. There should have been pictures of their wedding, pictures of their beautiful children. But, there was nothing. The man Vera loved was dying and there was nothing she could do about it.

Vera slid off the bed, not disturbing Robert, and wrung out the washcloth in the basin. The antique dresser her mother gave her was covered with bottles of different medicine for Robert. None of them seemed to be working for him, or either he had just given up. Vera stood over him; he barely opened his eyes to see her as she wiped his face with a cool towel. His eyes closed slowly, and he began to cough erratically, so much so that he lifted himself up from the bed.

"Vera!" Robert yelled out, not seeing her standing near him.

"I'm right here, Bobby." Vera rushed closer to Robert with the pail she used when he got sick and couldn't get out of the bed. He spotted Vera's hand and took hold of it.

He looked up in the aging woman's eyes and then placed her warm hand on his face. Vera put the pail down then placed her other hand behind his neck and pressed his face into her rib cage.

"We're gonna make it through this, Bobby. You and me, one more time."

Robert buried his face even deeper against Vera's body.

"I know, V." Robert pulled away from her and sat up on the edge of the bed. He focused his eyes on the dresser full of drugs. The doctors told him that he had a forty- percent chance of living for more than a year without chemotherapy. The pills were his only hope. Vera stepped into Robert's view, sorting through the array of bottles, gathering Robert's prescribed dosage.

"I'm not taking anymore of that shit. I can feel my body dying. My mind is so drained, I can barely make myself think of moving." Robert's anger fueled his strength, enabling him to lift himself off of the bed.

"Bobby, please get back to bed. You can catch pneumonia in this cold house." Vera eased herself under Robert's armpit to help him stand.

"What the hell you talking about, Vera? If I go back to bed then I may never get up again." Robert felt his legs weaken and put the bulk of his weight against Vera's ailing body. She gasped at the grunt of his weight. Robert was still a big man, even though he'd lost a tremendous amount of weight. Vera helped him sit down in a chair near the window.

"I'm not ready to die, Vera. There are too many things I have left to do." Robert stared out at the evening sky, holding himself up with the help of the windowsill. Vera watched Robert, and couldn't take her eyes off of him. She couldn't count how many times she'd seen him sitting in the same spot, staring out at the sky. She couldn't imagine being without him. She had been everything to him, but his wife. Vera wondered if this would be her final role in his life.

"I'm not ready for you to die either, Bobby." Vera was tired, drop-dead tired. She hadn't slept in days, worried that Robert wouldn't make it through the night. She walked over to him and put her arm across his shoulders.

"There's so much we have to do, Bobby." Vera squeezed the man she loved with a force of love that could endure anything.

"I promise I'll try." Robert turned his eyes back onto the darkening sky.

*****

Anthony cut the ignition of the car and turned around to see Jasmine fast asleep in her car seat.

"God, you look like Syd." Anthony admired the curly black hair his daughter shared with her mother.

"This has to work for us, baby girl. I don't know what else to do." Anthony took the key out of the ignition and then stepped out the car and opened the back door. Sydney stood hidden in the window of the apartment watching Anthony get Jasmine out of the car. Her heart raced as she watched him. The sight of him with his daughter filled her heart with emotion. She decided she would meet her family at the steps. Sydney let the lace curtain fall back in place and grabbed her jacket.

Anthony walked in through the entrance of the building and began stomping the snow off his boots on the huge rug. The apartment building wasn't one of the things he missed about the city. Wayne stepped out of his apartment as Anthony passed by. Anthony turned around to see Wayne behind him. Jasmine lay asleep on Anthony's shoulder.

"I think you got off easy with Sydney." Wayne moved away from his open apartment door and closer to Anthony.

"What?" Anthony responded quickly with much aggression. Wayne knew he was way out of his league, but he had to let him know how he felt. Wayne tried to hold his ground while Anthony moved toward him. Anthony could see the fear growing in Wayne's eyes, but he respected his sudden growth of balls.

"Sydney should have never let you back into her life or Jasmine's life." Wayne stood his ground as Anthony came closer to him. He'd been harboring his feelings for this man's woman for too long. In the back of his mind, Wayne knew that Anthony could beat his ass to a pulp, but he didn't care. He hoped that since he was holding Jasmine in his arms that would limit the violence that he'd been known for.

"I think you need to mind your own damn business." Anthony got in Wayne's face, "Unless you need me to show you how to do that." Anthony was chest to chest with Wayne then suddenly pushed him hard in the center of his chest. Wayne's frail body sort of lifted off the ground, nearly knocking him off his feet, but he caught himself before falling.

"Stop it, Anthony!" Sydney yelled at the top of her lungs as she jumped down the stairs. She snatched Jasmine out of Anthony's arms with urgency and then rushed over to Wayne who was barely standing up.

"Are you all right, Wayne?" Sydney touched Wayne's shoulder

tenderly. Anthony watched in dismay. He felt as if Sydney was slowly cutting his heart out of his chest.

"I can't believe this shit!" Anthony threw up his hands in disgust. Sydney continued to pamper and see to Wayne, who was putting on the biggest act of being hurt.

"You haven't changed one bit, Anthony. You still think you can just go around beating up on people. I knew it." Sydney rubbed Jasmine's back as she lay over her shoulder. It was obvious that Sydney had hurt Anthony. He was at a total loss for words.

"I'm outta here." Anthony walked to the door. "Fuck this shit," he mumbled.

"Leaving again? It's that easy for you, huh?" Sydney rolled her eyes and then turned her back to Anthony. Anthony stopped to see Sydney's back to him. He shook his head and then continued on out the door. Sydney turned around slowly when she heard the doors close. He was gone. She suddenly felt a sense of wrong rush over her. What had she done? The very man she'd used her prayers on each and every night was gone from her life again.

Anthony made his way to his sister's car realizing why he had her car. "Damn."

He looked at his watch. He was late picking up his sister from her job.

"Damn. Everything is fucked up, now." Anthony started the ignition and pulled off. Sydney watched him from the doorway. She hugged their daughter tightly as tears rolled down her face.

Why didn't I run after him? Why did I go to Wayne? Sydney thought, as she continued to eye the spot where Anthony had just gone from. Tears continued to cover her face as she watched the marks on the street from his car.

"What have I done, Jasmine?"

Jasmine wrapped her arms tightly around her mother's neck. Sydney was startled when Wayne put his hand on her shoulder.

"Wanna come in for a minute, Sydney?" He pulled his body closer to hers. She could feel him against her behind. She turned around suddenly.

"What are you doing, Wayne?" Sydney politely removed Wayne's hand from her shoulder and faced him.

"I thought this meant that you were choosing me now," Wayne stepped back somewhat annoyed by Sydney's new attitude toward him.

"Choose you? I didn't know I had to make a choice." Sydney put her hand over her forehead. "Lord, what have I done?" In a matter of minutes, so much had gone wrong.

"What's up with you, Sydney? I'm not good enough for you now?" Wayne let his disappointment surface.

"I'm sorry, Wayne. But, I thought I made it clear to you how I felt about Anthony from jump street. So, don't try and act like you didn't know," Sydney was getting louder with each word. "I'm just as confused as you are right now, Wayne. I come down the stairs to greet my man and my daughter and here I see him getting ready to whoop your ass."

Wayne jumped in quickly. "I was not about to get my ass kicked, Sydney." He resented her for saying that about him. "So, what was all that with us then, Sydney? I was only good enough for you until your baby daddy came home?" he said matter of factly.

"Don't even go there, Wayne, because I didn't even like your ass. You came after me," Sydney headed toward the steps with Jasmine awake over her shoulder, looking at Wayne.

"Wait, Sydney," Wayne felt like a real fool now. Sydney stopped just short of the stairs, but didn't turn around to face him. Jasmine gave him a bright, smile helping to ease his pain. Sydney took a deep breath. Her head felt like it was spinning. She was realizing that she might never see Anthony again. He'd been back for a month, but she still couldn't trust him with her heart. Anthony had all her love, but not her trust.

"I'm really sorry, Syd. But, what was I supposed to do? Not fall in love with you because you told me that? I couldn't help myself. I'll admit it. You broke my heart Thanksgiving Day."

Sydney knew that day would come back to haunt her soon. She turned around to see Wayne. She saw her friend standing there before her.

"Everything was going so good. We were becoming a couple. Then, he came back and you dropped me like a hot potato."

Jasmine lifted her head from her mother's shoulder to look at Wayne.

"How was I supposed to feel, Sydney?"

"Wayne, I am so sorry. I never meant for any of this to happen."

Sydney looked at him with sincere eyes.

"I know you were straight with me from the start. But, I thought I could change your mind and make you forget about him," Wayne stood in front of Sydney and then put his hand on the banister of the stairwell.

"Then all I can say again is that I'm sorry for leading you up a dead-end street. You may get what you want after all. Anthony is probably gone for good this time." Sydney didn't wait on his response before she rushed up the flight of stairs. She mumbled under her breath, "I ain't about to argue with you, Wayne."

Wayne watched her from the bottom of the staircase in silence. Sydney wasn't the only one who had lost someone.

*****

The morning's sermon was just what Sydney needed after all that went down Thursday afternoon. Maxine and Indira were both in other worlds that night, so girls' night wasn't much of anything that past week. Sydney hadn't been able to take her mind off of Anthony. She hadn't heard from him since Thursday, and her stomach had been full of stress and worry over it. Jasmine stood in the aisle, leaning against her mother's leg. It was obvious that she was ready to go.

Pastor Davis spoke his words through the sweat that poured from his face. He blessed the congregation one last time and sat down behind the podium. This was the cue for the choir to rise and end service with a song. The gowns of the powerful choir swayed back and forth as they sang in harmony. Pastor Davis and the deacons left the podium and walked past the standing congregation. Sydney sang along with the choir as the men passed her row then headed out the front doors. The elders in the front pews soon followed them. Sydney sat back down because it would be a while before it would be time for her row to clear out. She didn't see Virginia stop in front of her row.

"Grandma!" Jasmine yelled out loudly, causing Sydney to look up to see her mother standing in the aisle holding up the remainder of the large congregation. Totally surprised, Sydney turned her eyes to her daughter away from her mother. She couldn't help but wonder how she knew who she was. Papa Joe must have taken her to see her.

"Can we talk, Sydney?" Virginia was dressed to the hilt in her cream colored suit with hat to match. Sydney could barely see her eyes under the hat, but she knew her voice all too well. Without saying a word, Sydney and Jasmine moved over in the pew and let Virginia sit down. Whispers began to surface from the congregation as they passed the two sitting together. Virginia's stubbornness was well known by the members, and they were all pleased to see her sitting with her daughter. Virginia noticed that they had the attention of everyone in the church.

"I think you and I need to go somewhere else and talk," Virginia stated as she eyed the eyes that were on them. She always worried about what other people would think of her. Sydney didn't.

"No. This is fine," Sydney responded with confidence. Virginia turned her hidden eyes on her daughter. She could see that Sydney had grown up during the time of her absence.

Sydney and Virginia sat in silence until the congregation was out of the church. Virginia took off her lavish hat and held it in her hands. Sydney lifted her eyes from the floor, and for the first time in more than two years, she looked into her mother's hazel eyes.

"Sydney, I don't know where to even begin. But, I know I want us to begin somewhere." Virginia turned her body near her daughter's. Sydney began to relax and felt a sharp pain in her chest. It was her heart. It was so full of love for her mother that the pain of not sharing it with her mother ailed her. Sydney sat still in silence as Jasmine looked on knowingly.

"I wanted to come to you a long time ago. But after Anthony came over the other day, I..." Before Virginia could finish her sentence Sydney stopped her.

"Anthony! What does he have to do with this?" Sydney asked in confusion.

Virginia could see that she was unaware that Anthony had come to visit her last week.

"Sydney, I thought you knew. Anthony brought the baby to see me last week and he wanted to patch things up between him and me. We did. I thought you knew." Virginia realized that Sydney was probably totally confused right now about everything.

"No, I didn't know. We had a fight when he brought Jasmine home that night and I haven't seen him since." Sydney started to cry suddenly, and Virginia put her arms around her shoulders. It felt good to feel her mother's touch again, Sydney had missed it so.

"Oh, Sydney, I'm so sorry. Things will work out. Believe me. If God can bring us together, he will do the same for you and Anthony."

Sydney lifted her arms and hugged her mother tightly.

"I'm sorry too, Mama," Sydney whispered into her mother's ear as she hugged her. Jasmine felt left out and put her arms around her mommy, too. Pastor Davis and Brother Frank stepped back into the church and started clapping at the sight.

"Praise, God! Praise, God!" Brother Frank spoke as he clapped.

"I will second that, Brother Frank. I am glad to see God's work in action," Pastor Davis touched the trio as they let go of their embrace.

"Yes, praise God for giving me my daughter back." Virginia touched the pastor's hand.

"Thank you for everything, Pastor," Sydney said as the pastor made his way back to his office. He had another two hours before the afternoon service began.

Sydney and Virginia walked hand in hand to the parking lot with Jasmine holding onto her mother's purse. Sydney was beginning to feel some of the weight of stress lifting from her shoulders.

"Mama, would you join us tonight for dinner?" Sydney stood in front of her mother's pink Cadillac DeVille. She'd been one of Mary Kay's top sellers for more than twenty years.

"It's funny you ask, especially since your daddy eats with you just about every Sunday. I haven't had to cook in so long. I would love to, baby." Virginia squeezed Sydney's hand.

"Thank you, Mama." Sydney lifted her hand to her lips and kissed it softly.

CHAPTER NINETEEN

Indira and Omari wrapped up their lunch meeting with Glen Johnson who represented one of the largest black-owned hotel chains in the country. Glen was a handsome brother with a low cut, and gray eyes to start. His six foot two inch frame gave insight to his past basketball days. Glen had always admired Indira and treated her with the utmost respect. Omari made sure that Indira chaired the meeting, simply because he knew that Glen had an eye for her. He was right. Glen couldn't take his eyes off of her the entire meeting. It was obvious to Indira that Omari filled him in on her pending divorce from Robert. Glen happily signed a contract with the gallery to hang their paintings on the walls of the hotel's main lobbies and inside the rooms.

Omari watched Glen sign his name on the dotted line of the contract. Indira slowly lifted her eyes from the paper, and saw Robert standing across the street looking at the double glass doors of the gallery. She dropped the coffee mug of raspberry tea to the floor.

"Excuse me, guys. I am so sorry about that." Indira picked up the mug from the floor and dabbed at her blouse with a napkin.

"It's okay, just as long as the contract didn't get wet," Omari said as he laughed, although he was quite serious.

Indira quickly turned her eyes back out onto the street, but Robert was gone. She wasn't sure if she had imagined him standing there or if he really had been there. So much had changed in such a short time, Indira felt like everything was moving so fast in the opposite direction of all her hopes.

"Is everything all right, Indira? I mean, if there is anything I can do to help, just let me know," Glen tried to sound as sincere as he could. Indira woke up to Glen's concern for her.

"Thanks so much, Glen. But, I promise you I'm doing just fine." Indira touched Glen's hand, thoughtfully. Omari stepped out of the conversation and headed downstairs to a client who had just entered the gallery.

"I'll take care of them, Indira. You take care of Glen," Omari said sarcastically then sort of snickered like a kid all the way down the stairs. Glen laughed softly and then turned his attention back to Indira.

"Okay, Glen. I think everything here is all in order, and I will be getting in touch with you just after the Christmas holidays." Indira tried to remain focused on the business at hand, but Glen had something else on his mind.

"I don't really know how to say this to you, but here goes anyway. I would really like to take you out sometime." Glen could see that this wasn't what Indira was looking for, but he thought he would put it out there anyway. "Don't say anything now, Indira, but keep me in mind."

Indira was about to speak, but Glen put his finger up to stop her from saying a word. She could only smile at his actions. Glen got up and put on his thick overcoat. She had to admit it, he did have it going on.

"I'll see you next year," he said as he leaned down and kissed Indira's hand and then started down the stairs.

Indira was positive now that Omari told Glen that she was getting divorced. He had never kissed her hand before. Omari waved up to Indira at her desk just as Glen left the gallery.

"Real funny, Omari!" Indira yelled out over the balcony of their offices. Indira had so much work to do before her date with El that night. She was leery about starting up with El, but he insisted on seeing her. She wasn't ready to begin another relationship, just yet.

*****

Clarissa decided to take Maxine up on her offer to come to the shop and get the works. She was in dire need of a perm, manicure, and pedicure. Clarissa stepped into the waiting area of the shop, and took a good look around.

"Maxine, this is nice. Real nice," Clarissa walked past Stephanie at the desk to head to the back. Stephanie gave Maxine a questioning look.

"Clarissa is Indira's baby sister," Maxine whispered to Stephanie so she could take the ugly look off of her face. Stephanie nodded, and went back to the phone. Clarissa appeared from around the corner.

"I love it, Maxine. Ms. Mable would have loved this," Clarissa ran over to Maxine and hugged her.

"Yeah, she would have loved it," Maxine felt a strange sense of pride.

"Girl, I'm so proud of you; Sydney and Indira, too. All of y'all turned out good." Clarissa continued to go on about the trio, wishing that her life had gone as well.

"So are you ready to get you hair, fingers, and toes taken care of?" Maxine asked, as she and Clarissa stood at Stephanie's desk. It was still early, so Maxine had time to talk and catch up with Clarissa while she did her hair. "Let me tell you, if you want to make any money as a dancer, all of you had better look good."

Clarissa playfully shook Maxine's hand and the two stepped into her station. Maxine and Clarissa had always gotten along well since they were more alike than Clarissa and Indira. Clarissa climbed into Maxine's chair, as Maxine ran her fingers through her coarse hair.

"Damn. When was the last time you had a perm?" Maxine looked at the reflection in the mirror for her answer. Maxine thought back to when she used to practice braiding on Clarissa's thick head of hair.

"It's been a while. I wore wigs most of the time when I danced." Clarissa touched her hair and stared into the mirror. She sort of leaned back and focused her eyes again. She felt as if she didn't know the person who was staring back at her. Her face was pale without any makeup, and her body had become so frail and skinny. To make things worse, her hair was standing straight up on her head.

Maxine watched Clarissa closely. She could see all the things that Clarissa was seeing. She'd been down that same critical road herself once or twice. Maxine put her hand on Clarissa's bony shoulder.

"I'm glad you're home, baby girl," Maxine said aloud. Clarissa lifted her eyes to her.

"Thanks, Maxine. I'm glad to be back."

Maxine wrapped a smock over Clarissa's scantly clad shoulders then spun the chair away from the mirror and started parting and basing Clarissa's scalp.

"Tell me about D.C. and all the crazy shit you did at that club." Maxine changed her direction quick. She wanted to know the nitty gritty about the club.

"You still crazy, Maxine. It's so much to tell, but I don't know what you can handle," Clarissa joked.

"What? Can I handle it? You must don't remember who you

talking to. I taught your ass everything you know. "

Maxine and Clarissa gave a high 5 and started laughing loudly, so loud that Stephanie poked her head into the room.

"What are you two cackling about in here?" Stephanie would be a millionaire if being nosey was a job.

"Nothing, girl. Go on about your business," Maxine waved Stephanie away with her comb. Clarissa covered her mouth and laughed. "She is so damn nosey. Ain't nobody even talking to her," Maxine tried to be serious then she laughed when Stephanie stuck her hand into the room giving Maxine a bird. Clarissa couldn't hold it together any longer, she cracked up. Maxine was glad that Clarissa was there, she needed to laugh.

All morning Maxine had been staring at the clock. The only thing that had been on her mind was her mother. Today was the day that she was to visit her. Maxine had promised her Aunt Betsy that she would, at least, make an effort to visit—easier said than done. After almost fifteen years, Maxine would have her chance to let her mother know how she really felt and how much pain she'd caused her.

"So I hear that you knocked up," Clarissa said it so nonchalantly that Maxine dropped the comb onto her lap.

"Clarissa!" Maxine put her hand over her heart.

"What? You pregnant, ain't you?" Clarissa turned around in the chair to look at Maxine.

"Yes, fool. You just shocked the hell out of me when you asked me like that." Maxine looked at Clarissa and cracked up again.

"Ain't quite got used to it yet, huh?" Clarissa shook her head and laughed, too.

"Girl, let me do your nappy head before this place starts to fill up." Maxine went back to preparing Clarissa's hair for shampooing.

"I don't know what you talking about. I got good hair." Clarissa batted her bright eyes playfully.

"You ain't changed one bit, still a comedian. Now come on." Maxine led Clarissa
back to the bowls down the hallway. She put her arm around her shoulder.

"We've got plenty of time to catch up, Maxine." Clarissa knew this for sure. She had no intentions of going back to dancing or D.C. anytime soon.

*****

For once in a long time, the day seemed to breeze by at the shop. Maxine parked under the dimly lit street in front of her Aunt Betsy's house and then turned down the car stereo. The anger she'd harbored inside for her mother seemed to be fading with time. There had been so many questions in her mind, so many things she'd needed her mother for and she wasn't there. Maureen had left her at her grandmother's like some sort of UPS package. For years, Maxine thought she was just staying for a while. Then, one day, she overheard her grandmother on the telephone saying that Maureen wasn't ever coming back to get her child. Maxine put her face into her hands. Her emotions seemed unclear more so than ever. Where was the hatred and resentment she felt not more than an hour before she arrived? Maxine lifted her head above her praying hands.

"Lord, please help me tonight. I can't go on feeling like this." Maxine pulled her coat together and stepped down out of her truck and into the freshly fallen snow on the grass and sidewalks. The minute her feet touched the ground, she felt an awful urge to pee. The pressure in her bladder was becoming unbearable. Maxine made a dash for the house. Luckily her aunt was standing with the door open for her.

"What's wrong with you?" Betsy eyed her niece strangely as she ran past her.

"I gotta go to the bathroom." Maxine had unbuttoned her pants before she got in the door of the bathroom good. She dropped her pants and landed on the padded toilet seat.

"Whoa! I guess I can't forget that I'm pregnant." Maxine washed her hands then splashed cold water over her face. She took a deep breath. She didn't know what to expect next. The minute she opened the door of the bathroom, her aunt greeted her. Betsy took Maxine lightly by the arm and pulled her aside in the hallway.

"Are you all right?" Aunt Betsy rubbed her hand against Maxine's jacket then helped her take it off. Maxine could see that her aunt was more nervous than she was about seeing her mother.

"I just want to warn you before you go in there. Your mother looks really bad, and the doctors haven't given her much time." Aunt Betsy folded Maxine's coat over her arm neatly.

She'll Learn

"Don't worry. I'll be just fine," Maxine had an arrogant tone, causing her aunt to give her a shameful look.

"I know you are pissed off at your mother, but she is still your mother and I want you to give her that respect."

Maxine nodded in compliance and started to move away, but Betsy snagged her arm again.

"Do you hear me, Max?" The seriousness in her aunt's tone rendered the correct response.

"Yes, ma'am," Maxine watched her aunt walk ahead of her and sort of tiptoe into the TV room that was now transformed into a bedroom for her mother.

"Maureen, are you awake, honey?" Betsy fluffed up the pillows behind her sister's head. Maureen groggily opened her eyes and focused them on the figure standing in the doorway. Betsy saw Maureen staring at Maxine as she just barely stepped in the door.

"Maxine has come to see you, Maureen. I told her how much you wanted to see her."

Maureen's eyes lit up the best they could at the realization that the figure in the door was that of her daughter. She tried to lift herself up, but she was too weak. Her arms slipped down as she sat up on them. Aunt Betsy helped her sit up in the bed as Maxine looked on.

"I'm going to fix you some dinner, so I'll be back in a little while," Betsy was talking but no one seemed to be listening. Maxine and Maureen said no words, but only stared at one another. Betsy touched Maxine's hand on the way out of the room. Maxine searched desperately for the anger, hatred, and pain that lived in her body to devour her mother with. That was impossible for her to do the moment she laid eyes on her mother's sunken face and bruised body.

Her beautiful caramel skin had dark spots and healing cuts instead of the glow she used to wear. The shoulder length hair that moved when she spoke was now a dried-out ball of wire on her head. Aunt Betsy hadn't prepared her enough in the hallway. As a child, Maxine thought her mother looked like Diana Ross in the movie *Mahogany*. Now, she was shaking at the sight of her. She looked like a black holocaust victim. The only difference was she'd done this to herself.

"Maxine, is that really you, baby?" Maureen struggled to speak. Her voice sounded raspy and rough. Maxine looked as if she were frozen where she stood. Her eyes were locked in a deep stare on her mother. Maureen was embarrassed and ashamed for her daughter to see her like this and after so many hard years. She dropped her eyes from Maxine's, knowing that this wasn't going to be easy.

"Hello, Mama," Maxine finally got the words out of her mouth. Maureen lifted her sad eyes back to her daughter's face.

"I'm so sorry. I am deeply sorry, Maxine," Maureen mustered up the words in between her burst of tears. "I was strung out and I didn't need nobody depending on me." Maureen started coughing hard and grabbed her chest. "I just hope you can forgive me for giving you up, but I had to."

Maxine felt her guard weaken. She loved her mother, but she'd made herself believe she didn't. She rushed over to her mother as she continued to cough and struggle to breathe. Maxine got the cup of water from the nightstand and held it up to Maureen's dry mouth. Maxine let her eyes roam over the healing sores that lined her mother's arms. There were so many scars from years of drug abuse. Her arms displayed the many times she'd shot up, destroying them. Maureen sipped from the cup and then got her breath back.

"Thank you, baby."

Maxine put down the cup and remained seated on the edge of the bed. Years of thoughts, words, and questions filled Maxine's mind, but they wouldn't or couldn't come together for her to say something.

"I hear you've done good for yourself," Maureen struggled to keep the conversation going. She knew she'd failed miserably as a mother, the most precious of relationships, but the underlying hurt was the same for both of them. They were both left feeling hopeless and not worth anyone's love.

"Yeah. The shop's been doing well this year," Maxine kept her answers short.

"Mama passed her love for doing hair down to you. Me and Betsy didn't like to do hair." Maureen nodded her head as she watched her child, now a grown woman barely able to speak to her.

"She passed on plenty to me. Doing hair was just one thing," Maxine sounded sarcastic, but she really wasn't trying to be. Plus, she didn't want to disappoint her aunt.

"I know, baby. Mama was a good woman. Something I didn't know how to be." Maureen dropped her head low to her chest. She awaited Maxine's response to cut her deeply. After a few awkward moments of silence, Maxine spoke.

"You did what you had to do, and it worked out best for me. Grandma gave me enough love for the both of you." She put her hand on top of her mother's hand.

"I couldn't smoke dope all day and be a mother, too. That shit took over my mind and my body. This and this hasn't belonged to me in a long time." Maureen had tears rolling down her cheeks as she pointed to her head and body. "Mama tried to help me, but I was too far gone by then. I knew I had to give you up or who knows what would have happened to you."

Maxine wiped the tears from her mother's face with her bare hand. She wasn't afraid anymore.

"It's all right, Mama. I'm here now."

Maureen smiled at Maxine, knowing that this would probably be the highlight of their newfound relationship.

*****

Clarissa cut the volume of the stereo down when she heard the telephone ringing.
She managed to answer it on the third ring.

"Hello," Clarissa said.

"Hey, Claire, I'm running a few minutes late, and Eldridge will be there at 6:30 sharp, so let him in and fix him a drink or something until I get there." Indira sat at her desk surrounded by legal documents and clearance forms all awaiting her signature.

"Oh, is this the artist?" Clarissa asked mischievously.

"Yes, and mind your manners," Indira responded in a playful tone.

"Better hurry up and get here, then. I've been feeling a little lonely lately. An artist would be right up my alley." Clarissa checked herself in the hall mirror as she talked on the phone to Indira.

"Well, you need to close down that alley to all traffic."

Clarissa and Indira laughed on the phone.

"All right, girl. He'll be fine," Clarissa reassured.

"He's already fine, that's the problem." Indira laughed again.

"Bye, Indi!" Clarissa hung up the phone and pumped up the stereo once again. Jay-Z was bumping through the speakers. She used his music on stage a lot. Clarissa loved hip-hop and the thugged-out brothers who came with it.

*****

Eldridge checked himself in the rearview mirror of his rented Jaguar and then stepped out of the car. He walked up to Indira's front door then rang the doorbell, to no response. He then resorted to knocking on the door. He could hear loud music coming through the front door, but he knew it wasn't Indira's style at all. Before he could knock for a third time, the door opened wide. El sort of gasped when he saw another beautiful woman at the door and it wasn't Indira.

"Hi. You must be Eldridge." Clarissa extended her hand. El obliged by shaking it softly. "I'm Indira's younger sister… Clarissa." Clarissa moved aside to let him come through the front door.

"Very nice to meet you, Clarissa. Is Indira home yet?" El strolled past Clarissa and then caught a quick glimpse of her frame just as she closed the door behind him. The little sister was gorgeous too, but El's heart belonged to the big sister. Clarissa turned around to catch El leaving his glimpse of her. That was all she needed, a hint of interest.

"No. She's not here yet, but she's on the way home now. She just called a few minutes before you got here."

Clarissa sexily strolled by El, and led him into the living room. Her one-sleeve tank and hip hugger jeans sang a song. El followed her closely and then sat down on the couch. Clarissa knew she was looking good, especially since Maxine hooked her hair up. She loved her new short cut because it was frisky like her.

"Would you like something to drink?" Clarissa stood damn near between El's legs awaiting his answer. He said yes just to make her move. That wouldn't be too good for Indira to walk through the door to see him going at it with her baby sister.

"Yes. I'll have some cognac." El thought of something fast, and Clarissa disappeared, giving him time to catch his breath. Clarissa usually had that effect on men.

"So, I hear you're a big time painter," Clarissa yelled from the den as she fixed El's drink. He felt awkward yelling through the house, so he waited until Clarissa returned with his drink.

"I wouldn't say I was big time," he tried to be modest.

"I would. The paintings Indira showed me were beautiful." Clarissa sat down on the couch next to El.

"Thank you. I'm glad you liked them." El could see Clarissa sliding over closer to him.

"I have a few talents, myself." Clarissa crossed her legs and smiled flirtatiously at El. He took a big swallow of his drink, nearly spitting out the strong liquor at her last move. He seemed to be having a hard time with Clarissa's games. It was a game she'd played often and she knew exactly what she was doing to him. She treated every man she came in contact with as a potential customer. It was sort of an occupational hazard for her. It seemed as though she was preparing El for a lap dance.

"I'll bet you do have plenty of hidden talents," El responded, deciding not to take another drink because he could feel the last gulp taking effect on him already.

"Let me show you one of them." Clarissa jumped off the couch in a hurry. She left El in a state of shock. He followed her with his eyes out of the room. He hoped she wasn't coming back with anything that would get him into trouble. After slipping out of his coat and adjusting his pants, he checked his watch to see that only fifteen minutes had gone by.

"Maintain, El. Keep cool. Indira will be here soon," he whispered under his breath. Clarissa burst back into the room with a notebook in her hand and a shy smirk on her face.

"I wanna read some of my stuff to you if you don't mind." Clarissa didn't seem like the type of person to take no for an answer, so El nodded his head in agreement. In the back of his mind he thought it might be kind of fun.

Clarissa put her notebook down and positioned herself in front of the coffee table and got into character. El was taken aback at the sight of her.

"Ain't life grand when you're holding the world in the palm of your hand?" Clarissa was in another world. El could see that she was serious and became more interested as she went on.

"Ain't life grand when money is plenty, the sun is shining and your man is treating you as sweet as honey? Ain't life grand…ain't life grand?"

He watched the expressions on Clarissa's face and could see the emotion she was feeling with each word. It was kind of sexy. He took another sip of his cognac and sat back into the couch.

"…Then all of a sudden shit just hits the fan. What you gonna do?" Clarissa was standing with her shoulder shrugged as if she wanted El to answer, but he didn't. After a long pause, Clarissa started up again, with El hanging on her every word.

"Time is moving by slow now. Your heart is aching. Your money is short and your phone ain't ringing." She was putting on a real show for El in the absence of her sister. They both seemed to be loving every minute of it.

"Peace be with you on your journey of life. What you gotta learn? What's your lesson in life?" Clarissa knew she had El's attention from the boyish smirk on his face. She went on rolling her body with each word.

"Life is real. Life is true. Life is grand! When you're holding the world in the palm of your hands," Clarissa took a bow, revealing her perfect breast pushing near the edge of her shirt.

If I didn't really like Indira…, El thought to himself and shook his head. He caught a full view of Clarissa's bosom then swallowed the last of his drink, staring into the bottom of the glass.

"So did you like it?" Clarissa bounced her way back to the couch happily and plopped down next to him.

"Oh, yes. That was good." El was feeling good now that the cognac had helped him to relax. He put his arm over the couch and turned his body toward Clarissa. "I loved the way you recited your poem. I could tell there was a lot of feeling behind it." He allowed himself to get comfortable, and somehow let Indira slip from his mind. "So how long are you going to be in town?" El seemed to be making chitchat now, just when he heard keys at the front door.

Indira walked in to see El and Clarissa sitting on the couch. She put her briefcase and purse down on the chair.

She'll Learn

"Well, hello, you two. Has my baby sister entertained you while you were waiting?" Indira joked. Eldridge eased his body back to the front position.

"You know I did. I read Eldridge one of my poems." Clarissa rose off of the couch to remove El's empty glass from the table. She brushed Indira's shoulder as she went by. "Girl, he has got it going on. Let me know if you don't want it," Clarissa whispered to Indira and then laughed out loud. Indira smiled and turned her attention back to Eldridge, who was looking as handsome as ever. Eldridge didn't waste any time. He got up from the couch and extended his arms out to Indira.

"I have missed seeing your face these past weeks," El said in a sweet tone.

"Oh, really? And, what have you got planned for me tonight?" Indira welcomed his strong arms around her. She had been longing for that feeling herself.

"It's a surprise." El let go of his hold on Indira's small waist, slowly. He then eyed her from head to toe.

"Oh, it's a surprise, huh? Can I invite my sister?" Indira asked in a hurry, just as Clarissa walked back into the room. Clarissa could see the hope in El's eyes, the hope of being alone with Indira. She decided to answer for him.

"No, that's okay. You two have fun tonight. I'm going to chill out here." Clarissa spread out across the couch. El gave her a wink as sort of a thanks for turning down the offer.

"Maybe next time," El said to her slyly.

"Well give me a few minutes to change, and I will be right back." Indira made her way up the long staircase with El's eyes following her every step of the way. He walked over to Clarissa and gave her a high 5.

"Thanks for doing that. I need to spend some quality time with your sister. I'm going back to Atlanta in the morning," El sounded sincere. Clarissa could tell that he liked Indira. Any other man would have jumped at the chances she had thrown at him.

"Let's just say, you owe me." Clarissa started up the stairs. She was feeling guilty for flirting with Eldridge after she saw how much he liked her sister. Clarissa hoped Indira wasn't mad at her; that would be all she needed at this point.

Indira undressed from her suit and searched through her closet at the same time. She saw Clarissa enter her bedroom.

"Oh, good. Let me take a shower and you find me something to wear." Indira yanked off the remainder of clothing on her body and slipped into her silk robe. Clarissa hadn't started to move yet. "Get to it, girl. Find me something to wear, will you?" Indira pointed to the closet and then slipped into her bathroom.

Clarissa ran her fingers over the gorgeous suits and dresses. The shelves were filled with matching shoes and purses. Clarissa took a peek at the shoe size of her sister's Versace pump.

"Size 8! Thank, God." Clarissa pulled out a full-length sequined dress and a mini halter dress. She found matching shoes for both and then laid them out across the bed. The bathroom door flung open as Indira rushed out with steam following her. Still rubbing lotion on her body, Indira stopped in her tracks at Clarissa's choices.

"I really don't feel like wearing either one of those. But since you picked them..." Indira put her hand on her hip and then picked up the maroon halter dress.

"That dress is too sharp. You gonna have to let me borrow that one." Clarissa took out Indira's hairpins while she eased on her sheer stockings. Indira's curly locks fell around her shoulders.

"I hope you're not mad at me for flirting with your man," Clarissa sort of blurted out the statement. In her line of work, flirting with another woman's man could be deadly. Indira snapped the top of the stockings as she stood up.

"I couldn't care less about that, and he's not my man." Indira stood in her mirror over her vanity table and dabbed two drops of Issey Miyake on her neck and breast before slipping into her dress.

"He sure does want to be. Believe me. I was throwing his fine ass some fast balls, but he wasn't having it," Clarissa talked as she watched Indira turn into the princess at the ball. Indira hadn't changed one bit. In Clarissa's eyes, she was still the prettiest girl she knew. Indira checked herself once more in the mirror.

"Well, that's too bad for him, because friendship is all I want right now." Indira rolled her neck and eyes and then switched hard out the door of her bedroom.

"You go ahead then, Indira. Don't take no more bullshit from anybody." Clarissa met Indira in the hallway and led the way down the stairs.

If El ever lost track of what he wanted earlier, he knew it now as Indira gracefully came down the flight of stairs. Her velour halter dress hugged the right places and showed enough leg to drive El out of his mind all evening long. He glanced at Clarissa and nodded his approval of Indira's dress tonight. He automatically knew that this was her doing and not Indira's choice for the evening.

"Don't she look sharp as hell?" Clarissa danced around Indira proudly, just as she did when they were young girls preparing Indira for a date. In a family like theirs, they only had each other.

"Yes, she does. She looks fabulous, or like my man used to say… she looks marvelous!"

Indira sort of felt like she was fifteen again. El and Clarissa looked up at her as she stood on the stair above them.

"Okay. That's enough of that." Indira split the two and went to the closet to retrieve her coat.

"Damn, Indira. You still don't know how to take a compliment," Clarissa smacked her sister on her back playfully.

"Get used to it, because I'll be dishing them out all night long." El eased Indira's coat over her arms and shoulders. Then he held onto her. "You smell so good."

Indira blushed as El turned her around to face him. He held out his arm for her.

"Let's go, baby," he said. El and Indira stood by as Clarissa opened the door for them.

"Have a good time," Clarissa said as the couple strolled out the door.

*****

Maxine thought back on the week and decided that this was one of the most eventful weeks she'd ever been through. It would be good to just sit down and relax with the girls tonight. She didn't want to think about much of nothing. But how could she not? Maxine thought, as she straightened up around the house. She couldn't wait for Sydney to tell her what really happened between Anthony and her and why his thuggish ass was gone away again.

Sydney hadn't finished telling her about when Virginia came to talk to her after church, because Jasmine had started crying. Indira, the new independent woman, had some changes in her life with Clarissa coming to stay with her and with that painter guy who she couldn't seem to shake, though she didn't want to get involved with anybody just yet. Maxine turned on the evening news, but cut the volume down.

"She's got a point, though," Maxine said under her breath, as she thought about Indira's past relationship. "I would definitely take my time in finding someone this go ‘round if I was her." Maxine sat down on the couch in front of the silent television.

After seeing her mother for the first time in nearly fifteen years, everything that seemed to matter to Maxine had new meaning for her now. Her grandmother used to say that life is just one big lesson and every day you learn something new in it. Whenever Maxine did anything wrong you could hear the old woman gossiping on the phone saying, "She'll learn next time.”

Maxine smirked at the thought of her grandmother. She felt a rumble in her stomach and then placed her hand over it. The phone ran, and Maxine reached over to the end table for it.

"Hello," Maxine sounded somber.

"Hey, Maxine," Indira's tone was the opposite. She sounded upbeat about something.

"Are you and Clarissa on your way, yet?" Maxine asked, not letting Indira speak.

"Clarissa isn't feeling good, so I'm going to stay home with her tonight. Plus, I don't want her to throw up in my car," Indira stated, and then there was silence.

"Oh, okay, then. I guess it'll just be me and Sydney tonight." Maxine started on her bag of chips for tonight's gathering. She nearly dropped the phone from her shoulder trying to open the bag.

"How are you feeling today? Still sick?" Indira was feeling guilty about canceling out. The last time she missed coming over was because Robert had kicked her ass and she was too embarrassed to show her face.

She'll Learn

"Let's see. I'm down to throwing up only three times a day, instead of five times, so I guess that's better," Maxine tried to be funny, but she was upset.

"Eat some crackers or some bread, like I know what to do, right?" Indira reminded herself that she'd never been pregnant.

"Whatever! You'll know one day. Remember I wasn't trying to know about this myself."

Maxine and Indira laughed on the phone, just as the other line beeped.

"I'll talk to you tomorrow, Indi. My other line is ringing," Maxine said hurriedly.

"Okay, bye." Indira hung up as Maxine clicked over to the other line.

"Hello," Maxine answered.

"What's up, preggo?" Sydney boasted loudly over the phone.

"Shut up! Why is your ass still at home?" Maxine crunched the chips rudely in Sydney's ear.

"Don't get mad, but Mama wants me to go to something with her tonight so she can show me off all of a sudden." Sydney knew she was glad to go with her, but she knew Maxine would be pissed off. "You, Indira, and Clarissa won't even miss me," Sydney sounded reassuring.

"They're not coming over tonight, either. Clarissa is sick," Maxine had an unsympathetic tone.

"I'm sorry, Maxine. But, I'll make it up to you," Sydney pleaded with her friend.

"It's all right, really. I'm kind of tired, anyway, so I'll be fine," Maxine tried to convince herself of that.

"Are you sure?" Sydney asked.

"Yes and I'll call you tomorrow," Maxine moved the phone from her ear.

"Bye!" Sydney yelled. "Mean ass."

Maxine heard Sydney say that just as she switched off the phone. Maxine yawned and then picked up the remote from the table and cut the television off. She looked around the empty house and then made her way to the stairs. She grabbed the four pregnancy books Indira bought her, and carried them up to her bedroom.

"Might as well read about what's going on inside of me." Maxine cut the hall lamp on and slowly climbed the steep stairs to her bedroom. “I’ve got a feeling I’m gonna hate these stairs pretty soon.” Maxine touched her stomach as she reached the top step.

CHAPTER TWENTY

Christmas Eve arrived in traditional Detroit fashion. Snow fell from the sky every day leading up to the big day. It made for a white Christmas like everyone dreamed of, but it was impossible to drive in it. Anthony had been depressed since he and Sydney had that stupid fight a couple of weeks ago. They hadn't spoken to each other since, and he missed both her and Jasmine. Anthony didn't care what went down between them, he refused to miss another Christmas with his family. He had been putting up money ever since he started his job at the plant. He'd managed to put up enough to buy Sydney a ring and planned to do so real soon.

*****

Sydney burst through the door of her dimly lit apartment with Jasmine hoisted high on her hip along with her too large of a purse on her shoulder and two bags of groceries for tomorrow's dinner. Sydney put the bags on the kitchen table and then laid Jasmine down on the couch.

"Girl, you are getting so big, my hip is broke," Sydney joked to her sleeping daughter as she took off her winter apparel. Sydney kept Jasmine up just about all day since she had so much running around to do for tomorrow. It worked, Jasmine was fast asleep, so Sydney could get started cooking. Tomorrow wasn't just Christmas. It was going to be a very special day for Sydney; a big day indeed for Sydney and Virginia since they would be spending Christmas together for the first time in more than two years. Sydney wanted everything to be perfect for her. She wanted it to be perfect for everyone she loved, but everyone she loved wouldn't be there. She'd had Anthony in her hands, and then he seemed to slip through her fingertips again. She stared at her fingers on the turkey's pale, thick skin, as her mind locked on the thought of Anthony. Sydney took Jasmine into her bedroom and changed her into her warm Elmo pajamas. She looked at Jasmine as she lay still in the single bed against the wall of the room. She then closed the door halfway to be able to hear her. Sydney switched on the lights in the dining room and the hallway. She eyed the turkey thawing out in the sink.

"You look like a winner, my friend," Sydney washed her hands in the basin next to the turkey and then massaged it gently. "Just right. You are ready for the stuffing, so am I, for that matter." Sydney stopped at the realization of her words and thought about what she had said. She covered her mouth and laughed. She retrieved her apron and tied it around her waist.

"Let's see. It's six-thirty now, so I should be done at the crack of dawn." Sydney pulled out a stalk of celery, a bag of breadcrumbs, and a huge plastic bag spilling over with fresh collard greens. She washed the empty side of the sink to begin picking and washing the bushel of greens. Sydney wanted to be finished by the time Papa Joe got there so she could give him a hand putting Jasmine's toys together. Papa Joe was going on sixty-seven and he still insisted on doing everything himself. He would just say that Sydney was in his way, regardless of what she said. Sydney laughed at the thought of her father still climbing those five flights of stairs nearly every day. He'd always been there for her, no matter the problem.

She washed the celery then put it on the cutting board to chop. She remembered to chop them very finely because Maxine hated the large pieces in the stuffing. Plus, she had to make another pan of stuffing with chicken gizzards for her daddy and Indira. Just as she began mixing the bowl of breadcrumbs and milk, the doorbell rang. Sydney glanced at the clock over the stove.

"It's too early for Daddy." Sydney rinsed the mix off her hands under the water and then rushed to the door. The doorbell rang a second time.

"Who is it?" Sydney dried her hands on her apron.

"It's me, girl. Open the door," Maxine barked from the opposite side of the door. Sydney popped the three locks that helped to make her feel secure, and opened the door.

"Hey, Maxine, I didn't know you were coming over tonight." Sydney was surprised to see her.

"How come you didn't know? I called you and told you that I was coming over after I closed the shop." Maxine stepped inside the apartment, taking her coat off before she was all the way in the door. Sydney looked at her strangely.

"You did not call me, Maxine. But I'm glad to see you, anyway." Sydney tried to go on with her schedule.

She'll Learn

"I did call you, Sydney." Maxine tried to convince Sydney that she'd called. Sydney stood shaking her head in disagreement. Maxine turned on the faucet and washed her hands. "Damn, Sydney. Did I call you?" Maxine couldn't recall this event herself.

"When you pregnant, you forget stuff. Get ready for a lot more, my sister." Sydney went back to the mix in the bowl.

"That's messed up. I really thought I called you today. I kept saying it all day, too…call Sydney." Maxine sat down at the table and then slid the garbage can to her. She shook her head in disbelief.

"Start picking those greens for me." Sydney pointed to the bag on the table.

Maxine gave her an annoying look. "What does it look like I'm doing?" Maxine pulled the bag toward her side of the table. Sydney laughed but tried to stop before Maxine could notice.

"What you laughing at?" Maxine eyed Sydney at the sink.

"I thought you pulled the trash can over in case you had to throw up." Sydney laughed and turned to Maxine laughing. Maxine tried to act mad, but she started laughing, too.

"I came over here to help your ass cook. Not to get picked at." Maxine went back to picking the greens, with Sydney laughing even harder at her now. She could see that Maxine's emotions were suddenly on her shoulder.

"Well, I am sorry, Maxine. And, thank you for coming over to help me," Sydney playfully changed her tone.

"You're welcome." Maxine pulled the leaves off the stem in a rhythm. The two pans of stuffing were ready for the oven. Sydney placed the turkey in its pan and seasoned it well. Maxine got through the bushel of greens quickly. She and Sydney were both pretty good cooks, but Indira wasn't interested in Ms. Mable's cooking lessons. But on the other hand, she could clean almost anything. Sydney filled the sink with water and salt and then pushed the collards under the water to wash them.

"I'm tired already," Maxine wiped her forehead with a napkin from the table. Sydney started on the macaroni and cheese.

"What? Girl, I'm just getting started." Sydney put the macaroni on the stove to boil. She walked past Maxine to the stereo in the living room and cut on some music. Not loud enough to wake Jasmine, but loud enough to create some positive atmosphere. She put one of her favorite CDs of all times into the player and stepped back into the kitchen.

"Who you playing?" Maxine asked.

The music started and Sydney began to move her body to the beat right away, "A Motown Christmas."

"I should have known. You've been playing it all month." Maxine got up from her chair to go to the bathroom. Sydney stirred the boiling macaroni on the stove. The doorbell rang. Sydney looked at the clock on the wall.

"Still too early for Daddy," Sydney wiped her hands on her apron and rushed to the door. Without checking the peephole, she opened it.

"Hey, Daddy," Sydney was surprised to her father so early, but yet there was another surprise.

"Hello, Sydney. I hope you don't mind me coming over with your daddy." Virginia was holding one of her homemade cheesecakes in her hands. Sydney lifted her eyes to her mother and then smiled.

"No. I'm so glad you're here, Mama… Maxine!" Sydney led her mother into the apartment and yelled for her best friend. Maxine rushed to the hallway to see Virginia and Papa Joe.

"Hello, Mrs. Hastings. Hey there, Papa Joe," Maxine hugged the old man as she usually did, but only nodded to Sydney's mother. She and Maxine had never seen eye to eye, even over the years.

"You're looking good, Maxine," Virginia nodded in approval to Maxine and then sat down on the couch. Virginia looked around the tiny apartment and recognized plenty of the things that her husband swore he was throwing out. She couldn't blame him. She'd been the fool for giving up her daughter, not him.

"Thank you, Mrs. Hastings," Maxine politely replied and then stepped back into the kitchen.

"Where is my grandbaby?" Virginia asked with excitement.

"She's asleep in her room," Sydney responded quickly.

"With that music on?" Virginia's disapproval was evident in her voice. Sydney looked at Maxine, and then her father.

"Yes, ma'am," Sydney said, damn near in a whisper.

Virginia knew she was starting off on the wrong foot already, so she took a step backward.

"Is that The Temptations singing?" she decided to loosen up and give the evening a chance. Sydney lifted her eyes and nodded her head to her mother.

"Yes, they're singing *Rudolph the Red-Nosed Reindeer*." Sydney hoped she wasn't going to regret having Virginia back in her life. Papa Joe looked strangely at his wife of more than thirty years then rested his arm behind her side of the couch.

"Your daddy and I love The Temptations." Virginia turned playfully to her husband. "Don't we, Joseph?" she asked slyly.

"Yes, we do, sugar." Papa Joe put his arm on his wife's shoulders. Sydney and Maxine looked at each other almost embarrassed by their affection for one another. They both laughed like silly girls, while at the same time feeling sort of jealous of her parent's bond.

"Let me get back to work. Daddy, Jasmine's tricycle is in the box in that hall closet." Sydney went back into the kitchen with Maxine following her closely.

"Girl, I didn't know what to say to your mama. Am I supposed to still call her Mrs. Hastings?" Maxine put a piece of celery in her mouth as she thought.

"How do you think I feel? She's my mother." Sydney took the pot of macaroni off of the stove then poured it over the strainer in the sink. The steam from the boiling water rushed Sydney's face, giving her a facial. Maxine buttered the glass pan for the macaroni and started slicing the cheese.

"I mean, I have to get to know Mama all over again." Sydney poured the macaroni into the pan Maxine had prepared.

"For that matter, I would have had to get to know Anthony all over again," Maxine said.

Sydney emptied the pot and sat it on the counter top.

"But, Maxine. That's what I want to do. I want the chance to get to know both of them again. I prayed for both Mama and Anthony to come back. Now, I only need Anthony." Sydney noticed that Maxine had stopped slicing the cheese.

"Sydney, I know you love Anthony, but have you ever thought that he may not come back this time?" Maxine knew this would hurt Sydney, but she would rather for her friend to be hurt now than in the long run.

Sydney ignored Maxine's question as she mixed the eggs and milk for the macaroni. That same question had been lingering in the back of her mind ever since he left her last week for a second time. Sydney suddenly stopped mixing and turned to Maxine sitting at the table.

"No, Maxine. I have not thought about that. I have put the thought so far in the back of my mind it can't come true." She poured her mixture in the pan and layered it with cheese.

"Sydney, I just don't want you to..." Maxine was trying to prepare her friend for the worst, which is what she'd seemed to have gotten used to herself.

"Maxine, I don't want to hear it tonight. Just let me finish cooking the food and I will think about Anthony never coming back later, okay?" Sydney was becoming agitated with Maxine's negative views. "After two years, Anthony came back. I'm not going to give up on him just yet." Sydney let Maxine know that the conversation on Anthony was over.

Virginia walked through the door of the kitchen just as the tension between Maxine and Sydney was too thick to stand.

"You're right, Sydney. Don't give up on Anthony just yet." Virginia stood between her and Maxine. "Anthony was a different man when he came over to my house and apologized to me. I felt that he was sincere and genuine. Sydney, for the first time ever, I know for a fact that the man loves you and his daughter." Virginia put her arms around Sydney's shoulders. Sydney had missed her mother's touch and wisdom.

"Then, where is he now, Virginia?" Maxine said with confidence. "Why get her hopes up all high again for that runaway to never show his face again?" Maxine was obviously upset with Virginia's take on the situation. She had hoped that Virginia would talk some sense into Sydney's head. Virginia looked Maxine over thoroughly.

"Are you sure that you're talking about Anthony, Maxine?" Virginia hit Maxine where it hurt and Sydney felt the blow like it had hit her. Maxine was thrown off by the sassy woman's comment and was at a sudden loss for words. Sydney knew she had to do something quickly, before Maxine went off on her mother.

"Mama, can you rinse those greens and put them in the pressure cooker for me?" Sydney put her mother to work while Maxine looked as if she were about to boil over.

"Sure, baby. I came here to lend you a hand." Virginia tied the spare apron around her petite waist and began her task.

Sydney fixed a glass of ice water and handed it to Maxine. She drank it down as if it were the last on earth.

"Thank you." Maxine calmed down with the realization that Virginia was probably right. Maxine's cold stare that had been buried deep into the wiser woman's back, turned to an admiring glance.

The doorbell rang.

"I'll get it!" Papa Joe yelled from the front room as he struggled to lift himself from deep within the cushions of the couch. Sydney heard her father and then put the pan of macaroni and cheese into the oven. The room was silent as the three women prepared more dishes for the next day's feast. Each of them stopped as the kitchen door crept open. Their eyes dropped to knee level as Jasmine pushed through the swinging door. She was still very much sleepy, but she was related to Virginia, one of the nosiest women in town.

"Grandma," Jasmine rushed over to her grandmother's leg. Virginia kneeled down and picked up her only grandchild.

"Hello, brown sugar. You look so pretty in your pajamas." Virginia squeezed Jasmine's chubby body close to her face and neck. Maxine and Sydney watched in amazement. Jasmine had Virginia in the palm of her hands as she did Papa Joe. Sydney glanced at Maxine and smirked. They were both thinking the same thing.

"Did you see your grandpa out there? He's watching TV." Virginia carried Jasmine as she pushed the door and then stopped in her tracks suddenly. Sydney became concerned.

"What is it, Mama?" Sydney wiped her hands on her apron and walked over to her mother. She followed her mother's eyes to see Anthony standing at the front door with Papa Joe. Sydney's heart rushed to her mouth, damn near choking her. Virginia felt her daughter behind her, and rushed to move aside. She and Jasmine sat down on the couch.

Maxine got up to see what all the drama was; she let her mouth drop to the floor when she saw Anthony at the door.

"He came back," Maxine said in a loud voice, breaking the silence in the room. Suddenly everyone's eyes were on Maxine. She dropped her head.

"Yeah, Maxine. I came back. I came to get my family back, for good this time." Anthony stepped in as Papa Joe closed the door behind him. Sydney swallowed her heart back into her chest and then moved out of the kitchen door. She knew he'd come back because the love they shared was unbelievable.

"Sydney, I love you and none of that other bullshit matters to me." Anthony turned to Virginia and Papa Joe on the couch due to his loss of respect. "Oh, sorry folks," Anthony said.

"That's all right, son. Go on," Papa Joe waved his hand for Anthony to continue. Sydney walked over to Anthony who was standing in front of the closed door. Anthony focused his attention back on Sydney.

"Syd, you and Jasmine are all that matter to me. I came back because my chest hurt me so bad every day that I was away from you. But, I didn't have a choice, baby. I had to leave."

Sydney was about to speak just as he put his index finger to her lips. She kissed it lightly. Anthony smiled, and then in the coolest manner possible, he dropped down on one knee in front of her. Both Virginia and Papa Joe moved to the edge of the couch. Maxine moved so close to Anthony and Sydney, she looked like she was being proposed to.

"Sydney. I love you with all I have to give, and I want you to be my wife." Anthony reached into his jacket and pulled out a small, blue velvet box. Maxine stood next to Sydney, closely. Anthony opened the box to let out the perfect cut of ice for Sydney's hand. Maxine's eyes filled with tears as she looked at Sydney, who was as cool as a cucumber. Anthony lifted out the ring, and took hold of Sydney's hand.

"Yes," Sydney whispered in such a calm manner that no one else heard her, but Anthony. Anthony pulled at his oversize jeans to pull himself up and into the arms of his future wife. He put his hands around her face, gently.

"Thank you, baby," Anthony whispered, and then kissed Sydney's mouth with the passion of their last kiss. Sydney's eyes were still closed when Anthony pulled his lips from hers. Maxine slapped Sydney across her back.

"Open your damn eyes, girl, and take a look at that rock on your finger." Maxine held up Sydney's hand as Virginia and Jasmine rushed over to see it. Anthony took hold of his daughter and hugged her tightly. Papa Joe shook Anthony's hand.

"It's about time things worked out for you two," Papa Joe said in a stern voice. Virginia and Sydney hugged each other, as Maxine continued to appraise the ring.

"Well, Virginia. We can go on home now. This young fella here can help Santa out tonight." Papa Joe slapped Anthony across his back. He was officially passing the baton of fatherly duties to his future son-in-law. Anthony welcomed the invitation.

"That's right, sir. I can help him out." Anthony continued to disguise the task in front of his daughter, who was on her way to sleep again.

"Good, good. I'm an old man, now. It's time for you to take over." Papa Joe retrieved his leather cap from the coffee table and flipped it onto his balding head. Virginia continued to daunt over her daughter's happy news.

"I'm ready to go now, Virginia. I'm tired," Papa Joe said in an aggravated tone. Virginia stopped, and then turned to her daughter.

"See what you have to look forward to," she said sarcastically.

Papa Joe got his wife's coat from over the back of his old recliner, and draped it over her shoulders.

"I'm so glad we're together again, too, Mama," Sydney spoke sincerely, and then hugged her mother.

"Me too, baby. I'll call you in the morning," Virginia said then looked to Anthony and smirked.

"Well, maybe not too early in the morning." Virginia laughed, and then followed Papa Joe to the door.

"Let me walk y'all out." Sydney walked her parents to the front door. Maxine stepped to Anthony, who was still holding Jasmine in his arms.

"I have to give it to you, Anthony. You proved me wrong."

Anthony didn't know how to react to Maxine's comment.

"I'm glad you did, my brother," Maxine reached out her arms to Anthony and hugged him. He hesitated, and then hugged her back.

"You must be going soft, Max. I can't believe you admitted you was wrong about something," Anthony joked.

"Well, I am having a baby," Maxine said with a small sense of pride.

"What? Then that explains it." Anthony hugged her again. "Congratulations," his deep voice connected to Maxine's ear.

"Thanks, Anthony." Maxine meant that sincerely. She didn't have a choice but to give him a chance. He'd proven to be a step above the brothers she dealt with.

Indira and Clarissa made their way through the front door, just as Papa Joe and Virginia started down the stairs. Indira hugged the old couple and said her goodbyes to them.

"Hey, girl. What's going on?" Indira's hands were filled with bags as she came in the apartment ahead of Clarissa.

"Anthony!" Clarissa yelled, and then rushed over to him.

"Little Clarissa. What's up, ma?" Anthony took a good look at Clarissa, who was all grown up now, and then hugged her lightly.

"Are you and Sydney straight again?" Clarissa asked on the low low. Anthony leaned near her ear.

"Go check out the ice on your girl's finger." Anthony was filled with pride, and it was showing on his face. Clarissa yelled out.

"Sydney, get over here!"

Indira led Sydney over to Clarissa. She acted as if she was blinded by the size of the diamond on Sydney's hand.

"Oh, man. You went all out, Anthony. This is beautiful." Clarissa held out her arms to Sydney, and then hugged her. "I'm so happy for you, girl." Clarissa hugged her again.

Donnie Hathaway was singing about hanging all the mistletoes, as the music continued to play under the excitement. Anthony and Sydney put Jasmine to bed, together, and then embraced each other in a tight hold as if they never wanted to let go again. No words were needed as Anthony kissed Sydney lightly on her wanton lips.

*****

Vera pulled her weakened body from her bed, which was filled with the stench of sickness. Robert lay next to her, in the king-size bed, just barely lifting his lungs in and out to breathe. Vera promised Robert that she would stay by his side until the end. Robert had made it to another morning and another year. Vera leaned over against his arm and touched his forehead lightly. He slightly opened his eyes to see her over him. In Robert's delusional state of mind, Vera looked as young as she had when they used to fall asleep in her father's barn after making love in the hay. Robert let a smile come over his tired face. Vera could see in his eyes that he was thinking of something good, because his eyes were filled with laughter.

"I love you, Robert. I have loved you all of my life, even before I met you in Lafayette." Vera felt Robert's head become heavy against her arm. He held his eyes on her with all the strength he had left in his body. Vera put her weight under Robert to lift his head. She could see that she was losing the man she loved more than herself.

"Robert. Please, baby. You got to want to live, Bobby. I don't want to have to be here without you," Vera's words were drowned out with saliva and the tears that poured from her eyes. Robert froze into a locked stare as his body succumbed to death. Vera felt the coldness in his eyes and then lifted her hand onto them and closed them lightly. While easing her arm from under his head, she put his hand on his lap. She wasn't a stranger to death. Three of the five employers she'd taken care of had all died under her care. This was too surreal for Vera, as Robert lay dead next to her. She slid off of the bed, and stood gazing at Robert's body then covered him with a blanket.

Vera closed the door of her bedroom and made her way to the kitchen. She felt at peace, knowing that she had helped Robert to get his house in order during his final days. He made peace with himself and God. After smoking most of her cigarette at the kitchen table, Vera dialed the number for McPhall Brothers Funeral Home to come and get Robert's body.

CHAPTER TWENTY-ONE

The holidays seemed to have left as fast as they had come. For Indira, it turned out to be one of the best holiday seasons she'd ever had. It was great to see Jasmine filled with excitement as she opened all of her toys and gifts. She even knew how special it was to see her mother and father together. Indira made glances at Maxine, lovingly caressing her stomach and connecting to the child growing inside her. Papa Joe was relieved to see his daughter and wife together again after so many mistakes. Indira felt blessed to have her baby sister home with her.

Last night was just fine for her and Clarissa. It was the first New Year's Eve where they both weren't working, in the since of, working for a man. Clarissa joked about giving a record number of lap dances and splits last year at the club. Indira stretched and laughed about her sister's stories of The Paradise Lounge. She was hard at work herself last year, trying her best to keep Robert off of her. He was so drunk he couldn't see straight ahead of him.

Indira sat up against her thick, goose-down pillows and took in the blessings that rested upon her circle of friends and family. They were all blessed to have each other, and Indira was realizing that more than ever. The morning sunlight beamed in as she covered her feet with the bronze-colored satin sheets, while reminiscing about her past days and the happiness they had brought her. Clarissa knocked on the door of her sister's bedroom. Indira responded cheerfully.

"Happy New Year!" Indira yelled from the top of her lungs. Clarissa smiled.

"Someone's on the phone for you. It sounds important." Clarissa must have been on the phone since Indira hadn't heard it ring. Indira reached over onto the nightstand that used to belong to Robert, and picked up the cordless phone.

"Happy New Year," Indira said pleasantly to the caller.

"Thank you, and Happy New Year to you."

Indira caught the caller off guard with her holiday greeting.

"Is this Indira Carr?" The seemingly strong voice got back to business.

She'll Learn

"Yes, this is she." Indira felt in her stomach that something was terribly wrong.

"This is Harold Sterling, your husband's attorney." The attorney tried to jog Indira's memory about himself.

"Yes, I remember you well." Indira felt somber and numb as she spoke to him.

"Well, I wish I were calling you on better terms. But I'm calling to inform you that Robert died last night, just after midnight." The attorney became silent. He didn't hear any response from Indira, so he continued on. "The arrangements for Robert's funeral have been made, and are scheduled for Thursday of this week." The attorney was trying to be all business with Indira. She was puzzled by his last comment.

"Who made the arrangements?" Indira let the sheets slip to the floor. Indira asked the question knowing good and well who had made the arrangements.

"A Miss Vera Jackson, and Robert's eldest son RJ." The attorney fell silent, awaiting the next questions. Indira became upset that his woman made his final resting arrangements.

"Will that be all, Mr. Sterling?" Indira became more angered with every word that flowed from her mouth.

"One more thing, Mrs. Carr," the attorney kept her from slamming the phone down on the receiver. "Your presence is requested for the reading of Robert's will at my office, following the funeral." Harold's voice cracked at the mention of his longtime friend's name. Indira recognized his obvious emotions.

"Are you okay, Harold? I know that you and Robert had been close for years." Indira genuinely cared about his feelings, and Harold felt it in her words. Robert had told him on more than one occasion, that his young wife was a cut above the rest.

"Yes. I'm fine, Indira. Thank you for asking." Harold appreciated Indira's concern. "I will see you Thursday, and have a Happy New Year," Harold was speaking through a much needed smile. Indira held the phone close to her long after the other line disconnected. Clarissa opened the door and came in, sliding her bunny slippers across the glossy floor. She crawled onto her sister's bed in her skimpy top and shorts. She got under the cover with Indira.

"Is everything all right, Indira?" Clarissa had such an innocent face. It was amazing to Indira that she'd been through so much in her life. Indira smiled at her sister, pleased to have her there with her after getting the news.

"Robert died last night, just after midnight." Indira's eyes began to water up, but the tears remained in her eyes. She lay on her back staring up at the ceiling as she had done a million times.

"How do you feel about Robert dying, Indira?" Clarissa sat up on her elbow next to Indira. With the sun on Indira's face, she resembled Arnelle in her best ways to Clarissa.

"Good question. I wasn't ready for that one." Indira was looking at Clarissa on her pillows.

"Well, the man who loved you and beat your ass, all in the same motion, is dead. How do you feel?" Clarissa acted as if she were interviewing Indira. She spoke into an imaginary microphone in her hand. She dreamed of being a news reporter, and Indira was going to be a famous model and actress. Indira turned onto her elbow and played along with her sister.

"True, true. He did beat my ass, but I loved that mean-ass man. When he was a good man, he was a good man. And I will try to remember that first, over the ass whoopings." Indira let the tears fall from her eyes. The pain of his death reached her heart, and she felt his death through her body. The man she'd loved for nearly six years was dead. Indira stared at Clarissa, who dropped the microphone and wiped Indira's tears from her face.

"He never loved me," Indira spoke through her light stream of tears.

"He's not the last man who won't love you. Love yourself." Clarissa smiled and then rolled over onto her back to stare at the ceiling. Indira heard her wise words loud and clear, knowing that she was right.

"That's why I can't be with anyone right now. I need to get to know myself again." Indira joined Clarissa in watching the ceiling.

"Me, too. I don't know who I am no more. The best thing I have done in a long time was leave D.C. and that fucked up club." Clarissa threw up her legs, raising the sheets off of both of them. "Well, I do need somebody to love me from time to time." Clarissa playfully nudged her older sister's arm.

"El took care of that for me." Indira turned her eyes in a deviant manner.

"What! I don't believe you." Clarissa put her hand over her mouth.

"Girl, that is one fine man if you didn't notice, and I know you did," Indira touted her mouth out.

"I am shocked, Indira. I just knew you wouldn't be giving up nothing," Clarissa joked about her sister.

"I need somebody to work it out every now and then, but I don't need nobody telling me what to do. That man is dead," Indira caught the words coming out of her mouth. She tried to retract them, but couldn't. Clarissa saw the embarrassment on her bright skin.

"It's okay, Indira. Ain't nobody here but me and you," Clarissa smirked to Indira.

"You ain't right, girl." Indira smiled.

*****

Indira strolled into the large office of Harold Sterling, Robert's attorney. She silently nodded to the other women sitting in drab black suits, as if they really cared that Robert had died. Indira was dressed to impress, she didn't want to look as if her life was over. Robert left her to be with his other woman, giving her a chance for a new beginning. She wore her cream Donna Karan wrap dress and let her long, brown locks straddle her shoulders. Harold greeted her with such intensity that she felt he was glad to see her.

"How are you, Indira?" Harold led Indira to the seats placed in front of his desk.

"I'm doing well, thank you." Indira surveyed the room quickly, without letting her eyes lock on any one person. Bridget and Robert Jr. were sitting closest to the desk, and Cynthia sat on the opposite side. Her son and daughter weren't with her. The first two wives didn't get along with each other, for some reason. If Indira's memory served her correctly, she recalled Robert Jr. saying that his daddy was living with Cynthia while he was still married to Bridget. Indira never bothered with either one of them, so she never got in that mix of drama.

Attorney Sterling went to the back of the room with his vivacious secretary, and she handed him two vanilla envelopes. Indira sort of laughed to herself, noticing that Harold and Robert had the same taste in women…the younger, the better. Harold was a handsome man, sort of reminded Indira of Ed Bradley on *60 minutes*. Harold slightly brushed Indira's crossed legs to get to his desk.

"We will be getting started shortly. We are waiting on one more person," Harold spoke clearly with his eyes on the entire room. He watched the door for the last invitee. Indira got comfortable in the chair, though she wasn't anymore. She knew exactly who the person was they were waiting on. Robert's other woman, and she'd been just that, through all three of his marriages. Robert never made good on his promise of marrying her before he died. He was unable to have their divorce carried through that fast.

The funeral had been uneventful. There were plenty of prestigious people who had come to say their farewells to a colleague, not truly knowing the type of man he was. Indira had let Vera have the honor of sitting on the front pew at the church. Robert was her man more so than any of the women in this room, it was only right.

She and Vera had no words for each other, only knowing glances. The other wives in the club sat on the front row, right along with her. Robert Jr. gave a touching eulogy for his father, who he just recently started to see again. Robert was very hard on his children and made it difficult for them to even deal with him. Indira noticed that Robert Jr. had his eyes on her. She looked up to him and smiled. He smiled back, but only when his mother wasn't looking his way. Indira remembered the times when Robert Jr. would come over to visit with his father, and end up spending his time with her. Robert never showed any of his children much love except when he needed them for publicity. His books and his awards meant the world to him.

The door of Harold's office opened slowly, with all eyes closely on it. Vera walked into an observant crowd, and she held a fur coat in her arms.

"I do apologize for being late." Vera sat down in the center of the chairs that had been set up. She could feel the eyes against her, and then lifted hers to Indira. Indira didn't blame Vera for the breakup of her marriage, Robert was to blame. He was to blame for all the heartache she and Vera had suffered; two totally different women, but with the same pain left as scars in their hearts. There was a hushed reverence, and the formality of speaking in muffled tones as though any type of noise would be taken for rudeness was ensued.

"Okay, let's get started. First off, I just want to say that Robert was a dear friend of mine for many years and I will truly miss him." Harold unbuttoned his jacket, and then lifted his pants legs to sit down. He cleared his throat, and then began reading aloud:

"I, ROBERT S. CARR, of the City, County and State of Michigan, do make, publish and declare this to be my Last Will and Testament, hereby revoking all wills and codicils at any time heretofore made by me."

Harold paused a moment and glanced around the room. He could see the anxious and greedy looks on the faces of both ex-wives. He cleared his throat again and went on, **"FIRST: A. I give and bequeath to my friend, attorney Harold (Frog) Sterling if he survives me, in appreciation of his many years of loyal friendship and legal representation, if owned by me at the time of my death, my antique 1963 Chevelle and my 1965 Malibu."**

Harold had to take a moment to regain his composure before he burst into tears. Robert's thoughtfulness was a sad reminder of the friend he had lost.

Indira watched Harold, and empathized with him. It was appropriate for him to break down. Bridget folded her arms and let out a sigh to let the attorney know that she was becoming annoyed.

Harold took a deep breath and continued on, **"B. I give and bequeath to my first wife, Bridget, if she survives me, my complete ownership of two Express Cleaners and Laundromat, if owned by me at the time of my death."**

Bridget let out a different type of sigh this time. It was a sigh of relief. It was obvious that she didn't expect Robert to leave her anything. Indira rested her hands on her legs. She didn't want to let on to anyone that she was unaware of Robert owning dry cleaners, let alone, two of them. She didn't know what to expect either, but she really didn't care one way or another. She was unsure of whether she would even have her house after the reading of the will.

"C. I give and bequeath to my second wife, Cynthia, if she survives me, my complete ownership of the Forest Lake Apartment Complex, if owned by me, at the time of my death."

Harold stopped reading at the sound of excitement coming from Cynthia. Bridget rolled her eyes and snapped her finger twice at her. Once she was finished doing her winner's cheer, Harold went on. Indira watched the two women eye each other, no longer interested in the reading. Harold sort of smirked to Indira and Vera.

"D. I give and bequeath to my third wife, Indira S. Carr, if she survives me, my home in Bloomfield Hills that we once shared to include my furniture, furnishings, rugs, pictures, books, silver, linens, china, glassware, objects of art, wearing apparel, jewelry, automobiles and their accessories, and all other household goods, our joint Roth IRAs and stocks. I also direct my Executor to set aside the amount of Five Hundred Thousand Dollars ($500,000) for her future expenses, if owned by me, at the time of my death."

Indira was speechless. She was shocked beyond belief at the kindness of Robert after his death. Maybe this was Robert's way of asking for forgiveness, by making amends with everyone he'd ever hurt.

"Here you are, Mrs. Carr," Harold stood behind his desk, handing Indira a long white envelope. Indira stood up, nearly falling, not realizing that her knees had gone weak. She could feel the knives being lunged at her back as she stepped toward the desk and retrieved her check. Indira never even acknowledged the other women in the room. She sat back down in her seat, placing her eyes solely on Attorney Sterling at his desk. He smiled at her classy demeanor. The sighs and hisses came in unison, and then ceased to exist.

Attorney Sterling continued reading the will, but Indira left the scene in her mind the moment she sat back down. It felt as if the wind had been knocked out of her. The same way she felt when Robert hit her in her stomach, the wind was gone again. The whole scene became so confusing in her mind. She could see Harold's mouth moving, and Robert Jr. being hugged tightly by his mother. Indira let her eyes roam the office filled with Robert's past, all waiting to be paid off for his years of cruelty. Before Indira realized she was crying, tears were rolling down her face. She saw a tissue being shoved in her face. She lifted her teary eyes to see Vera behind it. Their eyes met for one strong moment, allowing them to see that they were in the same place of thought and life—so many things in common, but yet a world of difference between them. Without anger in front of her eyes, Indira could now see why Robert loved Vera. She was very beautiful, sitting before her dressed in her trademark red.

When she sang in the nightclubs back in the day, Vera became known for her red dresses, and attire. It was the one part of her past that was the easiest to hold onto. Indira reached her hand out and accepted the tissue from her. The room filled with loud cheers as the attorney read off what Robert had left each of his children. Indira wiped the tears from her face, and remained focused on Vera. She wondered what Robert would leave his woman. He had so much that Indira never even knew he had.

The room quieted to a respectful tone, with everyone now having what was coming to them, except for the last person in the room, Vera. She sat calmly and watched the other women in silence. Vera never asked Robert for anything, and in the thirty some years that they were together, he never gave her much of anything. What she gave him in return was her undying and unconditional love. Vera gave Robert her life, for just a portion of space in his.

She was becoming nervous, but she didn't want to let on to anyone that she was unsure of what was to come. Robert didn't give her much when he was alive. Why should she think he would in death? Vera closed her hands tightly across her lap. She felt a sharp pain through her chest, and lifted her arm slightly in reaction to it. She loved Robert, for him, and he knew that all too well. Robert knew she loved him even when he was too drunk to remember who she was.

Attorney Sterling slid another folder into his view and then opened it. He lifted his eyes to Vera who sat just beyond his desk. Her face showed no expression, but the anticipating worry she felt inside was eating at her. Harold had known about Vera for as long as he'd known Robert, and he knew the love she kept for him. Robert never worried about Vera leaving him. He knew she was his, wholly. Harold focused his attention back on the job at hand.

"F. I give and bequeath to my longtime friend and confidant, Vera T. Jackson, if she survives me, my restaurant Paris Black, ownership of eight boarding houses near and surrounding the campus

of Wayne State University, and ownership of two homes in Ann Arbor, Michigan, if owned by me at the time of my death."

Before Harold could finish, Vera's face was shining bright from the glaze of sweat that covered it. She used the remaining tissue in her hand to wipe her face. The shock was nearly unbearable. Vera let out a slight yelp, and started crying. Indira figured out that Vera had no idea of what to expect here. She'd been with this man for most of her life, and had never known her worth with him. Marriage was what she wanted the most, but marriage cost the most.

Indira watched as Vera broke down into tears, crushing her mirage of courage and confidence. The same mirage Indira had lived behind for the past five years. Indira slid over to the chair near Vera, and tried to comfort her. Indira believed that each woman in the room loved Robert in some strange way, but Vera seemed to love him the hardest.

Harold watched Indira comfort Vera, and sort of smirked at the sight. Robert would have loved this whole set up, he thought. His young wife and his woman finding comfort in each other over their loss of him. Robert had the mentality of a player and the mind of a hustler.

Robert was always the first to say the hustling was heaven sent, and it was the only way to make it. The ladies loved him and the men respected him. Robert had it all. Harold remembered feeling envious of his lack of care for life and the lives of others. Everything seemed to come so easy for Robert, but the envy disappeared with Robert's personal heartache. His money couldn't buy him the happiness and peace he yearned for.

Harold felt blessed to have loved the same woman for 23 years and never anticipated having a scene like this after his death. Harold blindly wrapped up the final formalities of the reading, and stood up from behind his desk. It was all over. Robert paid off his debts of sin in hopes to be resting peacefully in heaven. Vera took hold of the package of documents handed to her by Sterling's secretary. Indira stood up to leave, but not without Vera grasping her right hand lightly.

"Thank you, Indira," Vera spoke softly, just above a whisper. Indira didn't respond with words, but with an assuring nod instead. It seemed that Bridget and Cynthia had settled their differences in the wake of their ex-husband's death, and, in the wake of being left lots of money.

Who needed to fight when there was money? Indira thought the words through, and then smiled to Vera, who was already smiling back at her. In a way, Indira and Vera had settled their differences at the same time. Indira left the office with a feeling of confidence and readiness for whatever was to come next in her life. She had learned her lesson all too well.

CHAPTER TWENTY-TWO

The first day of spring couldn't have been a better choice for a wedding. It was perfect, regardless of what the weatherman on the television was saying. Sydney stared out the window of the church dressing room. She looked to the trees and the clouding sky before her. Even if it was raining cats and dogs, it would still be a perfect day for her. It was the day she'd been waiting for nearly all her life. It was the day she would marry Anthony. Tugging at her dress, Sydney tried to move closer to the window.

"Stand still, Sydney." Indira and Virginia worked on the final two pearl buttons that lined the back of her wedding gown. Sydney turned her head slightly to see the back of her dress.

"Oh, you look so beautiful. It reminds me of the day your father and I got married." Virginia clapped her hands together and then stared at her daughter. Indira stood next to Virginia, eyeing Sydney, in agreement.

"You do look beautiful, Sydney. I can't wait to see Anthony's face when he sees you coming down that aisle." Indira continued to primp and fix at Sydney's gown.

Maxine interrupted. "Well, I don't feel beautiful. Look how big I am in this dress!" Maxine yelled from in front of the full-length mirror with Jasmine by her side. Since she'd been pregnant, Jasmine wanted to be right under her. Maxine turned to the side and gave everyone a glimpse of her body from the angle. The dress Sydney had chosen for her and Indira, her maid and matron of honor, was not planned around Maxine looking like she was due at any given time.

"I made an arrangement with the photographer not to take too many pictures of me and my stomach," Maxine spoke with her hands, waving all over.

"Girl, I don't know what you look like in that dress," Virginia joked to Maxine. Virginia came to Maxine's aid in the mirror.

"Let me see what I can do for you, honey." She took hold of the satin sash around Maxine's stomach meant for the waist, and then moved it up decoratively around her neck.

"She looks like she's trying to hide somebody under there," Sydney joked.

Maxine rolled her eyes in retaliation. Indira and Sydney watched Virginia work her magic. The girls could remember when they were little that if you gave Virginia some fabric, she could damn near make you anything.

"That works, Mama," Sydney said as she stood like a princess in the center of the room.

There was a knock at the door first before it barely opened. Clarissa stuck her head in dressed in her bridesmaid attire to see Sydney before her.

"Sydney is looking all like a princess and shit," Clarissa quickly covered her mouth. Maxine and Indira were both staring at her angrily. Virginia let out a giggle. Sydney turned around to see her mother holding back laughter.

"I'm sorry, Mrs. Hastings. It slipped out."

Virginia couldn't hold back any longer and laughed out loud. Clarissa saw her, and started to laugh, too. Sydney and Indira looked at each other as Maxine also began to laugh.

"It's okay, baby. You ain't the first person to curse in God's house." Virginia dried her eyes, being careful not to ruin her makeup. She wanted the wedding pictures to be perfect. They would represent the reunion of their family. Clarissa remembered what she came to the dressing room for.

"I came back here to tell you that the director is ready to line us up. Come on, Indira and Maxine." Clarissa held her small bouquet of flowers in one hand. Indira and Maxine stopped at the door, and then turned to Sydney, standing in the bright sunlight beaming through the window.

"What are you two staring at?" Sydney felt strange enough in the getup, but she didn't want to look like she felt.

"I'm looking at a scraped-up knee tomboy dressed up in a wedding gown," Maxine spoke through the huge smile on her face. Indira and Maxine walked over to Sydney and then hugged one another as if it was the last time they would see each other.

"I love you two broads," Sydney was never short of I love you's, but this time she wasn't alone.

"We love you, too," Maxine and Indira nearly said in unison. After releasing their hug, Maxine and Indira stepped into the hallway to line up with the rest of the wedding party. Virginia waited for the door to close. Jasmine was holding her grandmother's hand as best she could, in total awe of her mother all dressed up. Jasmine looked adorable in her white lace dress, and patent leather shoes. Virginia reached into her purse and pulled out a tiny box and handed it to Sydney.

"Hurry and open it up. Me and Jazzy have to get to our seats." Virginia awaited the reaction from Sydney as she opened the blue velvet box.

"I'd forgotten all about grandma's ring. It's beautiful." Sydney admired the robin's egg blue topaz stone.

"I wanted it to be your something blue someday." Virginia was about to cry.

"Someday is today. I remember when grandma gave it to you."

Virginia helped Sydney put the ring on, and then hugged her daughter tightly.

"I am so proud of you, Sydney and grateful to have you back in my life. And you, too, Jasmine." Virginia lifted her granddaughter on her hip. "Kiss, Mama, we got to hurry and get to our seats."

Jasmine kissed Sydney and then let her straighten her dress. Sydney touched her mother's hand, and then Virginia rushed out the door holding Jasmine's small hand. Sydney could hear the whisper of voices out in the narrow hallway when Virginia opened the door. The door closed. Finally, Sydney was alone.

"Lord, I thank you for giving me this beautiful day and for bringing my family together. Please continue to watch over us and guide us through life. Amen." Sydney took a deep breath, and then made her way to the door. It opened suddenly, with Indira behind it.

"Let me get your train." Indira hurried to the back and fixed Sydney's long train. Indira was enjoying her duties as the matron of honor, all but the part of not being a matron anymore. Maxine came through the door next, rushing to sit down in an open chair.

"My feet are killing me. These shoes can't hold me." Maxine adjusted her shoes.

The director bursts in through the door next.

"It's showtime, Sydney. Will you ladies please line up?" Lamar, the flaming wedding director, began putting all the players in their places.

She'll Learn

"It's going to go smoothly, you'll see," Lamar assured Sydney, and then sashayed to the door.

"Thanks, Lamar!" Sydney yelled out, and caught herself.

"*Are you reaaaday?*" Maxine sung. Sydney laughed, and then sang the next line of the song.

"*Yes, I'm reaaaday.*"

Indira stared at the two women in amazement.

"Then let's get this over with. These shoes are killing me."

Maxine and Sydney moved to the door as Indira kept her train intact behind her. The wedding party, standing in the corridor, gasped as Sydney stepped to the foot of the door. Papa Joe sat in a chair against the wall. The minute he saw his daughter, he got up to take her side.

"You look beautiful, sugar." Papa Joe leaned over and kissed his pride and joy's cheek. There were six bridesmaids and groomsmen ahead of them, so Sydney held onto her father's hand loosely.

"Thanks, Daddy. You look mighty handsome yourself in your tux." Sydney pinched her father's arm playfully.

Maxine slid her arm through the arm of her escort, who, of course, was much shorter. It never failed, Maxine recalled being in at least five weddings, and every time, the guy had been short. She let her eyes roam the people-filled church and they all seemed to be staring back at her and her stomach. The little guy led the way, and Maxine wobbled down the aisle next to him. Knocking hard on the door of nine months of pregnancy, it was all she could do to manage. Maxine spotted Billy sitting near the back of the church. He winked at her when she made eye contact. She didn't now what to think about him and why he wanted to be with her now. When the two finally met up after Christmas, Billy poured his heart out to her and admitted to being wrong for dropping her before. She told him she was pregnant to get rid of him fast. Instead, he'd been coming around the house ever since.

Maybe he thinks I'm safe or something, Maxine thought. She continued to smile for the many cameras that flashed from the audience and the photographer ahead of them. Maxine shook her head at the thought of rekindling an old relationship, especially an old bad relationship. Why not, Maxine thought? What else could happen? Life goes on with or without you. The little fellow let go of Maxine so she could walk to her designated spot alone, as he went to the other side, next to a nervous looking Anthony.

Indira exuded nothing but confidence on the arm of her escort. She even looked to be leading him down the aisle. This day had been a long time coming. Indira took deep breaths to keep from crying at the sight of Anthony awaiting the woman he loved to make her entrance. The last seven months had been filled with some up-and-down days for Indira. Robert's death served as a reminder for her as to how precious life was and the need to be happy in it. Indira had learned to love herself, first, before trying to love another.

El had made her believe that his friendship was well worth its weight in gold. Clarissa got herself a job at Channel 4 as an administrative assistant, and Indira felt proud that her sister had gone on with her life, also.

As Indira stepped gracefully down the aisle, she could never forget the day she had walked down this same aisle to Robert. It was perfect...the wedding, the reception...everything but the actual marriage. Indira winked to El sitting in the second row, as she took her place near Maxine.

The wedding march rang out loudly in the large church, as the room occupants stood to the bride's attention. Sydney stood on the arm of Papa Joe at the entrance of the church, smiling from ear to ear at the faces in the audience. There were so many people there to share their day. Sydney nearly forgot what she was there for, until her eyes met with Anthony's.

Over the years, their love for one another had never faded. Though many obstacles fell in the way, they managed to make it here. Sydney tugged her father's arm, and then started their path down the aisle. She felt like a real superstar while the flashes went off and the cameras clicked with her every step.

Indira and Maxine had tears coming down their cheeks, nearly making Sydney start, but she had promised herself to make it through for the sake of her pictures. Sydney concentrated on making it down the aisle to Anthony who was standing there so handsome and debonair. Tears started falling from Sydney's eyes when she passed Virginia holding Jasmine on her lap. Jasmine waved at her. Papa Joe squeezed Sydney's hand when they reached the altar. Thugs aren't supposed to cry, but Anthony and his boys behind him were all on the verge of tears. Reverend Givens began the service with the attention of all in the church, but Sydney.

"We are gathered here today to witness and celebrate the joining of Anthony and Sydney in marriage. Today is the day that Anthony and Sydney will declare their love and commitment for one another," the reverend's deep voice carried through the church as if he were speaking through a megaphone, but his words weren't loud enough to wake Sydney from her daydream. It had to be a dream, Sydney thought to herself, as she watched Reverend Givens speak. Papa Joe let go of his daughter's hand and then kissed her. She watched him step away and then sit down next to her mother. Sydney completely missed Reverend Givens asking the question of who giveth this woman away.

Where was she? She missed Papa Joe saying I do. Sydney blinked her eyes wide as Anthony took hold of her arm, pulling her close to him. She was back. Her mind sort of came back from what she thought was a dream. No, it wasn't a dream. It was her wedding day.

Sydney turned and handed her bouquet to Maxine while she and Anthony lit the unity candle. Sydney's friend from work sang Nat King Cole's, *When I Fall in Love*, almost better than he had. Anthony helped Sydney with her train as they walked back to the altar. Reverend Givens put his hands together and lightly touched the shoulders of Anthony and Sydney.

"As the song says, when I fall in love, it will be forever. With the love of God and love for one another, your love will last forever. Do you, Sydney Angela Hastings, take Anthony Reid Carter to be your lawfully wedded husband, promising to provide him with sustenance, to console him in his moments of sorrow, to strengthen him in his time of weakness, and to share with him all of your happiness?" Reverend Givens ended, and then eyed Sydney over the rim of his glasses. Sydney didn't have to think twice about what she was doing.

"I do," Sydney said loud and clear. Anthony squeezed her hands and smiled. Some of the audience chuckled at her eagerness. Reverend Givens nodded his head to her, and then turned to Anthony.

"Do you, Anthony Reid Carter, take Sydney Angela Hastings to be your lawfully wedded wife, promising to provide her with sustenance, to console her in her moments of sorrow, to strengthen her in her times of weakness, and to share with her all of your happiness?"

"I do." Anthony lifted Sydney's hand to his lips and kissed it. Reverend Givens could see that Anthony was anxious for this to be over.

"Do you have the ring for Sydney?"

Antonio reached into the pocket of his tuxedo jacket and handed Anthony the ring.

"Would you put it on Sydney's finger and repeat after me?"

Anthony took his time sliding the ring on Sydney's finger, as he stared into her hazel eyes. Reverend Givens said the words for Anthony to repeat to Sydney.

"I, Anthony Reid Carter, take Sydney Angela Hastings to be my wife, and with this ring I thee wed and give my love to you."

Anthony repeated the phrase with tears falling from his eyes. Sydney wiped them away with the tissue in her hand.

"And your ring, Sydney," the reverend prompted.

Indira slid the ring off of her thumb and handed it to Sydney. Maxine held onto her bouquet.

"Would you put it on Anthony's finger and repeat after me?"

Sydney slid the diamond ring on Anthony's thick finger. Reverend Givens said the words for Sydney and she repeated them.

"I, Sydney Angela Hastings, take Anthony Reid Carter to be my husband, and with this ring I thee wed and give my love to you." Sydney kept cool and said the words so Anthony could hear her. Anthony knew that they were coming close to the end of the ceremony.

"May the love that you feel and share today continue to grow deeper and stronger with each passing day. With the power vested in me, I now pronounce you husband and wife." Reverend Givens closed his book and smiled at Anthony and Sydney. Maxine and Indira were both crying their eyes out now, along with all the other bridesmaids. Anthony smiled coyly at Sydney and then placed his hands on her face and eased her to him. He kissed her for the days and nights that they had been apart and for the lonely moments they had spent apart. The audience stood up and cheered the union.

Sydney learned to trust her heart to God and know that He would come through for her. Jasmine ran over to her mommy and daddy. Anthony picked her up and led his new bride down the aisle, showered under the storm of bubbles blowing through the air.

About the Author

Sybil Barkley-Staples believes wholeheartedly that God has equipped you to do the job, but it's up to you to recognize what he's given you and to start using it. ***She'll Learn*** is her debut novel, but you can expect much more from Sybil, she has plenty of stories to tell.

Sybil was born and raised in Detroit, Michigan by her mother and her grandparents. It was instilled in her that she could do anything she aspired to. Growing up Sybil had two loves in her life, basketball and writing. They both served as an escape from everyday life for Sybil, helping her to ease her way through the awkwardness of adolescence. Her first love, basketball, gained her a athletic scholarship to college. During her freshman year, Sybil met and fell in love with her husband. After a year, Sybil transferred to Clark Atlanta University in Atlanta, Georgia to concentrate on her goal of becoming a journalist. Upon graduation, Sybil became employed with The Weather Channel as a Technical Director. After nearly nine years with the company, Sybil is presently positioned as a web developer for the company's website, weather.com.

Sybil grew up listening to and loving all types of music, with hip-hop serving as the soundtrack to her life. She is an avid reader as well as a movie buff. Her favorite book and movie is *The Color Purple*. Some of her favorite authors are Alice Walker, Beverly Jenkins, Florence Scovel Shinn and the many authors bringing new voices to the literary scene. Meeting Terry McMillan gave her the motivation to try and get her stories published. Sybil has always been inspired by women like Oprah Winfrey, Susan L. Taylor, her mother Lena, and grandmother Mable, to guide her development as a woman and a mother.

Sybil Barkley-Staples is married with two daughters and lives in Jonesboro, Georgia. Sybil is currently working on her second novel ***Candy for My Soul*** and the untitled sequel to ***She'll Learn***.